I0822277

RAE AMBROSE

Earthborn: Kovenn

First published by Rae Ambrose 2024

All art is by Rae Ambrose, except the cover. Which is by Sonia Mohan.

First edition

Cover art by Sonia Mohan
Illustration by Rae Ambrose

This book was professionally typeset on Reedsy.
Find out more at reedsy.com

Acknowledgments

To that little black girl in English class and her bedroom who always daydreamed of her own characters In place of the established ones. The same little girl who loved and wanted to see Vampires, Witches and werewolves that looked like her. The same little girl who loved fantasy and anime. You did it! This is just the beginning.

And thank you to my mom, Thank you for never stifling my creativity. Thank you for always supporting me. Thank you to my friends who had to hear me info dump for eight years about my ideas. Thank you so much for listening to and supporting me.

Enjoy the Earthborn series.

* * *

Also, if you're anything like me and enjoy listening to music to connect better with characters I made character playlists for the three main characters! Aubrey, Saint and Rouge. This is completely optional, I just love music and making character playlists! I hope you enjoy them!

I also did a soundtrack type playlist for the vibe of each chapter! Again it is fully optional, I just love music!

Would you like to see the characters and support my art at the same time? I made portraits specifically for this book, I hope you like them!

I

Part I

Welcome Home.

1

PROLOGUE

Nevermore was always a quiet little sleepy town. It was placed on it's own little island a couple miles from Sin City. The town had a river of lava running through it, a few old stone bridges connecting the two sides. This place single-handedly shaped my love for Gothic architecture, from the businesses to the beautiful neighborhoods. There were beautiful boats on the lava at all hours, just a fun little attraction. You'd think I'd be over all the lava, considering it's everywhere. Pouring from every crevice of the rock formations surrounding us, like a bowl filled with cracks. Stepping foot back through those giant black Iron gates near the ferry drop-off felt so good, I missed this kind of heat. I can understand why it's such a shock for the new comers, the heat on the surface just doesn't compare. We're so far down South we might as well be isolated, most people ain't too fond of where the dead reside, But to me this is home.

Nevermore's Island was placed delicately under the palace

island. The Valley is made up of five floating islands all surrounded by constantly flowing lava. The Palace Island has been dormant and abandoned for quite some time now, you can barely see past the jagged sharp underside. The Giant island was anchored to Nevermore, giant old chains. Yet they still had this silvery shine to them, If I wasn't so sure I'd assume my father was cleaning them for the King, even if he'd never see them. Unlike the rest of The valley, The Palace Island had stunning purple and green flowers littering the perimeter. They were so luminescent, completely healthy and untouched, they're considered sacred flowers. The King's Nightshade garden. Dad always told me to never touch those, He didn't have to tell me twice. Though I was tempted, The palace grounds is the only place through out the whole Valley that has stunning luscious blue-green grass. I was enchanted by it. I wanted to touch it, I wanted to play in it. I wanted to be around it. Then I learned, It's everywhere on the surface. The contrast is almost overwhelming.

Honestly, It's good to be home. This is home.

Past Nevermore is a dark abandoned Island, Dad told me to steer clear of there too. Now as a teen, I didn't take to that as well as the sacred Nightshade plants. I remember how all the kids dared themselves to go there and touch the run down stone gates. It was always dark there, like a cloud loomed over it. It was so eerie. Rocks fell from it often, they'd *plunk* In the lava below. While the Lava flows from the other Islands, it doesn't flow from there. I don't believe it ever has. I learned my lesson going there though, my dad let me have an ear full. It was nothing special though, just a run down pile of rocks with a destroyed gate.

A good few miles from there is Sin City. That's the place. I never thought I'd miss that capitalist hellscape. That's the biggest island so far. It holds the Seven sin cities there. Gluttony, Greed, Wrath, Lust, Sloth, Envy, and Pride. All plopped on that one island, every one of the cities are the size of Nevermore, Hell maybe bigger? There are neighborhoods, schools, downtown areas, and what have you. We always went for the commodities, every sin has got their thing. Gluttony was my second home, a beautiful and delicious town. Everywhere you went it smelled heavenly, Aside from sloth, their denizens are probably the most content.

Then of course the entry island. That one doesn't float, but it does have a Hermes portal. I'm sure the gods forgot all about it, I'm happy it still works or I'd be fucked. And of course a dock for the Ferry. Five Islands, All connected by the ferryman's river, River Styx, like a sewing needle and thread. They drop you at all the islands, for a small price of course. Hell, I'm shocked I managed to keep any spares. I got lucky tonight, Charon wasn't working. They'd talk my ear off, or yank it off.

I took a deep breath. *Welcome home I suppose?*

The air always smelled of firewood and heat, a strange descriptor I know, but how else to describe the smell of constant burning lava. Such a comforting smell. I walked though Nevermore's grand gates, They had a giant three headed dog welded to it. The gates reached high towards the dark blue sky. Ravens and Crows sat perched on the gates, their talons clawing up the dark metal, Years of it caused wear but they're still recognizable. The town was basically empty at this hour. Unlike Sin City, this city sleeps.

All the shops were dark and the dirt roads were settled. I walked through the silent town, gripping the strap to my bag. I always felt safe here, but now I feel panicked. I could feel my stride slow down the closer I got to the outskirts. The closer I got to my house. I stared down at my scuffed boots. One of my oldest pair, the dust kicked up with every drag of my feet. I focused pointlessly on the wrinkled worn leather.

It's been four years, no contact. *I know he's furious at me, I would be too.* What kind of son am I? The lava was dim and sky darker, it was night now. *You dumbass, of course you'd wait until he was asleep, you coward.* What's that saying? '*Easier to ask for forgiveness than permission?*' just a cheap saying to make bad people feel better.

For twenty four years, this man clothed and fed and raised you, and you can't even write a letter to tell him you're Ok? Did he change the locks? *Gods, I'm such an idiot.*

Before I knew it, my boots stopped short of that dirty worn down wooden fence. I slowly moved my eyes towards the gate, staring it down, not moving an inch. Guilt is creeping in.

A gentle breeze passed by in the silence. It was barely enough to rustled the flowers, yet it was so loud and harsh in my ears. Almost like it was telling me, *Just do it already.*

I stood stiff in front of the house. My sweaty palms rubbed against my jeans. Anxiety is at an all time high now. I finally flicked my eyes up at the dark house. The tan house sat proudly, the moon peering down at it. *I hate being watched.* It had a dark brown roof and tall glass windows. It was a wrap around porch and off to the side was a simple building, Dad's shop. It never had a name, he's so damn goofy. He always said *"They know where I am, They know I'm a Blacksmith, why I need a name?"*

I shook my head. Every light is off in the house, probably asleep. Or could be gone for work? His life doesn't stop just because I'm not there. The Shop was dark as well, so obviously he wasn't in there, no sounds of metal either. *Stop stalling. You're already here, you can't back out now.*

I gripped the bag tighter, slipped my fingers between the planks and flicked open the flimsy lock. It was two seconds from falling apart. He still hasn't fixed it. I always felt so clever, then I grew up and realized anyone can do that. He always made it feel special though.

The old gate creaked open, the distant sound of wings fluttering filled the air temporarily. A few ravens floating past before settling back in, I took a step and headed towards the two story house. *Well, I'm Home.*

"Window." I muttered and slipped around back, stepping over the chains and discarded metal and materials. I never realized how much supplies dad goes through. The dark kitchen window caught my eye. Auburn locs down my back, two toned purple eyes. Small pupils and freckles on my copper skin. My yellow sclera seemed duller. Is it from lack of sleep? Who knows. Not much has changed appearance wise, just a constant look of shame and guilt etched on my face. *How pathetic.*

I turned my head away and continued walking again, trying not to brush up against the dirty paneling. My hands gripped the old tangled vines that trailed the side of the house and balcony. Memories began to flash back to me, years of sneaking home after missing curfew, sneaking in after a date, or after falling asleep at my best friend, Saint's, place. He never got mad, just pretended he couldn't hear me.

I tossed the bag over the brown wooden balcony rail and climbed over. The view from here was always beautiful. There's a cliff formation with Lava constantly flowing from it. It's stunning to see in the mornings, It also obscures the moon from time to time. Not sure why but it always brought me comfort. After slowly tip-toeing towards the window, I placed my fingertips on the glass and pushed up. I flinched slightly at the old panes creaking. *Please. Please. Please, be quiet.*

Breath left my lips as I got it fully open, My fingers lingered for a moment in anticipation. Nothing came. I gently lowered the bag inside and took a deep breath before entering myself.

The walls were painted green, my favorite color. LED lights were circled around the ceiling, the gray floors were slightly scuffed from my boots and desk chair. I had a few musician posters on my walls and a bunch of collectible guitars lined up. Music has always been my passion. My old glass case was still closed, the top shelf had my guitar pick collection, the middle had an old Dragon statue my dad made for me and the bottom shelf was empty, It'll be perfect for my gift from Briar. I'll never forget those four years with her and her family.

The light was off, the closet door still open, and the bed unmade. Just how I left it. He hasn't touched it at all. A lone picture sat next to my computer, the light hitting it just right. The glass reflected it back in my eyes and I squinted. I sighed quietly and dropped down on the bed, rubbing my face.

"You're a horrible son." I muttered, "He didn't raise you this way."

I laid back on the familiar springs and stared at the ceiling. Sucked in a deep breath and let it out, but the unease was not subsiding. I'm back home, *I should be happy,* yet I'm terrified. Will they all hate me? Four years is 48 months, 209 weeks, and 1,461 days of radio silence from a supposed friend and family member and it was all for what? Nothing? I could feel that revelation sinking in, *He* wasn't there. *Is he even still alive?* My eyes began to sting with tears. *Fuck, why do I even care? It's not like I know him.* He's a stranger as far as I'm concerned. But that's not true is it? You lied and ran away to find him and it amounted to nothing. *Fucking Pathetic.* You're still in the dark, you're still alone, you're still confused. Was it even worth it?

I sat up quickly, eyes wide and shocked as the door slammed open with a loud *bang!* A tall dark skinned man stood in the doorway, He could barely fit in the six foot door. His deep empty golden eyes were narrowed in anger. The golden rings that acted as his iris' scanned the room in disbelief they matched his golden freckles. His black and Scarlet mixed locs were in a low ponytail and of course he was in his shark set pajamas. His fists were clenched and his eyes were glowing in the darkness. The hall light was shadowing his front, That unease was bubbling over the surface now. I could hear blood in my ears, my hands clutched the bed sheets tightly.

"Aubrey..?" Tartarus questioned and took a step forward, I dropped my head in shame and refused to meet his gaze.

He slowly closed the distance between us and dropped to his knees. His big hands gripped my shoulders and he pulled me into an embrace. I could feel his familiar warmth from the natural heat that radiates off his body. His arms wrapped around me in a nearly bone crushing squeeze. I used to whine about, but now? I didn't care. I dropped my head on his shoulder and hugged back as tight as I could.

"Yea..It's me." Small and pathetic, actions have consequences, you knew that. You aren't a child anymore Aubrey.

"Gods, you can't just break in here. You know I keep important shit in here." He grumbled out, Tartarus pulled away and squeezed my shoulders. "Where have you been, why didn't you say anything, why did you disappear like that?" The end of his sentence was laced in pain, I dropped my head once more in shame.

"I.." I shook my head, "I'm sorry.. I'm tired..dad."

Tartarus sighed and dropped his hands and nodded slightly, "Yea."

He stood up, towering over me. His body blocked out the hall light once more, I kept my gaze down but I could feel his stare lingering before he walked out the room.

"Fuck. I'm a terrible child." I dropped back on the bed and slung my arm over my eyes.

* * *

Nevermore. Bright lava, a busy and social city. Everyone needs something and everyone is selling something, just trying to make ends meet. Nevermore is very different from Sin City, It's calm, quiet and sleepy here. The town is full of Reapers, Sorcerers, and a few unassigned sinners or refuge sinners with no sin to serve. When a sin is MIA the town shuts down and basically falls apart, many Pride Demons migrated here because of it.

This is the region that keeps death running smoothly. The Reapers are born and raised here. They attend school, graduate, get assignments, sort and deal with death in every aspect. Except for Blacksmithing, that duty falls on my dad.

Tartarus Kovenn, He's the god's Blacksmith. He makes scythes, swords, guns, anything you could imagine, all in the shop in the backyard. He's been in this business long before I was born. I'm pretty sure he's considered a Celestial, but I'm not too educated on how the gods work. He doesn't talk about that much. He barely claims the Kovenn name, unless it's in relation to the Earth Celestial, she's long deceased now.

I personally never met any of the other Kovenn's, dad always says they won't accept me, they wouldn't understand me. I respected that, I still do. I mean, why waste time on something I know is fruitless? I remember when I was a child, My dad brought me into the shop, I was sick that day and couldn't stay alone. I sat and watched him make weapons. I was so intrigued. A Reaper came in and requested a scythe, my dad was on it. He wasted no time. That's when I learned he was literally made for this. I looked up at him and declared I wanted to do what he does. He lit up that day, I don't think anyone else too much interest in Blacksmithing, I could imagine his son finding it interesting made his day.

The Reapers work very closely with my dad. Tartarus supplies graduated and decorated Reapers with weapons, all made with Death metal. Only He is allowed to own and use it. After Reapers graduate and get their clearance they come straight here and ask for a weapon to be forged. The Reaper academy pays him directly, The academy was created by a family friend. Jasper Sawyer, the Celestial of Death. Death Themself if you will. Jasper is their own can of worms, their accomplishments and victory over death rights made them quite famous down here. They used that money to fund the education system and the town, It's why Nevermore is a Reaper heavy town.

There are two Academies in Nevermore, Reaper and Sorcerer, respectively. While the Reaper Academy is open to all and anyone can apply and learn how to become a Reaper in one way or another. There's the opposing school, The Sorcerer Academy, that one you need to be a special type of Demon. That school was Created and funded by Hecate Kovenn, The celestial of Magic. She isn't as kind and welcoming as Jasper, So I've heard. She's incredibly allusive and Icy, there was an *incident.* Jasper recalls it, It put the two at odds. It's a very *hush hush* scandal, The papers barely reported on it. Rumor has it Hecate threatened the press, she's one Goddess you don't want to anger.

A Blacksmith, Death, and Magic. All sharing this same space.

The bright glow and heat of the lava bled through the open window. The heat warmed the side of my face and I squinted while slowly sitting up. *I fell asleep?* I sighed and breathed in, the smell of food trailed up the stairs and filled the house. I rubbed my face and took a deep breath before walking over to the door and peeking out then heading downstairs.

Tartarus stood by the old stove, the smell of potatoes and bacon fresh in the air. He leaned against the counter next to the coffee maker, holding an old mug I made for him when I was six. He was in a tight black shirt and his favorite worn out denim jeans and his black scuffed up boots. He shifted his gaze towards me.

I smiled lightly but quickly dropped my head.

"Well, morning, shocked you came down, figured you sneak out the window again."

I stayed silent. The room stayed silent, but it was so loud in my ears. That blood rushing feeling. That same feeling you get when your hand is caught in the cookie jar, but infinitely worse? My dad always made me feel like a child, no matter what. Maybe it's parental power? Who knows.

"I'm sorry."

He hummed and put the mug to his lips, "Mhmm, you said that."

"I.. I shouldn't have left like that, I really am sorry dad.." I finally looked up at him, gripping my hands nervously out of habit.

"Why would you do that? You can't…" Tartarus breathed out and sat the cup down then leaned forward against the dining chair, gripping the top. "You can't just, disappear like that Aubrey."

"I-I know..I know, I… Um, I know." I said quietly, "I, do you remember when you told me about that laboratory?"

He stiffened slightly, He sat in the chair and motioned for me to sit as well, we both took a deep breath and let it out, looking at the table. The sound of sizzling bacon lingered in the background. I stared at the brown wooden table while I quietly searched for the right words, *gods you're a fool, you didn't even think this through.*

"I got a letter, before graduation." I finally spoke up, he

looked at me in confusion and I pulled a folded up piece of paper out of my pocket, the paper since worn down and crinkled, folded and unfolded countless times. I sat it on the table and pushed it to him.

"I apparently had a brother in that lab?"

He looked at the letter, skimming it then looked back at me.

"And before you say it, yes I checked its credibility. I asked Sullivan about it." He made a face, I chose to ignore it. "It wasn't sent from the lab though, I even went there, it was still destroyed, like how you left it all those years ago. I asked her if she could track him, she couldn't. I searched, and searched and searched, for years. Nothing."

"I see." Tartarus rubbed his face, "Why didn't you tell me this before instead of lying about going to college then going radio silent for four years."

"Because if I told you, you wouldn't have let me leave."

"Of course I wouldn't have. That girl is clearly unreliable!" He dropped his hand on the table, "You can't go and chase dreams or ideas with no thought. I could have saved you the four wasted years, there was nothing left. It was all destroyed."

I sighed, "You don't get it."

"How can I? You don't communicate Aubrey! You could have died, or been taken. What would we do then."

I fell silent.

"I'm your parent, and you will always be my child, I don't care how grown you get or how grown you think you are, I'm always going to be your Dad." He looked up at me, his face looked hurt, I looked down once more.

"It won't happen again, I didn't find anything anyway.."

The room fell silent again, he eventually stood and pulled me into a hug, not as tight as last night, but still comforting and warm, "Believe it or not, I'm attached to you kid."

I laughed a bit, "Oh, who would've thought."

"Please, do me a favor." He looked at me, "Just, talk to me next time. Don't just get up and leave like that again, please."

I nodded slowly, "Alright, I promise."

I could feel my smile slowly fading with the sounds around me but heard a faint echo in my ears,

'Alright...One last time.'

I blinked slowly and glanced towards the clock that ticked faintly on the wall. The clock struck twelve. *high noon.*

"Here kid, you must be hungry, potatoes and eggs, no meat, like always."

I blinked once more and looked down at the plate, then smiled, "Thanks dad."

It feels good to finally be home.

2

ONE

It's been too long since I've been here, everything has moved so fast. It feels good to slow down. The hot rocks felt casual on my palms, the molten lava had a gorgeous glow and rumbled lowly as it flowed down the rocks and formations. From here there's a good view of the River Styx, A beautiful blue stream that travels all through The Valley, the lava caused it to shimmer in the light. Charon would float by every now and then, giving a big sweet grin to me, waving a hello, every time. Ever since I was a kid they always kept an eye on me out here.

"It's been so long, I missed you!" A cheery voice spoke up.

I turned my head to the dark skinned girl, she had long purple hair, her eyes were a bright stunning silver. She wore a puffy black baby doll cut dress with matching black pumps and gloves. She had her hair in a slicked back ponytail tied in a matching bow. Her make up was simple, light foundation, white liner and dark purple lipstick, It was her signature look at this point. She's truly a princess. Saint Sawyer, my best friend since grade school. We became friends because of our parents. Her dad, Jasper, and my dad, Tartarus, knew each other since high school, I guess it's only fitting we became friends as well.

She usually has bangs to cover her third eye, but seems she couldn't be bothered this time. It was never said but I always assumed her mother was an Angel or at least had some Angel DNA. All angels have multiple eyes, they're the only species on the planet with that trait. Her having a random third eye was so strange. She says the third is blind, that probably comes from her Reaper side. Blindness and Galaxy patterned hair or, rarely, body parts are telltale signs of Reaper Demons, but unlike other Reapers her galaxy is white. The white starry strands blended perfectly into her natural dark purple hair. She's so unique, she's stunning. I always thought so, she's so different from the other girls down here. To think she use to make me so nervous until our parents finally introduced us, we became fast friends. It didn't take long to learn that underneath the beauty lies a goofy kindhearted girl.

"How was the search..?" Saint asked. She sat next to me, and hugged my arm, laying her head on my shoulder and smiling up at me with those gorgeous eyes and pearly smile, her legs elegantly pulled to her, like the princess she is. I felt a small smile form on my lips as she spoke, she always had such joy in her voice when she spoke to me. Like I always mattered, like she was always so excited to see me. It felt good, especially now. I couldn't love and cherish her more if I tried.

I hummed quietly in response and shook my head, "Not good, amounted to nothing."

"I'm sorry Aubrey, I know finding him is important to

you... but I am happy you're back." She smiled, "Just in time to enroll into the Sorcerer academy with me!"

I blinked and turned my head to her, "Eh? You're going there? Why not, ya know, the Reaper Academy."

She looked away, "I don't want to, I never really wanted to. I want to perfect my Possession magic."

"And how does your daddy feel 'bout this?" I questioned, glancing over at her, "All things considered."

"They're supportive.." As always, Jasper would support anything she did, a doting dad through and through.

"Mm, well, if you like it baby, I love it." I leaned back on my hands again and watched the lava, Saint adjusted and laid her head comfortably on my shoulder, "But why would I enroll, I did my jail time."

"Oh haha," Saint rolled her eyes, "Because I'm there and I won't have anyone else there with me, it's a new environment.."

"I'm not even a Sorcerer sugar-" I raised a brow.

"True! But you have Earth magic, you'll fit right in! And you can stand to practice your little vine tricks more."

"..." I narrowed my eyes at her, "Implying?"

"Nothing sweet face, nothing at all~" She hummed, her southern belle accent rolling off her tongue, "Anyway! You don't even have to try, just be there 'Cuz I'm there."

"Mhmm. I'll run it by dad, don't hold your breath. He never really approved of Hecate's Academy, or her.."

"I'll take it!" She grinned ear to ear.

"How have you been though? You look great." I messed with a lock of her hair, perfect as always, not a single strand out of place, she hasn't changed a bit. She instinctively leaned into my touch like always, her skin was so warm and soft.

"Hah, thanks, wanted to try something new. Not much has changed since you left. I took a gap year after high school, went on vacation with my dad before work called Them away again, tried community college for a year, didn't like it, and now I'm going to the Sorcerer Academy"

"Mm, what about the ranch? How's that goin'? Are you going to do school and ranch stuff?" I dropped my hand and crossed my legs, sitting up and leaning against my hand, keeping my eyes on her. To the contrary of her girly and feminine exterior, She and her Dad are ranchers. The one and only, Reaper owned Sawyer ranch. Just like every Reaper needs a Scythe, every Reaper needs a horse.

"Mhmm, like always, I've met a lot of cool Reapers over the years, you were close to being replaced." Saint chuckled, I snorted out my nose quietly and shook my head.

"Oh really? Guess I'll have to step up my game." I instinctively checked the time on my phone, "How's lunch on me sound?" I got to my feet and put my hand to her.

"Phenomenal, always such a gentleman." She took my hand and dusted off her dress, I pulled her to her feet gently and put my arm to her.

"Oh shut up." A memory came to mind, "Oh shit, ya know, the surface is so strange."

"Huh?" She looked at me while we walked, tilting her head slightly. Her dainty hands gripping on my jacket slightly.

"I have an...*acquaintance*, up there, I asked her to locate my brother, but it didn't go anywhere."

"What was it like?" She asked.

"There's plants everywhere. Saint, I felt so.. at ease? Happy? They have newer cars and stuff too, it's not too much different though, but there's stars and moons up there, like more than just Aides' moon. And beautiful sunsets, we should visit one day for the hell of it." I smiled

"I'd genuinely love too, I don't think any of us get the chance to leave The Valley, my dad would lose their mind." She sighed out, "Well, aside from the Sinners, it seems they can come and go as they please."

"And the Reapers." I hummed.

"…"

"Why are you so against it? Your dad is literally Jasper, Ya know, Death itself. You'd excel and graduate with the highest degree possible." I asked.

"Exactly, I already know what to do. I can ride, I can do funeral preparations, I know dead languages, soul searching, sorting and philosophy, and crow and raven whispering. I'd just be relearning everything for what? A piece of paper. What a waste." She rolled her eyes and waved it off

"And Necromancy and Blacksmithing?" I mused.

"I didn't say I knew EVERYTHING, I know *enough*, besides they banned Necromancy, and I can't step on your toes, Blacksmithing is kinda your thing yea cowboy?"

"Oh how sweet of you," I opened the door to a diner for her, leaning over her as she walked past and followed her with my eyes, Saint hummed and put her hand up to her lips and blew a kiss. Her purse swaying on her arm. I chuckled and followed her inside and shook my head.

"Hm, maybe I need to go to the Reaper Academy, maybe I'll get better at Blacksmithing and won't be a complete disappointment to my dad." I muttered.

"Whoa, where did that come from?" She looked up at me, blinking her eyes in confusion.

"... I broke another one. He's running low on metals because of me." I groaned quietly, "Not as easy as it looks honestly.."

"Nothing is, especially Blacksmithing, don't force it love."

"Anyway.." I sighed.

"I mean it, stop being so hard on yourself. Gods you haven't changed a bit, and that's a good and bad thing, before you ask." She put her finger up and nodded her head.

"Oh gee, thanks."

"Stop being so fucking hard on yourself gods, you always on that *'I ain't shit'* bullshit and it's not befitting." Saint said.

"...Thanks." I snorted quietly.

"What are best friends for?" She smiled.

"Draining my wallet apparently, I swear one of these days a moth gon' fly out, then we both gon' be looking foolish."

"Oh! Do not speak that into existence! I'm too pretty to work, and you're my sugar daddy, you have one job"

"To provide sugar, yes darlin', I hear you." I laughed. Saint got a table for us and we sat by the windows, her in one booth and me in the other, she sat her purse down and I rested my boots on the other side of her. I took my hat off and sat it on the seat.

"But, maybe I'll spot you tomorrow." She grinned "Oh, Look at your hair."

"Hm? What about it?" I asked.

"It looks great! Your hair care routine must be heaven." Saint hummed, "It's so long now, I just realized."

"Ah." I laughed quietly, "You'd be shocked what retwists and a good Loc Technician can do. I'll have to go back soon, kinda slacked up on it the past year."

Saint nodded, "Well, maybe I can take you on a salon date

and help you out." She hummed then snapped her fingers, "Oh, talk to Mr. Tartarus fast, the window will close next week. Orientation is the following week."

"I can just text him now, we can talk about it when I get home." I pulled my phone out and shot him a quick text, "Anyway, fill me in, what's been going on with everything the past four years."

"Girl, too much, Ok so obviously most people are applying for colleges, yada yada, but I heard the palace got a lil active!"

"Oh?" I asked.

"Yea!" She moved her hands exaggeratedly, "Apparently the prisoners up there thawed out, Like, it's been how long since it was alive?"

"Thawed huh?" I hummed, "Dad says hundreds of years. He said it'll probably stay empty for a long while, and we better hope it stays that way."

"Why?"

"The king is complicated, he likes to play dollhouse and I doubt you wanna be a doll." I said, "And dad says when he stays, a snowstorm moves in with him. I bet those guys are happy to be out of that ice. They must've really Pissed Aides off. Or, If the legends are true, he gambled them out of their souls."

"Probably, Imagine being dammed to an ice sculpture for all eternity." Saint laughed nervously, "Makes me a little happier I'm not Earthen."

"You're telling me."

"Ehh anyway, Oh, Rouge is also back in town-" Saint spoke up.

"Ugh- wha-" I stiffened instantly, feeling a wave of anxiety rush over me. Flashes of the past immediately popped into my head.

"Yea," She hummed, "Her dad relocated, I think? But she's back in town! We should visit."

"………" I went silent almost instantly, and looked down at the menu, "No, that's Ok."

"Huh? Boy." Saint deadpanned.

"….."

"…." Saint narrowed her eyes at me, "Aubrey."

"……" I put the menu up to cover my face and groaned quietly.

"Aubrey you fucking dunce." She rolled her eyes, "You didn't tell her why you left, did you."

"Only you and dad know the truth, safe to say…our breakup wasn't great." I muttered

"…" Saint went silent, "Of course."

"…"

"Makes more sense now."

"I… I was scared Saint, it's not exactly easy telling your girlfriend that you're not actually a Demon, but a science experiment gone wrong, cosplaying as a Demon and yes I've technically been lying to you since day one, no that doesn't mean I lied when I said I love you-"

"Oh, you had a whole scenario in that movie theater upstairs." She said

"Be so fucking for real, you know Rouge." I dropped my head on the table, "I knew my actions would have consequences. I'll just..deal with them, like always."

"If you say so.." She said quietly, "But you know as well as I do, she will love you no matter what."

"Yeah.. that's the problem."

"…"

"Speaking of dunces, you back with that bum ass nigga?" I glanced up, hoping to change the subject, it was her turn to go quiet.

"... He's better.." She muttered.

"Fifty-seven."

"Wha-?" She questioned.

"That's how many times I heard that." I spoke up before she could, "And thirty-eight"

"He's cha- oh go to hell."

"When are you gonna move on? You are too pretty to work, but not too pretty to raise your standards? Does that bitch even have a job?"

"He's looking..." Saint trailed off, then looked down at the menu in front of her

"Mhmm, ya know, I can set you up with some hot girls, you know I know plenty." I grinned.

Saint smiled and waved her hand, "That ain't necessary, I can meet pretty girls all on my own, thank you."

I leaned against my hand with a small smile, "Well, I guess birds of a feather and all dat hm?"

"Huh?"

"Seems we both make bad decisions, I'm being for real tho, break up with him." I glanced at her, "You know I don't fuck with him, but I can see you sneak glancing your phone and I remember his number."

Saint sighed and shook her head, "Anyway, I know what I want.."

I eyed her for a bit before looking down at the menu. We sat in silence for a while before she eventually spoke up.

"Hope you like school uniforms."

"Oh fuck you."

* * *

“Hey dad,” I walked in the house, Saint behind me, “ You get my tex-?”

I tilted my head, Dad was sitting on the couch with Saint’s dad. They were dark skinned like saint, they had big voluminous curls with that galaxy pattern peaking through them. Their eyes were the same shade of blue as our sky with stars twinkling in them. They were dressed down this time, in simple flared out pants, a button down shirt and ankle boots. They were talking and laughing, Saint peeked over my shoulder and gasped in surprise.

“Dad!” She smiled, Jasper looked up, Their curls bounced when they turned their head to look at us with a warm smile.

“Oh, I was going to surprise you back home, I didn’t expect you to stop by princess.” They sat their cup down, “Aubrey, It’s wonderful to see you as well.”

“Hello Jasper.” I nodded, I took my hat off and placed it on the rack by the door, “What made you stop by? I coulda walked Saint home.”

“Oh, no need. I’m just here to get repairs on my scythe, no one else can fix it properly, might as well go to the best Blacksmith I know. Right?”

“It’ll be fixed by tomorrow, not a problem, I can drop it off for you.” Tartarus spoke up.

“Thank you sweetie,” Jasper smiled, “Oh sweet face~ I can meet you at home if you wish to catch up for awhile, I’ll cook your favorite for dinner and we can do anything you wish, I’ll be home for awhile.”

Saint’s eyes sparkled and she grinned wide, “No no I can

come with you, I can help." She smiled at me and I smiled back, "Umm, I'll meet you outside dad."

Dad took the cups to the kitchen as Jasper headed outside.

"Do you see what I see?"

"Eh-?" I asked

"Aubrey. Your dad, my dad." Saint pointed at me then herself.

"You think my dad is making moves on Jasper?" I asked with a snort, "He can't even speak to men and you think he's flirting with your dad-?"

"Obviously, dad was doing their hair thing, ya know, the thing. Imagine! If they get together~ we can be step siblings~!"

I laughed quietly, "Cute thought, but I'm sorry sugar we both know that ain't gon' happen."

She pouted but waved it off, "Ok~ Ima head home with dad, talk to Mr. Tartarus about the school!"

"Yes, of course, of course." I waved it off, she narrowed her eyes then left. I shook my head and headed into the kitchen. The kitchen, like most of the house had a rustic southern vibe. When the Earth Celestial, Terra , died she left this house to my dad. The only thing I know about her is her relation to my father. I never got to meet her. She apparently had it built centuries ago. It's probably the most expensive thing we own. We aren't rich by any means, but we do well enough. The house is certainly a luxury. It has three bedrooms, two and a half bath, Her and my dad lived here before I came along.

I walked over to the stainless steel fridge, the old wooden floors creaked under the weight. I pulled open the fridge and scanned the area for a drink. I grabbed the last cold soda and sat on top of the stone counter tops. Dad made sure the gas stove was off and placed the cups in the deep sink.

"So did you get my text dad?" I popped the top of the drink open and took a drink.

"I did, And you're sure you want to go *there.*" Tartarus scowled then turned his body towards me.

"Hm, at first, not really, but after thinking it over, yea, I do need to work on my Earth magic. Sorcerers are all about elements and shit." I laid my head back against the brown and white rustic cabinet, "Plus you won't let me leave The Valley, and you won't teach me…so not many options for teachers."

I could feel his eyes narrow at me in a side eye, Tartarus sighed and leaned against the sink, "I don't like Hecate, you know that she's…"

"Untrustworthy and weird, I know dad. But isn't she technically like your sister or something?" Iron, our Doberman hellhound, made his way in the kitchen. He yawned, he looked up at me with bright brown eyes and walked over wagging his tail and laying his head on my lap, I grinned and pet him happily.

Dad grunted, "Something like that." Tartarus muttered.

"Besides, she's not in charge anymore, a woman named Petra is the Headmaster, seems the student body loves her. So I won't come in contact with Auntie dearest." I snorted and hopped off the counter.

"Fine, I'll send in the paperwork, only because you want too and Charon approved it." He looked at me, "They miss you, you know?"

I glanced over at him, "I missed them too… I missed you

too dad."

"Hm. If you go to this school, I expect you to do your absolute best, yea?"

"...Yea.."

"Pace yourself, don't let those pompous assholes tell you that you ain't good enough, don't over do it, just...do your best. Alright?"

"Yes yes, I got it pops." I nodded, Tartarus placed his hand on top of my head and ruffled gently.

"Great." He walked off.

"Guess I'm going to school." I smiled a bit at Iron, "How bad could it be?"

3

TWO

"Alright kid, this is one of my easier orders, got plenty to spare with the metal. Want to give it a shot?"

I made a face and glanced away. Dad has been trying to get me back into my Blacksmithing lessons but I can't lie, I'm getting more and more discouraged each time I fuck up. I sat in a chair in the corner, my head rested against the hot wall as Tartarus went through his metal drawers.

Dad's shop was placed behind the house in a big glass gazebo, He said this was originally Terra's tea room, but she gave it to him so he could work from home. He never gave a reasoning, or told me where he worked before that but I never felt the need to ask. He split the gazebo in two, and lead a path to the house and to the front gate. He put up wallpaper and curtains over the back of the gazebo and uses that as his work space and the front half is a check In or waiting room of sorts. Dad is fast at his job so why have people stand around and stare at him when they could sit and mind their own? Just makes sense.

"Don't worry, it's just a training sword." Dad checked the

receipt then skimmed through his different metals, I shook my head.

"I think I messed up enough swords this week." I muttered, I could feel dad look at me sadly, he sighed quietly and nodded his head. He grabbed the metal for himself and looked back at his anvil.

"Alright, if you're sure."

I sighed, how pathetic. I can't even properly make something as easy as a damn training sword? Dad always makes it look so easy. I guess it's because he was literally made for this, the God of Blacksmithing and Imprisonment, all that jazz. I don't even know why I keep comparing. I'm not a god, just his kid trying to learn. It feels discouraging watching him though, he creates the lava from his hands, beats the swords and finishes it all within minutes. No one can really live up to that huh? But I *want* to. I just want to make him proud, it's the least I can do after disappearing like that.

We both looked up as the shop bell rang. We turned our head towards the shop front. Dad walked out, metal still in his hands, and met a taller male as he walked in. I followed after him and peeked over dad's shoulder. He had a scythe in his hand, a very elaborate one. His dull brown curly hair was braided at the top and the rest pulled in a messy bun, his chiseled face shimmered from the lights off the shop's glass windows, his most defining features were his mouse ears and tail and the vitiligo on his face and hands, I've never seen that around here before, the animal features of course. He's an Earthen, all the way down here? He wore a flowy elegant shirt with high-waisted fancy pants. He's a rich boy, new client?

He bowed his head respectfully then smiled charmingly, dads hands began to glow around the metal as he looked at the other male. His cheeks were slightly red but hard to see from this angle, he snapped out of his stare after the melted metal thudded on the ground.

"Hello? Is this the Blacksmith place?" He had a thick Latin accent, he's from the surface, interesting.

Dad cleared his throat, "Oh- uh. Yes. Can I help you?"

The male smiled and held up his scythe, "Need a repair… " He tilted his head, his ears twitched. "Say, you look familiar?" He tapped his chin, "Wait, I know those eyes anywhere, Tartarus?"

Dad blinked and looked up, "Huh? I'm sorry, do I..?"

"Oh uh, we went to high school together." He chuckled and rubbed the back of his head, "I uh, I was the small nerdy kid your friend always picked on."

"…" Dad took a minute then nodded, "Yes, I remember you, I asked to borrow your book when you were done and you kinda just threw it into my hands immediately."

"Heh! Uh! Yes. That was me." He scratched at his cheek as they heated up.

"Well, um, it's certainly wonderful to see you again, uh, you um, certainly matured-" Dad glanced away, I held down a laugh that came out as a small snort and avoided dads look.

"Oh, uh thanks." He smiled then put a hand to him, His brown eyes shimmered. "Mateo, Mateo Brown."

Dad took his hand gently, the smaller male had a quick look of pain on his face before dad quickly pulled his hand away and shook it to cool it down. I dropped my head in my hand. *Good on him though, he took that like a champ.*

"Sorry, sorry, Uh, how have you been?" Dad asked, taking

the scythe gently, "What would you like repaired?"

"I've been good, I work at the school nowadays... oh, um the blade is a bit loose and dull, can't cut anything."

"Well that's good, and an easy fix." Dad nodded and laid it down, he began to do his usual inspection on the weapon while Mateo shook his hand too cool it as soon as he could.

"Uh, how about you?"

"Huh? Oh! Heh, great! Uh I'm uh, ya know." Dad began stuttering and motioning to me, "Married, married- not, uh- with child. Like uh, I mean I'm not pregnant haha, uh I have a son now." He finally got it out. "I-I uh, I'm not married. Heh-"

I blinked slowly in complete shock then walked over, "Hello, my name's Aubrey."

"Nice to meet you Aubrey." Mateo smiled and I shook his good hand.

"Um, this should be done by tomorrow, it was nice to see you." Tartarus nodded, I shook my head.

Mateo smiled, "You as well, I'll be back tomorrow then." Mateo bowed his head and smiled, then left, his tail swaying behind him as he did.

I looked at dad and raised a brow, "Dad, what the hell was that?"

"I...have no idea. I just felt nervous all of a sudden." He whined and turned around heading towards the back to begin working on the repairs. I followed behind him, I've never seen dad react like that before, and I'm pretty sure he's had a crush on Jasper, Charon and Leviathan. He kept his cool each time, but that? I nudged him and grinned. He gave me an annoyed look before turning away.

"You should ask him out, he's kinda hot."

"Date? Me? No." He shook his head.

"Why not?" I asked.

"Dating doesn't work well for me kiddo."

"Well, maybe this time it will." I hummed, he kept working.

I looked down as my phone buzzed, a message from Saint flashed on screen and I looked back at him, "Oh, that's Saint, I gotta meet her. You cool if I go?"

"Oh, yea, be safe alright?"

"I will!" I waved and left.

4

THREE

"Hello Tartarus." Mateo smiled.

I handed him the scythe, perfectly fixed and wrapped for him. Ever since I saw him yesterday I've been a bit distracted. He's handsome. That's a given, I'm use to handsome men, but I don't know, maybe he feels different? All I could do was horribly distract myself by working on his repairs, almost eagerly. I don't know whats gotten into me, it's not like I have a shot, I already know how this song and dance goes.

"As good as new.." I nodded, I handed him the weapon and felt his soft hands brush against mine, I cleared my throat as he unwrapped the blade slightly before giving a satisfied grin.

"Fantastic, how much?" He asked.

"Uh, no charge." I stupidly spoke, I mentally slapped myself.

The smaller male laughed to himself and shook his head, He was dressed more casually today, a simple stunning embroidered button down shirt tucked into casual dress pants, his white boots peeking underneath, he's very well put together.

He tilted his head to the side, his hair flowing as he did, he had a playful glint in his beautiful brown eyes.

"Now, I don't think that's how business works." He joked.

"Uh- think of it as a discount?" I stuttered out with an awkward shrug.

"Well, again, not how it works..." He laughed quietly, "Hm, well, how about I buy you dinner? I know it's not the same value as Blacksmith work, but I don't mind buying multiple dinners."

I blinked in surprise and looked at the smaller male, he had a big grin on his face. I honestly couldn't tell if he was serious or just joking, I glanced away almost like I was waiting for the punchline, but one never came. I pointed to myself.

"I'm sorry, did you just ask me out-?" I asked dumbfounded.

"I guess I did... unless you're not interested-?" Mateo rubbed the back of his neck.

"N-no no! Um," I thought for a moment, maybe Aubrey is right? I mean, this is a once in a lifetime opportunity? How many handsome men actually pay attention to you Tartarus? Aside from the only other man you thought you had a shot with friend zoning you twenty years ago. And Aubrey is grown, and doesn't seem upset at the idea of me dating?

If I'm honest, I've never had this feeling before, is this a crush? Should I explore it? What could go wrong? No hard feelings if it goes the way it always does? I rubbed my head and glanced back at him, his eyes were hopeful and bright, I rubbed my arm and nodded a bit.

"Uh, sure, I'd love to."

"Really?" Mateo asked.

"Yea.. what can it hurt?" I nodded.

"Wonderful." Mateo's ears twitched and his eyes sparkled, "How's Friday? It's a weekend so I can stay up past my bedtime." He joked.

I shook my head with a small laugh, "Sure, sounds perfect." *How cute.*

"Great.."

"Great.." I nodded.

Mateo bowed his head and hurried out, looking quite giddy. I felt my face immediately go red. I covered my face in embarrassment and leaned against the counter. No going back now, Oh gods Tartarus what did you get yourself into?

Gods before I knew it, it was Friday. The days didn't creep along at all, that usual mundane snail pace was absent. All I felt was nerves, my stomach was in knots, my hands were sweaty, my heart was pounding. But alas, Friday came.

'Have fun dad!' Aubrey texted. I locked the phone and breathed out, I adjusted my hair and clothes before getting off the ferry, the smaller male had all his hair pushed back, He wore a nice black sweater and jeans. He got to his feet, his heeled boots clicking on the pavement.

"Sorry I didn't keep you waiting, did I?" I asked.

Mateo smiled and shook his head, "Not at all!" his tail swayed behind him, "I was hoping you'd let me choose the place."

"Sure." I gave a small smile and nodded.

"Fantastic! How does dinner in the Gluttony Ring sound?" He asked.

"Bit pricey?" I asked a bit shocked.

Mateo waved it off and grinned, "Nothing to worry about."

We headed towards the gluttony ring and walked towards a restaurant, I followed awkwardly. Mateo checked his phone then looked up at the building, and nodded then turned to me. I looked up at the building, *Bee's* written across the top, that little Sinner. I narrowed my eyes slightly.

"Is this Ok? I did a bit of research and saw this place had great reviews."

"Bee's? I didn't even know she had a restaurant?" I spoke then looked at him.

"It's new!" Mateo smiled, "A friend of mine said the food is to *die* for."

"I'd imagine..." I rubbed my neck. *Oh Honey, you have no idea.*

"Not interested?" Mateo asked, his tail lowering slightly. "We can go somewhere else?"

"No no, you seem excited..." I waved my hand, "Besides you're paying so... I just kinda feel bad about the pricing, Bee isn't exactly cheap with her skill."

"I promise, money is no issue, if you let me pay for the scythe repair we wouldn't be here." He closed his eyes with a cheesy grin. I felt my eyes softened and shook my head with a small smile.

"Alright, fine, fine."

Mateo opened the door for me and motioned me inside, the area was dim and more modern than her bakery or the den. The walls were white and draped in curtains. Tons of Grey booths and chairs. The floors and table tops were white marble. The wait staff was in white and black attire, diamond chandeliers hung from the ceiling. This place is leagues above her cozy diner and bakery down the street. What even made her invest in this place? *Oh gods it's gonna be incredibly expensive.*

Mateo walked over to the waitress and got a table for us. She buzzed and grabbed menus and headed to a booth in the back, I looked around curiously then sat at the table. The waitress took the drink orders then walked away with a smile.

"It's really nice here, not really her southern kitchen vibe." I said scanning the area.

"I'm sure she's trying to capitalize on the food industry, in all honesty I ain't too mad at it, who better than the Queen of Gluttony?" Mateo looked over the menu, his ears twitched.

"Right…" I looked at the menu and moved my fingers over the words. Lots of fancy foods, definitely not her typical menu. Hundreds of dollars steak and lobster meals, crab, and things I can't even begin to pronounce. I felt my finger tremble at the prices and fought the disapproving look creeping up on my face.

"Oh? You're blind?" Mateo asked.

"Umm, something like that? My vision is more like, heat signatures, doesn't make reading all that easy haha.." I rubbed the back of my head in embarrassment, "Ya learn to live with it, works wonders to keep your kid from burning themselves or knowing when to put the right type of jacket on when the cold front comes in."

"Interesting, I'm blind in my right eye, but that's just the Reaper genes." He nodded, I looked at him and gods, I can't believe I didn't notice the galaxy in his eye, of course.

"Ah yes, you're half right?" I asked.

"Yep, my momma was a Reaper, and somehow she ended

up with my dad." Mateo shook his head.

"What made you want to be a Reaper?"

"My mom. She was my hero as a kid, she was everything I wanted to be. Bit of a momma's boy I guess." Mateo laughed awkwardly. I shook my head.

"Don't feel bad, I'm more of a sister's boy? I suppose? My sister is the reason I live down here in all honesty." I glanced away, a small sting in my eyes. I blinked it away.

"Really?"

"She was wonderful." I sat the menu down. "She loved this place, shockingly so."

"Was it the heat?" Mateo joked.

I chuckled, "Probably. She loved volcanoes."

"Ah, that makes sense."

"So, how is your mother? I remember that scythe, it was one of my first concepts." I asked.

Mateo went silent for a minute before smiling gently, "She passed away, she got really sick, so I took over her job."

"Oh, I'm so sorry, Mateo."

"Don't be." He waved it off, "But it does mean a lot it was easily fixed, I was worried I'd have to retire it."

"Well, I'll be sure to keep it in working order for you." I nodded.

"Thanks..." Mateo sat his menu down and leaned against the table, "So, what have you been up to? Aside from working?"

"Not much, that's basically all I do nowadays." I waved it off, "Especially after my kid grew up."

"Does he have a mom?" Mateo asked.

"Nah, he's adopted. Just me and him, and Iron of course." I said, "And you?"

"Oh, I'm a teacher now, I work down at the Reaper academy with Erebus." He smiled, "And I reap sometimes, mainly my mom's assignments."

"How does all that Reaper stuff work? Jasper never really talks about their job."

"Ah, well, it's a random thing, once you graduate and get your scythe you're automatically put on assignment, I was assigned to war deaths. My younger years were not nearly as peaceful, my dad was ecstatic." Mateo rolled his eyes, his ear twitching.

"Oh, I'm sorry…"

"Kinda in my blood, didn't take long to get used to." Mateo waved it off, "Then I retired from that when a new guy came on the scene, Erebus approached me about teaching and offered to give me my moms old assignment, which was reaping children in a hospital on the surface, I like to put them at ease, they're so sweet, and they're kids so they can see us. Mainly chalked up to imagination until they inevitably pass away."

"That sounds rough…"

"Nah, I love kids, I love seeing them happy and content, but seeing them suffer with illnesses or injuries took some getting used to, I had to remember where I was stationed. They're all so sweet." He pulled out his phone and leaned over the table, showing some drawings.

"They draw me a lot!" Mateo grinned proudly, "I keep all of them in my house, it's bittersweet, but at least I know they're resting."

"Yea…" My eyes softened.

"Heh, sorry, that's probably depressing."

"No no, it's Ok, I asked." I said, "Say, why don't you order for me?"

"You sure?"

"Surprise me." I nodded.

"Alright." Mateo smiled.

* * *

"And that way, it keeps it sharp so you don't have to waste time with repairs every month." I spoke, as I waved my hand, "Ah, sorry, rambling."

"No no." Mateo smiled, "I don't mind it."

"I don't think you're supposed to ramble about your job in a relaxing time?"

"If your job doesn't stress you out, and you're passionate about it, I'm more than delighted to hear your voice." Mateo said smoothly, hell I don't even think it was intentional, but I still couldn't fight off that blush.

I blinked and glanced down at him, and cleared my throat quietly.

"Uh, talking about your passions and what not- of course... *heh.*" Mateo rubbed the back of his head. He awkwardly tried to backtrack. *So cute.*

"Mm, I like your voice too." I joked, "Your accent is cute, you're not from here?"

"Oh, nah, born and raised on the surface, in the Latin region, until I turned 15, I took after my mom." Mateo smiled proudly, "But it is beautiful down here, mom was so excited to show me her old schools and the Reaper town, well, Nevermore..."

"I used to visit the surface often, but once I adopted

Aubrey, I limited my time. Not many friends, and my two closest friends had kids of their own and worked just as much. But at least I could work from home..."

"Two closest?"

"Oh, Jasper and Leviathan, but Charon helped out anyway they could, they bonded so well with Aubrey, Aubrey loved them so much as a kid." I smiled to myself.

"What's it like being a dad?"

"Personally? It's wonderful, I never thought I'd be here, having a kid and being domestic. I assumed at this point I'd be working nonstop, alone with Iron and living in a shitty baron house."

Mateo laughed, "Well that's depressing?"

"Mm, well bright side, it didn't turn out that way." I looked over at the lava, the glow illuminating our features. It was warm but the glow was dimmer, it was getting late. I guess we finished dinner just in time. I blinked and turned my head towards Mateo, he was looking up at me, almost mesmerized, he had a gentle smile on his face, the lava lit up his eyes and stunning features.

"You Ok?"

"Yea... um," Mateo looked at the lava, "Have you tried lava rocks before?" He suddenly asked.

"Lava rocks?" I tilted my head in confusion.

Mateo walked over to the lava and shoved his hand in it. I felt my eyes widened in surprise.

"Mateo-?"

He pulled his hand out and sat on the rocks, in his hands were two red crystal looking things, he patted the rock next to him and I hesitantly sat next to him in confusion. Mateo put a piece in my hand and bit his, it crunched between his teeth and I looked down at him.

"It's a bit spicy, but it's good." Mateo grinned as his burnt hand began to heal.

I took a bite and cleared my throat as it began popping with a small hint of spice behind it. "Oh?"

"Good right?"

"It's certainly interesting." I covered my mouth a bit.

"My grandpa used to fish them out for me." Mateo laughed and made a fist as his hand finished healing, "My grandpa was a Dragon, he said it's a delicacy to them."

"A Dragon?" I asked in shock.

"Heh, yea, my dad is half Dragon, half War Demon, I only got the height from my Dragon genes. I don't fit in well with *most* mice, really awkward growing up. Women love it, men not so much."

"Tell me about it." I shook his head, "Most men avoid me, especially the ones that are my type. So I just stayed single, plus random men don't need to be around my kid."

"Men would call me a catfish, what a joke right?" Mateo snorted through his nose, "They see mice and assume they're all small and tiny. Not my fault my genes worked out how they did."

"So, you're single? Is that why you asked me out?"

"Yea, me and my girlfriend broke up a couple years back, two different places in life, she wanted kids and marriage and this fairy tale, and well, I realized I didn't want that with her. Hard realization but, it is what it is I guess..." Mateo leaned back on his hands.

I nodded slowly and glanced away, "So was this a date?"

"I hope so." Mateo glanced over.

"Why?" I asked.

Mateo sat up and smiled, "Is that an honest question?"

"Yea…" I nodded.

"…." Mateo smiled and glanced away, "You'll laugh."

"Huh?"

"It's… a bit.. Embarrassing?" Mateo rubbed the back of his head.

I raised a brow. *Oh gods, please don't be a weirdo.*

"Well, I used to have the biggest crush on you in high school." He glanced away. "But in high school, you always seemed so untouchable?"

"What do you mean?"

"Well, for starters, you were best friends with Leviathan, I hated him." He rolled his eyes, "And I assumed you two started dating at some point, you were both really close…"

"Oh! No, no, never. He was too involved with Scotus to notice me." I shook my head, I tried to lessen the bitterness in my statement. Too many memories, so much frustration, I still don't understand it now.

"So you did like him?"

"Yea, I guess so? At one point, I'm not really good with romantic feelings, how to discern them or anything like that. I rarely feel them." I sighed and rubbed my face, "Which also makes dating hard."

"Should I back off?" Mateo asked.

"Huh? Oh, no no, I'm sorry I didn't mean to come off like that." I signed a bit, "It's complicated?"

"Oh?" Mateo asked.

"I've never really had an official boyfriend before, so I'm not sure, how to go about it?" I rubbed at my face, "Jezabelle. This is embarrassing."

Mateo smiled softly, "Well, would you like too?"

"Err, have a boyfriend I mean?"

"I..."

"No rush of course, but I don't want to confuse you or make you second guess, I am very interested. And I'd love to take you out on a few more dates if that's Ok?"

" I um..." I glanced away in thought, "Sure..."

"Really? Like, you actually want to?" Mateo asked.

"Yea, I do..."

He couldn't hold back the big grin on his face, his cheeks were rosy and his eyes were bright.

"Great... I'll go at your pace, you're fully in control here, if you ever want me to back off, just tell me.."

"Thanks..." I gave him a gentle smile, "Um, I should head back, Aubrey is probably worried, I'm never gone this long." I chuckled.

"I can walk you back?"

"Sure.." I went to stand but Mateo beat me to it and put a hand to me, I gently took his hand and Mateo pulled me up like I weighed nothing.

That sent a shudder up my spine, the only guy to toss me around like nothing was Levi, and even then, he did it to be an ass, while with Mateo, it felt more natural, like that's just how he is. He will certainly be a new experience. Am I excited? Is this a crush?

He walked me back towards Nevermore and made small conversation here and there. I notice when he talks for too long, his language changes, he's bilingual, how fascinating. Then he'd get embarrassed and apologize profusely, *how cute.* We got to the house and I placed my hand on the gate before looking at him,

"Choose somewhere cheaper next time?"

"I will make no such promises." Mateo grinned. I laughed quietly and shook my head.

"How's next Friday?"

"Perfect." Mateo smiled, "You have my number."

"Yea.." I waved a bit, "Goodnight Mateo."

"Night…"

I bowed my head a bit awkwardly and headed inside, I could hear Aubrey stumbled before plopping down on the couch, I blinked and looked up. Then narrowed my eyes. *That little-*

"The couch is cold, and this spot is warm." I pointed to the area in front of the door.

"I dunno what you mean." Aubrey grinned, "Soooo second date? I'm assuming."

"Uh huh, don't you got school tomorrow? Bed."

"Fine fineee." Aubrey huffed then headed upstairs, I smiled softly to himself. Maybe this'll be good? Maybe some change would be nice? I guess we'll see.

5

FOUR

I looked up at the massive building, it was a gated property, a fountain with a statue of Hecate in the middle sat at the entrance. The school had Gothic architecture like everything important in The Valley, students wandered around in their appropriate coven uniforms. *Uniforms.* Ugh.

I headed inside, gripping my old backpack and rubbed my face, feeling nervous like the first day of high school. Palms sweaty, anxiety spiked, heart pounding, head hurting, the whole shabang. I took a deep breath and avoided as many people as possible. I hate being touched. It's not as busy inside as the entrance and the courtyard, but it was still loud with chatter and footsteps on the linoleum floors. I looked down at my paper and looked around the location, just open hallways and chatting people.

The school was massive, the main entrance was nothing more than a glorified hallway with archways circling the courtyard. The stone walls housed many portraits and by the entrance, flags of the different covens to join. By the front steps was The Headmaster's office, A little to the left was the library and the rest of the halls were covered in lockers and memorabilia from wands to hats and spell books. I can already tell I'll find much solace in the court yard. From here it looks like there's a green house on the opposite end, That might be the best spot for me. Already planning my escapes. Saint is *so* lucky I love her.

"Aubrey?" I turned to a mature feminine voice, I blinked as a brown skinned woman with grey and black hair stood beside me, she had a soft smile on her face, "Long time no see?"

Her ears were winged and she had two extra closed eyes placed under her own. She dragged black wings behind her, She was a curvy woman. She wore a slimming dress that covered her modestly. I guess those old Angel habits die hard. I bowed my head quickly to her in respect. Even now, her angelic energy commanded respect.

"Oh! Mrs. Eve, hello, wow.. What are you doing here?" I asked, straightening my posture out of instinct.

"I'm a teacher here now," She beamed, "The corruption coven teacher."

I nodded, "Oh, congrats, what made you want to teach?"

"Mm, my twins go here, you remember them, yes?"

I nodded.

"Keegan…she isn't taking this…change well.." Eve looked away, a look of hurt and worry in her eyes. *Keegan fell too?* Oh she must be **devastated**. I remember how important that Angel scholarship was to her back in High School.

"She..?"

Eve nodded, "She fell, yea, devastated her for years. Her mother and I had to do a lot of convincing to get her to enroll. But her brother is ecstatic, you should try reconnecting, maybe seeing a familiar face will put her at ease.."

"Of course, gods it's been so long, we haven't talked since?" I took a moment to to think, "What, graduation day?"

"I'm sure they both would be so happy to see you dear, just, go a little easy on the Angel Academy stuff yeah?" She smiled and patted the top of my head before walking off. I watched her go then looked back down to my paper.

I can't believe she fell. She was by far the most angelic person I've ever met. Being born here? That's saying something. I guess those programs and that place really is bullshit if they managed to outcast Keegan of all people. I shook my head, not my business. Not my business.

"Alright." I decided to wander around, a little exploration wouldn't hurt. I took in my surroundings, it's a beautifully made building, not a single sign of wear or tear, a few portraits of Hecate and the history of the school lined the walls by the entrance, I decided to head towards the library. Past it was the cafeteria, and what looked like a gym? Big place.

I felt a slight bump and shock on my shoulder, I met eyes with a taller slender mocha brown woman, she wore a witch hat with bird feathers on it. Her face was soft, her lips were full and stretched into an irritated frown. She had her gray hair curled over her blue eyes, barely showing them as she glared down at me. Her long black dress hugged her curves elegantly. She paused there, her stare boring into me, all I could do was blink and slowly step back to give her space.

"Apologies child.." Her voice was quiet but harsh, she turned her head forward and continued walking ahead, She made her way towards the Headmaster's office. I raised a brow but decided to go in the opposite direction.

"Ok.." I made my way towards the library, of course it was huge, quiet, and nearly empty. There was two levels, A few students were sat at the tables by the upper balcony. All the book shelves were floor to ceiling, filled with as many books as one could imagine. A few gargoyles were perched with torches next to them. They must be guardians. I guess even in college these morons can't be trusted with something as delicate as books. The old carpet muffled my foot steps as I wandered in.

Oh I can definitely learn more about plants here. I walked around and peeked at the end of the shelves for the catalog book. A couple of students were studying, others were listening to music or just reading. I hummed then smiled as I spotted the extravagant book. The pages were open and the book had a soft white glow to it. The pages were blank, I spoke to it gently and watched as it settled and words bled onto the page. I read over the instructions a few times before the book reset itself. Then made my way towards the earth section. Hundreds of books lined the shelves, perfect. I skimmed the books with interest, but one of these books was out of place.

I went to reach for it, but another hand got there before me, I looked over and tilted my head slightly. A smaller caramel brown chubby girl stood next to me, she had wavy hair past her shoulders, a dark brown with pale gray streaks. Her eyes were two different shades of blue, one bright the other dark. She was covered in freckles and had a small beauty mark under her right eye. Her nails had simple bear and bow designs on them. Unlike her mother though, she didn't have multiple eyes. Her harsh stare flickered to me then she blinked in realization, I know that stare anywhere. She hasn't changed a bit.

"Keegan?" I chuckled a bit, "Well, look at you."

"Aubrey?" She questioned before dropping her hand, "Oh wow, it's been awhile." She said back.

"I just bumped into your mom, you're really her mini me huh?" I leaned against the bookshelf, looking down at her. She was even in the plum purple variation of the school uniform, She's a conjuring student. She moved her hair behind her ear and glanced away, her cheeks got a slight red tint to them, even if she did try to hide it.

"Well thank you. And you've certainly matured.." Her eyes trailing over me before making eye contact again, "Blacksmithing does a body good?" Keegan trailed off then her face got red, her baby blue winged ears flaring in embarrassment, "I mean-!"

I chuckled, "Easy. Easy."

I crossed my arms, "I could say the same for you, maturing wise. Gods I still remember your awkward teen phase, the braces, the too big wings"

"Oh my goodness, shut uppp." Keegan whined and covered her face, "Don't remind me."

"Don't worry, you were still beautiful back then, we were all awkward teens."

"Beautiful?" Keegan tilted her head slightly, and messed with her hair, "No boyfriend out of town?"

"Eh, nah, boys ain't been on my radar since graduation, turns out comphet was kicking my ass, put a lot in perspective. Guess that Bi with a woman lean was kind of a sign in retrospect." I snorted.

Keegan nodded, "I get that, at least you know now? Gods

don't ask me." She shook her head.

"Well. I wouldn't be against talking to you about it, or, talking about anything." I grabbed the book she was reaching for before, a fire spells book. I put it to her and she looked up at me before taking it. Her soft hands brushed against mine.

"Really?" She hugged the book to her chest, "Well, I like coffee, if you ever want to talk."

"Noted."

Keegan gave a small smile before walking off, maybe this school won't be so bad. Saint's notification chimed in my pocket. She's probably looking for me. I looked back at the books and took a mental note before heading back out to the main hallway then turned my head towards the sound of my name.

"Aubrey! You came!" Saint exclaimed happily, already in her Possession coven uniform, The ghosty blue variation.

"Hey baby girl, I just got your message..." I nodded awkwardly and followed behind her towards a section of lockers.

Saint beamed, "This is going to be so exciting, have you chosen a coven?"

"Uh-?" I looked at my basically crinkled up paper and shrugged in confusion, "No? I honestly have no idea what my schedule is or where I would go."

"Oh, let me see." Saint took the papers and looked over them, "Ok, we have the Shadow Coven, Hexes, Curses, and Poisons Coven, Possessions coven," She motioned to herself and smiled, "Madness coven, Pain Coven, Blood Coven, Conjuring coven and Theft Coven."

I narrowed my eyes, *eight is a bit excessive*. I shook my

head a bit, noticing the name on Saint's paper, "Holloway..?"

She waved it off, "It's the name daddy puts on all our public stuff, I don't want people knowing I'm a Sawyer, it'll make things incredibly unbearable. Plus people ain't the… nicest to Reapers nowadays." She muttered the last part.

She looked back at the paper as I nodded in understanding.

"Anyway, Yes, most people already know their covens, 'cuz ya know, sorcerers are born into specific ones. You not being a Sorcerer makes this difficult." Saint tapped her lips with her nail, "Ok, we can put you in one and fake it till we make it." She read over the papers.

"You don't have Ghost or Possession magic, so Possession is off the table, you don't have Shadow magic, you don't have Fear, Pain, or Blood magic, or Conjuring magic, and you definitely don't have Theft magic. Soo, Curses and Hexes might be your Trojan horse, it's all spells and stuff! That's like basic magic." Saint put the paper to me and smiled widely. I took it from her and rubbed my head.

"Alright, uh, what do I do now-?" I looked around the space, people were walking in and out, opening and closing lockers, grabbing and putting books back. I looked at saint as she opened her own locker, the inside empty and dark before she put her bag inside, then it lit up with a purple hue and customized to her baby doll aesthetic, neat.

"You'll have to see Headmaster Petra, she'll get all your stuff in order, geez, been out of school that long?" Saint laughed.

"Uh, yea, high school is a distant memory now." I deadpanned, "Plus I went to the public Demon schools, not fancy Sorcerer schools."

"Well, welcome to your first fancy Sorcerer school!" Saint snorted.

"It's a bit much, ain't it?" I raised a brow, "Y'all are certainly extra."

Saint shook her head and began to organize her locker, "You'll get used to it babe." She glanced past me then turned her head completely, "Oh, don't freak out."

"Huh?" I asked, glancing back, I could feel my eyes stretch wide. *Rouge*. A tall dark skinned, curvy woman was walking towards us, surrounded by people as always, the kindest smile, the sweetest eyes, hair and clothes always perfect, she always seemed like she was floating above everyone else, to me she was the people's princess. The cheer captain, The prom queen, The valedictorian, The everything. Her green hair was pulled back into a neat Bantu knot style, her red lip gloss glowed in the natural light beaming from the corresponding arches, The lighting made her look like a goddess. Of course she could make a school uniform look runway ready.

I instantly turned around and covered my face in panic, I could feel my face getting hotter in pure embarrassment and unease.

"No no no." I groaned quietly, "Not now."

Saints eyes were amused, she closed her locker gently and patted my shoulder, "Hi Rouge, how was your trip love?"

I could hear the smile in her sweet voice, "Hi Saint, it was great." She stopped behind me and I wanted to curl into myself and fucking die. "Look at your new tattoo, oh it's so you! love the roses!"

"Oh girl stop." She laughed and waved it off, "Thank you~

so, how did those scholarships go?"

"Full ride, daddy is so proud, but." Rouge sighed, "Took a lot of convincing to let me go here."

"Well, I'm ecstatic you're here! I was worried I'd be alone, also happy belated~ not sure if you got my message."

"Oh, shit, I did, I forgot to respond, I'm so sorry love, thank you so much, the big twenty-four. Basically growing into my fangs now." Rouge laughed, Saint laughed with her before it went eerily silent in my ears, of course I couldn't just snake by.

"Aubrey?" Rouge questioned. I rubbed my face and took a quiet breath out before turning around and awkwardly leaning against the lockers to put some space between us. "Oh wow, you're back?" Her stunning green eyes sparkled in surprise.

Her long lashes and soft makeup elevated her beauty. She smelled so good, like always. A faint Vanilla and Shea butter, lotion and perfume combo she's always done. She always radiated warmth. I could feel my breath catch as I took her beauty in after all these years. She's just matured with age, still a goddamn stallion.

"Heh, hey Rouge.." I smiled awkwardly. Her eyes were so soft and kind, Rouge smiled back and nodded

"Hi Aubrey.."

"Hey- uh-" *You dumbass you already said that.* "How...have you been?"

"Good, went on vacation, convinced my dad to let me move back home while he worked. Turns out his job relocated down here anyway, lucky me" She shrugged cutely, "And you? How was college out of town..?" She placed her hand on my arm, she had black powder and glitter on her fingers like most Sorcerers, but she has her magic glyph tatted on the top of her hand, maybe all of it is a tattoo? That's smart, she'll never have to draw it.

"College-?" I internally slapped my hand on my forehead and groaned. I could see a Saint shaking her head in the corner of my eye, "OH! College, oh uh, yea…it was uh, not for me." I glanced away.

"I see, well, it's wonderful to see you again, I won't keep you." The same look she always gave me, "Saint we absolutely have to catch up soon, coffee on me?"

"Love too~"

With that she walked on, My eyes followed her like a lost puppy. Fuck, she still has that damn hold on me. The clicking of her heels slowly faded down the corridor, I instantly turned around and dropped my head against the lockers with a thud.

"Way to go, Romeo"

"Shut up."

"She genuinely alters your brain chemistry, huh?" Saint had amusement in her voice, all I could do was send her a weak glare.

"You could've told me she'd be going here. I can't believe she goes here." I dropped my head against the locker once more.

"Well, we found out together." She stood straight and walked ahead, motioning me to follow. "But, there was always a chance. She's a Sorcerer dummy. Or did you forget that with your alibi too?"

I groaned quietly, "Shut up."

I followed behind her with an embarrassed and defeated look on my face.

"Any who~" She chimed, "I'll take you to Miss Petra, get your schedule and what not before orientation and stuff." She turned me around and led me out towards the front of the school. We headed to the front office, Saint knocked lightly and slipped in. Petra closed her laptop and looked up at us.

"Morning you two." The lady who bumped into me earlier, *She's* the Headmaster? Why do people who obviously dislike people, work with people?

"Hi Miss Petra." Saint smiled, "This is Aubrey, he's a new student, he needs to choose a coven and get a locker and schedule."

"I see, you weren't already assigned?" She queried and leaned back in her chair, her gaze felt icy, even behind the bangs. Her voice was sharp and the energy around her was dark and uneasy.

"Uh, new to Sorcerer schools." I muttered.

"Oh, a public sin school kid, hm." *Oh, yea that felt like a slur.* I narrowed my eyes slightly as she stood and walked to a bookshelf. She picked up an old worn down hat, it looked like the same hat Hecate wore on her statue, it had a dim blue glow in her hands as she walked over.

"Well, as you should know, a Sorcerer's hat means everything to them, it shows their power and capability to graduate and learn as much as they can." Petra dusted off the old hat, "This is the original hat Her majesty Hecate used to create the eight covens. Some have called it a sorting hat or something, I call that foolish." Petra rolled her eyes.

I nodded slowly, "So, this hat just puts me in a coven."

"Not exactly, it accepts you into the coven, it's only used for those who are unassigned or undecided." Petra gave me a sly look, she placed the hat on my head, "What coven have you chosen?"

"Oh, Potions?" I questioned. The hat took on a green glow and I felt something drop around my neck and chest. I looked down at the green and silver key and raised a brow.

"That is your school key, if you lose it you will be expelled or perish." Petra sat the hat on her desk, "It allows you entry to the school and classrooms. It can also put a cap on your power level and regulate the power flow through your body, think of it as training wheels before graduating." She sat back at her desk and adjusted her laptop.

"The key will give you a schedule and locker."

"Miss Petra-?" We turned our attention to a thicker pink haired girl, She had bright pink eyes and darker brown spots on her mocha brown skin. She had a strange crescent shape around her right eye. Her hair was in a ponytail and she was in uniform. She had a dark pink powder and glitter on her hands, Her appearance was familiar but I can't quite place it.

She seemed a bit nervous and timid. She had her hand on the door and a slightly confused look in her eyes, she looked at both of us then the Headmaster.

"Oh, Rue. Perfect timing, This is Aubrey. He is new to the academy. Be a doll and get him situated, yes?" With that she opened up her laptop and motioned us out, I glanced at her but followed Saint out.

"Oh, uh, sure.." Rue closed the door behind us.

"Bit of a bitch isn't she?" I muttered

"Miss Petra? No, she's literally the sweetest, she.." Rue rubbed her arm, "She might be in a mood today. Who are you to even say that." She narrowed her eyes her thin eyebrows furrowing.

"Someone who's a people person." I deadpanned, and Saint elbowed me and shot me a look, "But please, show me the magic key stuff."

Rue rolled her eyes, "Just ask it for your schedule, it'll automatically take you to your locker."

"Thanks, so helpful."

"Um, thank you Rue." Saint spoke up and pushed me away before following, "Do not provoke her."

"Huh?" I asked

"She's a top Sorcerer, like super powerful. Just, keep your head down Ok?" Saint asked. I sighed, and nodded.

"Hey." We turned around and looked at Rue, "She asked me too, so I can still show you around."

* * *

"And here is where you'll be spending most of your four years." Rue spoke up and motioned to a hall, "The potions wing. Your first class should be glyph writing."

I looked up at the arch, "Alright, thanks."

"Yea sure." She responded before turning around, "Oh, and, good luck. This school will tear you apart."

I narrowed my eyes at her and rolled them, so tired of these pompous overrated witches. I rubbed my face and breathed out a heavy sigh. Half a day gone already? Didn't even have orientation yet and I'm already exhausted.

"See not so bad! You didn't melt yet." Saint smiled

"Yea, *'yet'*." I followed her back to the lockers and claimed mine. The inside turned green, some of the walls having a scale pattern on them, checks out. I closed it and looked towards the courtyard.

"Come on, it should be starting now." She hugged my arm close, I felt a bit of calmness wash over me, I took a breath and nodded before following her. We took a seat in the bleachers and I tried to drown out all the loud chatter. Saint was holding my hand and rubbing soothing circles on top of mine, she knows I hate crowds, she always tried her best to pacify me, I don't mind it, if not her, then Rouge.

I sighed a bit and leaned back.

"Afternoon students." Petra spoke up, everyone quieted down and took their seats, "Another successful semester with so many happy faces, and eager learners. As you all know, the next four years will be for advancing your born skill. Be it Possession, Hexes, Darkness, Madness, Pain, Blood, Conjuring or Theft magic, you will leave this academy as a prodigy." She motioned to the teachers on stage.

"Our staff is full of alumni who are here to be guides, you are expected to do your best and succeed. And if you work hard enough you'll be offered opportunities most can only dream of. I plan to keep this brief, but you are our futures. And you *need* to keep it bright."

"This school has no room for error or subpar sorcerers, if you believe this will be difficult, it's best to turn back now. I, or Hecate, will not accept below average skill." Petra smiled and bowed her head, the area stayed silent save for a few concerned murmurs. After that everything else just blended together, meeting a teacher there, exploring a new place here.

I can't wait to get back home.

I'm not too sure how I feel about the school and the

Headmaster, but I'm in it now. All to please that dork I call a friend. I smiled at her as we walked back home, she was going on and on about something but honestly I couldn't focus, if I'm honest my mind kept lingering back to her. Rouge. It's been so long, and even now she still looks at me like I matter, even after everything I've put her through.

Maybe Saint is right? I should just be honest, maybe then we can start over? Or should I just leave it? I don't deserve her and her patience anyway, who the hell do you think you are Aubrey, fucking hell. You left her with no contact for four years with a bullshit excuse of a break up. Why would you even try again? Hell, why assume she's single? Someone like her? No way. I was lucky, and I fucking blew it. What a fucking joke.

"Aye, Saint to Aubrey." I blinked as she snapped in my line of sight, I didn't even realize I was looking at the ground, "Requesting communication. You good?"

"…" I gripped my bag and took a deep breath, "Do you think I should let her go..?"

"Huh?" Saint tilted her head, "Rouge?"

"Mhmm.. I've been thinking about the options and possible outcomes.." I shook my head, "Should I just drop it..?"

"Aubrey…" She sighed and placed her hand on my back, rubbing soothingly, "Let's… let's get lunch? And relax for a while? I can see the exhaust in your eyes."

"…Yea…sure."

6

FIVE

It was a typical warm night, back when Aubrey was four and Tartarus was a new dad.

Jasper hurried in, "You're sure you don't mind watching Saint?" They spoke up, Their hair bouncing as they looked up at Tartarus. He nodded to them and took the small girl's bag.

"It's no problem, you seem stressed Jasper..." Tartarus spoke.

Saint looked around the brightly lit hallway, photos lined the walls and a key bowl sat on a side table next to the front door. She kicked her tiny shoes off and sat them next to Tartarus' boots. She messed with her lilac purple dress and held Jasper's hand. She's never been here before, It smelled like pie and air fresheners.

"It's just a lot going on right now." Jasper said, They rubbed their face and shook their head.

"Hecate?" Tartarus asked.

"Tsk. Yes, She's being incredibly difficult. I told her I'm handling it but she won't back off. Like you have a kid at home, don't you think you got more important things to worry about." Jasper said bitterly, "I didn't even make the call, ugh. I'm sorry Tartarus, Um, she has no allergies, but she's not fond of peanuts, or Brussels sprouts, bedtime at 7:30."

Saint looked up at the taller male, His golden eyes peered down at her. She hid behind Jasper's leg but they gently moved her towards him. Saint looked back at her dad in fear and uncertainty. Jasper just smiled and kneeled down.

"Princess, this is Daddy's friend, Tartarus." Jasper pet the top of her head, "He's going to watch you tonight while I work, Ok? I need you to be a big brave girl. He has a son you can play with too."

"..." Saint made a face of disapproval. She messed with her skirt and looked down.

"I'll be back in the morning, Ok?" Jasper smiled softly.

"Fine. Ok..." Saint rubbed at her eye.

"I can't thank you enough." Jasper stood, They smiled apologetically and took their leave. They turned towards them and blew a kiss to the purple haired little girl. They put their hand on their head and summoned their Reaper hat and with that took their leave.

"Alright..." Tartarus looked down at the small purple haired girl, her hair was curled to her shoulders and she was in an adorable poofy dress. She nervously gripped at her skirt.

Tartarus gently placed his hand on her shoulder and lead her to the cozy living room.

"Aubrey!" Tartarus called out, small pitter patter came down the steps, A little kid with auburn hair and bright purple eyes stood on the bottom step, his little hands gripping the banister. A big dog sat behind him on the next step. That made Saint even more nervous. They don't have dogs in her house.

"Hi daddy." Aubrey spoke cheerfully.

"Hey Kiddo, This is Saint, she's going to stay the night. Can you play with her and be nice?" Tartarus asked with a smile. Aubrey shrunk back himself and looked a bit nervous. He messed with the loose button on his overalls.

"Um, Okay…" He said.

"How about you two play outside and I'll get some dinner started?"

Aubrey got off the bottom step and put a hand to her, "Hello, my name is Aubrey I'm four!"

"Saint…" The smaller girl said, she hesitantly took his hand and shook it, "I'm four."

"We're the same age! Good already! Iron can play hide and seek! He's our Hellhound!" Aubrey pet the top of the dog's hand.

"We hide from your dog?" Saint asked.

"Yep! He's well… um, tr..trained." Aubrey nodded.

"Ok." Saint finally agreed. She slipped her shoes back on with Aubrey then followed him outside with Iron close behind.

"We stay away from the front and back gates, that's off limits!" Aubrey explained, "Iron will bark really loud if we get too close. Also we can't hide in there." Aubrey pointed his tiny finger towards the gazebo.

"Aw but I like those." Saint pouted.

"We will die. And death is permanent." Aubrey said.

"Not for me!" Saint said triumphantly, "My daddy is death."

"Hmmmm." Aubrey puffed out his cheek, "Well, I will die, and you will get in trouble."

"Okay." Saint huffed.

Tartarus sighed out, He kept an eye on them from the window. He's out of food and definitely can't go somewhere this late to pick up groceries. Especially not with two little kids. Hell, Charon is probably ferrying all night. He rubbed his face in exhaustion. One little firecracker is one thing, but two little kids is another. He's never watched Saint before, she's new to him. He knew Jasper had a daughter but he was usually on top of her child care. Until that **incident**. Things have become complicated.

He paced around the kitchen as the two kids ran around in the yard, a few occasional warning barks filled the area from Iron, be it they ran too far or too fast. Tartarus would be significantly more lost if Iron wasn't so helpful. He would watch Aubrey whenever Tartarus passed out from exhaustion, He'd follow him around to keep him safe when Tartarus was working. He alerted Tartarus to any and every possible danger and now he's basically a babysitter till the kids tire out.

Tartarus grabbed his phone and scrolled down his contact list. Not a long list, but a list nonetheless. Just four names, Leviathan, Charon, Jasper and Beelzebub. He dragged his hand down his face. Dear gods, he had to call her of all people. His finger lingered over her contact. He closed his eyes and pressed his thumb down and put the ringing line to his ear.

"This is Beelzebub! Hi Tartarus~" She buzzed in his ear. Her sickening voice rattled his ear. He debated hanging up, maybe contacting the Queen of Gluttony for kids isn't wise.

He kept his mouth shut,

"Is this about my adorable little nephew~? You never call otherwise!" Bee Buzzed once more.

Tartarus sighed this time, "Yes, I need food. Are you open? Is it safe for four year old's to consume?"

"Oh I told you, I would never harm a hair on Aubrey's head. Any little friend of his, is a friend of mine. I can whip up his favorite nuggets and mac and cheese and be there in two nibbles of a fly bite sugar~!"

"Alright, thank you. He's sensitive to meat-" Tartarus began.

"Plant based chicken my love, don't worry! There's a reason he loves visiting Auntie B's so much!" Bee bragged, smugness coated her tone.

"Just, Thanks." Tartarus spoke.

"Of course sugar, see you soon!"

Tartarus looked outside and up at the cloudy sky, "It's gonna storm tonight.. Better put them to bed early." He muttered to himself.

As promised, Bee was there quickly. She flew in with a basket of food. Her blonde hair was in a low ponytail. Her yellow and black skin glimmered under the lights, she was in a floor length nightgown, covering her insect legs. Her wings fluttered behind her and she landed delicately on the floor. Her bright red eyes flickered to Tartarus. Her antennae flickered towards the kitchen.

"Go ahead, Thank you for coming so late Bee."

"Don't mention it!" Bee flew towards the kitchen and happily set the table and made the kids their plates. Tartarus went to the side door and called out for them.

"Saint, Aubrey! Come inside you two!"

The small children happily ran inside, Iron close behind. He shook off his fur and laid in his bed next to the table.

"Aubrey, Take her to the bathroom and help her wash her hands alright?"

"Ok!" Aubrey took Saint's hand and led her down the hall.

"Who's little girl is that?" Bee asked, placing the hot plates on the table.

"Jasper's."

"Need any extra help with her before I go?" Bee asked.

Tartarus thought for a moment, "Oh, would you be able to stay while she takes a bath? She doesn't know me well and another woman might make her more comfortable."

"Of course." Bee smiled and sat at the table, "I cooked for you too, have a seat big guy."

"You didn't have too."

"I'm aware." She smiled.

"Hi Auntie!" Aubrey said joyfully, he walked over and hugged her waist. Bee pet his head softly and held him close.

"Hi my little prince, I brought dinner for you~Your favorite."

"Yay! Thank you! Look I made a friend! Her name is Saint." Aubrey said, climbing up in his chair. Tartarus helped Saint in hers and gently pushed the plates towards the two children.

"It's nice to meet you Sugar Plum."

"You too!" Saint smiled and looked at the nuggets, "Oh, whats this?"

"They're my favorite! Chicken nuggets!"

Saint tilted her head in confusion, Aubrey scratched his cheek and glanced away awkwardly.

"She's kinda weird, but she's nice."

Bee laughed quietly.

"Be nice." Tartarus said, "Eat up honey, it's just chicken and mac and cheese. I'll help you both to bed afterwards."

"Yes sir." Saint said.

"Well, at least she's well behaved, why haven't you met her till now?" Bee asked.

"Jasper never asked for help with her, Hell I didn't even know they had a daughter till two years."

"I see. She certainly looks just like them, she's adorable."

"She is." Tartarus leaned against his hand, He went to say more but decided to purse his lips instead.

* * *

"Sorry princess, You'll have to share a bed with Aubrey." Tartarus said, tucking the two in. He walked around and made sure pillows were on the side of the bed in case either of them rolled over. He turned on Aubrey's night light and smiled at them.

"It's Ok sir!" Saint snuggled into the covers. Aubrey put his stuffed Dragon between them.

"Your father should be here in the morning, so rest up Ok?" Tartarus kissed the top of Aubrey's head and flicked the light switch off.

"Goodnight daddy!" Aubrey said, turning on his side and hugging his plush. Tartarus left the room and gently pulled the door up and turned off the hall light before heading to his own room for the night. Iron laid in his dog bed by Aubrey's closet but he was fast asleep. Saint was looking around Aubrey's room. In the dark you can see the figures of his boots, his hats, his toys and his posters.

She noticed Aubrey really liked music, he even had a record player. Saint has one in her living room, it's her daddy's though, but she still loves listening to it with them. Lightning caught Saint's eye from behind the curtain on Aubrey's patio door. A loud *BOOM* followed behind it. Saint instantly covered her ears, she could feel the tears welling up in her eyes. She doesn't like storms. She never has. Aubrey's eyes were closed. He didn't seem bothered one bit. She rolled over and tried to cover her head with the covers. It began to rain brimstone shortly after that first thunder clap. It became a steady sound since.

Saint couldn't stop the tears this time. She whined and whimpered quietly at all the noise. She tossed and turned to ease her discomfort but her dad wasn't here and she wasn't at home. She was scared.

"Saint?" Aubrey asked quietly, "Why are you moving all around?"

"I'm scared..." She cried.

Aubrey blinked at the darkness and noticed the bits of brimstone hitting the roof, "Oh, It's raining..."

"You don't like the storms?" Aubrey asked her, Saint shook her head. Her hands were over her ears. Aubrey immediately gave her his stuffed dragon and pulled her into a tight hug.

"It's Ok... It's Ok. I'll stay up with you." Aubrey rubbed the top of her head. Saint was trembling in fear but Aubrey held her close.

Aubrey gave her his little green stuffed Dragon. Saint rubbed at her eyes and sniffed while Aubrey hummed some of his favorite lullabies until she fell asleep.

The next day Saint couldn't wait to tell her father about her new best friend Aubrey while she held the green stuffed Dragon.

7

SIX

"So kid, how'd it go?" Tartarus asked.

"Uh, it went." I muttered and dropped my bag next to my chair as I plopped down, "Haven't been in a crowded environment like that in awhile."

I leaned forward against the back of the chair. I rested my head on my arms and watched him cook, the smell of vegetables and shrimp filled the room.

"Huh? Are you making dinner already?" I asked.

"Mhmm. Gumbo, separate pot for you of course." Tartarus hummed, cutting up the vegetables. "Figured you'd enjoy it after a long day. Just a little bit though, the grocery fund is a bit low."

"Low?" I questioned, "Dad I can get another job-"

"It's fine, you're going back to school. I can just take more clients." Tartarus said.

"Dad-" I watched him move around and cook, "It's seriously no problem, I can probably get my old waiter job back in Gluttony."

"Aubrey." Tartarus sighed, "You've been working your

whole teenhood, just.. enjoy this year? You're back in town, you're back in school, you need a social life." He put up a finger, "That isn't me or Iron, or Saint."

I sighed and laid my head back down, "My social life is *buzzing* thank you."

"Mhmm. speaking of which, Charon should be back with Iron any minute."

"Oh?"

"Yes, go make yourself presentable for them, they have been asking about you since you left, so get your story straight and don't worry them."

I huffed and stood, slinging the bag over my shoulder, "I got it dad, I'll be the finest motherfucker on the block." I grinned and shot my finger at him.

Tartarus' face fell into a frown. He rolled his eyes and shook his head, "Oh hell, get your ass upstairs."

I laughed and headed up to my room, dropped my bag and plopped on the bed. It really does feel good to be home. It's nice seeing the surface but nothing beats *your* own bed, your own bathroom and your own domain. Maybe Dad's right, I should work on my social skills. I'm twenty-four and I shouldn't be this exhausted from being in a school building. And I can't always rely on Saint to be glued to my side, most of the denizens are the same? I could try to reconnect with a few people?

I glanced over at my nightstand, the lamp was off and a small cathedral ring was laying next to my old white charger, I grabbed my phone and plugged it up before sitting it down and getting up to shower. I pulled my shirt over my head and tossed it in the hamper with my other dirty clothes. I rubbed at and scratched my chest as I walked into the bathroom. I turned the dials and let steam slowly fill the room.

I'll need to spend money too huh? I'd have to get that old job again anyway. I huffed out, compromise? I can work less hours. Or take up a job in greed? They pay out the ass for basically nothing. Well, no dad would lose it, tends to be a bit shady. Fuck it, that's a tomorrow problem.

I stepped into the shower and laid my head back and closed my eyes, enjoying the water falling on my skin. It felt nice to see the familiar walls, dim green lighting and enjoying the soft music. I always loved showers. My shower thoughts were incredibly chaotic, but also creative, who doesn't like a good shower thought turned painting right? I've got a lot of shit to work on. I know that. This is a second chance, why not take it? A new job, new friends, new things to learn, a new me.

Charon would be proud of that, I got out and got dressed in simple jeans and a button down. plopping back down on the bed I let my eyes close. So much is in my mind at once and honestly it's too much to keep up with.

I sat up after a moment and grabbed an old notebook and scribbled down on it a small list: *make some friends, get a job, make parents proud.* As much as I hate those pompous assholes, I am excited to improve my earth magic. It's been stunted since I was a child, a few plant conversations and vine growth and not much more. I'm the only plant person in the family, Dad is technically an Earth Elemental but he has a lot of gray area. His main choice is lava, not very helpful. Lava is something I never clicked with. Earth is a spectrum, and he isn't on my side of that spectrum.

"Aubrey! Come eat." Tartarus called down.

I hopped up and tossed the notebook and headed downstairs and instantly smiled and hugged Charon. I could feel them squeeze and hold me there for a moment. Their dark, almost black skin glistened with starry blue, purple and white freckles. Their black hair flowed behind them like the River Styx itself, It still has that holographic glow like the River. They were still in their work robes and took their hat off. The small ghost and river design flowing as they did. Dad placed it on the rack for them and smiled. Their coin covered chest rattled with every motion.

Their pure white eyes glowed in happiness as they looked at me, It's been so long since I've seen Charon. They're one of Dad's old friends. They use to watch me when I was a child, They took me on the Ferry often and taught me sign language. They never talked but we had so many conversations. Hell, They're the one who gave me dating advice, Gods know Dad couldn't.

"Welcome Charon, I hope this isn't too inconvenient for you."

"Not at all! I heard Aubrey was back and just had to stop by~" They signed eagerly.

I smiled and signed back to them, "I'm happy to see you, I'm sorry it took so long."

'How have you been?' They signed, *'How was college?'*

"It was alright, I prefer being home though." I signed back, They smiled and nodded.

'We prefer you home sweetie! We missed you very much' they laughed quietly, *'Your father was a mess'*

"Oh?" I spoke and signed, "Now that doesn't sound like him."

'Oh hush now,' They patted my chest and smiled. *'Am I free*

to join y'all for dinner Tartarus?'

"Of course, you know you're always welcome. I figured you'd enjoy some Gumbo, like old times." Tartarus smiled and led the smaller person towards the kitchen, Their hair shined off the tiles.

I followed close behind and sat in my usual chair, I noticed Charon stayed close to Dad and didn't sit right away. I nodded to myself and took the hint before getting up and going back in the living room. I decided to feed Iron for the night, I kneeled down and pet behind his ears.

He nuzzled my face and licked at my cheeks.

"Aw come on boy, I just showered." I snorted, and stood up, making my way over to the pantry closet and began to fill his bowl by the hall. His tail wagged in appreciation and I decided to head upstairs to clean up my face and wash my hands.

'He's so big now, my gods, I don't want to cry'

"Yea.. feels like just yesterday he was learning how to ride a bike and learning how to read chapter books..." Tartarus looked at them and smiled, "He paints still ya know? Goes through spray paint like crazy."

'Does he?'

"I was thinking of adding a studio to the house for him, so he doesn't have to keep painting out back." Tartarus snorted, "A belated birthday gift."

'Sounds absolutely perfect! He'd love it!' Charon took their seat at the table, *'Is he here to stay?'*

"I believe so, I think he'll enjoy the academy, it can teach him things we never could.."

'That's wonderful to hear.' Charon signed, *'How are you feeling?'*

"I'm fine.." Tartarus muttered and sat the bowls down and Charon gave him a sad look, 'Better? I guess?'

'Tartarus...'

"Just happy he's home safe, I've had a pit in my stomach ever since he left…Charon, I don't have a good feeling." He sighed and sat at the table, "Something feels… off? The feeling subsided since he came back, maybe I was just worried?"

'It's normal to be, he didn't contact us for years, he could have gotten hurt.' They signed and touched Tar's hands gently. *'He's home now, things can go back to normal?'*

He chuckled lightly, "Define normal?"

Charon smiled and patted his hand.

I dried my hands and face and walked in, "Alright, let's eat?"

* * *

"Hey Auntie B." I smiled as I walked in her shop.

BeeBees Bakery, It was an old Retro shop. The booths were well worn in, the granite floors were scrapped up from the Bee's skating around. Honeycomb tiles littered the walls. She had many retro posters on the wall and of course the giant front glass windows. It was always cozy in here. The counter was glossy clean as always with a cake of the day under the glass case. Usually there's a line down the block for this place, It's been standing and popular since she's been down here, apparently that's a long time.

The shop was full of little bee trinkets. It always felt unauthentic to Auntie's personality. I personally feel like she isn't a Bee, and knows little to nothing about their culture. She tends to be very disrespectful in all honesty, but she's still the queen nonetheless. No one will dare question a Head sin, let alone the Sin who created The Valley famous Nectar. Naturally I wasn't allowed any, something about it being highly addictive and deadly? I'm not sure I'll ever know.

My boots clicked on the granite floors as I made my way to the counter, I smiled at her and leaned against the cold counter.

"Closed for the day?" I asked, flicking my toothpick from one side of my mouth to the other.

"Oh! Aubrey! When did you get home Honey Bee?" She beamed, her big red insect-like eyes shined, she held a jar in her white gloved hands, her wing's fluttering behind her as she sat the unlabeled jar down and made her way to me, pulling me into a bone crushing hug.

I laughed quietly and rubbed her back, She left kisses all over my face and I tried to endure. *Gods I'm not five anymore.* I smiled through it until she pulled away and cupped my cheeks.

"Auntie please. I just got back." I smiled, "I'm sorry, I would've visited sooner but Saint's been hogging all my time."

"Oh yes! Your little girlfriend who likes my chocolate and pumpkin cakes~I remember."

"Not my girlfriend." I shook my head and sat at the booth.

"Ah yes, The "*Best Friend*" You casually have matching tattoos and rings with." She teased. I waved it off.

Auntie Bee, Or Beelzebub, whatever, has been in my life as far back as I can remember. Probably the closest thing I've ever had to a mother. She taught me how to cook and clean and she used to babysit me for dad sometimes. She always had a soft spot for me even if that made dad uneasy. He said he respected her but I know he's scared of her and what she's capable of. She single handedly made the 2nd most addictive drug in The Valley and sells it for profit. What does she do with the patrons who buy? Not sure. Some disappear though. She told me to never ask her about that again. I was eleven then, and I'm still too afraid to ask now.

"Anyway." I snorted.

"How was school?" She asked, making her way back around the counter and going back to labeling her nectar jars. I began twisting absentmindedly on the stool as always.

"Eh, it wasn't for me." I shrugged, "Say, I was wondering if you could give me a job at the den?"

"A job?" Bee tilted her head.

"If you can, my waiter job again?" I asked.

"Hm. I'm not too sure if that's open, I don't do much stuff." Bee shrugged a bit and continued labeling, "Why do you want another job?"

"Dad's been budgeting for stuff lately, funds are low. Figured I'd help. And I need pocket change."

"I see, well it's best to ask Blanche." Bee hummed.

I blinked and looked at her. Blanche? Wasn't aware she was still there. Well, I guess that means Auntie co-owns? I assumed when she bought little birdie out she'd skip town. I remember she was way too pretty to work, way too nice to deal with moronic asshole customers who think taking their frustrations out on service workers will make them less pathetic. I've had one too many of those types of customers.

"Blanche? She still works there?" I rubbed my chin and

glanced across the street at the Den. The bold BeeBee's on the glass obscuring the view of the front door. Can't tell If they're closed or not.

"Of course, she runs it well." Bee nodded.

"Alright, I can ask, thank you Auntie B." I glanced away, "If you're closed, does that mean they're doin' a shift change?"

Bee hummed in response, "They should be closed for it, they might be cleaning the front now."

I haven't seen Blanche in years, she was a really nice work friend. A nice change of pace from the jackasses I went to high school with. Heh, I still remember how we met, she had the brightest smile on her face, served me a strawberry shortcake milkshake, homemade and gods did it taste like heaven. She beamed so bright when I complimented her. every time, on every little snack or drink she made. She had a talent, one I feel can never truly be replicated.

Though, Her being a cupid always made me nervous. The Cupids migrated down here a couple decades ago and set up shop in dens in all seven cities. Rumor has it they're children of Aphrodite to spread love throughout The Valley, others say they are demigods who died and made a name for themselves. Either way, they are different from other Demons, Hell I don't even think they're demonic in any way shape or form. They don't speak about their origins, and they don't open up avenues to ask questions. They're Sweet talkers, they blend with their respective Sin, took me years to realize they're all related.

Blanche is the only one I met personally, she's easy with words and her vibe is very intimidating. She always says sly things and gives me those side glances. I never understood why, I always assumed it was because of work and it's in character for her, considering she runs the den. Turns out all the Cupid's are like that. I assume they're just Succubi until I'm informed otherwise. It ain't up for me to speculate on. I mean, that's the whole shtick.

Although her with other people doesn't seem as organic. Like she's doing this because she has too, not because she wants too.

I stood and stretched my arms before taking a breath and glancing across the street at the Cupid's Den. Now's probably the best time.

"I'll head over and chat with her then."

"Alright! If you need anything Honeypot you let me know, I'll bring dinner anytime." Bee's wings fluttered happily behind her. Her antennae flickered in sync.

I smiled, "Hah, thanks. Dad would love it, he can't get enough of your treats."

I made my way across the street to the quiet diner, it had a lively orange, brown and yellow 70s aesthetic. like most of the dens, but hers was always my favorite. It was calm and sweet, guess that's why she bunkered down in the gluttony city. The neon Den lights were off in the window and the sign was flipped to closed. I pushed the door open anyway and scanned the area.

The neon orange lights illuminated the old checkered floors. The old red booths were already wiped down and prepped for the dinner rush. The low hanging lights all had soft orange colored bulbs in them, the floor was scuffed up worse here because of the amount of wait staff that still roller skate around. Soft music played from the jukebox. Lines will be out the door before long, these Demons can't wait for after hours Den activity.

I walked towards the jukebox, hands in my pockets and read over the cue.

"Sorry, we're closed!" A voice called out from behind the counter, I glanced towards it.

"Closed, yet won't turn up the music?" I made my way over and leaned over the counter a bit, "What I tell you about that Blanche? You know shift change is boring as hell."

I grinned as I heard commotion before quick footsteps darted in my direction. The small chested bleach blonde looked surprised to see me, Her insect-like eyes reflected the diner's chill lighting. Her hair was curled past her shoulders, she was in a short retro dress with white bangles and boots to match.

"Aubrey!" She pulled me into a tight hug and basically jumped in my arms, I braced myself and instinctively wrapped my arms around her upper waist.

"Hey Sugar.." I smiled and sat the smaller girl down. Her wings fluttered behind her.

"It's been so long! How are you!" Blanche asked, her big yellow eyes sparkled before she turned to make her way to the counter. She stood no taller than five feet, Her iridescent arms shined in the light. Now she's an *actual* bee Demon. She one hundred percent fits the part better than Auntie.

My eyes naturally trailed her, then I noticed her fuller waist and bigger, *gods.*

"*Damn-*" I coughed a bit then fought the urge to slap my forehead, *you said that out loud you creep,* "Oh- uh, doin' good.."

"Mmm~ what can I do for you?" Blanche giggled.

"I was actually wonderin' if you had any job positions

open?" I leaned against the counter and rested my head against my hand, messing with the cathedral ring on my thumb.

"Job positions?" She tapped her lips in thought, "Well, I have some night spots open."

"Only night?" I made a face. She nodded less enthusiastically.

"So far, yes. I can let you know when a day position opens?" Blanche asked.

"How long could that be?"

"Eh, months." She said.

"…I'll take the night position." I sighed in slight annoyance.

"Alright~ I'll send you a uniform and you can start next week?"

"Perfect, thank you.." I rubbed my head, dad ain't gonna like that. But hey, money is money.

"Of course~ and don't worry, I'll keep you safe, you'll be spending a lot of time with me." Blanche smiled, her voice smoother. *There's that vibe again.*

"Behave yourself, little Bee."

She giggled, "I'm just sayinggggg, We can take breaks together and what not~"

"Strictly Breaks." I chuckled and stood straight, "Considerin' all that commotion in the back, I assume you got a lot to do for shift change, I won't keep you too long."

"It's alright, You just caught me off guard, I haven't heard that delectable voice in years."

"You flatter me, Little Bee." I grinned, "I'll see you next week, We can catch up on that first break together yea?"

I placed my hands back in my pockets. She hummed and

nodded.

"Looking forward to it~ talk my ear off dear!" Blanche hovered above the ground momentarily.

"I'll be sure too." I walked towards the doors, "I should head back to Auntie's, You behave yourself now."

"Always~!" She basically purred. I chuckled and shook my head. Leaving, I headed across to the bakery. My boots scuffed against the road and I took a deep breath out.

Working the night shift ain't ideal. That'll take some adjustment. Those customers are different, way worse than the day shift customers. I rubbed my face and pushed the bakery door open,

"I'm back, Auntie. Got a job."

"Oh! Did she have the position open?" Bee asked, holding newly folded Pie boxes.

"A night position, I'll take it."

"A night one? I know what happened last time, why not just work here baby? I can find you something to do." Bee asked, her wings low.

"Don't worry yourself Auntie, I can handle it. Just, keep it between us?" I asked with a smile.

"Fine. I will be keeping an eye on you."

"Wouldn't have it any other way Auntie." I sat at the counter again and began folding the new boxes. I rested the heel of my boot against the metal rods of the chair. My hands methodically folded the branded boxes. Not the most eager about the night shift, but the other workers say they tip better and those tips will come in handy. Especially if Saint is back in my budget. That girl can bankrupt me if she so wished. I laughed quietly to myself and glanced at the ring on my thumb. It's been four years, I guess I do have four birthdays to make up for.

"What are you giggling about over there?" Bee asked with a smile. I shook my head gently.

"Ya know Auntie..." I pushed a finished box aside.

"Yes?" Bee asked, stacking some of the finished pie boxes.

"I never use these recipes you teach me." I laughed a bit.

"But you know how to cook don't you~? That's better than nothing." She moved the pie boxes to the back and came back with a warm pie for us to share. She sat the cinnamon apple pie down between us and searched for a knife.

"Besides lots of men...oh." She trailed off and I felt her glance at me. I laughed and nodded.

"Mhmm..." I hummed, folding another box and pushing it away.

"When did that change?" Bee asked while cutting slices.

"When I left. I realized men just weren't on my radar. They weren't connecting. Yea I dated and fucked men but it didn't feel right. At first I thought I was just Ace, but then I have sex with women and that is significantly better." I leaned against my hand, running my finger over one of her jar labels, fixing it slightly, "I can see myself spending my life with women, but I can't see myself spending a day with men. Like shit, guess I'm not bisexual." I laughed quietly.

"I see, well, women like people who cook too~" Bee sat a slice down for me, "Try it for your little Saint friend, she might swoon."

"Hey. Auntie, please." I pouted, "Besides, you know better than anyone I've had my eye on Rouge for years."

"Oh, Yes. You mean that Vampire girl?" Bee asked.

"..."

"Whatever happened to that?"

"I fucked that up." I muttered, "Probably forever."

"Oh I'm sorry honey, I doubt that. All it takes is communication, *maybe*." She trailed off, "I don't do relationships."

"Heh, it's fine." I shrugged, "I decided to ask a classmate for coffee..."

"Oh, Saint?"

"Auntie. No." I poked at the pie with my fork "Keegan, Eve's daughter."

"Eve... Eve?" Bee hummed to herself in thought, "The Angel? Oh, yikes. Why?"

"She's cute, and it's a nice change of pace" I hummed. "Can't be stuck forever right?"

"I suppose that's true..."

"Speaking of hung up, how's your crush?" I laughed, she shot me a look. My turn to tease.

"It's over. He told me he isn't into women, why didn't you just tell me" Bee Huffed to herself.

"Well, I wasn't aware of your feelings at first. I just thought you were nice to Dad 'cuz of me, but man. When you notice?" I shook my head, "It was painful"

"Oh haha." She rolled her eyes.

"Oh, before I go, I'm going to that Sorcerer school."

"Huh? Hecate's school..?" Bee looked at me, she gave a disapproving frown.

"Mhmm. Saint begged me too."

"Ah...well, if she does anything-"

"Nah, I doubt she even shows up. She's been a recluse for how long?"

"Eh, she's still got eyes everywhere, such a self centered weirdo, who has that many statues of themselves." She rolled her eyes.

"Auntie B.." I chuckled quietly and shook my head. "Anyway, I better head back, pops worries when I'm in the city too long."

I stood up and stacked the boxes for her.

"Of course my sweet precious baby~" She walked to the back and pulled out a big basket and topped it with an orange bow, "Oh, and here take this to your father, I put some sweets in there for you too."

"Oh, Of course.." I smiled and took it from her gently.

This will definitely soften the blow on the job. Maybe we'll hold off on the night shift part, he'd have a heart attack. Gods. I waved and left the shop, adjusting the basket to grab my phone. I felt a sudden bump on my shoulder and foot.

"Oh- shit.. Uh sorry-" I blinked and looked up, feeling my face slowly go hot. "Rouge.."

She stood tall in all her glory, She was in a bat shaped shirt, with a high waisted skirt and black boots. She smiled softly, her afro perfectly maintained, like always. She still smelled fantastic and still made my breath catch in my throat. I cleared my throat and stepped back to give her space.

"No no it's alright, I wasn't paying attention…" Rouge smiled softly. "What are you doing here?"

"Oh, uh," I shrugged a bit and adjusted the basket, "Just running errands and picked up Dad's stuff from Auntie B's, he can't get enough of her pies and shit.. yea.."

"Ah, me too, kinda addicting" Rouge smiled.

"Yea, be careful with that, she ain't the most….ethical" I trailed off.

"A lil blood ain't hurt me none." Rouge waved it off

"Oh, yea I forgot." I laughed awkwardly then internally

face palmed when her face slightly fell.

"Oh I'm sorry, that was-" She started, then looked away, resting her hand against her lips gently.

"Uh? What?"

"...Nothing, sorry.." Rouge trailed off.

"Rouge... are you still..." I looked at her then sighed lightly, "Rouge, I..I'm not angry at you.. I never was. I was worried about you."

"..."

"I won't drudge it up but, if it does make you feel better, you ghosting me for 3 months hurt more than the bite." I messed with the ribbons and glanced away.

"...I could've killed you.." She muttered. That hurt my heart. Gods I wish i could just hold her and tell her the truth.

"Nah!" I waved it off, "I mean, I'm fine clearly, just got some sharper teeth, ladies love it"

"Hm.. you are so goofy.." Rouge smiled lightly "Haven't changed a bit.."

"Good..?" I asked.

"Good."

"Well, good." *Dumbass, why do you do that?* "Um, what made you move back..?"

"School, convinced dad to let me go, plus a family friend is setting up shop here in Daddy's old town."

"Town..ain't your dad a Sin?" I looked at her, she nodded.

"Mhmm, one of the firsts, Envy I believe. So it'll be lively again before you know it."

"Never been to envy..."

"Neither have I, but he's excited to show me~" Rouge smiled, "Supposed to have a daddy daughter day tomorrow, it's been so long.."

"Well, I hope you have fun."

"Thanks, um, how is your dad?" She rested her hands gently in front of her and met my gaze.

Her eyes sparkled that soft beautiful green, her eyes were always soft and gentle. It was one of my favorite things about her. She's always been patient and loving to me, and I discard her like a moron. Hell, I got lucky the first time. She can and could have always done better than me.

Beauty alone she could do better than me. She could marry a big time prince and live a princess fairy tale if she wanted. Add her caring and kind personality, she's a one in a million chance.

oh fuck. you're staring Bozo.

I blinked and dropped my gaze, "Oh, he's good…yea. Same old dork as always…"

"You're stressing him out aren't you?" Rouge laughed quietly, *so sweet.*

"Ain't that a kid's job?"

"I guess so.." She hummed.

"Ya know, you haven't changed a bit.." I spoke softly, she looked at me, a small spark in her eyes.

"Good?" She asked

"Great." I sighed out, *you're staring again.*

"Well, great.." She smiled and nodded her head gently, "Um.. Anyway, I should uh.."

"Oh, yes of course, sorry.." I stepped aside and opened the door for her, "See you?"

"Bye Aubrey.."

I let the door close and breathed out a heavy sigh and rubbed my face.

"Dammit… way to go air head."

8

SEVEN

It was a warm day in The valley, Leave it to me to get suspended from High school for a week.

This is so fucking embarrassing. I huffed and plopped down in one of the Den's booths. The old leather seat whined under the weight. I ran my hands through my locs and looked out the big windows towards Auntie B's bakery. She's going to be so pissed with me. *Fuck*. She's going to pull at my ear too. I irritably slammed my boot on the ground. I dropped my backpack next to me and tapped at the table leg with the tip of my boot. I absentmindedly twirled the cathedral ring on my thumb.

Gods Saint is going to be so angry at me. Hell *she* might pull my ear.

"Hi sweet pea.." A sweet voice spoke up, "You doin Ok?"

The soft sound of roller skates hummed next to me. The place was damn near empty aside from a few wait staff. I glanced over at the girl. She was a small thing, five foot nothing. As feminine as they come, brown skin with black and yellow markings like other gluttony Demons, her bouncy curls framed her face perfectly, her bright yellow eyes sparkled with a sweet contagious happiness.

"Hm. I've been better." I muttered back, tapping my nail on the table, eyes bored and glancing back out the giant windows.

"Oh, I'm sorry to hear that, was your day bad?" She asked sweetly.

"Uh….uh. Hm. I've had better days-" I trailed off, thinking of the events from earlier.

"Hm..well, how about this." I turned my attention towards her, as she held a milkshake glass in her hands, presenting it to me, "A Strawberry shortcake milkshake~"

I felt my mouth water at the shake, I shook my head and patted my pockets.

"Oh, uh I don't have any cash, hon. I'm just here waiting on my Auntie." I glanced away, "My dad's out of town and I ain't got a job so."

"Auntie?" She asked.

"Auntie B, yea, she said she had to count inventory here or something." I waved it off as my foot began to tap the table again.

"Miss Bee is your aunt… well, consider this on the house." she looked away before nodding to herself, "I needed someone to try it so~"

"…" I looked around the spot, Auntie spent a lot of time in here and her shop, it was definitely dated, retro trinkets and furniture, all orange, definitely captured the gluttony vibe. "So, what's this place? What's with the dated look."

"Oh, it's a Cupid's Den, the Gluttony branch." The bee smiled.

"Cupid's Den, ain't that sex clubs or sum. And excuse my

assumption darlin' but I don't think pretty young things like you are legally allowed to run such clubs." I glanced at her and looked her up and down. There's no way she's older than me, since when was teens running sex clubs.

"Only at night sugar." She giggled and put the shake to me.

She leaned down as she did and her name tag caught my eye. *Blanche huh?* I raised a brow before taking it. I hesitantly took a sip as if she'd hit me with a bill immediately, I blinked and looked at the shake before sipping some more, the sugar immediately activated my tongue. It's the perfect amount to stimulate taste for me. I took a few more sips in surprise.

"Holy shit, this is delicious." I muttered around the straw.

"Ya think??" Blanche beamed.

"I haven't had many milkshakes, but this is definitely unforgettable." I glanced up at her and nodded.

"Eee~ that's wonderful, I was nervous, I've been experimenting with recipes and our menu, my siblings don't do much change but I love making things~ I was thinking of adding milkshakes." She squealed and explained pointing to the board behind the counter. Her wings fluttered in excitement.

"I highly recommend it." I said between sips

"Can I get that in writing?" She giggled

"Where I sign?"

"Mm, no job you said?" Blanche smiled, "Well cowboy. You're pretty charismatic and I've been looking for day waiters, if you're interested."

"Never had a real job before, is it hard?" I asked, glancing at her.

"Nah just be nice and serve plates and take orders for a couple hours a day." Blanche responded.

"I'd have to run that by my pops, he don't like me bein' in Sin City too much." I hummed, looking back at the shake.

"I understand, especially here…" She tapped her lips with her nail, "Hm, so you said you're Miss Bee's nephew?"

"Yea basically, got in a lil bit of trouble at school," I snorted through my nose and shook my head, "Smacked a kid in the face with a skateboard, apparently that's a troubling offense, can you believe it?" I shook my head and rolled my eyes.

"Hit a kid in the face…" The bee spoke slowly, "With a skateboard? You are certainly her nephew."

I laughed and sat the milkshake down, "Should I be offended?"

"Dunno, you got any more skateboards?" She joked back. That tickled me I can't lie.

"My pockets are empty. May Aides himself strike me down if I'm lyin'."

She giggled and shook her head, "Tell me, Is it weird being related to her?"

"Not really, why?"

"Well, she's Beelzebub, one of the Main sins." She started and glanced away before looking back at me, "She isn't all up there…"

"See, Auntie told me not to ask her about anything she does outside of me, such as her job and connections. She just had to say that once, and I ain't ask no more. So I'm not sure what you're referring to, darlin'."

"Smart boy.." Blanche smiled.

"Heh, don't see them often do ya?"

"Out here? Not at all." She laughed then put a hand to me,

"My name's Blanche by the way."

"Pleasure. So tell me, Is it French… Or Spanish?" I took it gently, her hands were soft, she's not a Demon. Usually they feel insecty. she felt more… *flower like.* Touching her felt familiar, like laying in a field of fresh dew covered flowers, a comforting feeling. I gently let her hand go and she moved her hair behind her ear with a sweet giggle.

"Spanish?"

"Means white don't it, I ain't fluent in Spanish, but I can read a crayon."'

"It's french.." She smiled.

"Ah see I had a 50/50 shot, I like them odds." I smiled, "Aub-."

I felt a chill go down my spine as an icy glare found it's way on the back of my neck. It felt like the room instantly fell silent. Blanche and I turned our head as soon as Auntie spoke up.

"AUBREY MAXWELL KOVENN!"

"Oh fuck."

* * *

"Aubrey, what the hell were you thinking?"

Tartarus paced the room as I sat against my bed on the floor. I kept my eyes on my pile of boots by the closet. I avoided eye contact all the way home. I immediately went upstairs and he took a moment before coming into my room, hands on his hips and face exhausted. Still in his work clothes.

"…I wasn't." I muttered.

Actions have consequences, and I'm fully prepared for these. and I wouldn't have changed anything about that day. But it still sucks seeing dad being so distressed about me.

"I told you to lay low. This is the second school in the past 3 years. You can get kicked out again." Dad rubbed his face, breathing out calmly.

"..."

"Why did you do it?" He asked.

"..."

"Suddenly you're quiet as a church mouse? Aubrey. Not only did I have to come home 2 days early, you interrupted Bee's day too. The hell is going on. That ain't like you." Tartarus said, standing in front of me.

"..." I sighed and laid back against the bed, looking at the ceiling, "He left bruises on Saint."

I felt my fingers spin the cathedral ring on my thumb.

"What..?"

"We were talking before her dad picked her up from the coffee shop, she had bruises on her arms and I kind of just." I sighed and turned my head to look at him with dull eyes, "And I'd do it again."

"..." He went silent, "Kid..."

He sat on the floor next to me, rubbing his face and looking at his lap before turning to look at me. He opened his mouth to speak but closed it shortly after. I sat up and pulled my legs up to my chest and rested my arms on my knees. I began to mess with my hands nervously.

"You told mc, that type of behavior is unacceptable and cowardly and that cowards deserve hell. Right." I muttered, "Why is this any different."

"Because you're in school, and you don't assault people.

It'll be on your record if that kid's parents press charges." Tartarus sighed.

"So , who gives a fuck about records, most of the people down here a dirty Demons. Or dead." I looked back at my lap.

"Aubrey.." He sighed once more and dropped his head, looking at his hands then back at me, "Look. You aren't... a normal kid.. Yea?"

"..."

"And, raising you is... A bit tough, I can't lie to you." He turned his body to face me, "I am proud of you for being there for Saint, I won't punish you for that. Hell, I can't."

"But." I muttered.

"But, you're..." He tried to find the words, "No one else is like you, You can do so much damage, I don't want you defined by you being different, I want you to fit in and be normal like the other kids, I want you to feel normal, I want you to succeed like those other kids."

"What if that's not what I want." I asked, looking at him.

"..." Tartarus went silent and looked down, turning his body forward, "I guess, I didn't think of that.."

"Yea, I'm not five anymore pops, I got thoughts and opinions. I ain't worried about being different." I sighed, hugging my legs to my chest. "I know I'm different."

"Aubrey." He spoke up, "Can I be honest?"

"..."

"I'm..terrified." He said, keeping his gaze down

"Huh?"

"That... They'll find out about you or find out about what I did, and once one person knows everyone does and then the wrong people do, and if it gets out, I'm terrified they'll take you away from me." Tartarus messed with his hands, then took a breath, "I love that you have individualism, I'm happy you're headstrong and outspoken, I'm happy you're my son, but, I'm attached to you kid. I can't, I don't want you to disappear from my life over a snot nosed fucker with no love at home."

"They can take me away..?" I asked.

"You... are technically supposed to be *dead*." Tartarus shook his head and I blinked in confusion, he waved it off. which means not now, don't ask, "It's a lot."

"Dad.."

"So please, for a little while, just lay low. For me? Especially when I'm out of town." He looked at me.

"..." I sighed and nodded, "I understand.."

"I assume you don't want Saint to know about this?" Dad asked.

"No no, she'll never talk to me again!"

"My lips are sealed." He smiled then nudged my arm, "Good job kid, I bet he'll think twice fuckin up like that again."

"Heh" I laughed quietly, shaking my head.

"Maybe I'm good at this 'raising a kid' thing."

"Oh I surely hope so." I joked and leaned into him.

"Not sure where you get that violent streak from-" He dropped his arm around my shoulders in a hug, tilting his head in thought

"..?" I stared at him with a raised brow.

"What?"

"Pops be for real."

9

EIGHT

It was Fall in our second year of high school, I remember her creeping up behind me with a,

"Whatcha readin' tiger~" Her voice was so cheery when she spoke up from behind me, she placed her soft hands on my shoulders and leaned against me, startling me a bit. I gripped the book in my hands and glanced at her before shaking my head.

"Gah- hey. Doctor's Monster." I glanced away then back at the book, "You wouldn't like it."

She plopped on the picnic bench next to me and leaned on her hand, looking at me attentively. The breeze felt nice, her afro ruffled slightly in the breeze. Rouge, her blood red lips were pulled into a delicate smile. She wore her Greed school uniform, A black uniform dress with a white long sleeve underneath and a simple golden tie. Her hair in two afro puffs with a satin gold ribbon tied around it. The puffy white sleeves caught the wind as well. Her stunning green eyes narrowed at me in question.

"You're always reading something weird, what's it about?"

Rouge asked and tilted her head slightly to the side, her guillotine earring swaying slightly as she did. I got those for her as a gag gift a couple years back, I'm glad she likes them. They suit her style well, everything fits her well.

"A Doctor trying to play god and create life and issues occur. It's one of my favorites." I hummed, she nodded and lifted her head off her hand slightly while making a face.

"I see..."

I hummed in amusement and closed the book, leaning on my hand.

Rouge, Rouge Bellrose, the gem you are. As smart as you are beautiful, as kind as the first born Doe on a misty winter morning. The highlight of my day is always seeing that gorgeous smile she always reserves for me. I still remember when we first met, she always had this big bright nervous smile on her face and she was so eager to talk to me. I remember when I approached her at that game, I didn't know it, but that small moment changed my life for the better, she made everything better.

"Anyway, what are you doin' on my side of the tracks. Ain't skippin' school are ya?" I asked, tapping my boot against the metal railing of the bench.

"Maybe~ I can be a bad girl sometimes." Rouge nodded and grinned.

I laughed quietly to myself, "Oh really?"

"Mhmm~" Rouge hummed.

Saint approached while holding her school bag and sweater, In the exact same uniform but somehow it looked so different on her. Her purple hair was slicked back and cut to her shoulders, she rarely does short hair but I can't lie I think it suits her the most. She had a gold headband in her hair. Her silver bow earring caught the light perfectly. She sat on the other side of the picnic bench and sat her items beside her.

"No she can't, they let us out early 'cuz a teacher got that Demon plague thing goin' around right now." Her sweet belle voice spoke. Rouge huffed in return.

"Well, better luck next time, Sugar." I chuckled, "Maybe one day you'll be bad enough to hang with me and Saint."

"Oh I'm plenty bad! I got a C on my test last week because I fell asleep studying." Rouge boasted with pride, until Saint chimed in, which she again huffed to.

"B+" Saint hummed and I snorted out of my nose, I eyed Saint and noticed she was keeping her hand out of my sight.

"Mhmm, Studying?" I leaned against my hand, watching her in amusement. "Nah, not bad enough."

"You two are such jerks."

I smiled and motioned for Saint's hand. She seemed shocked and hesitated.

"Don't lose it again." I gave her a look, between my fingers was her black cathedral ring I got for her in eighth grade. Her eyes looked relieved. She happily took it from my hand and slid it back on her ring finger.

"Oh! I was so scared I dropped it on my way home! Oh, you are a jerk."

I chuckled, "You left it on my dresser darlin'."

Saint rubbed the ring before smiling, "Anyway~ you wanna get lunch? On you of course beloved." She perked up once it was placed back in her possession. I hummed in response and began packing my backpack.

"Would I expect any different?" I stood and slung my bag over my shoulder and put my hands in my pockets, "Yea, the Den should be empty, and Blanche is sweet on me and will give me a discount if I ask nicely."

"Cuz she wants to fuck you." Saint retorted, I shook my head and waved it off as she and Rouge stood.

"Aw, you sound jealous." I grinned, She turned her head to me but Rouge began walking, I watched her go momentarily before focusing on Saint, tilting my head slightly. Her brow was raised and had that look in her eye. *Oh geez, here she go.*

"Don't make me hurt you, nigga.."

I put my hands up and grinned, "Easy easy baby girl. We're just friends."

"Yea I'm sure she wants to be more than friends." Saint rolled her eyes and walked ahead of me.

"Nahh, nah." I waved it off and followed after her and walked to catch up to Rouge.

I'm not that naive, she drops *hints.* More like outright asks me all but to fuck her. She's a beautiful sweet girl, but my sights have been set on the same girl for the past year, I can't even imagine paying much attention to other women the way I do Rouge. She's just truly something special. I unbuttoned my gluttony uniform, A simple black button down with an orange vest and brown pants. Still wore my boots, they'll complete every outfit.

"Um, So, that test?" I asked, arms behind my back and looking at her, Rouge blinked and glanced over at me.

"Hm?" She slowed her stride and turned her bright gaze to me. I felt a wave of pure bliss wash over me, I adore how she looks at me and she probably has no idea. I smiled at her slightly.

"A B+ ain't like you princess, what was it about?" I nudged her arm gently.

"Oh.. it's uh. Something I'm not that great in.." She twirled some of her hair around her finger and avoided my gaze, a nervous tell. I nodded and took my gaze off her. "I was lucky to get the B, let alone the plus, I've had nothing but C's all year."

"Well, enlighten me, maybe I can help?" I chimed.

"Science, mainly elements, chemicals and periodic tables. Too much shit." Rouge sighed and rubbed her face.

"Well why didn't you say so? I can help you at any time."

"You do science?" She asked, looking at me.

"Oh you have no idea." I laughed a bit, "Yea, one of my best subjects next to English, Gym and Art. Ya know, the useful shit. Now don't ask me 'bout math, that Saint's area."

"Well..color me intrigued.." She mused, "If you're free Saturday night, we can study?"

"Sure, just call first. Iron gets testy." I squinted and glanced to the side, recalling my schedule before nodding, we got to the quaint diner and I opened the door for her. She smiled sweetly and nodded her head, hair bouncing as always and eyes glinting. She placed her finger against her lips gently and walked in.

"Noted.."

I watched her go and kept the door open for Saint, she hummed and met my eyes. She had a grin on her face and I felt a frown stretch on mine.

"Oh look at you not choking up for once." She teased.

"Wha-?" I blinked and tilted my head in confusion, leaning slightly against the door. She frowned in annoyance, something I'm used to at this point. Especially with this topic.

"Rouge asked you on a date and you kept your cool." Saint

raised a brow and crossed her arms.

....

"....What."

Oh shit, did she? Did she actually? What the hell, I didn't even catch it. Of course she wouldn't care much about studying? Or maybe I'm just a bozo for getting my hopes up and listening to Saint, I glanced away and rubbed my face and groaned quietly. No, no. Don't overthink it, you embarrass yourself when you do. She chuckled quietly and patted my shoulder and shook her head.

"Oh my gods, go inside."

"Wait, dammit, you can't tell me that, I'll fuck it up." I groaned and followed her inside, she hummed and headed to our usual booth. Rouge was already sitting and looking at a menu, she kept her gaze forward as I followed behind and narrowed my eyes at her.

"I didn't say a thing"

"Come on you two, I already ordered drinks!" She waved us over, Saint smiled and put up a finger, she knows she ain't getting out of that accusation too easily.

"You really think she's interested in ME?" I prodded and looked at her slightly distressed, *gods you're such a fucking loser.*

You've dated countless women and men, and what have you. But Rouge is where you fumble each and every time. What the hell is wrong with me? This is the most debilitating, painful crush I've ever had in my life. It's never been this hard. I've never tripped over myself so much, hell not even with Blanche's non-subtle flirts she throws at me out of the blue and her suggestive advances. Not to mention all the girls that clamor for my attention, hitting on them is easy, almost second nature. *But Rouge?*

I can barely form sentences around her. She takes my breath away every time I see her. Her eyes, her smile, her personality, her everything. She's so intimidating. But why? Is it her height? Her kind eyes? Her curves and confidence? No. I just don't get it. Besides, What's it even matter? She's never shown interest in me past a friend, she's never made any gestures or flirts to indicate it? Unless I missed it? *Gods I'm such a fucking loser.*

"Uh. Duh, I go to school with her, she literally avoids any relationship opportunity. I thought she was maybe aromantic or something, but nah the way she looks at you is very telling." Saint hummed and adjusted her bag on her shoulder, I instinctively took it and held it for her while in thought. Then shook my head.

Don't get your hopes up loser, she's your friend before anything else, and that's something I'd never trade. If I can't date her, that's more than enough. I walked with her. Saint happily sat next to her, and I sat across from them. They instantly sparked up a conversation about the menu options, I could feel my eyes soften at them.

Saint adores her, maybe that's a good sign? They became friends without me having to convince her. She spends more time with her than I do, and they look like long lost siblings, giggling and joking together. A small smile appeared on my face as I watched them. They are definitely two of the most important people in my life. They both make me happy in different ways, and their friendship is absolutely priceless to me.

Their smiles could light up rooms, their laughs are contagious, their personalities are infectious in the best kind of way. Gods I could never be angry or hateful around these goofballs, I recall I was pissed one morning about a guy ruining my coffee and these two decided to tell me the most horrid, unfunny ass jokes and stories to see me smile, it's the small things I cherish with them. Every laugh, every awkward moment, every sleepover, every walk. Just, the small things.

"Ready to order Aubrey?" I blinked and glanced at the menu, then nodded a bit.

"Yea."

* * *

It felt like Saturday bulldozed through the rest of the week, she was bright eyed at my house by noon. In a simple bat print dress and black heels, Her hair was done in a simple half up half down style and she had her backpack over her shoulder. Dad was more than happy to give her some lunch before work and left us to our devices. A couple hours went by, she was sitting on the bed with a frustrated look on her face and I read off the homework papers, these private schools ain't no joke it seems.

"Then you take the compound and-"

She let out a long groan and plopped back on my bed, her arms stretched behind her, I leaned back against my hand and raised a brow at her.

"Ughhh Aubrey, you're saying too many big complicated thingsss" Rouge looked up at me and grinned, "Take a break~?"

"Alright, fine, fine." I huffed out then glanced at her and

grinned playfully, "Starting that bad girl streak huh?"

"Long overdue dontcha think?" Something flashed in her eyes and she turned to lay on her side and smiled at me.

"Nah, I don't think bad girl is a good label for you, I think you're a phenomenal good girl.." I leaned against both my hands and looked off at the wall and hummed quietly before catching myself, "Eh, not in a weird way of course-"

"Mm…" She laughed quietly then sat up and looked around the room, "I never been in your room before…"

"Oh uh-" I glanced away in embarrassment, "Yeaaa it's a bit childish, still working on it-"

"No, no I like it, it's so…you." Rouge mused, I glanced at her and scratched my cheek gently with my finger.

"Good?" I asked.

"Good."

"Well, good.." I smiled as she stood and wandered around the room, it's been relatively the same since I was 13. Tons of rock posters, spray paintings, couple of pride flags, Bi and nonbinary, a few figures on my desk and my guitars, and of course my lights around the ceiling. I haven't really felt like changing it, like she said, it's very me and I'm not used to having girls like Rouge in here. Most of the girls that come in here are too occupied to give a fuck about my room.

I watched her walk over to one of my prized possessions, I remember when I got it. A cherry red antique bass from one of my favorite rockers, signed and in perfect condition. Dad gave it to me as a holiday gift and I've never seen him so proud. I just kept crying and thanking him over and over, I didn't even know he paid much attention to my ramblings. He's always had such a stoic face and vibe.

She delicately moved her fingers over the edge of the instrument, I slowly glanced away and mentally slapped myself for the split second thoughts going through my head. *But gods, the things I'd do to and for her is immeasurable.*

"Hm.. this guitar?" Rouge turned her head to me, moving her hand away from it gently.

I cleared my throat and sat up, "Oh, the real guitar from the front man in Goathell. And this one is the one used in that old MJ music video, took forever to find it. It's signed and everything~" I walked over and patted a silver iridescent guitar and grinned proudly.

"Oh and of course my posters, dad took me to this concert when I was 13. Changed my life.." I trailed off as I looked at the posters.

"I didn't know you were so passionate about music…" Rouge said gently.

"Oh, yea, mainly history… Bit dorky I know-"

She waved her hand and smiled brightly, "No no, I think that's actually really cool, I mean who else has vintage vinyls signed by the singers? 'cuz I surely don't."

She pressed her fingers together and looked back at my memorabilia, I tilted my head and glanced towards her.

"I can't tell if that's sarcasm-"

"It's not Brey Brey, what are these guitar picks?" She giggled then motioned to my jar, I smiled in a giddy way, most girls don't ask nor feign interest. The only thing they like is that I'm good with my fingers because I play, yeah it's nice having that assumption but not many connections get made when sex is the main thing on your mind. Rouge was never like that.

"Every concert I go to I buy a pick, I've been to a lot of

concerts"

"Well, take me next time. Rock is kinda fun." Rouge placed her arms behind her back and I chuckled to myself and shook my head slightly.

"Oh? Sorry, mainly took you as a Pop and R&B girlie."

She shot me a look and nudged my arm,"Mainly R&B, now you wanna hear dorky I can go into the jewel's. Mainly Jade. She's so iconic."

"JJ?" I beamed and looked at her, "I love her actually, she and Malekite are geniuses!" She made her way over to my vinyls, she gently flipped through them, her finger delicately sorting through them. Her eyes were soft, not a sign of feigning whatsoever, she moved her hair behind her ear gently, those same guillotine earrings I got her.

Gods.

"Couldn't agree more, favorite album?" She asked while picking up one of my limited edition never opened vinyls, I walked over and picked up the original copy behind it.

"You're holding it." I flipped it around, showing the cover.

"Holy shit really?" She looked at the one in her hands and laughed quietly "This ones my least favorite."

"Really?? Come onnn you don't like it?"

"She was a skip for me I fear, but since you like it maybe I should revisit it." Rouge hummed and placed the other vinyl back. Something about that made my heart flutter.

What the hell are you doing to me Bellrose.

"I can put it on for background noise, if you want." I asked gently.

"Sure, do you mind if I get some water?"

"Oh, I can grab it, would you like some snacks or?" I put the vinyl in the player and lowered the volume to a soft hum.

"Just water is fine.. Thank you.."

I headed downstairs and rubbed my face, *gods stop being a loser.* I grabbed a few bottles and headed back up and handed her one of the waters.

"Here you go." I glanced away and sat on the bed next to her, "We can get back to it if you'd like."

"Just a little longer, my brain hurts" Rouge pouted.

"Fine fine, I'm lenient." I laughed quietly and sipped my own water. She sipped hers and grinned in the cutest way possible.

"So benevolent~" She giggled.

I shook my head and glanced out the window at the distant fence around our property. It was tranquil and quiet, just soft music and her presence. Something I'm all too familiar and comfortable with, it always felt comforting. She always made me feel safe, be it my goofy hobbies, or jokes, or my personality. She always made me feel content. I leaned back gently on my hands and brushed gently against her arm. I glanced down at her as she leaned against me. Her soft coils fell in her face, her eyes were a bit tired but still lively.

Her normal scent of Vanilla and Shea filled my nose, her soft hands barely grazed against mine. She has no idea what she does to me, does she? She couldn't have a care in the world, she's just comfortable. And I can't stress enough how happy it makes me that she's like this with me. Hey who knows maybe there is a chance?

No. shut up.

I glanced away, fighting the heat rising to my face and focused in on the track, "Ah, this one's my favorite."

"Huh?" She asked.

"On the album." I trailed off, "It's my favorite song, the production and vocals are phenomenal. She's so talented."

"She is, isn't she..?" She smiled gently and closed her eyes, "So, aside from your music and guitar collection.. What else?"

"I read a lot, and I like spray painting. Lotta abstract dragons I think? That's what dad says anyway."

"You definitely give a spray painting rocker vibe, wow…" She laughed quietly to herself and sat her bottle on her lap.

"I hope that's a good thing."

"Definitely, I never thought I had a type till now…" Rouge hummed.

What did she just say? Did she mean it that way? I glanced down at her, she didn't move an inch.

"….." I scratched my cheek gently, "Heh- uh- y-yea um." *you fucking loser.*

"Oh, sorry, came out a bit wrong." Of course, stop jumping to conclusions.

She sat up and closed her bottle, eyes still content. She swayed her feet a bit and leaned against her hand and kept her gaze on the floor. I mentally slapped myself and held back a disappointed sigh.

"N-no it's fine.." I muttered, "I don't really have a type, I understand."

"Oh I can tell, your roster is so random." She giggled gently.

"You think-?"

Without missing a beat she said, "Mhmm, what do I have to do to be a part of it?"

She definitely meant it that way, oh gods. How the hell do

I even? *What.* I know the shock and slight confusion was heavy on my face, I couldn't fight back that blush anymore and dropped my head in embarrassment. She hummed almost triumphantly but picked up her textbook once more.

"........" I didn't mean for it to slip out, "Fuck..."

What the hell are you doing to me, Rouge Bellrose.

* * *

"Brey Brey~" I heard a cheery tone behind me. I blinked and turned from my locker and met Rouge's bright green eyes. A few students were muttering in the hall, I was just as confused.

"Hm? Rouge-? What are you doin her-"

"I was gonna wait till after school butttt, I saw this and thought of you~" She moved her hand from around her back and handed me a neatly wrapped box with a simple bee pattern, how cute. I smiled and took it, no need to play that game. She always has her mind made up when she gives gifts.

"What's this for...?" I asked gently, she basically beamed and moved her other hand and showed her test.

"I~ got an A on my retest. Thanks to you of course.."

"Oh, shit, that's great!" I smiled, "That's the good girl I know."

She giggled and waved her hand, I watched her and smiled, a small red tint was on her cheeks, "Oh stooop"

"But a thank you would suffice, you didn't have to-"

"Open it~" She pushed.

"Hm.." I looked down at the gift and gently pulled the paper off and blinked in surprise,"Oh… shit.. This??"

It was a shadow box with the most beautiful typography of my favorite song and a guitar pick in the corner. I stared at it and smiled, is this what it feels like to be in love? To be appreciated and listened to? Is this why she's so different to me? It's so small, and so simple, yet I feel like I could burst into tears if we were alone. She must've remembered the parts I subconsciously hummed, she genuinely paid attention. It wasn't just some ruse to get in my pants. Wasn't fake interest with an ulterior motive. Just genuine interest in, well is it smart to say friend?

I don't want to be just her friend. I know that.

"I got it commissioned, it's the lyrics to your favorite Jade song, and a custom guitar pick based on it… I hope it's not.. Too cheesy?"

"…." I felt a smile form, and noticed I was still staring at the shadow box, she got quiet then began messing with her skirt nervously.

Don't blow this loser.

"Aubrey..?"

I looked up at her with a big smile on my face, " I uh…do you want to go on a date with me..?"

"… Yea.." Her eyes lit up, and that filled me with hope and happiness. She said yes? Maybe this time saint was right, just this once. But I don't have to tell her that.

10

NINE

"Honey, I think you're overthinking it." Saint spoke.

"Nah, her face.. Did she say anything to you?" I nibbled my nail and bounced my leg.

Saint was on speaker. I kept staring at the ground. I'm such a moron, mentioning it like that. The ravens and crows flew by, a few Crows landed on my balcony rail every now and then. They cawed then flew away. It was a normal occurrence. I stood and began to pace on my deck as I talked to her.

"No. Those months she ghosted you, she fell off the planet. I'm sure it's sensitive for her. You know she ain't really a blood drinking type.."

"I just.." I sighed and looked towards the cliff in the distance. Lava slowly rumbled from it and pooled into the river below. I sat in one of the deck chairs with a harsh plop and rubbed my face. "I wish I could say something to make her feel better, I am genuinely Ok."

"Maybe if you told her the tru-"

I cut her off immediately, "Saint."

"Alright, alright," She sighed.

"Anyway, what are you doin tonight? Want to watch some old movies?" I leaned to the side and rested my head against the palm of my hand. I need to take my mind off this.

"Ooh canntttt, got a date"

"Oh?" I asked.

"Mhmm, that's all Ima say about that." Saint hummed, "We can definitely do it another time though~?"

"Of course, finally a decent man to spend money on you. I can have a break, my pockets are hurtin', baby." I joked. Her end went silent before she hesitantly responded. I raised a brow and sat up, adjusting the phone.

"M-mhmm."

"What was that?" I narrowed my eyes at the screen, Her photo being half of a photo we took in a bathroom during Hallows Eve. She was smiling wide and her eyes were bright. A drastic contrast to the suspicious tone in her voice.

"What?"

"That pause." I muttered.

"Nothing..?"

"Oh gods. Are you going out with that fucker-" I started but she instantly cut me off.

"Gotta go Aubrey see you!" With that she hung up.

"…..That son of a-" I growled low in my throat. What part of stay the fuck away from Saint did that bum not understand. Of course he'd wait till I leave to make moves on her. *That fucker.* But hey, the lesson worked the first time. Why not run it back right? I got time.

"Redbuck!" I looked towards the door and headed back inside. I closed the balcony door behind me and tossed my phone aside. I heard him making his way up the steps, he tapped gently on the door before opening it.

"Yea dad?"

"Oh, hey, are you hungry?" Tartarus asked.

"Depends, you cooking or?" I asked.

"Ehhh had a lot of repairs today.." Tartarus trailed off but shrugged.

I waved it off and hopped up, "I can cook pops, no problem."

"Oh- no-?"

"Dad. Please, I'm not that rusty, Auntie would have my ass you know that." I gave him a look, "She took the change well, honestly I didn't think she'd care much. Her sexuality is murder and death, please."

"Yeaaa always have been- wait. What change?" He asked. I looked at him, *oh yea I didn't tell him. Haha, that's embarrassing.*

"Oh- heh. Changing out the Bi flag for the Lesbian flag tomorrow." I scratched my cheek, "Probably gonna rehome it to Saint, she's Bi."

"No more snot nose boys? Oh thank gods." Visible relief washed over him, *damn tell me how you really feel,* "Uh… uhhh, I mean, congrats baby! I'll update accordingly."

"Yea uh huh." I rolled my eyes then laughed a bit, "Thanks."

"I heard Leviathan moved back." Tartarus glanced at me, "How you doing..?"

"…." I walked over and past him, heading downstairs to the kitchen. "Have you seen Saint around?"

He sighed softly but followed, "Saint?"

"Remember high school? When I got suspended the 3rd time?" I looked through the fridge to see what was available, seems dad restocked. Gods I hate to see him take up so many repairs, I grabbed a few things and closed the fridge.

"Yes." He sat at the table and huffed out, "No repeats please, hon."

"I think she's with that bastard again." I muttered.

"Aubrey…"

"Dad." I retorted.

"… I can ask Jasper about it. But."

"No… no, she'll get mad at me… I'll just. Chat. He can't snitch to a teacher this time." I began cutting up vegetables.

"Aubrey."

"Anyway. Um, I stopped by Gluttony, obviously.." I hummed, "I got my old job back.."

"Aubrey, I said-"

"I know. I know, I still want to help.. And I need spending money, pops. Plus I'm doin' what you said? Starting a social life."

"… At the Den." Tartarus asked.

"You know Blanche runs it, she's sweet, and Auntie B is always there."

"I don't want you mixed up in her operation, Aubrey." He bore into my back. I shuddered it off.

"And I won't be, just a server like always, smiles and tips and stopping the occasional bar fight, nothin' I can't handle. And before you say it. I told them 'bout school and got night shifts and short hours. I got it covered."

"…" Tartarus sighed and rubbed his face.

"Trust the kid you raised, I'm a big boy now. All grown up!"

"Yea… Alright, if it gets overwhelming, you can take a break. You SHOULD take breaks It's a-"

"Marathon. Not a sprint." I finished, "I know dad..um.

How about a father son night?"

It's been awhile, and he's finally home and not busy. So why not.

"I'd like that."

11

TEN

Ever since I was a little kid, I dreamed of the picture perfect life. A husband, kids, the big house, and fancy clothes. To uphold the perfection of The Sawyer family. To carry on the legacy of our family. It's just me and my father of course, never knew my mother, and father never mentions them. It wasn't something I paid much attention to, I never thought about having a mom or felt like I needed one, My father filled their role perfectly.

Jasper Sawyer, Death; peaceful. They are the poster child for Grim Reapers everywhere. My father used to apprentice under the original death, although they never really speak of them. I just know that the original god blessed my father, thus our family business began. My father has a very high reaping count, which causes them to be away often. Death never stops, everyone dies, all the time. I try not to be resentful, I understand the importance of my father's job and the organization they run, I know balance is important. I know.

From a young age Father was magnificent. A prodigy

from production, Quite literally made for this line of work, made to eat, breath and sleep reaping. They were the talk of the town, and far beyond. They couldn't comprehend how a beauty such as them thrived in such an environment. They got many betrothal offerings, many bribes to be better and see better. None peaked their interest, their first love will always be Reaping and the organization they built off their essence.

Without my father the Reapers wouldn't exist, Death as we know it wouldn't exist. Before my father it was said death was unruly, chaotic, overwhelming and exhausting to deal with. In some cases, death was sadistic. Mother nature was never so forgiving, eras of people dropping like flies and piling down here, cramped like a can of packed sardines, no one cared. The angels certainly didn't. For the longest time, death was their responsibility, until suddenly they began discriminating. Picking and choosing who deserved happiness. On paper that's a wonderful idea. Most people are disgusting, but their standards weren't normal. Anyone deemed a sinner, something as small as one cigarette as a curious kid, to the murderer down the street all ended up here.

Such a barbaric time.

It took father years to build Nevermore and The Valley and fight for the rights to death first and foremost. It was a long dispute I heard, until their teacher showed up and made a declaration. With that, Grim Reapers were the sole death bringer and managers. Death was ours and only ours, with minor Angel interference exceptions. Father eventually made the Reaper organization, and the Reaper school. So Reapers can be born and taught, not made.

It's a big role to fill.

I just want to make my father proud. I want to be as perfect as them. I want to continue our legacy, But with that as my competition, how can I? Clearly I'm an expert at all things reaping, would be an insult if I wasn't, but I don't think that's what I want to do. Once I learned I had Sorcerer magic, things became murky. Everyone knew what they wanted, but me. And because of that, I decided I'll just marry and uphold our status through ally ship and reputation. It worked back then, why not use it again.

Accomplishing that idea is of course tougher than you'd think. I know my family name holds weight, It's the most important name in The Valley. The only men who are interested in me are the ones who want to reap the benefits of my family's labor. *I'm not naive,* but what is marriage if not give and take and compromise? Love is a non factor when your goal is appearances and power. I want to make my father proud. It's always something I longed for.

Marry rich, have the best children, keep the family name untainted. *Simple.*

Yet, I keep making bad decisions. Why am I stuck in this cycle? *I'm not naive,* yet I'm very naive. I don't want a man with his life together, *why*? well I tell myself it's because I don't want a strong man fighting back against me. But in reality? I think I just enjoy a project. So I settled for him. He's tall, blonde hair, green eyes, a loser, a bum. A disrespectful jackass with no work ethic whatsoever.

But I can fix that.

I want to fix that. Fixing people is what I'm good at. It's what makes me, *me*. I've been fixing problems since I was old enough to comprehend. My father was always busy and very forgetful, very absent minded in their early years, so I picked up the slack, had my father take breaks, unload their problems, and be there for them. They always praised how mature my emotional intelligence was, and I take pride in that. Then came Rouge and Aubrey. More projects.

But they were difficult. Aubrey in particular. Every man I've come across has done nothing to wow me. Just empty promises and dull flirts, questions about my inheritance, our business, and my availability and their chances of joining the family. *I'm not naive,* but these business transactions weren't entertaining me, so I looked the other way, and like most people who don't get what they want from me, they left. I'm used to that.

Aubrey wasn't like that however, He never wanted anything from me. He was so different. He went out of his way to always spend his money and ask for nothing in return, it was so strange. Our class differences couldn't be anymore obvious, I knew that, and he knew that, yet. Without hesitation. I could look at an object for too long and it'd be a gift for my birthday, he'd save up his money just to see me smile. And never asked for anything in return.

It felt unreal, I'm very aware of the class differences in The Valley, they're amplified by the horribleness of Demons and the high capitalistic society that was created down here. My family has been blessed since creation, My father being death itself and basically one of the founders for The Valley naturally holds a lot of power here. Especially since they are Death's official successor. I know people of lower classes despise upper class Demons. I know the indifference causes a multitude of problems in our society, I know things aren't fair for the less fortunate, and I've accepted their disdain towards me and people like me. I don't blame them one bit. The sneers, snide and sly comments, the threats, all of it doesn't bother me, not one bit.

But even so, Aubrey was from a lower class, yet he went out of his way to treat me, like I wasn't already spoiled beyond belief. I've grown used to the class divide and hatred it brings.

I've educated myself on the struggles of others and fixed my world view accordingly, but this unwavering kindness and joy from Aubrey, seeing him light up when he gives me gifts I never expected, Is something I find so endearing. Him saving up as much money as he could to buy me something way out of his tax bracket moved me. It wasn't about the money though, it was the thought and his attention. It was all I desperately wanted, He wasn't a business transaction, his infatuation wasn't false, his expectations were zero.

I remember when we were fourteen, Aubrey got his first job. He got to help in the Lust Goat Sanctuary, It was farm work. Something he's use too and he loves Goats. The first thing he bought was two rings. They were Cathedral windows. My all time favorite thing is Cathedral architecture. My father's aesthetic takes after Cathedrals, stain glass and horses. I use to talk Aubrey's ear off about how our house was built. He listened to every second and saved up money to get custom rings made for us.

I'll never forget that, I'll never undervalue anything he did for me. I think that's when love became so evident to me. I realized I loved Aubrey, but I didn't love these men I swore I'd marry. So I decided not to pursue a love. Aubrey was enough.

He was my friend, and me being his friend was as valuable

as all the money in the world to him.

Maybe this is what unconditional love feels like from a person not related to you?

Someone who forever puts your care, needs and wants above their own, no matter the odds. That intoxicating feeling of being adored and cherished was wonderful. I didn't care about the gifts, I cherished them with my whole being, but the thing I loved most about him was how much he cared. How present he always was. Every long night of crying, or missing my dad, or having a cold, or just down on my luck. He'd drop everything to be with me and make me feel better. I swore to myself, I'd be that for him too.

This is where the business logic comes in, scout and recognize your client and what they're looking for, make an analysis on how to move forward, execute a fool proof plan of attack, and success. It starts with extravagant gifts, then spontaneous surprises, and of course, sneaky callbacks. Yes, I listened and acknowledged everything. Aubrey loved Rock, he loved guitars, he loved art, cowboy boots, and punk ideology, he loved his individualism. So what did I do? the only proper thing of course, catered to him. And gods the look of happiness and joy on his face with me reciprocating his intensity made me feel so warm and fuzzy, a warmness I've only felt with helping my father. I loved us, I love him, and I love our relationship.

Then Rouge showed up, tenth grade. It's embarrassing to admit now, but I was *so jealous* of her. Aubrey was infatuated. He couldn't wait to tell me he talked to her at a basketball game, he was ecstatic. His attention was on someone else and I wasn't coping with that well. He lit up every time he talked about her, His eyes sparkled with hope when I mentioned she asked about him that day.

See, Rouge and I are in the same class. Same tax bracket. Her family is well off, I'm not fully sure on what it means but I know she's able to hang. Being so, we attended the same schools and events, I wasn't too fond of her. What did she have that I didn't? What attracted Aubrey's attention so much? She's just a girl, yes a pretty girl, but just a girl nonetheless. Aubrey has seen plenty of those. Even back then she was radiant, she had the softest, kindest green eyes on any girl I've ever seen. She was intelligent, and she was opinionated. She was an all around nice girl. Which I found hard to believe, someone like her radiated mean girl energy, the give sly two faced compliments just to laugh behind your back type.

But she never did that. Quite the opposite actually. The other girls didn't like her and always made a fuss about her participating in events, especially *all girls* events. I noticed she would sit alone and wait for everyone to leave changing rooms or bathrooms before she went in. I noticed she'd never spend much time with other girls as well. Just Aubrey or by herself. I later figured out why and it softened my perspective of her. And I decided to give her a chance. She was alone like always, reading a book and keeping to herself, but her eyes were slightly dull and she seemed tired. Not only that, Aubrey hasn't mentioned her in days.

So I approached her, and gods I feel like a fool, she was as sweet as anyone could possibly be. No arrogance of a rich daddy's girl, no venom in her compliments, no side eyes or sly remarks. Just a genuine and kind girl, in need of a social circle. After chatting with her, I realized she and Aubrey are so similar, she puts others feelings and well being above her own. She'd have a gun wound and ask the shooter if they're Ok. She was so kind and soft. She had this deer in the headlights idea of life, she wanted nothing more than to make it to tomorrow because you never know what tomorrow will bring. *How silly.* We got closer, I sat with her in classes, at lunch, and took up for her when an ignorant lowlife had the audacity to disrespect her.

And naturally she returned the favor. Another client in the business model. Adjusting accordingly was easy, especially because she was just as grateful as Aubrey. I started off small, simple gag gifts that a toddler could purchase, then evolved to more extravagant things, her humbleness never wavered, everything was wonderful, she was wonderful.

I recall a time, back in sophomore year, I was sitting alone, Aubrey was in the gluttony school cities over, and I was stuck in greed with no friends and completely subtracted from these pompous people. I can't lie, Aubrey and Rouge humbled my way of life greatly, to the point I realized my own faults and logical fallacies. I thought I was educated on class divide and less fortunate individuals, but a sharp wake up call came knocking when I heard these moronic Demons sneer and talk down on the public school kids.

Without them, I imagine I would've felt the same way, made the same remarks or at least thought them. Turned my nose up at anyone below me. Well, thank Jezabelle that didn't happen. I can't stomach these imbeciles, how they made it into such a prestigious school is beyond me, but no doubt everyone speaks money. The first day was dreadful, I was alone and overwhelmed, surrounded by people I couldn't stand and my father was off on business again. I felt so alone.

Until I heard that familiar voice, and felt those cold soft hands over my eyes and smelled that Vanilla and Shea scent, "Guess who~"

That's how I knew we'd be inseparable. She stole my heart, just as Aubrey did, And just like Aubrey, I will do everything in my power to return all the kindness and favors on my end of the deal.

Aubrey and Rouge individually have taught me so many things, so why do I still settle when I know what I deserve and have experienced it?

Well. *He's* my project. I've worked so long to mold that bastard into my perfect husband, only for it to backfire tremendously in my face time and time again. He was a horrible person, good for business, bad for relationships. And maybe in my own twisted mind, I love him. Or do I love being in a relationship? Do I love the illusion of being a fixer in this situation? Is it my ego or my confidence that thrives off this? Who knows.

"Oh gods. Are you going out with that fucker-" Aubrey began. I hummed to myself and looked through my closet before cutting him off instantly.

"Gotta go Aubrey see you!" I hung up and huffed out.

I tossed the phone on the bed next to that old green stuffed dragon Aubrey gave me when we were kids. The plush slumped over slightly and I glanced at it, its old faded face seemed to contort in a frown. The same frown Aubrey would give me if he saw me on a date with Adam.

"Don't look at me like that." I huffed and slid the clothes on the rack, the loud screech startling my pet raven, Opal.

She cawed in discomfort before settling back in. I smiled

apologetically at her before grabbing a red skin tight dress. Not my style, never really has been. He prefers it. I rolled my eyes and pulled it on, I brushed my hair and looked at myself in the mirror. I could barely recognize myself. All I could think about was how Aubrey bought most of my favorite dresses, He even tried to buy shirts and boots that would match me, so we could go out together and match. He encouraged my style, He loved my style.

Then there's Adam.

I shook my head and grabbed my phone and bag. Don't overthink it. I muted my notifications and headed down the stairs, waiting on him.

Why? Who knows.

12

ELEVEN

"What would you like, Saint?"

I felt my eyes flicker up towards my boyfriend, pure annoyance at his voice ran through me. I can't believe I'm even here. Every time we're together all I can think about is being anywhere else. I think about Aubrey and how annoyed he'd be with me right now. He'd have that adorable frown on his face and telling me *'Be so fucking forreal right now.'* Looking at him from across the table all I feel is disgust and annoyance. Why do I even bother? I've given up on him, he's a failed project, something only a present father can fix. Out of my hands.

He sat in a pale brown suit and a horrid yellow tie. His blonde hair was messy, He claims he likes it that way. His deep green eyes used to make my knees weak, now all I hold is contempt. He studied the menu like he doesn't bring me to the same three star restaurant every week, feigning interest. This garbage restaurant is the only thing he's willing to spend money on when it comes to me, but according to Rouge, he's fine splurging on his side endeavors, why do I keep holding on?

I've declared him a failure, my friends hate him, and I've grown exhausted of his presence. I recall in Early high school I was so infatuated. I hand selected him myself, Adam, son of a local business man. I pursued him, and began to mold him into my perfect husband. Started off with clothes and postures, training him to compliment and cherish me, training him to speak with class and elegance. But slowly those feelings dissipated into disdain. On both ends. He was getting short tempered, more secretive. And that's when Aubrey's radar probably started going off. He never really hit me, but he did say a lot of things I'm ashamed to admit I took too personally. I thought I was in control, but that man was playing me like a fiddle. It started small, from him hating my braids, to hating my dresses, to wanting to change my accessories.

Aubrey would never.

Oh Aubrey. After he grabbed me that day and left bruises on my arm, that's when the perspective shifted for me.

Little did I know, my picture perfect idea, my perfect thoughts of a perfect family came crashing down at that moment. That won't do. A Sawyer being stuck with a disrespectful, untrained, disgusting rat who is overstaying his welcome? When Aubrey left and he dumped me I fell into a spiral, reading horror story after horror story. More women talking about the situations they found themselves in, and the advice they recommended. That dream died that day.

I remember a conversation I had with Aubrey three years ago. Right before he disappeared to find a lead on his past, we met at Blanche's Diner, like always, shared a booth, like always. He offered to pay and wouldn't take no for an answer, like always. He'll probably never change, and *I can't stress enough how happy that makes me.*

That conversation rang true in my mind as I listened to the buffoon talk. Just babbling on about nothing.

I remember him starting off gentle, overly gentle, no silly remarks, or harmless jabs, or goofy jokes. Just softness, like he was breaking bad news to me. I remember being worried and confused, I thought he was still upset over Rouge, or the accident, but no. It was about *me*. How can one be so selfless and considerate that they ignore their own pain and problems just to make you feel better and to help you? Is it noble? I'd say so. Is it foolish and unhealthy? Of course.

"I.." He shifted his gaze away in thought before speaking, *"I had a boyfriend, freshman year of high school. He was my first real boyfriend, the huge crush, the flirting in the hallway, texting till 3 am and being exhausted the next day, all that jazz."* He rubbed his face.

"But. He became rude, annoying, brutish, and loved making demeaning jokes at my expense. I thought that was normal. Then, we broke up and I dated other people and realized, that isn't normal, nor did I deserve to be subjected to it. Strangely, you and Rouge taught me that."

I blinked in surprise and tilted my head slightly to the side.

"Being loved unconditionally feels good. And I hope one day you get that realization with a guy you really like, and you can have that nuclear family dream you want." Aubrey laughed lightly. I felt my eyes soften at that, that perfect family.

" But." I looked at him slightly confused. *"I can't help you, if you don't want to be helped, baby girl."*

He spoke and turned his body to me, leaning back against the window, the chains on his belt and boots rattling as he did. His Auburn and blonde faded locs fell neatly past his shoulders. His eyes seemed tired, his speech was slower. *He's exhausted.* Yet he's here worrying about me and my foolishness. Suddenly I felt horrible. *Was I causing him upset?* Gods that was never my intention. I looked away from him and dropped my eyes to my lap.

"I want better for you." He continued quietly, almost timidly. *" But with how you're movin'... there ain't much I can do love."*

Something about that hurt, have I really been so one track minded? Have I really not been here this whole time? How long has he felt this way, gods does Rouge feel the same? Everything suddenly crashed down over me, that perfect family, the projects, the business. Was it really blinding me this much? How foolish of me. I'm usually the one giving these talks. I'm the one that takes on the emotional baggage of them with ease and happiness because my only want is to make them feel as safe and happy as I do. Yet this whole time I was causing upset in them and didn't even realize? *How narrow minded and foolish can you be.* I tensed up as Aubrey spoke up once more, I glanced at him. His lips were pursed for a moment in a thin line before he breathed out and moved his locs out of his face.

"I ain't gonna be here forever, and I want you to be taken care of. And that bastard ain't gonna do that." Aubrey messed with his hands, a nervous habit of his. It made me feel worse. Am I really this hard to criticize? Am I really *this* unavailable to them?

" Look baby, I love you. More than words could ever say."

Aubrey's voice was more firm, I met his gaze but remained silent, how can I respond when I'm blindsided like this.

"Aubrey..." Was all I could muster up under my breath. He rested his hand against mine, gripping my clenched fist gently. That same matching cathedral ring on his thumb rested next to my cathedral ring on my ring finger. The silver ring shone in the window light. He tightened his grip, the cold rings pressed to my hand.

"Saint, you are my best friend. The love of my life. You are one of the most kind, thoughtful, giving people I've ever met. You're as beautiful as a Magnolia in Taurus. You're so smart, so outspoken. Any man would be lucky to be your husband."

"Of course you'd think so." I muttered, *"Most men don't see my worth like you do."*

"Then they're idiots. Seeing you as a family name is bullshit, you are so much more than that name."

"Heh, I guess."

"Say it back." Aubrey demanded I blinked and looked at him as he repeated his statement. His eyes were determined and bright. *More than my name huh? That's the first time I've heard that.* More than a Sawyer. That thought has never crossed my mind before. It was always just the game plan.

More than a Sawyer.

"I'm more than a name?" I questioned gently. Aubrey narrowed his eyes.

"I'm more than a name."

"That's better, let that be your mantra from now on." He grinned goofily. I smiled gently and shook my head. He fell silent again, I looked at him and he looked like he was contemplating something, I could see the indecisiveness on his face.

" I am... so sorry if I made you feel any type of way over my disdain for him." He looked at me with somber eyes, *"I know I'm harsh with you about that boy, but I realized I've been too overbearing and overstepping in your life.."*

I gripped his hand instinctively and turned to face him, I understand now. This isn't an intervention, it's things he thinks he'd regret never saying before he goes. Him worrying for my well being in his absence, him making sure I won't hold disdain for him as time goes on. Aubrey gripped my hand back, which all but confirmed my suspicion. Like a book.

"Not once have you ever done that to me, and I have no right to do it to you. I want to give you time and space to make your own decisions, as you've allowed me to."

Trust. He's trusting me.

"Hm." I hummed, *"Finally trusting me eh? About time. I'll take a better late than never."* I said playfully, Aubrey suppressed that goofy ass grin he always gave me. His face relaxed and his eyes softened, he still had a gentle grip on my hand and kept his gaze locked on them while rubbing his thumb gently against the surface of my hand. Our rings gently rubbing against each other. I felt content. I always feel content with him.

"I just...I want you happy Saint. I won't always be here to protect and baby you, and my biggest fear is failing to do so." Aubrey sighed, *"I just worry."*

"I know, always have."

"Well you stress me out." Aubrey retorted, "M*m, what would you do without me."*

"Hmm, not sure, maybe go hungry and wear last season's fashions." I joked, he smiled and snorted through his nose

that time. He continued to rub his thumb soothingly.

"I have to be honest with you, before I go." He cleared his throat, *"I can't lie to you, it feels bad. I know you didn't take that break up well and I was nervous you'd be angry with me."*

I gripped his hand reassuringly.

"Seeing those bruises on you, seeing him sneaking around on you, disrespecting you." Aubrey gritted his teeth, *"I can't stand it. You deserve so much better."*

He got angry? That's a first. I remember him going to the hospital when my boyfriend was there, but I didn't think to put two and two together. Aubrey *never* gets angry, let alone on mine or Rouge's behalf, irritated? Sure, annoyed? Absolutely, but *angry*? Never. I didn't think that was an emotion he could even reach. That puts a lot into perspective, gods I've been so blind. What a fool I've been.

I asked as gently as possible, *"What did you do?"*

Aubrey tensed up, "..."

He sighed and looked at me, pain in his eyes and a small forced smile on his lips. He cleared his throat. *"I'm the reason he dumped you. I threatened him too. And told him not to tell you I said anything."*

"Is that so." I hummed, I looked back at the table. I see. I should've known, I remembered they went to the same school, and if Aubrey saw my bruises, that was a bomb waiting to go off. Gods.

I don't feel anger. Instead I feel the same I always do, grateful for him and his care. How can I be mad when he was clearly worried and told me on his own volition? How can one care so much for someone else while neglecting their self.

"Thank you for telling me." I spoke gently and gave him

the kindest smile I could muster. After that he hugged me as tight as he could and just held me there. Oh Yeah, that's right he's leaving after this. I don't know where he'll be or how long he'll be gone, so I squeezed back as tight as I could. Ignoring the cold buttons on his denim jacket and embracing that familiar warmth. Reciprocating as always, something I will always do.

"Besides, maybe when we're old and gray at like thirty, we can get married and reap the benefits." Aubrey rubbed my back gently and I just laughed quietly.

I thought about that conversation for a long time, a very long time. *If I have Aubrey, what am I putting up with this bullshit for?* Aubrey is already a fixed project, something I don't have to fix or remind to love and cherish me, he just does it because he's a good friend. And not having to fix something strangely feels good, very good. Maybe this is a sign.

That conversation followed me for years. Yet I foolishly got back together with this bozo, but this time, I know why. Aubrey was gone, Rouge was gone, My father was gone. Just me, alone with my unstable thoughts and feelings, of course I'd make such a foolish decision and delusionally believe this relationship is beneficial in any way. Gods Aubrey *still* doesn't like him, right back to the harsh push towards dumping him, but this time? I think I'm going to finally listen.

Aubrey's back. Rouge is back. And dad's back.

Most importantly, *Aubrey is back.* My second half, My soulmate. The love of my life is back. *So, What the hell do I need you for.*

"I want better for you." Yeah, me too. I understand what

Aubrey meant now. I heard you Aubrey, and I hear you now.

I sipped my wine and I glanced down at my phone and checked it as it chimed, silence came finally from the other end of the table. I sat my wine down and gave my phone my full attention. I sent a quick message to Aubrey and decided to take him up on that movie offer. I smiled softly to myself as I saw the little text bubbles bounce as he typed.

"Sure! Dad just crashed for the night, too much sugar for his old man heart, lol. I'll choose some movies and grab some snacks, text when you're outside."

"Who's that dear?" I blinked and felt annoyance almost instantly, I fought the urge to roll my eyes. His voice disgusts me now. Is this what that picture perfect marriage would've felt like? Gods how foolish I was.

"Hm, Aubrey is back in town. And we just made plans." I sat my phone in my purse and noticed him stiffen in the corner of my eye. What a coward.

"A-Aubrey..?." He began to stutter and dart his eyes around nervously, "Wait plans-?"

"Mhmm, Easy honey. He's with his dad."

This is the opening, take it.

"Is everything Ok?" I queried.

"Uh, I have something to tell you." He spoke nervously, I gave him my attention and picked up my wine glass once more, a sweet Peach Chardonnay, my favorite. I narrowed my eyes at him as he rubbed his hands on his pants.

"When we were in high school, he beat me with a skateboard and threatened me to break up with you." Adam muttered, "I didn't want to tell you because I didn't want to ruin your friendship or perception of him. I know you only saw him on weekends and outside of school."

Manipulation. I know that tactic well. Notice a weakness and attack it, cause doubt and then gaslight. That won't work on me this time though honey, I'm not a dumb sixteen year old anymore.

I hummed and sat the glass down, "Is that so?"

"Yes, he came to the hospital afterwards and made sure I did it. I never wanted to leave you, that's why I took a chance immediately after he left."

"So you're a coward." I hummed. He blinked and darted his eyes up at me, "And trust me, I'm very aware of what Aubrey is capable of."

"You expect me to fight the son of Tartarus for *you*?" Adam asked in disbelief.

"Of course. I expect nothing but the best. Correct?"

"That's insanity. He hit me in the face with a skateboard." Adam deadpanned, I laughed to myself. A skateboard, he was definitely angry, no way he was thinking clearly.

"Yes, he told me, look sweetie." I sighed and picked my napkin up off my lap, "I think this ship has run its course and sad for you, it hit some rocks."

Adam eyed me, "What."

"I'm bored of you, You are nothing more than a juvenile boy in the body of a man, and I think breaking up is the best course of action, you have nothing to offer to the Sawyer family."

"Wait- now hold on Saint, let's not be too rash?" He put his hands up as if to touch me and I instinctively pulled back. I sneered in disgust and pulled my bag to me.

"Let's make this easier, Ok? I'm sure Stephanie, or Charlotte, or Jackie, or whomever you keep glancing at your phone for is waiting for you." I bowed my head and stood while dusting off my skirt, "Have a nice night."

"H-hold on!" Adam stammered, "So it's over just like that?"

"Absolutely."

"Is this because of Aubrey, I knew you two had a thing going on."

I blinked in surprise and before I knew it I let out the loudest laugh I've ever heard come from my mouth. I quickly covered my mouth, I placed my bag on my stomach and snickered quietly.

I shook my head, "I don't appreciate your projection, accusing me of your acts is unbefitting."

"If you walk out that door, you will regret this."

"We aren't in high school anymore." I turned to him completely, eyes narrowed, "There are no teachers to cry to, and no limits on what violence one can inflict. If that is a threat, I will move accordingly."

He fell silent, then dropped his gaze. *Coward.*

"So again, have a nice night." With that I took my leave.

"Hm, well Ms. Sawyer. Let's see how the Sorcerer Academy appreciates the last name."

* * *

"Hey gorgeous! Thought you had a date?" Aubrey opened the door excitedly, then he raised a brow, "Lil' tight ain't you? That ain't your style." He motioned to my skin tight dress and I waved it off.

"Guess who's single?"

He blinked then grinned wide, "For real?"

"He didn't take it well, tried to threaten me." I dropped my bag on the couch and plopped down next to it, Aubrey fell silent momentarily before closing the door and sitting next to me. I yawned and stretched out wide.

"I probably got some of your clothes upstairs, if you want to change." He spoke softly.

"Thank you~! Where's little Iron~" I asked happily. Aubrey rolled his eyes.

"Do not baby our hellhound, he's a dangerous protector." He groaned as the pup in question padded over, I patted his head and scratched behind his ears while his tail swayed.

"A big dangerous protector who'll get belly rubbies~ hehe~"

"Gods." He picked up the remote and leaned back, "But I am happy you're single, let's stay that way for a while yes?"

"Oh that's rich coming from you."

"Wha-?" Aubrey looked at me, "I'm single right now!"

"Yea till next week." I rolled my eyes playfully, "I saw you flirting with Keegan."

"Whaaa? Nah, she's just sweet."

"Mhmm, so are you." I retorted.

"I-"

Arf.

13

TWELVE

Have you ever had a person in your life that you knew would be heaven and the stars to you? someone you know could be the death of you? Someone that made you say and do nonsense, just because they existed? Have you ever loved someone that much?

I love him. That much will always be clear. Aubrey is my heaven, stars, moons, sun, world, everything. I remember when we first met, we were fifteen, I was the new kid in school. The first time I saw him. He was in a music room practicing piano. I remember it being a crazy juxtaposition. This kid in a cowboy hat with an all black leather jacket and matching black cowboy boots and fingerless gloves sat at a piano playing the most beautiful tune. He piqued my interest immediately.

The second time I saw him he was with Saint, a gorgeous girl. Back then she always had her hair in braids. She wore a lot of edgy outfits, nothing near her current baby doll and soft style. High school was an awkward time. He was slamming a guy's head into a locker on her behalf. She didn't seem phased at all. He was expelled not too soon after.

In that small amount of time I noticed when he's with Saint, Aubrey's eyes are so bright and kind. Saint never dimmed his light, and vice versa. They were thick as thieves. Soulmates if I've ever seen it. As close as close could be. Gods, I used to be so envious. Kind of still am If I'm honest. I know if I were to fully lose Aubrey to anyone, It would be Saint. Though I doubt they know that.

I never had that, I didn't have friends to hold hands with or eat lunch with all the time. I was just the weird new kid, sitting alone. Nothing special, nothing unique, just a drop of rain in the ocean. I wasn't lonely though, Every late night, recital, or special events my dad was there, and of course the gang. My father's hands aren't the cleanest, at least that's what he tells me. He and My "Uncle" Titus formed a gang in their youth, they traffic weapons, drugs, the works. It's a bit funny how he found me because of a trafficking deal gone wrong. I was embraced with open arms.

Bit silly I know, a bunch of mobsters showing up and cheering on a nine year old little girl in a ballet or band recital? Being as loud as they can, showering me with roses and praises as if I was their little girl too. It was wonderful, but that's family, not friends. I never had those. Never stayed in one place long enough. With daddy's, *job* staying still was a risk. I never understood it then, I was even resentful for a time, but being older now? I understand. My dad has done nothing but protect and love me. I couldn't be too upset over not having friends or social stability where it mattered.

Until I saw him, The first time he ever talked to me, it was a chilly Tuesday, The Valleys climate was off balance and his nose and cheeks was so red, his eyes glistening, His hat obscured his deep purple eyes, he had his scarf tight around his neck and had on that same leather jacket. He was waiting outside the Greed school after his expulsion, Saint going here I completely understood. How he got in? No idea. He was way too rugged to be here on scholarship, unless he got in because of his music? That thought of him playing piano quickly came back to me.

He didn't even give me a side glance, he looked like he was waiting on someone. His hands was in his pockets and he was leaning up against the big stone columns by the stairs. I remember getting there early to request a new uniform, a girl's uniform.

I stood awkwardly to the side and I guess I caught his eye. Aubrey glanced at me then turned his head completely.

"Hey." He spoke up.

I turned my head to him then away.

"Yeah, You Darlin'." His voice was so smooth. His accent was adorable, it went along with his style completely.

"Um, yes?" I asked him. He stood and closed the distance between us. I noticed his boots. They were top tier leather, there was a skeleton design on them. Is he from money as well?

"You ain't from here are you?" He asked, His eyes seemed amused.

"Oh, No, we just moved down here." I responded.

Aubrey laughed to himself and nodded, *"Question. You got a lighter?"*

"A lighter?" I asked.

Aubrey pulled a cigarette out of his pocket and nodded his head. His blonde locks framed his face. I stuttered before shaking my head. I instead snapped a small flame between my fingers for him. He leaned forward and lit his cigarette.

"'Pprecaite it." He stepped back, *"Aubrey."*

"Oh, Um, sure..." I messed with my pants nervously, *"Rouge."*

"Rouge... It's nice to meet you."

"You as well." I smiled gently at him.

Saint showed up soon after and we didn't speak again after that. I never saw him on campus unless I happened to catch him there in the morning waiting on Saint or walking her. I assumed they were lovers, and the last thing I need is homewrecker accusations at a new school. I kept my head down.

Then I tried out for cheerleading. I'd see him at every game, He was a basketball player. If he wasn't there to play, he was there to hang out. Usually without Saint. Even back then I knew he was a player. He flirted with every girl on the squad, except me. I thought rumors got around to him and he wasn't sure about me. Like most guys. It's funny. I don't even like guys, yet I felt drawn to Aubrey. Something about him. I don't know if it was his calm and dark demeanor or his narrowed sharp eyes. They were almost deadly and I can't lie it made me shiver. He was always surrounded by girls or his guy friends, he felt untouchable. Until he recognized me at a game.

He was at the concessions and I was getting something to drink.

"Rouge right?" Aubrey suddenly spoke up behind me.

I turned around in surprise.

"The new girl?" He smiled.

"Oh, Um, yes." I said and glanced away, I patted my skirt

down instinctively, but his demeanor was off. He had that same smug and cocky energy he displayed with other girls but it seemed like it was faltering.

"How are you liking it here?" Aubrey asked.

"It's nice, It's certainly different from my home." I laughed quietly and sipped my drink.

"Where you from?" He asked, leaning against the bleachers.

"The surface." I pointed up instinctively, *"We moved because of my dad's job."*

"Ah, A city girl hm? You should be in your element here." He laughed.

I glanced away shyly, *"A little, Still getting used to everything."*

"I see, tell me." Aubrey's sharp eyes glanced at me, *"Has a girl named Saint approached you?"*

"Saint..?" I asked, *"No. She hasn't."*

"Alright." He nodded. He seemed to end the conversation with that but I was determined to keep his attention.

I never had friends, but I was determined to be his. I couldn't tell you now what I was so infatuated with back then. Maybe because he came off nicer than the others? Or was he so loud and fun from a distance? Or maybe it was because ever since the beginning he saw me, Rouge. And not *a boy in a dress.* He never bullied me, is that why? Who knows?

He was in a green sleeveless shirt, gods were his arms big. He was a toned guy, He had a baby face though. He had a constant deathly stare and frown on his face unless he was with Saint or his friends. His jeans looked like chaps, he had simpler boots on this time and an expensive watch. It was clearly not his style. He was holding a soda bottle and I noticed a cathedral ring on his thumb and a few silver rings on his pointer finger and a simple lock necklace around his neck, and of course he had a hat. His boots scuffed the ground as he crossed his legs.

"Sorry to bother, You're at these games a lot." I spoke. He chuckled and nodded.

"Yea, I'm not big on the social scene but the guys bust my balls when I don't show up. If I'm honest I prefer to be home." Aubrey waved it off, I noticed he had three long nails and two short ones on both hands. Strange.

"Really?" I asked.

"If I'm not at my best friend's place I'm at home." He shrugged, *"I have a shit social battery."*

"I see." I nodded, *come on Rouge. Think of something or he'll walk off.* I rubbed my wrist in thought but before I could speak he spoke up.

"You're a cheerleader?" He asked, motioning to the uniform.

"Oh! Yes, this is my third game." I smiled, *"It's pretty fun so far."*

"New city girl and already on the cheer team? Color me impressed. What's next. The prom queen?" Aubrey joked.

"Depends, can I count on your vote?" I joked back.

He grinned and I swear I noticed his cheeks heat up, *"Maybe, I like a girl who can joke."*

I laughed quietly, *"So, you transferred schools? I recall seeing you with... I'm assuming, Saint? On my first week."*

"Heh, Yea. Got expelled, I'm in the Gluttony school now. If I'm honest I like it a lot better." He hummed.

"Really?" I asked.

"Less pompous assholes." Aubrey nodded.

"Well, I hope I don't give that impression." I messed with one

of my coils, smiling at him.

He smiled a sweet smile and shook his head, *"No... Not at all..."* His voice was kinder. So were his eyes.

"I feel like I can talk to you for hours, but I know you got that whole cheerleader thing, half time is coming up."

I felt my face get hot, Oh gods. He's gonna see me at half time? I bounced on my heels slightly and nodded my head.

"Oh! Yeah! Yeah..." I trailed off.

Aubrey pushed off the bleachers and walked over to me, He adjusted my bow and smiled at me. He smelled so good. It was a nice mix of Hazelnut and mint, with a small hint of pine. The shadow of his hat made his eyes stand out so much more, they almost had a light glow to them, suddenly purple is my favorite color.

"Good luck." Aubrey tipped his hat to me and walked over. He turned his face quickly and I'm glad he did. I couldn't hold back that blush too much longer. *Oh he's dangerous.* I patted my cheeks and walked off.

It seems that's all it took. The next week Saint approached me, and we've been the three musketeers ever since. Went from never having friends to having the two best friends ever. I still kept my distance, even as their friend I couldn't tell If they were an item. They really blurred the lines. I learned they have matching rings. They spoil each other daily, Saint loves to brag about having him as a friend. While Aubrey is a lot more lowkey.

Contrary to the rumors in the halls, Saint is by far the sweetest person I've had the pleasure of meeting and befriending, She had an infectious vibe that was so calm and chill. Saint was always there, She'd comfort me through anything. I finally worked up the courage to ask her if she and Aubrey were together. She just laughed in my face. I immediately felt embarrassment wash over me. Saint apologized shortly after and shook her head.

"Not at all, He is super into you. Like a massive crush." Saint said.

That caught me off guard. He's so hard to read. I didn't believe her at first until I noticed how he gets nervous and stumbles around me. Saint heavily encouraged me to ask him out.

Now Aubrey, where to begin? while Saint was my sister and bestie, Aubrey was my other half. I was convinced we were soulmates. Him being more open and expressive with me made me so happy. Yes we were friends, but it feels like it didn't click as fast or easy as Saint and I's friendship. It always felt like there was this wall between us. Like Aubrey was tip toeing on eggshells around me. It took so long for him to warm up to me. I chalked it up to him being in a different school, until Saint informed me of his crush. I can't believe I thought he hated me the whole time.

How silly.

I could never tell what Aubrey was thinking, he was this strange anomaly in my life. When I fell in love with him? I'm not sure, any goofball moment of his could be a great guess. His compassion and genuine kindness always put me at ease and made me feel fuzzy inside even if his words and demeanor came off cold. He was a fighter, kinda cliche huh? Daddy's little ballerina princess running around with the bad boy biker who fights all the time? But gods I wouldn't ask for it any other way. *I love him, all of him.* His flaws, his goofiness, his pros, everything.

I thought he felt the same way about me, then the *accident* happened, and he broke up with me a few months later, at graduation no less. He couldn't even look me in the eye to do it. He probably sees me as a monster. A bloodthirsty gross vampire who sees him as nothing more than a convenient snack. *Gods, what a fool I am.* I wouldn't blame him if he believed the anti-Vampire propaganda. Gods he'd know first hand.

Saint was the first person I called when Aubrey and I broke up, that was my first heartbreak. That pain was unbearable and she was there through it all. She never made me feel worthless or stupid or like my feelings didn't matter. She was always a safe space. She's like the sister I never had.

Even so, even if he's afraid of me, or hates me, or we only stay friends, whatever he desires. I will ***always*** love him. Always.

"Rouge???"

I blinked at snapping in my face. Suddenly everything came back to me. My senses kicked in and the burning of my dry eyes became noticeable. The warm liquid leaking from the styrofoam cup and down my hands.

Zoned out again, I shook my head a bit and quickly sat the drink on the table and hastily grabbed napkins to clean it up.

"Sorry! Sorry, I wasn't here. Gods" I sighed and gripped the blood soaked napkins. *Blood.* Disgusting. After the accident I had to drink it. I used to be vegan, Ironic ain't it? A vegan Vampire, have you ever heard something so silly?

Even so, I stuck to alternatives, was never tempted by smells or anything, I fit in like a normal Sorcerer. The only ones who know of my vampire side are My friends and family, Who would've known The Valley of all places pushed the anti-Vampire propaganda. We're surrounded by disgusting Demons for goodness sake but *I'm* deemed the horrid one, because of my lineage I had no control over? What a joke.

I thought I could coast by and ignore that side of me completely. No Vampire urges no Vampire problems.

Then I met Aubrey. His scent, his blood, gods, it was intoxicating. It was the first time I've ever smelled blood in a living creature before, the first time I've ever felt my fangs twitch and my mouth water. Being around him was so difficult I had to buy suppressants to numb the urge. But nothing works forever. Now I'm sipping blood in disguised containers like a common fanged Demon.

"You alright honey? You've never been this checked out." Saint asked, she sat across from me. Her hair was in a long curly slicked back ponytail. She just got it done, probably on Aubrey's dime. She was in a simple two piece black outfit with a sweater and skirt and of course a big bow in her hair to match. She had a half eaten croissant and coffee in front of her, her nails were freshly done as well, now that I know Aubrey paid for. He use to all the time.

I shrugged and shook my head, "I just... There's a lot on my mind."

"Do you wanna talk about it sweetie?" She took my hands and gently pried them off the napkins and tossed them aside on her plate. I kept my gaze down and dropped my hands to my lap.

"..." I sighed quietly, "I ran into Aubrey in Gluttony the other day. It .. Was awkward. And the... Accident... Slipped in."

"Accident-?" Saint blinked in confusion then her eyes saddened, "Oh Rouge… Honey, are you still hung up on that?"

"How could I not. I'm drinking a blood coffee."

"Baby, you need to let that guilt go.." Saint said gently, "He holds no resentment towards you."

"I attacked him in cold blood and not only infected him with an incurable disease, I drank his blood and was ready to kill like a starved crazed animal." I muttered, clenching my fists tightly and kept my eyes on the table, "The thought of no resentment is foolish."

"Rouge, he's not…" Saint went quiet for a moment, making me look at her. She was looking away and had a slightly troubled look on her face, "You are the world to him. He would allow you to feast on him if you so wished it. Those 3 months of no contact hurt him more than your bite ever could."

"…" Of course, yea. That sounds like Aubrey, he's so. *He's so?* I don't know, he's so concerned with everything else and never himself, gods he probably didn't even realize the venom because of his worry for me.

"Look, I think you both have a lot of things to talk about, It's not my place of course, but I think clearing the air will give you closure and time to move on and forgive yourself." She looked at me gently, "If Aubrey has forgiven, why can't you?"

"Because I'm a monster. Maybe all those flyers were right." I muttered, "Some person you are Rouge. What kind of person attacks their boyfriend. Gods I'm such an idiot."

"Rouge. hey, no. stop that." Saint snapped her fingers and dropped her hand on the table. "Those flyers are bullshit and you know it."

"...." Now I'm not so sure, I still have no idea what came over me that day. What if it happens again? How can I ever trust myself again, especially around him? Because even after biting him and unlocking that blood lust, I haven't craved any other person, just him. I don't understand what's going on with me, I just don't understand.

"Anyway- I'm sorry that's- that's not why I asked you here."

"Rouge..." I waved it off and shook my head.

"I'll be Ok... how have you been? New boyfriend or anything?"

"Nah, single now actually"

"Oh?" I perked up. She laughed quietly and waved it off.

"And you? How was the surface?" Saint asked, leaning against the table.

"Oh, same as always! I was born up there so." I sat up straight, "Daddy was working a lot though, I met a lot of cool people I definitely won't forget." I moved the cup from my sight and waved my finger around, "Got kidnapped and I took tons of pictures~"

"I'm sorry?" Saint asked.

"Huh? Oh haha. Yea it happens sometimes." I grabbed my phone from my purse and opened the photo app, she just stared at me.

"Why- Wha-?"

"Mhmm" I slid the phone to her and motioned for her to scroll right, "Oh, I actually wanted to ask you for some advice?"

"Of course honey, shoot." Saint looked down at the phone and scrolled through the pictures. I rubbed my finger on my arm gently and tapped my nail.

"So.. It's always been you and your dad?"

"Hmm yea, as far as I can remember. I don't think I've ever met my mother?" Saint hummed.

"And your dad doesn't date..?" I asked.

"Nah, not that I know of. Why?" Saint slid the phone back to me and I sighed and tapped my nail on the screen.

"Well… You have a close relationship with them, like I do with my dad, so I wanted your perspective.." I muttered and rubbed my arm once more, "I think daddy has… an admirer? Or he wants to date.."

"Oh?" Saint asked, leaning against her hand.

"Hm." I muttered

"Is that bad?" She asked.

"I don't know… It's always been just us. Ya know? And Uncle Titus of course… He never really mentioned it.."

"I see.." She nodded.

"But he's my dad and I'll support him but what if this new person sees me as competition or tries to get rid of me? Or they don't like me? What if they lock me in a closet and I have to pretend to be Ok because my dad loves them-"

Saint waved her hands and blinked in an overwhelmed way, "Whoa whoa whoa there. Slow down hon."

"I just… I'm protective." I breathed out.

"You're a daddy's girl through and through hm?" She laughed a bit, "From how you talk about him he will choose you every time."

"You really think so..?" I looked at her.

"Of course, you're his main priority, which is very attractive. Maybe I should date a dad?" Saint tapped her finger on her lips and looked up in thought, I laughed and threw a napkin at her.

"Ewww well my dad is off the market"

"Hehe, why wouldn't want me to be your Step Mama?" Saint joked and I laughed once more. She's always been such a goofball, she's always able to help me through my emotions and thoughts, I'm not sure where I'd be without her.

"Ewww you loser!"

14

THIRTEEN

"Oh there you are ladybug." I looked up as I walked in the dusty old house. My dad, a tall dark skinned man with piercing blue eyes, dropped a box on the ground, dust clouds rose up and he fanned it away before clapping his hands together and dusting them off. He had dust on his blue shirt and jeans. He had a band of pearls around his black locs, He had Dragon adjacent features from the teeth to the ear shape but he wasn't a Dragon, just passed for one. I scrunched my nose and looked around the area.

Dad said he hasn't been in this place in hundreds of years. I personally have never been to Sin City, outside of school and one dinner date with Aubrey in senior year. Everything here is very. *Green*. What can you expect from envy though hm? Every sin has a gimmick, Sloth is winter and cozy, Wrath is a circus, Greed is stores and casinos, Lust is night clubs and red carpets, Gluttony is diners and bakeries, and Pride is out of commission. No pride sin as far as we know. Now Envy? Here is more, aquatic? It feels like an aquarium here. Something I never experienced before.

Dad mentioned wanting to open a few clubs for Uncle Titus to work out of, like on the surface. That is definitely more of Dad's vibe. I closed the door gently behind me and made my way over to the taller dark skinned man. His usual blue eyes were a vibrant green here, his body having this natural green glow to it. This energy is definitely something I'm not used to.

"Hi daddy, sorry I was hanging out with Saint." I coughed a bit, "Was escaping the dust orphanage."

He snorted through his nose, "Oh haha." He looked around then rubbed his face, "You're fine, You're just in time. How's dinner sound?"

"Dinner?" I asked, looking at all the boxes, and gave him a confused look.

The house was empty, It was a Gothic style home, The floors were dark and the walls had old dark green Gothic wallpaper. The kitchen was all black with silver appliances. The walls were tall, with high ceilings. It was covered in dust and cobwebs from dad's absence. It seems when a Sin leaves the City completely shuts down and the Demons are effectively left homeless. They tend to migrate to other cities in the meantime. The strangest thing about this house though were the amount of fish tanks in here. He's going to fill them up with Seahorses. I just know it. What can you expect from Leviathan, monster of the sea though I guess?

"Not here, got some business to take care of." Levi slid a few boxes out of his way with his foot and walked out of the kitchen area. I watched him walk past me and to the front door. I tilted my head and raised a brow.

"Business…?" Daddy never let me join his business meetings. Him or Titus. They think they're still protecting me from their dirty jobs and blood money. I'm twenty-four, I'm more than well aware. I was made aware when I was fifteen and a guy began stalking and harassing me way back when then he suddenly disappeared, and uncle kept making goofy jokes about sleeping with fishes. It freaked me out for so long because of my phobia of fish, he wasn't helping said phobia because in my mind I thought he was saying a band of fish came and kidnapped him.

I know, goofy. But I'm just a girl. A girl with a phobia.

"Personal." Levi smiled down at me, "Promise."

"Oh, alright.." I walked back over to the door, "Should we change-?"

"We can pick something up." Levi opened the door for me and motioned me out.

Unlike the rest of The Valley, Sin City had vehicles like the surface did. More things to capitalize off of I suppose, Moving here was definitely a learning experience, I've never walked so much in my life. Especially because unlike Saint I couldn't ride horses, and unlike Aubrey I wasn't a gym bro, but I didn't want to feel out of place so I walked everywhere. I've never been so exhausted and tired in my life. It eventually got better, I finally picked up exercise again, got back into dance and self defense classes. I most definitely needed those skills here.

Dad called a car to the steps, the green sparkly vehicle pulled up on the stone path and dad opened the passenger door for me before the Envy Demon got out of the driver's seat. I sat inside the car and took a deep breath.

Honestly, this place is worse than the surface. Up there I came in contact with a handful of Demons because they slipped between the cracks and got exorcised back here by the Angels. But down here they're on every corner, every inch of this city. It was an adjustment period but you quickly learn which Demons will cause you harm, or want to play tricks, or just want to get through the week.

Not too different from the surface in that regard.

I looked out the car window and watched as it left the green hued city of Envy and drove through the streets of the square. I spent a lot of time out here with Aubrey and Saint, mainly at the fountain. Lots of wishes were thrown in there. A lot of memories. We weren't allowed in the cities, plus in order to travel from city to city you need clearance, and we weren't old enough for that. If you knew a person though, you could come and go as you please. For us, Aubrey was our ticket in and out of Gluttony. It was not exactly the safest, but the better city to spend hours in. Miss B was an absolute sweetheart to us and gods were her pies to die for!

A lot of good memories out here.

The car headed towards greed, I perked up and tilted my head and looked towards my dad. Levi's face was softer than usual. He had a smile in his eyes as we sat, I glanced towards the window and narrowed my eyes.

Personal hm?

I looked at the city of gold that is greed. It was bright here, you could see the glow above the gates from the square. I always wanted to come and spend a day here. All the best dressed Demons come from here. Their golden skin sparkled with soft gold flakes, they looked like living statues with the best complimentary clothes I've ever seen in my life. Everything here radiated money and well, Greed. With one new trend here, another pops up there. Like clockwork. In the center of the town was this giant clock tower, but it didn't look like it was telling time. A few people were crowded by it and a few cameras floated around them. Interesting.

The store fronts were all lined with blue and gold clothes and accessories, odd.

We pulled up to a store front. I blinked and looked at him as he got out of the car then opened my door. I got out and stepped on the sidewalk, *solid gold!* But every step ripples to show golden snake skin. Looking closer a lot of the golden accents have snakes or snake skin printed or carved into it, how beautiful.

"Whoa.." I looked up at my dad, "Are we gonna shop??" I asked eagerly, gripping his hand. He chuckled and nodded.

"I figured you were old enough to see the Sins, and I have someone to meet here and if we look… non *greedy*, He won't let me live it down."

"He?" I asked.

Levi hummed and led me to a shop.

"This might be more your style Ladybug, go crazy."

I bounced slightly and happily headed into the shop, tons of racks filled with clothes. The area had a blue hue in the store from lights against the golden trim walls. Soft music was playing and a few Demons were shopping around. *As snooty as ever.* I hummed and walked around looking at the clothes. I raised a brow, everything was blue or gold. *No other colors?* I pushed a few clothes aside looking for any other color, *No way they've been bought up.* No one else on the streets were wearing other colors. *Gods, blue is definitely not my color.*

I pouted a bit as Levi slid his phone in his pocket. "What's wrong, Ladybug?"

"There's no other colors? No Reds, Oranges, Greens, not even Purples?"

"Ah well, that's because that's my color." A voice spoke up, Dad and I turned to them. He was an average height individual, with long black braids, with a few curly strands here and there. He had an all purple suit on with a hat to match, some parts of the suit were see through. His hat had golden chains dangling around him, obscuring his face for the most part. He wore a singular white glove and had furry cat ears and a tail swaying behind him. He had two big black cats behind him, cats in suits? An Earthen? How peculiar.

His appearance was so captivating, I didn't notice the Demons hurrying out and doors being locked at first. He radiated money and grace. He must be a noble, or royalty of some sort? Or he's the biggest breadwinner here, I'd imagine if you have enough coin you get royal treatment. This is greed after all. He was kind of intimidating, his eyes were obscured, but his gaze still felt icy.

Levi straightened his back, turning completely to the stranger and I looked up at my dad curiously.

"Well well. If it isn't Leviathan. Look at you.." His voice was smooth and calming, he wiggled his fingers and tilted his head up, a quick glance of his eyes showed a mischievous glow in them, "Been scarce for years and you show up and cross my territory?"

Levi snorted out of his nose and dropped his head with a sly smile, "Shiloh, you know it's nothing personal, I was actually here hoping we could talk about that. But naturally I have to look good for you right?" He motioned to the clothes before leaning against the rack, "I don't mind making this up to you."

"Oh?" He hummed, he dropped his arms behind his back and nodded slightly, "You haven't changed a bit, have you Tiger?"

Levi shrugged and smiled, "Know what they say about old dogs and new tricks."

Is he flirting right now? I narrowed my eyes.

"Oh hush." He laughed, his ear then twitched as I caught his attention, "Who's this?"

Levi stood straight and motioned me over, he placed his hands on my shoulders, "Rouge honey, this is Shiloh. An old friend from way back in the day. Shiloh, this is Rouge, my daughter."

"Daughter-?" He made a confused face, eyeing him.

"Adopted" Levi reassured and I nodded a bit.

"I see… well, look at you beautiful. It is wonderful to meet you, you can just call me Scotus.." Scotus instantly perked up and put a hand to me, his nails were painted a black to purple ombré, he smelled of vanilla and almonds, I could get a small glimpse of his eyes from here, they shined like stars. I took his hand gently, they were soft. Very soft, almost as cold as the chains around his hat when they brushed up against my arms.

"Hello…"

"Would you mind if we treated you to dinner, Kitten?" Dad spoke up, Scotus gave him a look. I know that look all too well, calling him goofy. I'm sure dad's used to that look. Scotus let my hand go gently and moved his hands back behind him. He hummed before responding.

"I'm not busy, sure. why not, especially if you're buying, Sugar."

Oh they are definitely flirting, oh gods is this the admirer?

"Don't I always." Levi turned to me, then patted the top of my head and I looked up at him, "Rouge, I want you to try this place out here, I used to go there in high school, you might like it."

"Oh hell, don't tell me you're heading to old Jimmy's Place." Scotus turned, crossing his arms and shaking his head.

"If it ain't broke don't fix it." Dad retorted.

He's definitely got to be dad's admirer, dad has never acted this calm and relaxed with anyone, not even Titus, and I'm sure Titus is just as flirtatious. An old friend from back in the day? How far, clearly way before me. Even as his daughter I've never seen his guard this down in public, let alone in a Sin territory. Dad always told me to keep a wall up in case things go to shit, and he looks like he's ready to drop to his knees and ask this person to marry him. He radiates elegance and charm, he's beautiful, clearly. *Who is this person.*

I cleared my throat and nodded, "Sounds fun daddy, I love seeing your childhood spots, who knew you had a whole life before me."

Levi smiled and pinched my cheek like always.

"She's so sweet... You sure you raised her and not a mama?" Scotus joked.

"Now what mama would be with me, A gay man, Let's be serious now." Levi raised a brow, "This was all me, and maybe a small tinge of Titus."

Scotus nodded and leaned back against one of the cat men standing firm behind him, he didn't even flinch, "So what I'm hearing is, you're single?"

"Absolutely." *No hesitation.*

I looked between both of them. A loud chime from outside startled me, I jumped a bit and turned my eyes to the shop window, a bunch of Demons hurried to the clock tower, once the chime ended, the area fell silent, an announcement sparked up.

" Blue is overdo, I wish to be seen in Green."

With that the store's blue lighting changed to green. The clothes seemed to switch out almost immediately and suddenly a rush of Demons came to the door to buy the new green garments. They pounded on the locked doors and wide windows, waving money and shouting dramatic nothings. *Yes, this is definitely greed.*

"Green? That wouldn't be for little ole me would it?" Levi asked.

"What can I say, it's definitely your color." Scotus pushed off the guard and strided over to a display, he moved his nails over a dark green tux, the light making it look slightly black and green. A snake pattern was lining the inside of the coat and had a matching handkerchief, definitely dads style. "I might like this one."

"Noted." Dad nodded.

"And for you~ Rouge dear~" Scotus walked over to a rack, sliding the hangers on the screeching golden bars, his eyes scanning the different clothes. He pulled out a mid length dress, looks like it'll stop just below my knees. "This might be more you." He moved his hand over it and changed the garment to red.

I gasped in shock and smiled. "Definitely! I have been told red is my color.."

"I can tell, I'll make an exception, just this once." Scotus winked and handed the dress to me. He waved his hand to the shop owner and pointed his men towards the door. "See you at 7?"

"6:50." Dad responded back almost instantly, Scotus smiled wide and laughed to himself.

"Nothing less." And with that, the guards pushed the doors open, parting the crowd of Demons with ease, a taller man waited by his car and opened the door for him. And just like that he was gone. I couldn't help but watch him go, panic aside, he's memorizing, absolutely stunning. Completely untouchable. Yet he was blushing and giggling at my old man of a dad?

I turned my head up to him and narrowed my eyes. Dad glanced down at me then away. He smiled and motioned me out of the store. *Oh he ain't getting out of that conversation that easily. A pin is in it.*

* * *

Ok, I have never felt like more of a third wheel in my life.

I huffed quietly and checked my phone. Dad was making conversation with Scotus. Bright side, the diner is certainly interesting, it's not 70s like the cupid's den. It's a bit different than that, a run down truck stop diner. Maybe it was a 50s biker joint? Black and red aesthetics and old license plates lined the walls. Red sparkling bar seats and a big jukebox against the wall, playing a soft song from dad's decade probably. But the food was good, the french fries were cooked and seasoned to perfection, and I'm a sucker for a good philly. The shakes are pretty decent, but after trying the shakes in Gluttony, nothing really compares.

I looked outside at the nearly empty parking lot, Scotus' lavish car sat outside with more of those cat men standing around it and by the door. Everywhere this feline goes, people clear out like he's death. If the staff didn't work here I'm sure they'd be out with a fire trail behind them. The bright red neon lights reflected off the cars and ground. If you squint it's a lot like the surface.

Feels nostalgic, like that night dad found me. He was outside a diner, smoking a cigarette. The red lights illuminated his face in the most intimidating way. He'd been watching the building for hours. I didn't know why, I do now though. He was sizing up the place. Everything happened so quickly after that. All I heard was screaming and gunshots then my hiding place being kicked in. I was six when I first met him I believe. He made eye contact with me and without hesitation he scooped me up in his arms and pulled his jacket over my head.

I've been attached to him ever since. He fed, washed and clothed me and I just never went away. It's always been just me and my dad, for as long as I can remember. Gods I remember for my 10th birthday he showed me the official legal adoption papers, I'm his daughter, and he wasn't going to leave me, not like *he* did. If I'm honest I don't have much memory of my life before Dad, it took check ups from a doctor the gang knew to even figure out what I was. Vampire and a Sorcerer, what a combination. Going to regular doctors was off the table since then, and dad cracked down on my protection as much as he could without overwhelming and scaring me.

He's always been so gentle and caring with me, all through my years. I was his soft spot, I'd take advantage sometimes. Sometimes I want some people to disappear. Sometimes I want a new pair of shoes, just bat your eyelashes and ask sweetly. Dad crumbles every time.

It's always just been us, sometimes Uncle Titus, but usually, just us. Father and daughter.

But now? He's being sweet and gentle with someone else, someone I don't know, someone who predates me. I know I'm his daughter, I know realistically I have nothing to worry about, but since when has emotions ever been rational? Emotions never made sense to me, feeling everything so intensely all the time was a big flaw of mine. Love, anger, jealousy, sadness. It all was too much. It hurt so much. My love for my dad and Aubrey nearly consumed me, I felt like I was suffocating without them. If my dad ever left me behind, I wouldn't know how to react. This crushing, suffocating, massive wave would just wash over me. It's like I keep trying to swim up and breathe but it was impossible.

Guess that's what happens when you're abandoned by your last remaining birth family? Over attachment, abandonment, whatever else. Maybe that what this dread is, an unhealthy response to my attachment, but can you blame me? How am I supposed to act when two becomes three, when you were happy with just two.

I looked across the table at them, they were smiling and sharing stories, catching up. I've tuned out at this point. Not to be rude or anything, but I feel like I'm intruding. *Gods I hope Aubrey and I never made Saint feel this way, how awkward. Oh, I'm not here again.* I blinked and glanced towards the distant voice ahead of me, my senses kicked in and I sat up.

Scotus was smiling sweetly at me, while dad was looking at me expectantly. I dropped my arms softly on the table and blinked once more. *Geez girl you weren't even paying attention.*

"I'm sorry? What did you say?"

"I asked how old you were.." Scotus spoke gently. Oh, I have to get to know him of course. I took a moment before smiling.

"Twenty-four, as of last month."

"Oh??" Scotus perked up, "I can take you drinking and clubbing how exciting~"

Dad shot the smaller person a look.

"Kidding kidding, loosen up Betty." Scotus laughed and waved his hand. "So Rouge, tell me about yourself, I can tell you're his world."

"Me?" I asked, he nodded.

"Oh, well, um.." I took a moment to think. "Well, I like performing arts.."

"Oh? Such as?" Scotus asked.

"Dancing, mainly Ballet, and I use to play the Cello in school." I dropped my gaze awkwardly. In the corner of my eye I could see dad smile proudly.

"You take after your father I see." Scotus hummed and leaned against his arms on the table, His eyes were a deep blue galaxy, seemed like they were swirling, and the stars I saw earlier, were actual stars. He must have Reaper genes. His sharp eyeliner really complimented his gorgeous eyes. He had different skin pigments ranging from dark to light. He's stunning up close. He eyed me, but I couldn't read his emotions.

"Leviathan, sweetie? Do you mind giving us a moment?" He asked, I tensed slightly. *Oh gods.*

"Oh, uh, sure." Levi glanced over at me before slipping out of the booth and resting his jacket on the seat and heading to the bar a little ways away.

"Ok sweetie, let's take a breath, yes?" Scotus spoke gently,

"You're so tense.."

"I'm sorry, I'm just.."

"A daddy's girl, I can see it all on your face." Scotus laughed softly and nodded, "Well let me assure you, No one, and I mean no one, is taking that man from you sweetheart, not even death themselves."

"I've been friends with that man for as long as I remember, as loyal as they come."

"You think so?" I asked.

"I know so sweetie, I mean, he's still kicking it with Titus after all these years." Scotus' eyes softened like he was recounting a memory, "Ya know those two met in high school on a random night. Your dad called me freaking about him bringing a drunk guy home and was worried his parents would hear them."

"A drunk guy?" I asked, intrigued. Scotus nodded and smiled.

"Yep, a dumb drunk Dragon named Titus, which he didn't know until the next day." I laughed quietly, yea that sounds like Uncle Titus. "And they've been friends ever since, ask them about that story, it's hilarious when they both try to tell it."

I smiled softly, he seemed nice. And his tone doesn't sound condescending or fake, more cautious and shaky, like he's nervous. Well that makes two of us.

"Now me and your father, We met before freshman year. I ran into him in Sin City. I was lost and confused." I looked at him, "I was reborn into this silly place, and your father was the first to help me."

"You weren't born here?"

"Gods no!" He laughed, "I used to be up there, living a

normal life. And next thing I know. I'm here. I mean, My Earthen features are pretty prominent."

"Interesting.." I laughed quietly, "Uh, Yes. Sorry… It's been so long since I've seen Earthens. They're usually souls down here…"

Scotus laughed, "Yea, well, I cheated my way into this position. Best way to become a Sinner right?"

"Heh, I guess so?" I smiled awkwardly.

Scotus smiled then looked at the table momentarily, "Look.. Rouge, I love and care for your Dad." He looked at me and sat up, "There's no reason to beat around the bush about it right?"

Scotus breathed out, "And, that man is crazy about you. And I want you to like me."

"Why? He's grown and I'm grown, you have nothing to prove to me." *Play it cool girl, do not show you're actually falling apart over this.*

"Maybe so, but I'm still willing to make an effort if you're willing, of course I won't step on your toes or cross your boundaries. I'd be stupid to play in your face. He'd notice it right away."

I breathed out as I felt some tension leave me. I nodded, alright he's not a weirdo, and he's not the person who will ship me off as soon as he gets the chance.

"I see."

"Can I be honest with you dear?" Scotus asked quieter. I raised a brow and tilted my head, "Your father is, Husband material, to me. And he's back… And he still looks at me the same."

I see. Old friend is an old love interest. I had a suspicion, but a lot of people are naturally flirty. But Dad's behavior should've been a tip off. The diner, the flirting, the avoidance of the topic. *Dad is crushing, hard.* I nodded to myself and looked at the table, would that mean someone else will make dad happy? Dad will be happy right? At the end of the day isn't that all that really matters? Isn't that all that should matter?

"I..will be honest." I met his eyes, "You will be an adjustment. I want my dad happy, but I'll need to adjust."

"I understand." He nodded, "I can't imagine what it's like having a single parent your whole life then someone else shows up in the picture suddenly, I'll give you space and time, but even if me and your father stay friends, I want to make an effort with you dear."

"Yea, alright.."

"Is there anything you'd like to know? Something to put you at ease?" Scotus asked.

I took a moment to think, "Um, you said you love my Dad? Why."

"Why?" Scotus blinked, "Gods where to begin? He's always been so kind and gentle with me, and I noticed that's something foreign to him. Unlike with others he puts up an effort to communicate with me. He treats me like I'm the most important thing to him." He sighed sweetly, "First kiss, first date, first crush, first love. Whole thing."

"Oh fuck." I rubbed my face, "Well, I." I laughed and shook my head, "I can't really hate that. You sound a little too familiar to me."

"Oh? Have a special boy?"

"Something like that." I shook my head and messed with my hair.

"I see.." Scotus nodded, "Soo, this person must be special

if they have you timid and shy?"

"You have no idea." I sighed, "But that's past, we're not together anymore."

"Oh..." His voice trailed off, "I'm sorry dear."

"It's alright, this isn't about me. Dad seemed really excited for me to meet you." I smiled, "So I won't disappoint him. You seem nice."

"Nice enough."

* * *

We sat quietly in the car, dad looked exhausted. I can tell his social battery is zero at this point. I watched as the city of gold passed by us. The city seems to be asleep at this hour, by now the surface would be full of stars and the moon would be shining so high, I think that's the only thing I truly miss about the surface, just the sky. Down here it's endless deep blue and twinkles, they kind of resemble stars, and of course Aides' moon, so it's not too bad. It's beautiful down here, but it's not the surface. I hummed quietly and rested my head against the window.

"I really appreciate this, Roro." Levi spoke quietly, "I was nervous you'd be indifferent."

"So, you really like him?"

"Have for years, probably always will if I'm honest." Levi hummed.

"I see..." I looked back out the window, "Well, whatever you choose to do dad, I'll support you."

"..." He smiled softly and pulled me close into a tight hug, "Thanks ladybug."

He rested his head on top of mine, and closed his eyes, "Fuck, I need a nap."

I laughed and patted his arm, "We'll be home soon dad. I can't carry your whole weight so stay awake."

He chuckled, "What did I do to deserve such a perfect daughter."

"Your blessings maybe?"

"Oh I have none of those to cash, they'd play against me." He laughed, "But maybe raising you redeemed me to the universe."

I laughed quietly, "Maybe old man. Maybe.."

I leaned against him and looked out the window as we drove back home, it'll take some time, but dad I promise I'll be Ok with another person in your life, just continue to be patient with me. That's all I ask.

15

FOURTEEN

A loud chime rang out in the quiet room. The aggressive vibrations on my desk dragged me out of my sleep. *12 am.* I groaned quietly and shut it off aggressively. Letting my eyes adjust in the dark and narrow them. *Oh, it was a calendar notification. Briar's birthday.*

That woke me up almost immediately, heh, usually I'm awake and wishing her a happy birthday. I rubbed the drool off my face and looked down at my textbooks. *Guess I was tired.* I rubbed my eyes and leaned back in the rolly chair and closed my eyes.

Briar, gods I wonder how she's doing, it's been what? Two and a half years? I smiled softly to myself and looked back down at my phone to send her a happy birthday text, not twelve on the dot but twelve nonetheless. I can imagine the big smile on her beautiful face when she reads the texts, I can see it now. Her sitting in her rose garden, she'd twirl her blonde locs around her finger and her piercing red eyes would light up with excitement. It was always the little things that made her the happiest. A sheltered rich girl with guards and no friends and home schooled? Yea, anything would impress her in terms of relationships. I never had to try. But I always did.. Guess it was over compensation for fucking up with Rouge as bad as I did. *I miss her.*

I rubbed my face and glanced back at the time, twelve in the morning huh? Yea, guess now is a better time than any to take a jog and recuperate for school tomorrow. Today. *Whatever.* I got up and threw on a T-shirt and shorts then climbed out the window towards the gate and headed towards the town. It's peaceful at this time, low glows of the lava, little to no people around, silent sounds of the birds and a warm breeze. I always took late night jogs to clear my head, especially when frustrated. Or just too tired to fall asleep.

Gods, I'm so tired. I'm so close to giving up on this school bullshit, I'm not even learning anything of importance. Like controlling my magic better. I'm not a Sorcerer so all of this falls flat. The only thing I'm good at is combat but that's useless to them without my magic being an assistance.

No matter what I try it's just vines and poisonous flowers. *Great* for potions, terrible for combat.

And the Headmaster isn't helping. Gods it's like she's constantly breathing down my neck, waiting for me to fuck up. Her stare is incredibly annoying and unsettling to feel. Makes my neck shiver.

But Saint is so happy, Rouge too. Everyday it's like she gets a little closer, I hear she's doing great in her studies, her and Saint both. They were born to do this after all.

I jogged past the Academy and noticed a sleek blacked out car in the road. A very nice car, too nice to be in Nevermore. I glanced up at the building, I tilted my head slightly to the side as I noticed a few lights on, I stopped my jog and narrowed my eyes. The campus doesn't open till nine. And closes at nine. Who the hell would still be here at this time? And what's that sound? I strained my ears slightly to make it out, but nothing.

Behind you..

I blinked and glanced behind me, *that whisper again*, and side stepped as a small pink haired girl stumbled in front of me, I instinctively caught her and pulled her to her feet then realized.

"Hey… ain't you that-?"

"Gods. The hell's your problem. Watch it." Rue growled out and fixed her bag. Not sure what she was up to, she's in the brightest beige coat I've ever seen with a pair of cream heeled boots and a matching purse on her arm. I raised a brow and stepped back from her.

"I was standing still Darlin', I think you're confused." Rue sucked her teeth in annoyance and went to open her mouth, "Plus, it's 1 am, the hell you doin out here bulldozing around for."

Rue pursed her lips almost immediately. She gripped her bag and her eyes darted quickly to the building then back down.

"None of your business, I can ask you the same thing." Rue narrowed her eyes, "Don't you have an exam to study for, you'll be kicked out if you fail you know. What a waste of an entry."

"Oh fuck off." I rolled my eyes, "And from what I'm hearing you're not as good as you think you are Pinky. Careful of that glass house."

Rue scoffed and dropped her fists to her side. Her eyes

narrowed, "Don't you dare, compare me to you lazy slackers. My grades and performance are *exemplary*." She stepped closer and poked my chest for emphasis.

I grabbed her wrist and moved her hand away, "Yea yea, tell it to your circle jerk overachievers, I couldn't care less."

"You vile little-" Rue stopped then snapped her head back towards the school as one of the lights suddenly flicked off, I dropped her wrist and turned away, crossing my arms as she let out a swear from under her breath.

"Seriously. What the hell you doin out here powder puff, trying to steal test answers or sum."

"I'd never! You delinquent." Rue protested.

I laughed to myself, "If you ask nicely maybe I'll help you."

"How about you shove it!" Rue pointed up at me, her cheeks puffed out in anger. How cute.

I laughed in her face and went to jog off, "Yea well, good luck to you princess. If ya get caught I didn't see ya, I might think you're a self absorbed, arrogant brat, but I ain't no snitch."

"You are so." Rue cut herself off at the sound of keys rattling, she grabbed my arm immediately and snatched me outta sight behind nearby rock formations.

"Wha-" Rue slapped her hand over my mouth as a heavy pair of footsteps stomped past us. Sounded like he was on the phone, Mentioning a book and did what he was told? I glanced at her then pulled away when the guy drove off.

"Forreal. What the hell's your problem." I demanded this time.

Rue hesitated a moment before speaking, "Something here... is wrong"

"As in."

"Keep an eye on your friend. The purple one."

I immediately got defensive and narrowed my eyes in defense, "Meaning."

"Not like that. Calm down, This place... It's not right. And Miss Petra has never been so cold and distant, especially to me.." Rue looked away, "I need to know what changed."

"So you were sneaking in there to look around?" She nodded sheepishly, I shook my head.

"Well you aren't going to be successful now."

"Yea no duh, I figured as much." Rue stood up and brushed the dirt off her jacket, I looked up at the school and watched the statue in the courtyard.

"You said she's never been this cold before?"

"Huh? No never, she's as kind as can be. She was so happy to get this job but she slowly started changing.." Rue shook her head, "I don't know, then there's the 4th year classes, they're all changed, and secretive."

"Is that so?"

I got to my feet and checked the time, "Look, school opens in about 8 hours, I wish you luck, but I have to go."

"8 hours.." Rue looked up at the school. She had an upset look in her eye, I watched her momentarily then glanced back down at my phone.

Dammit.

I sighed and rubbed my face. "Alright, Come on."

Rue blinked in confusion and slowly followed behind me, "What are you doing?"

"You have an Hour. If my friend is possibly in danger I want concrete proof of it. Understood." I glanced down at her.

She took a moment to process before nodding, "I'll try

my best."

I made my way to the building, wandering the perimeter for an entrance that wasn't so noticeable, that guy had to get in some kind of way. I narrowed my eyes and followed the mushed dirt trail towards a side door, I kneeled and studied the lock before pulling a hair pin from my pocket and began picking at the lock. Rue's soft footsteps came up behind me, I could feel her paranoia from here.

"What are you doing..?" Rue asked.

"Getting the door open." I glanced at her, "Can't let her dearest know we were here after her little henchman now can we?"

"Tch, I suppose. Well hurry up before we get caught."

"Has anyone told you, you're great with people?"

"Huh? I? No-?" I gave her a deadpan look as the door clicked open, she pursed her lips in an annoyed pout.

"Oh shut up." She walked ahead and slipped in the building. I followed behind her and took a deep breath.

"Alright, where are we going?"

"I'm not fully sure... I feel her office would be best. There's gotta be something in there."

"You *think*?" I looked around the place, all the lights were off and it was eerily silent aside from her quiet footsteps. But the small whirling of cameras echoed in my ears, I scratched at my ear and glanced down at her.

"Better than wandering aimlessly right?"

She seems to know the layout of this building pretty well, she purposely moved where cameras couldn't catch us. *Interesting*. She led the way to the office, of course it was locked. I kneeled down and fiddled with the lock as she stepped aside and motioned to it. The lock rattled a few times, sounding infinitely louder in the quiet halls, Rue kept her eyes out, scanning the halls before staring at me.

"Should I be concerned about you having this ability? Why are you good at this?" Rue crossed her arms. The door clicked and I pushed it open while standing.

"I'm a delinquent, remember?" I motioned her inside and followed behind, glancing around the dark room. No cameras in here. I flicked the light on and walked towards the desk. Rue began looking through the drawers and over the papers as carefully as she could.

I looked at all the tall bookshelves lining the walls and walked to them, scanning over the books. Interesting.. I picked up a dark green book, it had gold trim and intricate flower designs around a decorative cow skull ornament.

"Whoa…" Pulling the book open, the pitch black pages soon lit up with purple text. A bunch of plant spells and forms, I scanned over a few pages before hearing a soft whispering.

"Huh? Did you say something?" I asked, looking over at Rue who was rummaging through the bottom drawers.

"Huh? No."

"Then…" I glanced towards the other shelves and closed the book in my hands before putting it back gently and walking towards a pale purple book with gold trim on the spine. It looked like it had a golden eye and apple printed on it, but no title. It felt strange. It gave me an uneasy feeling, incredibly uneasy. Is it whispering to me? Why is this familiar, what is this book. I felt my arm instinctively moving towards it but I do not want to touch that thing. I couldn't keep my eyes off it, That's no regular spell book.

"Ah ha!" Rue exclaimed, making me jump in surprise and

turn my head to her, "I knew it, the fourth year's syllabus for the year."

"The syllabus? Really." I crossed my arms while walking over, glancing towards the book, "What's this prove."

"These aren't normal classes!" Rue pointed to the paper, "Fourth years are supposed to be doing job shadows, advanced classes, and exams to get their wands and hats. These classes are incomprehensible. And this is Dead language. Why would this be a mandatory course? Only Reapers need to know Dead language."

I hummed and looked over her shoulder then pointed to the bottom. "That. That's dead language, I'm rusty on it but that says death and Reapers."

"Exterminatio trucis messor vis, graduating classis" Rue narrowed her eyes.

"Sounds like a spell."

"No, it's definitely not, dead language spells only work for Reapers." Rue shook her head, "I haven't translated dead language in awhile, so give me a minute." She took a picture of the paper and I looked through the papers on the desk.

"It's on these too." I pushed the paper to her. She took more pictures and nodded.

"I'm going to look into translating this."

A small crack down the hall caught my attention, I instinctively shot my head towards the noise. I narrowed my eyes at the dark halls and watched silently. A small movement of a shadow immediately caught my eye and ears.

"Hey darlin' I think we should go."

"But-?"

"Now." I walked to the door and peeked out of the room,

"Fix everything the way you had it."

Rue did so hastily and scurried behind me, she loomed closely and I motioned her out. She went the way she came, avoiding the cameras once more, but this time one of the cameras was down. I raised a brow and walked over, examining the wiring. Short circuited? I narrowed my eyes and glanced around the area, listening intently.

Rue got to the door and turned, "Hey! Come on."

I waited momentarily before standing and following her out, closing the door behind us. She was looking at her phone, her pink eyes were sparkling from the late night lava and she giggled giddily.

"Oh wow! That was exciting!~"

"Ok. Calm down." I shook my head, "When you get that translated, you tell me. Alright?"

Rue nodded while bouncing in place. I rubbed the back of my head and glanced away, "Uh, you want me to walk you home?"

She blinked and looked up at me, "Oh. You're capable of chivalry?"

I grunted and turned to head home. She snickered to herself quietly and gripped the side of my shirt.

"Yes, please, if you don't mind."

I huffed quietly, *Why did you raise me right dad.* I rolled my eyes to myself and motioned her to walk. I followed close behind her, hands in my pocket as she kept her eyes on the phone. *"Exterminatio"* Rue tapped her lips. She was thinking hard.

"So, how do you know dead language?" I asked, glancing at her.

"My mom taught me." She responded without looking up,

hand still on her lips. “I find Reaper things interesting.”

I snorted through my nose and looked at her, “Seriously?”

“What.” She narrowed her eyes.

“Oh! Nothing, nothing Pinky, I just assumed you'd be elitist about them.”

“Tch!” She crossed her arms, “How do you think I knew about your friend dummy.”

“She's a Sawyer, most people know of her, well. At least I assumed so.”

“A Sawyer?” She echoed, “Well I knew she was a Reaper... but a Sawyer? And no one knows but you?”

“Mhmm.” I glanced at her.

“Why would she come here but not the Reaper academy.”

I shrugged, “That's her business and hers alone.”

“Keep an eye on her.” Rue looked up at me, she came to a stop in front of a gated property, “So, why do you know dead language? Did you steal a book or something.”

I scowled at her, then looked towards her house. It was far off on a hill. Of course it was huge, The spoiled princess had a big fancy palace. I pointed to the gate, the word Kovenn spelled in the solid black bars, a single raven sitting above it, peering down at us.

“I'm a Kovenn.”

She blinked in surprise, “What!?” She narrowed her eyes, “And who is your parent.”

“Is that any of your business?” I crossed my arms.

“That implies your parents are one of my aunts or uncles, and you don't look like any of them.”

“Uh huh. Well, nice to officially meet you coz'.” I turned on my heel and started for home. Rue tilted her head and watched me go.

I sighed out and rubbed my arm, walking slower. Well tonight was certainly eventful. I grabbed my phone as it chimed, Dads awake ,the message flashed on screen followed by a notification from my bank app saying I was sent one thousand gold from Briar, I frowned and shook my head. That girl. Leave it to her to send money on HER birthday. *What a goof.*

"Aubrey!" I turned my head to the waving pink haired girl, "Watch out for that snake!"

Dread washed over me immediately.

16

FIFTEEN

"Hey kid, there you are." Tartarus spoke up, "You alright?"

"Yea, sorry, I went for a morning jog. I got your message, everything Ok?" I asked.

"Oh, yes. I need you to keep an eye on Iron for a while, I'll be leaving for a few days." He looked tired, almost annoyed.

"Few days?" I asked, leaning against the couch.

"I'm out of Death Metal, I have to see if I can get some mined." Tartarus sighed and grabbed his boots by the door.

"But that's all the way in The Summit."

Tartarus shrugged, "That's business. It's why I'm low on cash, orders are backing up. I've been waiting."

"How are YOU low on Death Metal, aren't you the only supplier? It's illegal everywhere else." I watched him gather his things, his shoulders were slumped.

He hummed, "It's just a few days, a week tops. You'll be alright?"

"Yea, of course.." I glanced away, "Just be careful? The Angels are assholes."

"I know better than anyone." Tartarus shook his head,

"I'm going straight to Apollo then here, he doesn't give me shit."

"Alright.." Tartarus placed his hand on my head and smiled.

"A week tops." He said.

"A week." I repeated.

He gave Iron a quick pet and headed out the creaky gate. I looked at Iron and breathed out, "Well. I guess it's just us boy."

He barked and laid by the door and I headed upstairs to get ready for school. I kept checking my messages as I did. No word from Rue, guess she crashed as soon as she got home. I grabbed my backpack and headed out the door and towards school.

I headed inside and to my locker, opening it then checking my phone. She sent the pictures, no translations yet though.

"Morning Aubrey~" A sweet sing songy voice spoke from behind my locker door, I stifled a startled jump and pushed the door closed, revealing Keegan, her beautiful face was rosy, her hair curled flawlessly and her eyes bright and soft, her ears fluttered as she smiled.

"Sorry to startle you.."

"No no darlin, you're more than fine." I glanced towards my phone, "Actually I'd like your input on somethin'."

Keegan looked up at me and tilted her head to the side, "Sure?"

"Your brother does graphic design right? Posters and stuff."

Keegan nodded. "He does, his little hobby *you* used to tease him for?" She raised a brow.

I chuckled nervously then grinned cheesily, "I was misguided back then."

"Mm, Is that so?" Keegan shook her head, "Why ask?"

"Posters. I need information on the process." I smiled sweetly.

"Oh, well I'm not very educated on his stuff, you'd have to ask him." Keegan smiled gently, "Apologies."

"You're fine Sugar." I grabbed my books and pocketed my phone before closing the locker.

"I um, actually wanted to ask.." Keegan spoke up, She messed with the hem of her uniform skirt.

I turned my head to her, "Yes?"

"I was wondering if you'd still like to get that coffee?" She messed with her hair nervously, like she always used too. I smiled softly and ignored that little echo from Saint in the back of my head about being single.

This stunning woman is asking me out and I'm just supposed to say no? Yea, I ain't built like that.

I leaned against the lockers and smiled, "If I'm honest I figured you forgot, I'm sorry sugar, I shouldn't have let you get all worried like this."

She waved it off and glanced away with a blush on her chubby cheeks, "No no, I should've texted.."

I smiled at her, "I'd be delighted, I'm free today. Four o'clock?" I asked and stood straight.

She nodded eagerly, her curls bouncing.

"Perfect. I've gotta run before classes start but, four." I put up four fingers.

"Four." She smiled.

I nodded and walked towards the computer labs, maybe this is good. It's not like I have any shot with Rouge anymore. And being hung up isn't unhealthy. *Yes yes Saint was right.*

Like always. And she's an Angel, well maybe she can fix me. I laughed to myself and shook my head, *Oh shit her brother is going to kill me.*

Heading to class, I passed the headmasters office, I could feel her icy stare follow me. I refused to look in her direction, but I could still hear those small whispers. Is it that book? I glanced over slightly but kept walking, the door closed softly behind me and I turned.

A girl with puffy shoulder length dark gray hair was standing by the door, her hand still on the knob. Her eyes were strange, nothing like a Demon I've ever seen before. Her eyes were doe like, her body was soft I could tell from here. Her hair framed her face beautifully, her eyes narrowed at me before she turned and flipped her hair over her shoulder. When she did, her fluffy earrings revealed themselves. Just like Saint, it looked like she had a third eye on her forehead but her brown skin had lighter parts trailing from her neck to her face, looked like Vampire albinism spread. *She's certainly unique.* She's in the Potions course uniform. Is she new? I blinked but kept walking. *Strange.*

* * *

Gods, I can't believe I let Saint talk me into this shit. I huffed out, blinking slowly to wake myself up, staying out all night probably wasn't the best idea. *Lectures, quizzes, notes,* ***fuck.*** I told myself I'd never do this school shit *ever* again. Why am I such a caring and thoughtful friend. My eyes bore into the board ahead of me. My head rested in the palm of my hand. The potions textbook open in front of me, is it on the right page? Who knows. What is this teacher going on about? Who knows.

I never really read the textbooks, I've been so focused on my earth studies I haven't even thought about the potions side of this damn course, I groaned to myself quietly, ain't this shit supposed to be easy? Read a spell, put them in a cauldron and stir that shit up. Why does this shit look like mathematical equations, and these ramblings ain't making this better.

I sucked my teeth quietly and narrowed my eyes in annoyance, and dad isn't here to translate it either, he's got more important shit to deal with.

Fuck me.

"*Psst.*" I blinked and glanced towards the sound, "Struggling with this too?"

I blinked and turned my head to a brown skinned girl, she had long brown twists with a few lighter brown and blonde highlights throughout, her uniform was tailored to her smaller waist and her pants flared out the bottom but it was still in the school colors. Her eyes were a deep brown and freckles lined her cheeks. She smiled sweetly at me and I narrowed my eyes slightly in thought, a small thought scratching in the back of my mind.

"Uh, yea." I muttered and glanced away awkwardly.

"I can see the frustration on your face." She spoke quietly and leaned towards me, "It's really simple actually, practical potions can be like science equations, don't let the numbers freak you out."

"Huh.." I looked back at the book. I blinked in confusion as my brain tried to get back into school mode. She pointed her pencil towards the professor who's now going student to student. *Oh fuck, am I supposed to make what ever the hell they were talking about?*

"Page 53, think, H2O plus Carbon, that's all you have to do." She smiled and leaned away. I grunted quietly and quickly turned the pages, as the professor slowly made his way towards me. I read over the book with a squint, I looked at all my supplies and narrowed my eyes. Scientific equation huh? chemistry?

Now that I can do. Reading baking instructions do nothing for me, but chemistry? Can't tell me shit. I muttered to myself while looking for the right mixes, won't be an exact match up but as they say for scientific hypothesis, gotta try. I wrote a few notes down and muttered to myself quietly as the professor stopped in front of that other person in the corner of my eye, the kid's concoction turned pink, that's the goal. I nodded to myself and made a few tiny mixes on my paper.

A shadow suddenly formed over me, a throat clear made me look up, "Aubrey. Your potion please." He spoke almost irritably.

I glanced up at him, then down at the materials, test one was blue, test two was red, it's somewhere in between, using a deduction, adding A to B will give you C. *Right?* I slowly moved my hands over a few of the chemicals and slowly added the substances together, the teacher huffed out of his nose.

I hate school, I can already feel everyone's eyes on me, time feels like it's slowing down and my hands are getting sweaty. It's hard to focus when all eyes are on you. *I hate fucking school.*

I huffed out as I went to pour the chemicals, but suddenly my phone went off causing me to fumble the ingredients and add too much. It turned pink momentarily before turning red and blowing up in his face. I smiled apologetically and awkwardly. The teacher gave a gruff noise, he wiped his face with his handkerchief then began writing something on his clipboard and moving on to the next student.

I slid down in my seat and rubbed my face, the girl next to me smiled and patted my shoulder.

"Almost had it.." That quiet voice said, I glanced over at the brunette.

"Yea, it would've been fine if my phone didn't go off." I muttered, "The only one that would've worked since I wasn't confused this time, how frustrating." I moved the book over the now ruined notes and laid my head back against the bench.

She giggled quietly, I felt my body relax and eyes soften. Such a familiar safe vibe, "Poor timing, I get it, I'm a bit bad luck prone myself." She gave a soft and warm comforting smile.

"Uh, my name's Aubrey." I said quietly.

"Mi-" She cleared her throat then smiled, "Jonas."

"Nice to meet you Jonas." I blinked and looked back at my phone as it buzzed once more, then slipped out of the classroom, checking the texts. From Rue, guess she cracked it. I read the multiple messages and skimmed it.

"Destruction of the Grim Reaper force graduating class" I tilted my head to the side slightly. "Destruction of the Grim Reaper force, graduating class?" Gods have you people never heard of punctuation. I stared at the message, reading it in different cadences, I blinked as a shadow and a soft

sound caught my attention.

I looked up and stood to attention, watching that area. I slowly made my way over there, I didn't see anyone but I did hear subtle clanging. I followed the noise and the closer I got, the more familiar it sounded, it was clanking metal, and the smell in the air, ash and fire.

We don't have Blacksmithing classes here? I narrowed my eyes and walked towards the area the sound was coming from, it was an unmarked room in a darker part of the school full of cobwebs and dust, clearly unused. I pressed my ear to the door and listened. The metal is different. That's not regular metal. I closed my eyes and strained my ears. Sounds like dad's metal, it was denser, lighter, had a particular smell to it when burnt. *Death metal? Here?* I squinted my eyes in thought. *How would she get access to death metal, and how is she running a shop in the school with anyone none the wiser.*

I swore under my breath as my phone chimed again, the clanking stopped and footsteps approached the door quickly. I hurried back the way I came while silencing my phone.

Dammit Rue.

I glanced over my shoulder towards the room right as it closed again.

Yea something isn't right.

I slipped back towards the class as the school bell chimed. I felt that icy stare again, I turned my head to see that same gray haired girl from earlier, she had a dark look in her eyes, she clearly came from the opposite direction of that abandoned hall. She walked past me, kept her eyes on me before looking forward. Was she watching me this whole time? A chill ran down my spine.

"What's her deal." I muttered.

"Aubrey?" Jonas smiled, holding her books, and held up my backpack "Free for lunch?"

I looked at her then smiled a bit, "Sure."

17

SIXTEEN

It's been a couple days. Things have been quiet, but, my hunch was correct, Orien unintentionally confirmed those notes were for posters, Keegan worked fast to ask him for me. The concepts on her desk? Death, Reapers. What the hell is she making a poster for? And what was that room for? I tried to double back but that hall was blocked off now and Dad is still out of town so I can't even ask him about it.

Even so, no one mentioned that room though, no whispers or gossip about it at all. I've kept my ear to the ground, Rue has been a bit quiet as well, Now that I'm hyper aware, a lot of things here aren't clicking for me. The year four students are basically non-existent on campus, and if you see one of them they look drained, devoid of life almost. They're tight lipped as well. It's like a giant secret is being kept between them, something they're all in agreement of keeping quiet.

What the hell is that about?

I've been spending the past lunch and free periods with Jonas, and boy is she a gem. She radiates familiarity and kindness, and honestly it feels good. Saint and Rouge have been busy with studies and I'm taking every opportunity to avoid having that talk with Rouge, much to Saint's annoyance.

She seems well traveled, and incredibly educated on things I never thought of. She spoke to me about her clothing hobby for hours and I enjoyed every minute of it. She even offered to show me how to sew and to help me with my classes. She would share her notes with me and offer me advice. It was such a breath of fresh air compared to the other students here. All of them treated me like I was stupid, or incompetent. *What pompous assholes.*

I sat with her outside the greenhouse and sat my drink down. She was sitting politely next to me, her uniform skirt perfectly tailored. I leaned back against the warm glass and tossed a few bread crumbs to the crows as they cawed and bounced around. I smiled softly then turned my attention to her.

"They seem to like you." Jonas spoke up, putting her books away and picking up a water bottle.

"Oh, yea, Crows always hang around me, Ravens? Not so much." I laughed quietly.

"Is there a difference?" Jonas asked.

"Absolutely." I nodded, "For one, crows are smaller." I looked down at the birds as they tilted their heads and pecked at the bread crumbs.

"And Crows can remember faces better, I'm sure I've probably been feeding the same birds for years and not even realize it." I laughed and tossed the last of my bread to them gently, "The only Raven that likes me is my friend's pet, Opal, she's a sweetheart. The rest kinda avoid me."

"I see, are they your favorite animals?" Jonas asked, tilting her head at the group.

"One of them. I'm really, *really* fond of Goats. And these cute little things called Cats? They have them on the surface, they're so perfect. I want one so bad but I doubt they'd last here."

"Cats." Jonas asked in slight disbelief, "I'm sorry you don't strike me as a… Cat lover."

"You think?"

"Creepy Birds and Dogs? Sure. Cats? Not so much."

I laughed and laid my head against the glass, shrugging, "I just like animals. I mean, I'm a vegan for a reason, well not a full vegan. I only eat fish and chicken."

"Really?" Jonas asked, her eyes brightened, "So no beef or pork or anything like that? I understand the beef though, Do you follow Jezabelle?"

"Mhmm, Yea. Can't invoke her wrath right? I know Cows are sacred." I watched the River Styx flow above us calmly. It shimmered from the moon's shine. Aides' moon has been very prominent lately. I trailed the river flow with my eyes and relaxed.

"You are a very interesting person, Aubrey."

"You think so?" I shrugged, "Dunno, I think Ima dime a dozen."

"No, no." Jonas shook her head, "Not at all."

"Well, thanks." I smiled and lifted my head to look at her, "I think you're interesting. You tailored this one as well? Is that even allowed?"

Jonas grinned proudly, "Yep! according to the student handbook chapter 5 section 3." She patted her pants.

"I'm so jealous."

"Well I can definitely do some alterations for you?" She beamed.

"Nah, I wouldn't ask anything free of you and I'm tight on cash right now." I waved it off.

"No no, I don't mind."

"Really, it ain't that big." I shrugged. I sat up properly, placing my hand on the concrete steps and unintentionally knocking her water over, I grunted and tried to pick it up before it all spilled out.

"Oh shit, sorry I can get you a new one."

"No need.." She put her hand up and leaned forward, circling her fingers elegantly over the ground and pulling the water from it expertly. Her movements were so fluid and advanced, like it was child's play for her. I blinked in shock before narrowing my eyes and looking back at her, she put the cap back on the water and sat it down, good as new.

"See, no harm done." She smiled proudly.

"Whoa. You're a water elemental?" I asked, looking at the water then at her.

Water elementals are basically non-existent down here, all things considered. They don't tend to do well in the intense heat and lack of water. The air is always dry and there's absolutely no natural water sources here. I never even noticed that was an issue until I visited the surface. They had lakes, and oceans, and rivers made of water, ponds, all types of different water sources.

What is a water elemental doin down here?

The flap and wind from the crows' wings cut through the silence. She seemed to realize then turned her head to me and cleared her throat awkwardly.

"Um, yes?"

"How are you surviving down here? Do I need to get you some more water? Are you hydrated?" I asked.

"I'm fine, honest." Jonas waved it off, so nonchalant.

"How are you so calm?" I asked, brow raised.

"Oh this is nothing, I'm so in my element, no matter where I go." Jonas bragged, waving her hand.

"Even at such a disadvantage..." I looked down at my lap in thought, "Ok, but how."

She went silent for a moment, glancing around almost nervously. She glanced up at the greenhouse then leaned forward to me, I leaned forward to meet her and she put her hand up and spoke quietly in my ear.

"I'm a different type of elemental, I can't talk about it out here."

I blinked then looked at her, Jonas sat back then got to her feet, opening the greenhouse door. Jonas looked down at me and motioned me to follow her inside. I practically hopped to my feet and followed her inside, closing the door softly behind us.

She stretched and shook her arms then turned to face me, I tilted my head in question but stayed quiet.

"This stays between us, yes?" She spoke softly and stood in the middle of the room.

"Absolutely." I nodded almost eagerly, I've never been so intrigued by any Sorcerer before, what does she mean she's a different type? What other types are there?

"Look around you, what do you see?" Jonas asked, motioning around the area. I looked around and tilted my head in confusion.

"Uh, Plants?"

"Yes, but think harder." She moved her hand, her fingers danced elegantly as some of the plants around her began to move. I gasped a bit in disbelief.

"I see items filled with water." She walked over to a flower and plucked it, she held it between her fingertips and ran her finger down the damp petal. A small trail of water following her motion before the flower wilted and died. A glob of water sitting on her gloved hand.

I had no words, all I could do was watch intently.

"There's water, *and* earth, in places you *never* think about." Jonas moved the water around on her palm and up her fingers making them freeze then unfreeze, almost like she was playing with a toy.

I never met any water elementals formally, but I did know a family of Ice elementals, and Briar told me, freezing and unfreezing water is a high level skill, that even *she* hasn't mastered yet, she could never thaw ice and manipulate it. But here's Jonas, changing the mediums with no issue.

Not even my dad can transition like that, it's why he sticks heavily to lava. Cooling it and altering it in any way was something he's never shown the knowledge to possess. And she's doing this here, in The Valley. I was completely speechless.

"You… You're amazing."

Jonas smiled softly and let the water drip through her fingers, "I learned magic from the elements. From nature, like the goddess intended. My sources are the moons."

She put up a finger, "Jezabelle, her goddess, she made the Elements, this World, for us to appreciate and learn from. All of her and Aides' children made gifts for us, and we did nothing with them. Yes the sun rises everyday, water fills the planet, but what is the point of these gifts, if we learn no appreciation from them?"

"Uh?" I asked.

"Listen." She closed her eyes, I looked up and looked at the roof of the green house, "Do you hear that?"

"The plants?" I shrugged, "I always have."

"Ah, see." She pointed at me, opening her eyes, "That ain't normal, love."

"What do you mean?" I asked.

"That is her goddess, sharing her knowledge with you. You're like me." She smiled. "I can teach you, if you wish."

"Teach me how?"

"We are all connected, without Air there is no Earth, without Earth there is no Water, etc." Jonas moved her hands elegantly, moving like water itself, "When you're in tune with Jezabelle there's no limit to your capabilities."

She looked at me, "No need to draw magic from Hecate."

I felt my eyes stretch wide, "Are you saying?"

"She is no beacon to me." Jonas shook her head, "I don't pull power from Hecate."

"How is that even possible?" I asked, astonished and intrigued, I could imagine I sound like a child eagerly awaiting the end of a bedtime story. Not pulling from Hecate is a new concept, she's the goddess and giver of magic itself, without her magic wouldn't exist all throughout Ansastatiaus, without her, how could we even tap into the elements?

"Well, her goddess created the nature around her and she cherished it for us, so we need to be in tune with what she made, does that make sense?" Jonas asked, "You are an earth elemental, and you hear the plants speak to you,

you're already off to a great start."

"I'm sorry, I'm still not fully understanding." I spoke almost desperately.

She motioned me forward, I closed the distance between us and she placed her hands on my shoulders and lifted my arms, she adjusted my hands and faced my palms upwards. She hovered her hands above mine and closed her eyes, I took the hint and closed mine as well.

She spoke softly, "In order to connect with her goddess, you have to completely trust her and her creations, don't focus on the energy of this school and what you normally pull from, feel your body merge with the life around you, listen to them intently. Think of the cycle of life, what the elements represent, your element."

I listened to her and took a few deep breaths. I was never the overly spiritual type so this feels a bit strange, of course I believe in the gods and I respect them, but I never prayed or thought about my place in the universe like this. I listened to the plants when I was a kid, they were my only friends. They had a soft, ghostly feminine voice. I can almost hear it now. I always just assumed that was my inner voice. That part of your brain that keeps you out of danger, the fight or flight response.

Her voice was calming, I wasn't sure what she was saying but she seemed to calm the other voices of the plants, almost like they all accumulated into her empty whispers. Am I connecting? I feel light. Even at ease. I feel like I'm being wrapped in a blanket, swallowed by the vines I used to play with, or create. But this didn't feel like I was drowning, more like I was being swaddled, so comforting.

"Breath the air, feel the water, become the earth, burn like fire."

She spoke up, *"Do you feel it?"*

Her voice was distant and echoed now, I could still hear her but everything else was more clear. I took a moment before responding with a quiet, "I think so?"

"It's so much more clear." I spoke calmly.

"Good, good." Jonas hummed, "Now let's try something new, focus on the ground. Imagine the movements of it, the cracks, the shape, the formation."

I nodded.

"Now move it."

I took a few deep breaths and focused on the ground below us. The plants are all I hear right now, I feel them wiggling at my fingertips, I tried to ignore that feeling and focus down. I tried to imagine the rock lifting and cracking for me, moving for me. It's stubborn of course.

Move you dumb rocks. Move.

I could feel sweat running down my brow, I tried not to strain too much as I remembered how elegant Jonas was moving. But does that even apply to rocks? No element is treated equally right? If the rocks are stubborn, shouldn't I be? I could feel my hands slowly curling as I focused.

After a few moments, I still felt nothing. *I can't feel a connection to the ground..* I sighed out and opened my eyes.

"Damn.." I dropped my hands to my side and jumped as a loud *thud* crashed around us. I looked down and saw the rocks slightly shifted below us, a few cracks spreading from me and a few pebbles bouncing as they landed. Whoa? Did I just?

"Fantastic Aubrey." She smiled sweetly, her voice so familial, I looked at her, my eyes stretched wide. *That worked? That fuckin worked?*

"You have such potential, hon." She smiled, "I knew you weren't a Sorcerer."

I coughed a bit and glanced at her a bit nervous, "I-"

"This makes you a Witch." I blinked and looked at her in confusion. That word sent a chill down my spine.

"A what-?"

"A Witch. Like me." She smiled and grabbed her backpack, "A Witch is not a Sorcerer nor mage, a Witch is a person in tune with nature, a Witch is a follower of her goddess, Jezabelle. Your magic is pure and genuine. Not artificial and temporary."

Jonas explained, she picked up her backpack and pulled that same cow skull book out of her bag, the one I saw in the headmasters office. Jonas put it to me and pressed it in my hands. I stared down at it like a kid in a candy store.

"How did you...?"

Jonas smiled, "Earth witches are some of the strongest I've heard, considering that was Jezabelle's favorite element." She patted the book, "And honestly, this would probably be better with a supposed Earth Witch than sitting on a shelf collecting dust. Right?"

All I could do was nod and stare at it, the language on it was old, dads native tongue it seems. Was it written by Aides and Jezabelle? I gripped it protectively. But Jonas placed her hand over the skull, her fingers catching my sight. I looked up at her and she had a gentle look in her eyes.

"I can teach you, but you'll have to want it."

I looked at her then back down at the book then the ground. This is what I wanted, why I came here in the first place. This is the first amount of progress I've ever made aside from withstanding lava. I'd be a fool to pass this up. And that voice wasn't against it, she was quiet, I nodded to myself and smiled at Jonas.

"I do." I hugged the book to my chest, "Will you teach me, Jonas?"

Jonas bowed her head sweetly, "I'd be delighted, Aubrey."

The school chime made her turn her head right as I did a happy bounce, squeezing the book to my chest in excitement. I couldn't contain it anymore. She turned to me and motioned to the door.

"Come on, free period is over, I'm sure you have places to be." Jonas smiled.

I nodded and eagerly grabbed my backpack and put the book in carefully. I collected the rest of the trash and Jonas used her water bottle to water some of the plants, I guess putting the water back she took. She was so gentle, the flowers seemed happy about that.

She walked with me out of the greenhouse area, leading me towards the entrance.

"This is our little secret. Ok?"

"Of course." I nodded.

"Good." Jonas smiled.

I opened the doors for her and let her walk ahead of me. Jonas walked down the stairs, arms behind her back and she had a bright glow to her. Is it strange to be so grateful to her? She's really going to teach me how to better my magic? She's already been giving me pointers and now she's trusting me with such a revelation? Most people here would never be this trusting or this unconditionally kind. Yet since I met her, that's all she's been. She knows nothing of me, yet she took this book for me, showed her skills to me, and is willing to teach me. Most people around her treat me like gutter trash because I'm from Nevermore, but when I told her that she didn't bat an eye.

She wasn't arrogant. She didn't make snide remarks. She felt otherworldly in the back of my mind, almost ghost-like. Something like a distant memory. I've never felt this comfortable around a stranger, something about her is just so familiar. Does she feel it too? Is that why she's so kind to me? I genuinely can't put my finger on it. It's driving me nuts. She felt like a sister, or a cooler older cousin you desperately wanted to like you. *Jonas, who are you?*

I looked over at her, she hummed quietly and looked around the courtyard, she seemed to be looking for some-one. I watched her slightly then jumped at her suddenly slamming her foot on the pavement, I nearly stumbled at the impact and looked at her bewildered. Her eyes were narrowed and focused on the ground. I hesitantly glanced down then back at her.

"Uh?" I cleared my throat, "You good?"

"Huh?" Jonas blinked and looked at me then smiled like nothing happened. "Oh, sorry. Saw a snake creeping behind you."

Jonas hummed and I stiffened and shuddered in discom-fort. *Another fucking snake? That's what? Three this week?* Of course things you're terrified of just love being around you. I scurried off the steps and gripped my bag. Jonas followed behind.

"Don't like snakes?" She asked.

I shook my head, "Eh, phobia."

"I see, how interesting." Jonas trailed off and glanced away, "I've never been too fond of them either, always found them disgusting and useless. Slippery and evil. Just horrific disgusting creatures."

She had a soft look on her face but her words were full of venom. I gulped quietly and glanced away momentarily.

She waved her hand, a slight gold glint flickered off her wrist in the school lights, I narrowed my eyes slightly and rubbed my head in thought. She was just, nice. Being around her felt so natural as well, she was so comforting, so familiar. So calm and inviting. It was scratching my brain, she blinked and looked at me.

"You okay sweet pea?"

"Oh, um." I blinked and dropped my gaze, "Sorry, you just... You seem familiar, it's been eating me for the past few days."

"And I'm curious why you were so kind and helpful so soon. Why are you so trusting?"

She went quiet.

"Who *are* you Jonas?" I asked. I turned my body to her and gripped my bag, her lips were closed, but her eyes were soft.

"I'm just a girl, a girl who wants friends."

"Huh." I narrowed my eyes, "Well your accent, it's very distinct, not like mine and dads, more similar from further south. Are you from here?" I asked.

She blinked and rubbed her head gently and shifted her eyes away, "Wrath ring, yes."

"Wrath." I repeated.

Ok that explains that accent, but I never go to wrath, and she doesn't give wrath Demon energy. She hasn't cussed or yelled whatsoever, but she did just aggressively stomp out a snake. I guess that would be in character for them. But she's talking to me, wrath Demons don't like me much and make it very clear. They aren't shy about telling me I irritate them, it's funny I can't lie. They hate anyone they can't manipulate. But I don't get that energy from her,

The hell is her deal.

"Mhmm! Born and raised."

I eyed her slightly, she glanced at me and laughed nervously.

"I never go to Wrath, don't got clearance. So that ain't helping your familiarity." I said.

"Well if it helps? I go to the Gluttony ring often. I love BeeBee's Bakery, so many delicious pies."

I blinked, then rubbed my head. Oh, of course, Auntie's Bakery. So many people come and go, a lot of regulars. I rubbed my chin gently then nodded. That made things less ominous. I don't know, maybe I was overthinking, it was just feeling odd. I felt my shoulders slump as I relaxed, she seemed to visibly relax as well.

"That's probably where, I spend alotta of time there."

"Work there?" Jonas asked.

"Nah, Miss B is a close family friend. And my dad loves her gift baskets. I use 'em to soften blows." I laughed quietly. Jonas giggled and turned her head as a kid caught her attention.

He nodded his head and motioned her over, he was tall and slightly tanned, his clothes looked darker than the usual school color palette, his hair was jet black and falling in his mono lid piercing silver eyes. Strange, is he a vampire? A drastic opposition to Jonas though.

"Oh." She waved at the other guy and smiled gently at me. "Well, that's my cue. It was wonderful talking to you Aubrey."

"Oh, you as well." I glanced over at him then looked back at her, she nodded her head then made her way to the black haired male.

The boy glanced in my direction with the iciest stare I've ever felt. They exchanged a few words then He placed his hand gently on Jonas's back and led her away. Must be a boyfriend, they tend not to like me very much.

I glanced back at the stairs where Jonas stomped, the concrete was cracked now. I pouted slightly before walking off the grounds. I checked my phone and checked all my notifications. Shit, I didn't realize the time. A few texts from Saint and Auntie. I checked hers first while putting my earbuds in. Just delivery requests, guess she fired or *ate* another kid. Geez, I told her I can't deliver shit for her anymore, dad will pop a blood vessel.

I sent her a quick text before checking Saint's.

'Available for a sleepover?? You don't work today do you??'

'Nah, I work tomorrow though, I'll have to check on Iron and walk him and shit then I can head over. I met a really cool girl in my Potions 101 class, you might like her.'

'Oh really?? Can't wait to hear! Also Rouge is over, so don't freak out yea? Stay single!'

I narrowed my eyes and sucked my teeth at that as I went to type a response. I rubbed at my eyes as they began to blur. Hell, is my sight seriously still acting up? Been awhile, maybe I'm just tired.

I stared at the slightly hazy screen then groaned to myself. What the hell am I doing? I can't avoid her forever? Maybe Saint was right and I should just be honest? Maybe then I can apologize properly and get things off my chest? And hopefully put her mind at ease. This heart ache sucks. Not being her boyfriend is one thing, but not being her friend is another. I hesitate to call, I don't even look in her direction anymore. I can't live like that.

I can't live without her.

But she'll probably think I'm an abomination, something she shouldn't be mixed up with. Something that might be a deal breaker...

I stared at my keyboard, debating what to type.

Heh, what a joke. Ghosting, dumping her so unceremoniously, never properly communicating, entertaining petty flirts and going radio silent for days? Those should've been deal breakers. Leaving her like that for four years should've been a deal breaker. Yet she put up with me and my bullshit, why? I don't deserve her. I truly don't. With that track record I wouldn't blame her for jumping ship over my life long lie. Can't blame anyone but myself huh?

Actions and consequences.

I stopped in my tracks, looking up from my phone and glanced slightly behind me. I narrowed my eyes at the eerie quiet. *I heard that.* It was quick, very quiet. I noticed it, barely under my music and the sound of bird wings. I pulled the ear bud from my ear and locked my phone. The air feels different, someone is here.

I turned completely and looked behind me, nothing was there. No one was out. Odd. The streets are usually full, around this time.

Yea this don't feel right. I'm the worst person to sneak up on. Best thing about losing one sense, others heighten. I will definitely hear you before I see you. I stayed there for a moment, straining my ears for that noise again. I couldn't tell what it was the first time but I'll know it when I hear it.

I scanned my surroundings then turned my head towards the sound.

It was a hiss. Gods it better not be another fucking snake.

I stumbled and flipped back at the sudden attack in front of me. The hell, *a bullet*? I looked towards the direction of the shot and narrowed my eyes.

"You're bold for taking that shot so late." I got to my feet. "Don't be shy, I don't appreciate being shot at by strangers."

I stared down the shadows by the close buildings, suddenly all movement was silent. And before I knew it, snakes were lunging at me. I groaned and dodged as quickly as possible. I hate snakes. *I fucking hate snakes.*

I quickly moved from the open and grew a few vines as a distraction. *They felt different this time?* I almost lost my footing at how much and how strong they grew. My eyes sparkled before I stumbled back avoiding another gross scaly creature. *Focus Aubrey, you can thank Jonas later.* I threw my backpack towards them to free some weight off me.

The hell is this person's problem. What the hell do they think they'll gain from this? I'm not a royal, or a noble, I have no value on my head. So why the hell am I their target? I instantly leaned back, dodging a bullet. These snakes, brown with gold and white markings on the top. Incredibly distinct. From the Middle Eastern region? I narrowed my eyes in annoyance. The sudden spike around me makes sense, it was whoever the hell this bastard is.

That last bullet came from a different direction. Did they move that fast? Or is it more than one person. Fuck me. I darted down an alley, *I need high ground,* I could barely hear over all the hissing and my pounding heart. Hell I could already barely see, now I'm in this dark ass alley. I kicked down a few stray boxes and trash cans to part and slow the snakes down. I quickly jumped to a fire escape and gripped the bar, scanning the area.

Where are you fucker.

My eyes stretched wide and I grunted as I flipped up on the rail using the heel of my boots to anchor myself, dodging another bullet. I saw that one. I trailed the smoke and noticed a silhouette just a little past the snakes, on the other fire escape. I narrowed my eyes and used all my force to push off and jump towards the building, grabbing the window sill immediately and pulling myself up. I heard a noise and a clambering to pick up something.

Guess you didn't expect that huh. Shattering the glass with my elbow, I pulled myself in and looked around the area, I caught a glimpse of a black boot leaving the room. I gave chase immediately. Barely catching glimpses of them, basically skipping stairs to close the distance. They turned a corner and as soon as I did a bullet flew past me and grazed my ear, causing me to stumble back.

"Fuck." I rubbed the blood off and followed them down the hall.

Ok, snakes? Avoidable. bullets? Child's play. But fucking with my ears? That's a death wish. I slammed my body against the door and they turned to face me, a red and gold gun in hand, still smoking from the last bullet.

She was short, in a black tailored vest and matching pants with blacked out glasses. Her hair was a deep brown and curled past her shoulders. Her eyebrows furrowed and she raised her gun again. She already shot off five rounds. Oh honey that shot better count. Her golden tipped fingers pulled the trigger as soon as I came to a stop, I pulled the metal door closed, the bullet getting lodged. She swore to herself then I heard the hisses. I opened the door and stared her down.

The hissing is her hair? *What the fuck?*

Her obscured eyes stared me down, gun still in her hand. She didn't utter a single word. I couldn't see her eyes but I could feel the dark stare she was leveling at me. My breath was slightly labored and ringing was filling my ear, a burning sensation was slowly creeping on me.

"The hell. Is your problem? You jackass." I hissed out.

She stayed silent, then a grin flashed on her lips, but she didn't say anything.

"Get that slick look off your face before I knock it off you. You got the right one today." I growled. "Answer the question."

"..."

I glared at her, "What, cat got your tongue."

"You're pathetic." She spoke, her accent was middle eastern. The hell she doing all the way down here? I blinked then narrowed my eyes, "What does he see in you."

I grunted quietly, "The hell are you talking about."

"Look at what you've grown into. You can't even hold your own against some little snakes. I'm kind of disappointed. I can't lie."

"Say something worth listening to or I'm beating your fucking ass." I growled. She smirked and shook her head.

"Pathetic."

I instantly jumped on her and pinned her down, slamming her back against the ground. She let out a surprised squeal and began to hit at my arms, barely even noticeable. I see, she's only used to spaced combat. *Well too bad girlie. I like being up close and personal.* I slammed her down by her shoulders and shuddered in disgust at the snakes on her head coming alive and pulled my hands away quickly before it could bite.

Up close I could see the different skin patterns. Her dark black glasses reflected my pissed off face. She kicked out from under me and scrambled to her feet. I grabbed her ankle before she could get too far and pulled her down. She started kicking again. I grabbed her other foot, pinning her legs down. The hell am I supposed to do with this crazy dame? What the hell is she even talking about? Who is *he*? And why am I mentioned alongside him. She squirmed and fought under me, I glared harshly at her but ignored her sad excuse for fighting.

"Guess every accusation is an admission. You throw that word pathetic around loosely and you can't even shake me off, creeper."

She growled in response, "Get off me! You disgusting brute!"

"Then start talking. Why the hell are you shooting at me you freak."

She just kept squirming and trying to wiggle away. I huffed out in annoyance, I blinked slowly as my eyes slowly began to haze again, but this felt different? I could feel my grip slowly weaken and everything was ringing. What the hell?

I groaned and fell back as she wiggled her legs free and kicked me directly in the face. I held my nose and groaned in slight pain but mainly annoyance. I looked up as she took off, my vision blurry. I got up and stumbled at the sudden dizziness, something's not right.

I leaned on the building and opened my mouth to shout after her, but her figure slowly disappeared from my vision. I felt a sharp pain on my ankle and looked down as my eyes somewhat focused on a small figure slithering away.

What the hell did she do to me?

"Gods... I hate snakes."

II

Part II

What Is Going on..?

18

SEVENTEEN

"Aubrey?"

I groaned quietly and curled in on myself, my body felt numb around my leg and my arm felt hot and sore. That ringing in my ears finally stopped. That's good. *What the fuck was that even about. Who even was that? Has she been stalking me this whole time?* I moaned out uncomfortably and felt my body slowly roll over. The sheets were soft under me, but gods was it cold. *Unnecessarily cold.* As I slowly woke up I could feel my fingertips freezing.

I can hear subtle voices echoing in my ears, *oh gods did that asshole kill me?* Did I really get done in by a fucking snake bite and a bullet past the ear, how fucking pathetic. If I died? Where would I go, I already live in The Valley. Would dying even matter at that point?

"Aubrey, can you hear me?"

I slowly opened my hazy eyes, the lights all blurred together, a few figures were slowly forming in my vision as my body woke up. I rubbed my eyes and let them focus properly. *Where the hell am I? And why the hell is it so fucking cold*. The area had this icy blue hue to it, the Victorian styled walls glistened like crystals and the bed felt like the most expensive linen I've ever felt against my hands.

"Cold..." I muttered.

"Hey, Aubrey." Pure red eyes met mine, familiar red eyes. The voice began to register and I instinctively sat up but felt freezing hands lay me back down, "Easy there hon, try not to move too much."

"Bri...ar?" I questioned halfheartedly, I couldn't take my eyes off her. It's been years, about two and half right? I'll never forget those shining eyes and gentle voice, never. Her blonde lashes and albino skin glistened from the snow emitting off her body, her long black locs rested behind her as she sat. She dyed them? Her gloved hands remained gently on my chest.

Guess the cold makes sense now.

"Well, Aubrey. Hasn't it been some time." A male voice chimed in, he made his way in the room,wiping his hands down with a towel then placed them smoothly in his pockets. The head of the Wynter household, Briar's dad. Belial, his albino skin had a small red blush to it as he walked over to the side of the bed and placed his cold hands on my forehead, sending an intense shudder down my body.

He had gold charms attached to his locks, It complemented his blue vest and black shirt. His hands had that same Reaper Galaxy imprint on them. I wasn't aware their galaxy's could show up in different places until I met the Wynters. His icy brown eyes studied my face.

"Hm. Seems you got into some trouble, how lucky are you." Belial hummed, his pale brownish gray eyes filled with concern.

"Oh shit." I muttered, "Mr. Wynter... Um, nice to see you again."

"Hmm, I know you aren't too fond of doctors, all things considered. I gave you a few shots and let Briar bandage you up." Belial smiled, "How are you feeling?"

"Uh, *fuck*. I'm not sure. Never been bitten by a snake before." I groaned.

"Fascinating, the effects it had on your body slowed drastically, with that much poison you would've killed over immediately. You are such an interesting individual."

"Hold up. Run that back?" I asked and sat up anyway, gently taking Briar's hands off my chest and rubbed my bandaged ear, "Poison?"

"Yes, it seems you've been bitten by a viper, native to the middle eastern region on the surface, nowhere near here. How odd." Belial nodded his head.

"I found you passed out in an alleyway on my way home. Something felt...off." Briar chimed in.

"Uh, yea. I was walking home... From the academy... Then this person started shooting at me? And a bunch of snakes appeared? Hell, I don't know."

Mr. Wynter gripped my cheeks with his freezing soft hands and tilted my head to the side to look at my ear. He narrowed his eyes, "Well that explains your bite, but not your ear."

I shuddered once more, "S-she sh-ot me."

He let go gently, "A bullet grazed you. I see. Must've been coated in the same venom." Belial tapped his lips and nodded his head, "You're lucky Briar is obse-"

"DADDY." Briar exclaimed, cutting the older male off.

"Hm." Belial grinned devilishly, like he always used to,

then chuckled, "You're lucky her, *intuition,* is usually spot on. It's why she's the hunter of the home. Just like her mother."

I chuckled lightly, "Heh, she always had a knack for bailing me out of trouble."

Briar smiled sweetly, "You should rest and let the medicine work."

"Nah, I'm alright. Plus it's fucking freez-" I blinked and met Briar's sinister gaze and gulped quietly before dropping my gaze, "Uh, yes ma'am."

"Good boy." Briar placed her delicate hands on my shoulders and pushed me back into the pillows with zero effort. Still has that crazy strength I see, "I'll get some stuff to warm you up~"

Briar stood and basically bounced to her feet, her black dress hugged her curves and fell to the floor. The dress was low cut, showing off her chest and her unique Wynter family birthmark. I felt my eyes soften at her as she slipped out of the room.

Briar and Her family are a *special class* of Vampire. I don't know much about it, I just know they need to keep the Vampire part of themselves hidden. They pass perfectly for Reapers since all of them have that patented Galaxy trademark, aside from their Mother and Briar's twin If I remember correctly. They're a highly renowned family on the surface. A family full of Doctors, Lawyers, and Morticians. Ironic ain't it? Briar was training under her mother, the amount of blood on my hands from working there is insane to think about, yet they all take pride in their predatory behavior and trafficking business.

No way to sugarcoat it in all honesty. I was indifferent.

They were doing this to survive, who am I to judge? I have the privilege of not being a Vampire in this society. Staying with them for those two years I was away was genuinely a new and interesting experience. One I know I can't share with my friends and dad. Auntie B would be proud, but that tells me I should keep quiet even more.

Briar and her family updated me on a lot of Vampire side effects and customs. They were shocked that I was bit by one but never gained any Albinism. Apparently being bit by them causes those effects and the family's albinism comes from Belial and the Vampire venom, causing strange skin discoloration on some of them. Briar for example still has brown skin on her hands and feet, She isn't sure if it'll go away or not. I found it fascinating. Especially in the town they live in. There's many cases of Vitiligo there, the implications are chilling.

Belial wanted to run tests on me after that. He's been interested in my body ever since, on a scientific level. One day I decided maybe having Belial check up on me wouldn't be so bad. It ended up working in my favor because if I need anything I can go to him for a check up, sadly the Wynter's live on the Surface. I sighed out and looked up at the high ceiling but kept my head on the pillows.

"Well, some things never change hm?" Mr. Wynter spoke up.

"Guess so.."

"Good thing I ran a few tests on your body all those years ago. Your body is certainly a challenge to treat, but you intrigue me so much. I'm learning a lot." Belial tapped his finger on my ear, "This was nearly healed when we found you, your ankle as well, but your body didn't know what to do with the venom in your makeshift system."

"Huh?"

"You threw up a lot." Belial grinned wide and held up a vial with a dark liquid in it, I made a face and glanced away.

"Gross." I instinctively wiped my mouth then felt my eyes widen in horror, "Oh hell, did I vomit in front of-"

"Yep, a lot." Belial placed the vial back in his pocket and chuckled, "She's used to bodily fluids, she studies under her mother, and our hands ain't the cleanest."

"That's so fucking embarrassing."

"Mm, I'll give you some time, I'll hand her some pain medicine that should knock you out for awhile, I know it won't do much for pain, you don't register that properly yes?"

"Yea, nothing really changed."

"Oh silly!" Belial laughed and walked to the door, "Your body is changing and adapting everyday. That vampire venom is doing a number on your cells, even if you can't tell. So fascinating."

"Is it?"

"Mind her appetite. We dont need more samples in you." He nodded at me then gave a gentle smile, "It's wonderful to see you again Aubrey. Rest up."

With that he took his leave and closed the door softly behind him.

Wait. Oh gods, does he know she was? *With me*? That I was? *Oh gods does her mom know!?* I dropped my hands on my warm face, my nose was freezing, gods I know my face is beyond red right now. I rolled over and stared at the snowflake patterned room. The room was nice sized. It had basic Victorian furniture, from chairs, to the dresser to the bed. It had a cute bay window that faced towards The Valley's outskirts. It's no where as big as their manor on the surface, but hell it was still luxurious. The floor plan looks somewhat similar to Saint's aside from the lack of a balcony.

I shivered and hugged my arms to my body. Haven't been in this level of cold in awhile, and I was happy to be away from it. But it's a bit comforting, especially since it's Wynter's cold. Two and a half years, and Briar hasn't changed a bit. Still has those bright, sweet, starry eyes. Stunning pale skin like the first snowfall, but she dyed her hair black, it suits her and her whole vampire status, still short, I can tell from how she stood, she wasn't wearing shoes, she always hated how short she was compared to me, she swore she wouldn't be caught in her flats or socks around me. She got used to it.

"Ok~" Briar bumped the door open with her hip and walked in with a tray. "I remember the warm things you can actually taste, soo I have tomato soup, grilled cheese and hot tea~ and for your troubles I made some Macaroons."

My eyes sparkled, "Macaroons?" I sat up and adjusted my position, "Oh. Uh. Did you cook-?"

She pouted, "No, of course not. Blaire did.." Briar handed the tray to me gently and I smiled. She sat back on the bed and laid a shirt next to me. "And a new shirt~ blood got on your other one."

Briar's eyes flicked to my collar and she licked her rosy lips almost instantly, I cleared my throat and laughed nervously.

"Uh, thanks hon."

"Of course! But, how are you feeling?" Briar asked gently, placing her hand on top of mine, her eyes full of worry. "I know you can't exactly feel pain but.."

"I'm alright? I think." I shrugged a bit and sat the tray on my lap, "I don't feel any pain, but I do feel strange...I've never lost control of my body like that before..."

"Well, daddy told me to give you this medicine so you can sleep, maybe when you wake up you'll feel normal? Read over it, make sure It's right."

Oh yea, forgot about her blindness. I took the bottle from her and skimmed over it.

"Hopefully. I'm not fond of this feeling." I nibbled the grilled cheese and sipped the soup.

I breathed out content at the warmth and the deliciousness of the food. It's nice to taste things every now and then, it's kind of satisfying. But not having proper taste buds does not save me from whatever the hell Briar cooks. I think she's the bee's knees and the horizon's sun but *my gods* I've never had such rancid food in my life. Not even my body would keep it down, that's saying something. But her brother? And her mom? Food heaven. Now baking? You ain't touching her with that. She makes the most delicious cakes, and these Macaroons, never had them before her but I'm hooked.

Briar sat quietly, messing with the curly strands of her hair, looking at the floor. I looked up at her and glanced away awkwardly.

"Uh, what brings you down here? How have you been?"

"Oh. Um, we're on vacation." She smiled, "Erebus has a few weeks before he has to go back to work, so we wanted to surprise him."

"Does that mean *all* your siblings are here?" I asked, a bit hesitant.

"Nah, just me, my brothers and dad." She giggled, "Mom and my sisters are doing some last minute business back home, they should be here sometime tomorrow."

"Oh, that's good." I breathed out, "But how have you been?"

"Oh, sorry. Um, pretty good, I got another guard after you but he didn't last long, Juliet got bored and hungry." She rolled her eyes, "Met a guy, but I wasn't really impressed, then I learned he believed he was in opposition to you."

"Me?" I chuckled quietly and shook my head, "So what I'm hearing is, you're single annnd free on weekends?"

She giggled and let her hair go and rested her hands gently on her lap, "Yes, of course that's all you heard."

"You know my hearing is selective." I grinned, she cupped her rosy cheek and waved her other hand.

"Oh hush, yes I'm very aware." Briar smiled gently at me, "How are you?"

"Doing Ok, just got back home a couple months back."

"You didn't come straight home afterwards?" Briar asked.

"No." I finished the sandwich, "Had some business to check on."

"I see, my apologies."

"For what?" I asked.

"I didn't mean to intrude." She said.

"Never. I told you, if you ask, I will answer."

"Yea, as a guard." She muttered.

"And as a boyfriend turned friend." I gave her a look and moved my hand on top of hers, she was always in her own head. Guess we have a lot in common, made her take to me pretty easily. It's funny how I was told up and down not to take that job position. That they'd eat me alive and work me like a dog or chase me out of town like the many before me. But that's the second place I felt comfortable and at home.

The Wynter family was always so kind, her sisters were *very* kind. Her father took a liking to me almost immediately, I'm sure it's because he realized I wasn't normal. I was usually better at masking, but I guess I got too comfortable. He's been soft on me ever since, because of him I can taste a handful of things now, and as far as I know, they respected my secret and space. I hated to leave. I hated to leave the comfort and friends I've made. *I hated to leave Briar.*

I never thought it was possible after Rouge, but she weaseled her way in my heart. She was standoffish the first time, her eyes were cold and harsh, she didn't even bother to learn my name for the first few weeks. Then she suddenly spoke to me in her garden. She sat in the fresh snow at a black table, the deep green bush of red roses surrounded her and gods was it a sight to see. Her family pearls glinted just like her snow covered lashes. I never knew the cold could be so breathtaking. She asked me my name that day, I'll never forget hearing her voice for the first time. Made my blood run cold and my face burn hot. Her accent was so smooth, it was southern but not from my region, every word she said sounded meticulous and carefully pronounced.

She told me, *'I'll give you a week.'*

Something awoke in me at that sentence, I hadn't left her side since, not in those full two and a half years.

It was hard leaving the Wynter manor, I'll always remember and cherish my time there. If I'm honest I never thought I'd see them again, going back to the surface just wasn't an option, seeing Briar again didn't seem like an option. Seeing her now feels so surreal.

"I suppose... but your honesty was always...calculated."

I laughed quietly, "Guess we have that in common."

"I've always given honest answers!" Briar huffed and crossed her arms.

I raised a brow at her, "Like that time you told me your last guard caught a train out of town, and that was just code for his BODY parts was being shipped from your basement freezer?"

"..." Briar looked away, "Technically honest."

"Mhmm." I hummed and sipped the tea, "Oh, by the way. Happy birthday, Love."

Briar blinked and turned her head to me, her eyes seemed surprised, "You always seem to remember.."

"I have it saved in my phone, with other important events." I hummed, "I also saw that bank notification. Ya know, most people don't send a band to their exes on THEIR birthday."

"Well. I'm not most people."

"Oh baby don't I know it." I laughed quietly to myself. Then a thought hit me, *holy shit I didn't show up to Saint's.* Oh hell I didn't call or text she's going to assume I'm dead, then she's going to work up Rouge, *oh fuck*. I groaned and dropped my head in my hand.

"Are you Ok, sugar?" Briar asked gently.

I nodded and looked around the room for my phone, "Uh, I need to call my friends."

"Your friends?" Briar echoed.

"Before I got attacked I was supposed to stop by, I don't know how long I've been out. Also my dog, oh fuck dad's probably going to freak out if I haven't responded to a text in hours."

"Your dad..." Briar spoke softly then smiled, "Take this

medicine and I'll grab your phone."

I picked up the bottle and read over the label. She walked over to my backpack and jacket placed neatly on the bay window, she unzipped the bag and looked through delicately before gently pulling the book out and looking at it, she turned to me and tilted her head.

"What's this?" She asked.

Oh Shit, I forgot about that, "Oh, uh, it's nothing. Just an earth magic book, I'm uh. Holding onto it." I waved it off. She glanced back at it and raised a brow.

"The cow skull…?"

"Uh, yea, Aides. It's nothing Briar, really. Uh, Is it damaged? I threw my backpack Heh."

She inspected it carefully with her fingers then shook her head, "Doesn't look like it."

"Great, thank you…" I went back to reading over the bottle and breathed out.

Briar placed it back in the bag and began patting the extra pockets then checking my jacket. She grabbed the phone and walked back over as I drank the medicine from the bottle.

"You numskull!" Briar swatted at the back of my head and swiped the medicine from my hands, "You can't just chug it like beer!"

"I didn't have a cup-"

"Then ask for one goofy!" Briar groaned and handed me the phone. I grinned awkwardly and checked all the notifications. Yea as I thought. *Fuck I'm gonna get an earful.* Immediately texted my dad and apologized for missing his texts, then hesitantly called Saint. A few rings then immediate screaming.

"Ok Ok, Saint."

"ARE YOU OK!?" Saint exclaimed.

"I'm fine. Uh, got into a scuffle, baby girl, I'm fine." I muttered.

"What kind of scuffle?"

"The kind that knocks you out for a couple hours." I glanced away.

"Where are you?" Saint demanded.

"A friends, I'm Ok, I'll be leaving in a couple hours-"

"I'm on my way." And with that she hung up. I dropped my arms on my lap and rubbed my face. *I didn't even give an address,* I whined quietly and dropped my head in my hands.

Saint is gonna cause a scene and pull my ear. I just know it. Briar motioned me to lay down and I did, looking at the ceiling. I stifled another groan and focused on sleeping, I'll need that extra energy. So much to explain. Saint, Rouge and Briar all in one place.

Rouge and Briar in one place.

Rouge...

and Briar.

One place.

Oh fuck.

19

EIGHTEEN

Don't blow this loser.

I told myself not to blow it. She was here, Rouge was always here, wanting me, wanting to be with me. Yet, I got greedy. I became *Icarus*. It was like, since I had her I didn't try. How foolish can I be? Her smile got dimmer slowly but surely, I pretended not to notice. She put up with me, and I knew she would. I'm horrible for her, she deserves better, and I know she thinks so too. Knows so maybe.

"Aubrey..?" She spoke up quietly.

I looked up at her, but kept my mouth shut. She shifted her gaze away and cleared her throat quietly, *"I'm sorry, I.."*

"What is it, Rouge."

Rouge rubbed her arm and looked at the floor, *"I wanted to know if you'd be available after your game?"* Her voice was soft and nervous, yet I showed no empathy. Not a lick of compassion. I shrugged my arms and shifted my gaze to the side.

"Not sure, depends if the boys ask me to hang." Why did I say that? I didn't care for them anyway. But she never fought

back. Never opposed my decisions. She just nodded and stayed quiet.

You idiot.

It wasn't always this way. Ever since we talked for the first time at that basketball game, She became a constant in my life. Hell even Saint liked her, which was rare. When she was mine I took her on dates every Friday, anywhere she wanted to go, took a few extra hours at work, much to her dismay, but she deserved the best. Flowers every Thursday, surprise lunches every Wednesday, it was so sweet, so easy. Her smile meant the world to me, it still does. Then suddenly something changed?

Insecurity, ego, foolishness.

I know that now. But back then? I just lashed out, I stopped paying attention to her. I already had her, she wasn't going anywhere. Even when I blow her off for a party, forgot a date or two, even flirt with a few girls in front of her. She never fought me back. She never cared, at least that's what I thought. Before she started missing my games. When she wasn't cheering, she'd be in the bleachers smiling and cheering me on, eyes always so bright, wearing my jacket like always. Not seeing her there was a wake up call.

She stopped responding to my texts, even Saint was being cold to me, *I fucked up.*

I know I did.

But she still stayed here. *Why?*

Why did she stay. I don't have money, I don't have clout or influence. I'm just a guy. A guy she was in love with. *Oh gods, you idiot.*

I put in effort again after that, I made it my mission to win her back. Especially after Saint making it painfully clear, she has options. I'm not the only one to notice she's a catch. She's gorgeous, tall, kind, smart, everything you'd want in a friend and lover, someone who never puts herself before you, even though you tell her not to. She was selfless.

I was reminded of that, foolishly, after seeing a man try. She doesn't even like men, she never has. But him having the gaul to even query her interest? To be in her area, breathing her air, in her sight. That humbled me, knowing and seeing are two different things, and honestly now I know I didn't deserve her, hell I probably still don't. *But dammit,* I was going to convince myself I was good enough, no matter how hard I tried.

She slowly warmed back up to me, we got closer, and slowly but surely we were together again. Like she never left, like I never fucked up. And for Jezabelle's sake, I treated that woman like the queen she was. I didn't make that mistake twice.

Until graduation.

I couldn't look at her, I couldn't see her face.

A week prior I decided I was leaving, for as long as I needed to. I had questions, and I finally got a clue that I could get answers. A single letter signed from someone on the surface, I knew I wasn't a normal Demon, but I needed to know more. And dad wouldn't tell me, nor would he let me leave so easily. Was it stupid? Yea, most likely. Did I care? No, not at the time.

I didn't think about the consequences. Leaving my dad, my home, my friends... Leaving Rouge.

I kept my back to her, Rouge's voice was so confused and hurt, I couldn't meet her gaze. *I just couldn't. Fuck.* I couldn't even tell her why I was leaving or where I was going. The timing couldn't be more wrong. She avoided me for three months after that *Hallows Eve incident*, and she *just* started talking to me again. Yet here I am, as soon as she talks to me again I'm breaking up with her. **Fuck**.

"Aubrey..?" She spoke up quietly, that same soft worried voice, I kept my back to her.

"I'm leaving Rouge." I muttered, *"I'm going out of town for college, it's best if we break up."*

"Break up..?" Rouge asked, hurt in her voice.

"There's no reason to do long distance right?"

Rouge stayed quiet. She dropped her gaze. I fought the urge to turn around and abandon the plans, but I have to know. I can't let this opportunity pass. Since I was a kid I've longed to know. I can't give this up. And honestly I can't trap her anymore, she deserves better and she shouldn't waste her life waiting on me. She would if I didn't do this now. And what if she finds out in the future? She'd blame herself for keeping me here. I just know she will, or do I? Hell, I can't even tell her. *What? Do I not trust her?* No. *Of course I do. I just...*

I sighed quietly, *"Look Rouge, I just, this is just best for now."*

"Best?" She echoed defeat. That hurt me. *"If..."*

She took a breath and I could hear her heels begin to move. *"Don't. Please."*

She stopped, her side of the room silent once more. *"I'm not sure how long I'll be gone, and college is different ya know?"*

"Yea..I suppose." Rouge spoke quietly.

"I'm sorry.."

"I'll support whatever you wish to do Aubrey." She spoke softly.

I nodded, and walked off. *Something I regretted for those four years, I fucked up again.* And it amounted to nothing. Nothing at all. The facility was destroyed and abandoned, the person who sent it apparently didn't exist. I wasted four years, and I still have no answers. What a fucking joke. I was so frustrated I could cry. Did I royally fuck up my life by leaving like that? My life I could have had with Rouge? *Fuck, it wasn't worth it.*

And I still won't be honest with her, after all that? What do I have to lose now? Briar knows, Saint knows, why can't she? And avoiding it isn't getting me anywhere with her, I need to fix this. Saint was right, *like always.*

I say I love her, and I feel I can't even tell her about this? If I can't be open, is she really in love with *me?* Or the version of me I portrayed to her? Do I actually love her, if I don't tell her the truth? I know I love her, that's something that will always be painfully obvious. So for logic sake, if I love her, I have to be open and honest, but gods that rejection from her is so scary. What would I do? What if she's disgusted by me? By what I am. What if my defiance of the gods, my whole existence turns her away? Or puts her in danger?

What if, what if, what if. Just tons of what ifs. Tons of excuses.

They're so scary, they're so halting. I don't want to lose her, I can't lose her. Telling the truth is the right thing right?

I shook my head, shut up. Silence the doubts. There's no going back now. How long will this lie go? I can feel that voice, she isn't speaking, but I know she's telling me to just tell the truth. Get out of my own head and talk to her. She's right there. Worried sick. She has *always* been right there.

I sat up and tried to rub the grogginess from my eyes, as

they ran in the room. Everything is a bit blurry and muffled. Don't think about it. Just do it. I took a breath and looked at her, my eyes as serious as I could muster. Worry was all over her face, she kept her distance, but that hurt me. She cares about you idiot. Just *DO IT.*

I cleared my throat, and just like all those years ago, I sat up and spoke, "Rouge, we need to talk."

20

NINETEEN

Rouge turned her gaze to me as the others slowly left the room. She was dressed down, her hair was in Bantu knots, she had a loose fitting tank and satin pants on with bat earrings. No matter what she wore, she was always stunning. Rouge sat and instantly gripped my hands. That calmed me a bit, I squeezed her hands in reciprocation. I tried to calm my rising anxious thoughts. She waited a moment before she spoke.

"Aubrey, are you Ok?" Rouge asked.

I smiled tiredly and felt my heavy eyes blink slowly at her.

"No big deal." I tried to joke, "Little venom ain't no thang, really."

She didn't smile, just gripped my hand tighter. I felt my foundation shake a bit at that, but shook it off and adjusted my position. I moved my hands from hers and placed them on top of hers.

"Look, I, I'm sorry." I looked Rouge in her eyes, "I haven't been honest with you."

"About?" She asked.

"Me."

Rouge raised a brow and tilted her head.

"Why I left, why I'm different, why I'm Ok right now." I breathed out and dropped my gaze to the bed.

"Why you're here." Rouge inquired.

I nodded. I glanced to the side and sighed quietly, "This has to stay between us. Ok?"

"Aubrey.."

"Rouge. Please. Promise me." I practically pleaded, she seemed taken back by that.

She nodded after a moment but kept her eyes on me, "Alright."

I took a moment to find the words and how to go about this. I've had four years to prepare this speech. I used to picture how this would go but in my scenarios I couldn't hear myself. Just the loud rejection I thought would come. I nervously fidgeted my hands, I could feel fear and doubt creeping in. There's that insecurity again. *Why does she do this to me? Why?* She's not shallow, she's never been, yet I always feel the need to be perfect for her. Why do I feel the need to contradict what I know about her. She hasn't said or done anything to validate these thoughts yet they still plague me. I took a breath and rubbed the back of my head,

"Um, obviously I'm different… than most Demons."

"Well.. I honestly, never noticed, I assumed you were just a Wrath or Pride Demon…" Rouge spoke softly. My turn to be taken back, I tilted my head in confusion.

"Wrath-" I asked.

She looked down sheepishly, "I said wrath *or* pride."

"Yes, pride, I guess I can understand they're an anomaly. But wrath?" I chuckled a bit at her, rubbing my hand on top of hers, the same old Rouge, *my Rouge.* That put me at ease.

"Well, you're very violent prone and that's before you get angry, and when you do get angry, it's explosive."

I shook my head and smiled gently at her, I looked down at her hands, her nails were perfectly done, the gems glinted in the light. Her hands were soft and warm against the harsh cold of the room, I felt my eyes soften as I caressed her hand gently, absentmindedly.

"No.. I'm not a sinner." I glanced at her, "Or an Angel, or Vampire, or Werewolf, Fae, nothing like that."

She tilted her head in confusion but stayed quiet.

"Remember when I left for college?" I asked cautiously, I could see a semblance of hurt in her eyes.

She nodded anyway and answered back with a small, "Yea.."

"I didn't go to college. I went to the surface to find the facility I was created in." I basically blurted out, no going back now.

"Huh? Facility?" Rouge asked.

"I'm ***NONE*** of those things.." I gave her a look, "I am what dad calls a Homunculus. I was made from science and alchemy, I wasn't *born*."

Rouge's green eyes widened in shock, I could see the information processing on her face. "You're not Earthborn? *At all*? How is that possible."

"I don't know, that's what I've been trying to find out." I shook my head, "Dad said the Kovenn's heard about a scientist defying Jezabelle's wishes so they tracked him down and destroyed his lab and killed him. But dad said when he found me, I was a baby so he kept me." I gently let her hand go and looked at her, bracing myself for the look of disgust. But it never came.

I took a deep breath and continued, "I'm... Technically supposed to be dead, which is why dad wouldn't tell me anything. And he made it clear I wasn't allowed to tell others."

She sat silently, I stayed quiet as well to let her process. That seemed to shake her up a little, might've softened the blow a bit. Rouge looked at her lap momentarily then back at me.

"Does Saint know."

"She does." I nodded.

"How." Rouge asked.

"She found out on accident actually. I cut through half my finger once." I put my scarred hand up and laughed quietly, "Didn't react, I couldn't feel it at all. Plus my blood not being red is a bit of a give away." I glanced away.

"Your blood.." Rouge dropped her gaze, "I thought.."

I blinked in realization, *Hallow's Eve*, yea. I shook my head. As the memories flooded back, She wasn't herself, and to this day I can't fathom what set her off, and by her reaction. I doubt she knows either. She avoided me after that, no one knew but me and Saint. I got a tattoo not too long after to cover the bite marks. I know the stigma around vampires and I didn't want her getting in trouble, or worse, dying. There ain't many laws and regulations down here but just like everywhere else, Vampires are considered illegal. Stupid, just plain stupid.

I still remember how horrified she looked after the fact. She was shaking, and I couldn't comfort her.

I looked at her, "I told you I didn't care about that Rouge, this is mainly why." I went to grip her hands but she snatched them away almost immediately. Rouge had that same look on her face, that hurt me. I just want to comfort her. *Please don't reject me.*

"I still don't know what I am, or what it means to be what I am, which is why I left four years ago. I got a letter from the facility. And I knew I couldn't tell you all why I was leaving." I put my hands up and tried to calm her down.

Rouge's eyes began to glisten, she dropped her head in her hands, her shoulders began to shake. She let out soft cries, "I.. I thought you left.. and avoided me because of..."

"Rouge, I never cared-"

"Bullshit!" Rouge exclaimed and stood up, "I attacked you, I bit you, I drank from you without your consent. And you're going to tell me you're not mad?"

Her eyes were full of tears, she hugged her arms to herself tightly, she looked terrified and panicked, I tried to stand and go to her but she darted her eyes to me, I stopped almost holding my breath.

Rouge turned away and rubbed at her face, I looked down at my lap and dropped my hands.

"I.."

"I thought this was your way of telling me you needed space." She shook her head and gripped her arms. "That you broke up with me because I fucked up."

"No. No.. I, Ok. Yes, maybe I should be upset that you attacked me. But I'm not. You not talking to me and avoiding me for those three months after hurt more." I looked at her, she glanced towards me.

"You just... shut me out." I looked away, "I just wish you talked to me. Maybe then I could've saved you the mental anguish."

"Yea. I get it. I was stupid. I know." Rouge wiped at her eyes and I shook my head.

"No. I… I should've told you sooner. I should've just been honest. I was terrified.."

She looked at me, "Of what."

I felt my body tense and I tried to choose my words carefully, "You hating me, being disgusted by me, scared of me.. I had a million and one thoughts in my head and I was worried one might come true. I didn't want to risk it, I didn't want you to go."

"Oh Aubrey.." She spoke up quietly, "I have and always will love you."

"No matter who, or what, you are. I thought you'd know that." Rouge went silent for a moment, "Did you not trust me?"

"No, I did, but. You make me insecure, Rouge." I muttered.

"Do I."

"I always feel like I have to be perfect for you, or to be with you. I'm not from your background or class, I know you can do better. You know you can do better. Who the fuck am I kidding." I muttered.

"Aubrey. I never cared about that. Any of that. I cared about YOU. How you treated me, how you made me feel. It was always just. YOU."

I sighed lightly and looked down, "Yea…"

She looked away and rubbed her cheeks, "Aubrey, I will always care for you, I just.. I need the same from you."

"What?"

"I need you to care too."

"I do, I always have, I always will." I spoke up.

"Then be honest with me." Rouge turned to look at me,

"From now on. Don't lie or hide anything else from me. We were friends for years. I want to be that again.."

I nodded eagerly, almost too excitedly. "I'd genuinely want nothing more. I just, I want you back in my life, seeing you but never talking or making eye contact was torture. I wanted to call you and tell you about pointless things, hang out with you and Saint again."

I looked down, "I don't have to be your boyfriend, I don't want to try to get back in your romantic graces. I just want you in my life."

Rouge remained quiet then took a seat next to me. She didn't look at me. But her eyes were deep in thought, she looked at the floor then closed her eyes. Turning her body, she put her hand to me and smiled gently, she was calmer. Eyes still slightly glistening.

"Then, Ok."

I looked at her and took her hand gently then kissed the top lightly. I breathed out as a weight lifted off my shoulders, I dropped my forehead against her hand and allowed calmness to overtake me, *Saint was right. Like always.* I felt her gently wrap her arms around me. I rested my forehead on her shoulder. Her familiar lotion filled my nose comfortingly, being around her felt peaceful. I missed this feeling. I missed her.

A small knock on the door caught our attention, Saint slowly opened the door with Briar and Mr. Wynter behind her. I sat up and breathed out.

"Ok, sorry about that.."

"Aubrey. What happened, why are you here? And who are they." Saint cautiously walked in, gripping the door handle. I motioned her over and immediately started doing damage control.

I waved my hands calmly as she sat between me and Rouge, she felt my face and looked over my neck and shoulders.

"Calm.. I was bitten by a snake." I gripped her hands gently and kissed the palm. That seemed to calm her a bit, but her eyes were still filled with worry, and near terror when the end of my sentence settled in.

"A snake!?" Saint exclaimed, I shushed her gently and rubbed her hand. I went to speak up but Mr. Wynter spoke first.

"A very venomous one." Mr. Wynter interjected with a smile, putting his finger up matter-of-factly. I gave him an annoyed look as he set Saint off even more.

"I'm fine." I quickly interjected.

"You passed out for hours in some strangers house!? You're clearly not!" Saint exclaimed, I smiled gently at her and rubbed her wrist and leaned into her touch, I gave her a gentle look and she calmed down, eyes still panicked.

I waved it off, "Besides, they aren't strangers. This is Dr. Wynter, and his daughter Briar Wynter, I use to work for them when I was gone."

"Oh, so that's how you know her." Rouge muttered while she crossed her arms.

I hummed, "Briar, Mr. Wynter, these are my friends, Saint Sawyer and Rouge Bellrose." I stretched and rubbed my legs, trying to wake them up. I can't tell if my body is just tired from the medicine, or if my body is practically frozen.

"Oh?" Briar chimed up, she eagerly made her way to Rouge and took her hands in hers, "You're the famous friends he told me about~."

"Oh. Funny he didn't mention you at all." Rouge said, a

small amount of bitterness in her voice. Briar laughed.

"A bit hard to talk with poison in your body right?" Briar hummed.

Briar couldn't see it but Rouge was not amused at that, I chuckled nervously and cleared my throat loudly, "Anyway."

"Sawyer, you said?" Mr. Wynter spoke up, "Oh wow, a Sawyer and a Kovenn in my humble home, what a pleasure."

Saint nodded gently, "It's a pleasure to meet you sir." She got to her feet and bowed her head gently.

I slowly swung my feet over the edge of the bed and stretched, I shuddered and pushed myself off the bed and steadied myself. I took a big stretch and let my joints loosen. Been out for way too long. I bounced on my toes a bit and shook my arms to loosen them. I walked over to my bag and shoes and pulled on my boots and zipped them back up.

"Leaving so soon Aubrey?" I could hear the pout in Briar's voice, I smiled apologetically

"Yea, gotta feed Iron and I've got a date."

I mentally slapped myself as soon as the room fell silent between the girls. *You moron, you're in a room of jealous women and Saint.* I smiled through it and grabbed my bag, slinging it over my shoulder.

"But we should definitely catch up Briar, you have my number just give me a time and day."

"Oh, sure.."

We turned our attention to the door as another Wynter family member stood there with a tray.

"Oh? Leaving?" Blaire. His blonde braids fell past his shoulders, pulled up in a ponytail. His deep brown eyes surveyed the room. He was in his typical house clothes, a

T-shirt and sweatpants. He held a fresh tray of brownies in his hand.

"Blaire! You're so sweet~." I took that as my opportunity to get out, I grabbed my jacket and slipped out between them and swiped a brownie from the tray, "Call me and we'll hang out."

Blaire blinked in confusion and watched me leave, I pulled on my jacket and nodded to myself. I breathed in the heat and relaxed, if I'm honest that cold is only nice when I'm *preoccupied,* preferably with Briar.

I looked up at the sparkling sky in thought, Aides' moon staring down at me, then a thought hit me. Of course. The Wynters. The metal. I can talk to Dr. Erebus. He'll have some information, no matter how small. I put the brownie in my mouth and began my walk home. I could hear Rouge and Saint slowly following behind me after saying their goodbyes.

"Aubrey, are you sure you're alright?" Rouge asked gently. I turned to them and smiled.

"Yes, I'm sorry. I don't know why she attacked me. But.."

"She?" Rouge repeated. I nodded.

"She was controlling the snakes, I've never seen her before." I shoved my hands in my pockets. Rouge nodded to herself quietly, did I do that on purpose? Maybe a little. Fuck her for that, and *fuck those fuckass snakes.*

"But that's not important." I looked at them, "Something is wrong at this school."

21

TWENTY

"So hold on, explain this again?" Saint spoke up, she was sitting at my desk, clearly confused but Rouge was quiet.

"I'm still thinking it over." I spoke, "But something isn't right. A few nights ago I was jogging and ran into Rue, the pink haired girl."

"Yeah, I know about her." Saint spoke with a nod.

"She was sneaking into the school, I helped her, and we found this poster. For the fourth years. It's dead language." I handed Saint my phone and Rouge leaned over her shoulder. "She translated it and told me to keep an eye on you."

"Me?" Saint asked.

"Mhmm, I think we're on the same page, the Headmaster is doing something with or against Reapers. A few days ago I found a Blacksmith in the school using death metal. That isn't normal." I paced back and forth, clicking my pen in thought.

"At all, we have no use for death metal, plus it's illegal for anyone to use it except your dad." Rouge spoke up.

"Exactly, but dad said he's low on metals and has to head

north to get more, he never runs low. Then I see the Blacksmith? Something is clearly wrong." I nibbled my nail, the pen clicking one last time, "Rue has been quiet about it, but it's bugging me."

"That is a bit...*Concerning*." Saint spoke up and handed my phone back, "But it's a stretch, Miss Petra isn't like that, students have said she's as kind as ever."

"I find that hard to believe." I muttered with an eye roll, "Her office is weird. She has a book in there, it's.. it made me uneasy. And she had Aides' Grimoire." I pointed out, they looked shocked about that.

"Y'know, the one that's SUPPOSED to be in the castle, locked away with everything else." I clicked the pen again. "Why would a random Sorcerer just *have* that."

"Ok, I can't argue against her having it, unless, maybe she got it from Hecate? It's a Grimoire after all?" Saint questioned halfheartedly, "Would make sense if a magic book was in a magic school."

I narrowed my eyes at her.

"And you shouldn't have been in there in the first place." Saint rolled her eyes.

"Saint." Rouge muttered, "This is something worth looking into, maybe we can talk to the Headmaster at the Reaper school?"

I nodded and looked up, "Yes, I was thinking the same. Mr Erebus, he's a Wynter, he'd definitely know something, even if it's small."

"You want to bother Mr. Erebus with this? Aubrey please, maybe you just have a bias 'cuz you hate school, there's no greater conspiracy here."

"I rather rule out all possibilities, especially if it means you stay safe." I sat the pen down and grabbed my phone before heading downstairs, Rouge following behind. Saint groaned and followed shortly after.

"Ok, hypothetically, what if there *is* something going on. What then? What if you get yourself hurt by being in a situation where you have no business." Saint said, stopping on the last step. Rouge stood beside her and looked at me,

"Well, frankly, It ain't about me." I looked at them both, "You, both of you, are my motivation and priority, if there's Death Metal just out on the loose, that won't sit right with me. If it gets too out of hand, we can talk to our parents."

They looked at each other, mulling over my words.

"Fair?" I asked.

Rouge nodded while Saint sighed, something flashed in her eyes momentarily before she nodded as well.

"Alright, fine."

I smiled a bit and took Saint's hand gently, "You're so sweet, Y'know that?"

"Just to you two." Saint gripped my hand, I kissed her knuckles and smiled.

"This caution extends to you too RoRo." Saint said, giving her a look.

"Of course." Rouge giggled and took Saint's other hand. "But making the adults aware won't cause too much harm."

"Right." I checked the clock in the kitchen, "Let's hurry before he leaves for the day." The girls nodded and I opened the door for them and followed them out.

We made our way to downtown Nevermore, heading directly to the school. Saint gave us clearance and we headed inside to Dr. Wynter's office. Family full of doctors, there is something so incredibly morbid about that in hindsight, now that I'm thinking about it. Saint knocked lightly and we waited awkwardly, the tall pink haired male answered a moment later. His dark eyes glistened as he noticed us. He was albino just like the rest of his family, but he had one brown spot over his eye. His lashes and eyes were two different colors, His left eye being that same blonde that Belial has, but his right eye matching his pink hair. He apparently gets that from his mother. His left eye was red just like Briar's but his right was brown. He was truly out of place down here compared to other Reapers and Demons. I always found him handsome with his chiseled face and pretty eyes. Now knowing the family secret it makes sense why he never uses his last name and why he looks the way he does.

"Well, if it isn't little Sawyer and her friends." Erebus smiled, we bowed our heads in respect.

"Hello sir, I'm sorry to bother you at your job." Saint smiled apologetically.

"Not a problem! Is your father alright?"

"Oh! Yes, they're heading back to work soon, this isn't about them though."

"Oh?" Erebus stepped aside to let us in.

I haven't been inside the Reaper school before, gods it's grand. The dome structures of the roofs and elegant floors made it a sight. It was on par with a Cathedral, Jasper's specialty. There were tons of stained glass pieces in the main area of the school, unlike the Sorcerer school there weren't any statues of Jasper, But there were a few photos by the main office showing the history of the school. Gods sometimes I wish I was born a Reaper, they are so interesting. It's very comforting, strangely, feels kind of like a coffee shop, that feeling of ordering coffee and using the free internet while doing papers, but a coffee shop in a bookstore kind of feel. Ironic for a place specializing in death, hell one of his students could be the last thing I see one day, kinda freaky to think about.

"What can I do for you kids?" Erebus smiled, he leaned against his neat desk, he had a bookcase lined on the wall and his PHDs behind him, he crossed his arms and looked at us expectantly.

Saint elbowed me and I blinked before remembering the reason we came here, this place always makes me existential.

"I'm Tartarus' son, a Blacksmith in training and I was wondering if you had any Death Metal shipments? We're running low."

"Death metal?" Erebus questioned, "No we never get any, I wasn't aware Tartarus had a child." He raised a brow but stood and walked around his desk and flipped through his files.

"I usually put in bulk orders for Tartarus often, at Jasper's request. And of course sign off on your fathers checks, I guess that's why he took on more jobs, had a mouth to feed."

I nodded awkwardly, "Uh, yea, he's very to himself, I'm sure only a handful of people know I'm his son."

"Well, We don't use death metal here, we use Iron and other simple metals for Blacksmithing. The courses are simple, and most Blacksmithing we do is for minor repairs, all the heavy stuff is your fathers job, through and through."

"So he's the only one who realistically can have Death Metal?" I nodded, "Has anyone else ordered any? Would you know?"

"Well, death in all forms is our business, if any metal got

in we'd know about it." Erebus sat at his desk and logged into his computer, "I assume this is a serious matter, hence your questioning?"

"Oh, yes sir." I nodded, "My dad left yesterday to get some more metal from the mines, he's never been this low before so I figured I'd ask, couldn't hurt right?"

"I see, that certainly is concerning, without death metal fourth years can't get their scythes. That's an issue." Erebus looked through his computer.

"Sir, if, hypothetically, Death Metal got into third party hands.." Rouge trailed off, "How likely is that?"

"Very unlikely, and for good reason." Erebus hummed while he typed, "The last time Death Metal was in the streets, we lost a few Reapers and my father nearly got taken out, it's been cracked down on ever since."

Mr. Wynter? Interesting. I tend to forget he's native here. I pursed my lips a bit and glanced away.

"Death metal can kill Reapers?" Rouge asked. I glanced over.

Saint nodded, "Yes. It's a very dangerous element, made by death himself. Death metal is mined from Obsidian crystal and Silver from Jezabelle's resting place, Aides gets it blessed by her aswell. She brought you in this world, and she can take you out, not even we are immune to their touch."

"Scary.." Rouge muttered.

"Huh.." Erebus hummed as he sat up, "Seems a shipment was redirected or intercepted about two months ago but it's like it was just dropped then disappeared. That's worrying."

"Intercepted two months ago?" I asked, that's dads usual replenish time, he gets constant shipments to stay on top of orders, yet this time it doesn't come? Then disappears?

Then the Blacksmith in the school using death metals. This can't be a coincidence. But how did they get a hold of it, they're just regular sorcerers, the least equipped to bypass Reaper protocols. I tapped my chin in thought, yea, something is definitely wrong here.

"Thank you sir, I'll let my father know." I smiled.

He nodded, "Saint, have your father contact me as well, yes?"

"Of course." Saint bowed her head respectfully, "We won't take up anymore of your time."

"Happy to help, thank you for bringing this to my attention." Erebus spoke up, his voice was serious but he smiled gently.

I quickly whipped out my phone and sent a text to Rue, asking her to meet us. She was right, and if the school is making death weapons, and has a goal to get to the Reapers... *I have a sinking feeling in my stomach.*

"Well this is certainly concerning." Rouge sighed, "What now?"

"I'm going to talk to Rue, maybe she can figure something out? She's got more leeway than us."

"Aubrey..." Saint warned.

"Trust me, Ok?"

Saint nodded slightly, I headed back home and rubbed my head. I kicked the gate open with the tip of my boot and rubbed my eyes. I made my way to dad's shop and looked through his files.

"Huh?" Saint watched me, "What are you?"

"Dad keeps papers of all his work transactions. Time stamps." I flipped through the papers and grabbed a file, "Something tells me, if this becomes more, dad will be on the chopping block, they'll try to blame him immediately."

"So? It's not like they can replace him, your dad is literally the only one with an immunity."

I shook my head, "He isn't immune."

"He's not?" Rouge asked.

"No one is. He has stitches from times the metal cut him when I was a kid, it takes longer to heal but he isn't immune."

We all looked up as Iron began to bark and growl, the gate creaking open, we looked out the workshop and noticed the pink haired girl pushing the gates open in disgust. I rolled my eyes hard and walked over.

"Down Iron, she's fine."

"Yes, this is precisely what I expected." She looked around and made a face of disgust. I rolled my eyes once more.

"Not important Pinky. We've got a problem." I motioned her inside the house. She hesitantly followed and basically tiptoed around Iron as he tried to sniff at her, "I'd offer you water, but my poor people cups might have ya pass out."

"Of course you'd drink tap."

"Nah, I just assumed you were too prissy for a bottle." I crossed my arms as Rouge and Saint sat on the couch. Iron sat next to me and laid down, she rolled her eyes and sat on the love seat by herself, she looked around the living room and seemed to curl in on herself. I sighed and shook my head.

"Look, this stays between us." I spoke up, "Clearly there's something the fourth years are training for and if Reaper weapons are being made, it can't be for a good reason."

"It seems that way." Rue hummed, "Why would Reaper weapons be involved, they're illegal for non Reaper use."

"Apparently they kill Reapers. The posters, the strange

behavior, the field trips?" I asked, not wanting to finish the sentence.

"No." Rue spoke up, "No, Miss Petra would never.."

"Seems she will." I crossed my arms.

"There's gotta be a better explanation. That's not on the table." Rue muttered.

"Fine, she wants to kick dad out of his field, that's another idea, but that doesn't account for the Reapers."

"She could want to sell to non Reapers?" Rouge asked, I raised a brow.

"It's The Valley, capitalism runs this place because of the king, it's very plausible the school is trying to run a smuggling ring." Saint spoke up, "And many Demons have issues with exorcists, she can make a killing off of them alone."

"Capitalism." I deadpanned.

"It's realistic." Rue nodded.

"Is it?"

"Oh so killing Reapers with death weapons for no good reason is more realistic?" Rue asked, annoyed.

"Maybe it's not Petra. And there is a reason."

The room fell silent, "I mean, whose school is it."

"Stop." Rue spoke up.

"Hecate."

"Stop." Rue repeated, but stern. We turned our attention to her, "Hecate hasn't been heard from in centuries."

"In public sure, but we all know what's coming up, and how she left the public eye."

"I don't know Aubrey, not even she is that crazy." Saint said, rubbing her neck. Rouge remained quiet but kept an eye on Rue, I did too, eyeing her carefully.

"She isn't crazy. She was heartbroken." Rue spoke up.

"Most of the population has been heartbroken, you don't see them funding a school and starting an *alleged* weapon trafficking ring." I challenged, Rue gripped her coat and looked away, almost enraged.

"These are just theories, there's no real evidence on anything. Nor her involvement." Rue stood abruptly, catching us off guard, "But I do agree, this stays between us."

Rue walked past the coffee table and practically stomped to the door. She kept her head down and gaze on the ground and her fists clenched. I eyed her suspiciously, until I noticed a lock around her neck, barely noticeable under her jacket, *a lock like mine,* she's hiding something. I immediately gripped her wrist and turned her around.

"Are you a Reaper." I asked. She blinked in confusion and went to snatch her wrist away. I tightened my grip and kept her in place.

"Let go."

"Are you a Reaper?" I repeated.

"Let go!"

"Aubrey, don't be ridiculous." Saint stood up while Rouge sat quietly, assessing the situation. I narrowed my eyes at her and stared her down. She had bright pink eyes, brighter than her hair, her tan jacket hugged her chubby body tightly, everything she wears screams money, from her name brand jacket down to her matching purse and name brand boots, why would she wear a cheap lock necklace, that doesn't make sense. I felt Saint place her hand over mine and pry my fingers off her. Rue's eyes were welled and she quickly turned around and left the house, slamming the door behind her.

"Aubrey have you lost it!" Saint asked, I looked at her then back at the door, "You could've hurt her."

"Sorry." I muttered then shook my head, "Sorry, I thought I saw something."

"Yea.. Just, apologize to her when you see her." She said and shook her head, I have to go talk to dad about the metal situation, You notified the adults and we did our part. Just relax, Ok?" Saint grabbed her bag and patted my shoulder before leaving. Rouge got up from the couch and walked over.

"You alright? That was out of character.." Rouge spoke softly.

"Yea, I thought I saw a lock." I muttered

"A lock?" She echoed.

"A lock is a spell, it changes your appearance temporarily, covers blemishes, acne, scars, what have you. I have one."

Her eyes narrowed slightly.

"For my Homunculus features." I interjected, I pulled the necklace from under my shirt, "Without it my flaws are more noticeable."

She tilted her head, "Flaws?"

I unhooked the chain and let the illusion fall. My eyes became two toned, my pupils are smaller, my teeth were pointed. I could feel that burning sensation on my back. Rouge blinked in surprise.

"Oh wow…" She touched my cheeks, "Your eyes…"

She stared into them, I could feel myself slowly getting embarrassed. She moved my locs aside and stared at my ears as well.

"And your ears are so small. Wow, Is this how you usually

look?" Rouge asked gently. I smiled softly with a nod.

"Yea, It's a bit inconvenient. Dad says it's kind of uncanny valley for him. I look normal but something is clearly off." I said, gripping her wrist gently and rubbing my thumb against her hand.

"No, No, not at all. I like you better this way. You're so unique." Rouge smiled, "I always loved your eyes, I didn't think they could get better. I'm kind of jealous."

I laughed quietly, then smiled at her. I just stayed there. She was taking in my features. Her soft warm hands stayed on my cheeks, I closed my eyes and pressed into her hand. It feels nice to be this close to her again without that lingering anxiety. Iron nudged at my leg and she pulled her hands away after a minute.

"Thank you for being honest with me, Aubrey." Rouge smiled.

" I, um, Yea…" I put the lock back on and rubbed the back of my head, "Um. Anyway, I have to walk Iron. He'll start growling before long."

"Alright…" She smiled then pet Iron's head before leaving.

I sighed, *Weapon trafficking, sure.*

22

TWENTY-ONE

"Mom! Have you seen my white and blue sweater?" I called down the stairs, I rushed from room to room hurrying to get ready, I took the curlers out of my hair and brushed it letting them fall past my shoulders. *White roots again, dammit, I just colored them.*

"Check your closet Keegan!"

"I did!" I groaned quietly and looked through my drawers and in my closet.

I looked through the white and blue shades in my closet, moving around the garments to look at the different racks, the lava pooled in like sunlight, it reminded me a lot of the dorms in The Summit. It was comforting but made me feel a level of unease so mom decided to give me black out curtains. I skimmed the articles of clothing then walked back into my room, bed was fully made, with pillows crowding the top, my bed curtains were tied open and the walls covered in posters. There were still boxes to unpack, but I'm pretty comfortable.

Being home felt good. Being back in The Valley felt odd,

especially after being surrounded by holy light, The Sun, Angels and clouds. Just to drop down to brimstone, lava and sin. But it's home, it'll always be home. Being back has been an adjustment, losing my scholarship was a slap in the face but in all honestly what did I expect? I was nothing more than gutter trash who snuck in the academy, never mind my grades, my skill, my talent, my power. Just a rat beneath their feet, and I foolishly danced for them, yearning to be in their ranks. What a fool I was.

I still want to be a part of their ranks, it was my birthright, how foolish of me right? But I wanted to be an Angel more than anything, I studied, prepped, hell I even moved. What a joke now it seems, I didn't stand a chance, what a fool I've been. All that work just for my scholarship to be revoked on the smallest of offenses, on something that wasn't even *my* fault, it's taking time to work past, my therapist told me to focus on the now and not the past. Not wondering about what ifs and what could be. She told me that was the quickest way to drive myself insane, she's not wrong.

I tell myself, in hindsight I'm happy it didn't work out. I know that place wasn't good for me, I lost weight drastically, developed an ED and enough trauma to last me a lifetime. Sometimes I can't help but wonder what it would've been like if I stayed here, how my life would've turned out if I just followed mom's footsteps and went to the Sorcerer schools.

Is my dad even proud?

But past is past, nothing you can do to change it, but you can always live and learn from it.

"Sis, is this what you're yelling about?"

I shot my head towards the door. Orien had his arms crossed, holding up my sweater, his eyes were bored and tired as always, he wore his food pajamas I bought him in high school as a joke. His hair was down and wet like it was freshly washed, must be getting braids again.

"Yes! Thank you!" I walked over and went to grab it, he took it back and shot me a look.

"All this for that jackass?" Orien asked.

I rolled my eyes, "Oh please, I know you don't like him."

I waved it off and snatched the sweater from his hands. He crossed his arms as I pulled the sweater over my tank top happily and fluffed my curls.

"Yes because he's an arrogant prick who overcompensates for all he lacks."

"So you've told me." I looked through my lipsticks with a hum, same thing as always. "It's just coffee, it might not even go anywhere."

"I can only be so lucky. If he hurts you-"

"Yes Orien, I know. I know."

He's the oldest, *by three minutes,* we're twins but by fate have two separate birthdays. The only children our parents decided to have.

Centuries ago, my mother was an Angel, she met my father up there, in The Summit. She said their romance was like a fairy tale, only something you read in the books. He was kind and gentle and a huge romantic. She said he got under her skin a little too easily. He took pride in her, he showed her off and worshiped the ground she walked on. Everything was great, until she got pregnant, before their marriage. *Big sin.*

My father couldn't have cared less. Mom said our father hated the hypocritical and misogynistic teachings of the churches, he saw everyone as equal, what is a man without a woman? How can a man be if not for the womb of a woman? She chooses who she wishes to bare for, and who are we to disrespect that? He tried to plead their case, they're married legally but no ceremony yet, no "Sin" was committed. But from how momma implied it, that didn't matter. I learned the hard way.

The misogyny is way worse than father ever described in his journals, even so he was angry at her mistreatment. My father wasn't naive, no, not at all. He knew My mother was beautiful, He knew she had many options, and she knew some powerful people had an eye on her. And well? What do horrible men do when faced with rejection? Well. they lash out. Mom was sentenced and fell, stripped of her Angel status and wings. They didn't expect it, but he followed after her.

They were together, happy and in love, until he got sick. The Valley is dangerous for angels, the environments are drastically different, Mom swallowed her pride and begged them to save him, they refused because he 'chose his side.' We were seven when he died. Orien was bitter towards them ever since. I understand, I do, but, I wanted to make dad proud and complete my virtues, just like he did.

Easier said than done. Once they found out who my mother was, it made things incredibly complicated. It's like they wanted me out since I got in. Targets painted on my back, eyes on me all the time, it was so stressful, my wings began shedding.

I adjusted my back out of habit, oh yea. *My wings.*

I sighed and shook my head, applying my mascara. *Happy thoughts, in the now Keegan, you have a coffee date with a childhood crush, focus on that.* I steadied my hand and breathed out, pushing the thoughts to the back of my mind. They'd stand out here anyway.

"If you're not back in 3 hours I will come and pick you up myself." Orien pushed off the wall and headed down the hall to his room.

I looked over at him and watched him go, I groaned and yelled out the door, "You will not!"

He waved his hand and closed his door. I groaned quietly and checked my phone, Ok, take a breath. Happy thoughts, happy thoughts.

I looked at myself in the mirror and adjusted my sweater and skirt, I smiled wide. I certainly look healthier, I got color back in my cheeks and don't feel light headed every time I move. The fat gain is new, but honestly I'm strangely not mad at it. I guess it helps when Pride is obsolete and we don't get predatory ads in greed anymore. I fixed my socks and patted my skirt down. This is probably the most beautiful I've ever felt, in a very long time. I looked at my roots once more and whined, I hope he doesn't think it's weird, I have to redye them. I tried not to look at the horns, those are new.

Happy thoughts, happy thoughts. I closed my eyes and took a breath.

I grabbed my perfume and spritzed it on my neck and wrists, gods I hope this isn't too much for a coffee date. Is this a date? I messed with my hair nervously. Maybe I should change? Or use a simpler bag? I went to look through my closet again but heard a knock from downstairs.

Gahhh he's here. I fixed my outfit one last time and hurried down the stairs.

"Oh- Honey, I was just about to yell up to you." Mom

smiled, "Aw honey~"

Mom kissed my cheeks and pinched them gently, "My beautiful girl~ Aurora look at your step daughter~"

"Mooom" I huffed out and moved my hair behind my ear and quickly put my shoes on, "I'm twenty-three, stoop"

"You look beautiful honey, have fun." Aurora smiled.

"But not too much fun!" Mom interjected, I huffed in annoyance and shot her an annoyed look. Orien is our mother's son, I can't stress that enough.

Mom and Aurora met when we were ten, a Demon from the abandoned pride ring, they clicked almost immediately and it feels like just yesterday when they met and got married, Aurora is a second parent, she's been very active in our lives without trying to replace our father. She's always been really sweet. She treats mom just as well as dad did. I honestly thought mom would just be single forever, but somehow Aurora made her way into our little family. I'm happy she did, it's nice having another parent to talk to about tough things without worrying momma all the time. She's so generous and kind, she always went out of her way for our family. Naturally it took Orien some time to accept her but now he loves her more than anything, funny how that works.

I quickly opened the door. There stood Aubrey, his locs were pulled back and he was wearing all black, and I saw he snuck in his boots, I held back a small laugh and smiled at him.

"Hey Aubrey."

"Hey, ready?" He smiled. I nodded and grabbed my bag, "Hello Mrs. Eve, Mrs. Aurora." He nodded and waved.

"Hello sweetie, make good choices." Mom spoke up. He

nodded awkwardly and waved, I closed and locked the door behind us and breathed out.

"I hope I didn't overdo it, this isn't too much is it?" I asked nervously, he blinked and looked down at me then chuckled.

"Nah, not at all. I just hope you won't get too hot..." He motioned to the sweater, "How long have you been back?"

"About a year, I'm alright, really." I messed with my hair.

He smiled and nodded, "Well that aside, I know you aren't big on flowers, but I thought it wouldn't be a date without them." He smiled and handed me a rose, I took it in surprise and smiled. "Don't worry, it's plastic." He chuckled.

This is a date! Oh gods girl don't mess this up. I internally squealed while taking the rose and laughed quietly, "Yea, allergies, thank you."

"So, I was thinking we take the ferry up to Sin City and head to a shop in Gluttony?"

"Sounds wonderful." I smiled, he put his arm to me and I took it gently. We headed down the trail and I tried to stay calm. I gripped his arm gently, he stood taller than me, at least a couple of inches and I could feel his muscle through his jacket. He smelled nice too, like pine or cedar, he hasn't changed a bit.

I haven't been on a date before, and if I'm honest I never thought I'd have one with Aubrey of all people, he always seemed so out of reach, either I wasn't his type or he wasn't single. He was always so sweet on me though, which I found interesting. He and my brother never got along. I never knew why, but I know Orien can't stand him. Always at each other's throats, but for Aubrey it seemed like it was just a joke, something fun to do while my brother got migraines just thinking about him and their confrontations.

We met as kids, in fourth grade I believe, when I still went to school here, he was always so nice but he was shy for a while. He didn't have class with his purple haired friend in that grade, so he spent time with us. I guess we became his friends, well I was, Orien was and always has been overprotective. Aubrey didn't mind though, He was always kind and considerate.

Even in high school he took time to speak to me, even if we were more distant, it's like I never left his mind, even the smallest amount of me was still there, he was so charming, but gods was he bad for me. I was applying to the Angel program and he was a temptation, *a lustful one.* If His grace Caelus was testing me, Aubrey would've been that test. As virtuous as I chose to live my life, even I wasn't immune to such feelings. Gods, I remember he asked me out in freshmen year and I nearly said yes. I wanted to so bad, he was so cute.

I let a dreamy sigh slip quietly out of my lips.

He didn't seem to notice and he helped me on the ferry and signed to the ferryman. They seemed friendly. I can't understand sign language but it seems friendly. I took a moment to calm my mind and swallow my embarrassment.

He smiled and sat next to me. I watched the stream pass us by, it's been so long since I've seen it. The deep blue mist, with white stars twinkling throughout, reminded me of an hourglass, or calming sand. It was quiet on the outskirts and gods did The Valley look beautiful from afar, it felt like seeing a dimming campfire from a distance. It's calming and comforting, I suppose such as death. I leaned against the edge and watched the pools of lava fall below, the glow illuminating the path beautifully.

"So you've been back for a year?" Aubrey asked, I blinked and looked over.

"Hm? Oh, yeah, finally got all my stuff back and cleared from the trial." I muttered

"Trial?" He asked.

"They accused me of sinning, lust of all things." I rolled my eyes in disgust. "I don't like talking about it if I'm honest.."

"Well that's bullshit." I jumped slightly at his words, "You're like, the most angelic person I know, like to a fault almost."

"Ah." I smiled awkwardly.

"Way too nice, you have no idea how many people your brother and I smacked in the mouth for you. Perverts or idiots, since you were nice they thought you were an easy target." He rolled his eyes.

"Oh?" I asked, leaning against my hand, the lava illuminated his face beautifully, he toned up, his jaw was stronger, his freckles were more prominent and his beautiful purple eyes shined, his locs were out of his face for once and *gods* is he handsome, always has been but he certainly grew into himself. He snorted through his nose.

"The only thing your brother and me agreed on. How is he by the way?"

I laughed quietly and glanced away, "He's fine, same old same old, he's been helping me settle in and navigate. Everything changed so much.."

"Yea, I can't imagine what The Summit looked like, but I hope you're happy to be home. Your mom missed you like crazy I'd imagine." Aubrey hummed.

"You have no idea.."

"I missed you too, you look great by the way, like wow.

Look at you." He smiled and nudged my arm, I giggled out of habit and blushed in embarrassment, I messed with my hair anxiously.

"Ah, thank you.. I know it's a drastic change…and my hair.."

"Baby. A/re you happy?" He asked, I blinked and met his gaze in confusion, "With yourself, where you're at, being female presenting?"

"Oh, absolutely, I think this is the happiest I've been in a long time." I looked down at my lap, messing with my skirt, the estrogen worked wonders, it's a drastic change and it certainly helped me gain weight, I feel a lot of things, but hatred for my body definitely isn't one of them, I look at the fat on my body in the mirror and just cry in pure happiness, I never thought I'd get to this point, and keeping my hair short? I love it, *I love me.*

"Then that's all that matters, and your hair is cool as hell, it blends so perfectly. I think it's cute." Aubrey smiled, I glanced away.

"It's not perfect, I usually have it dyed, I forgot to do it before bed last night."

"Perfect doesn't exist darlin', and if it did, we're nowhere near it." Aubrey waved his hand, "You look phenomenal, and you're happy, that's all that truly matters."

"I guess you're right.."

"Broken clocks and all that." He grinned goofily, I laughed quietly and looked up at the city, it's certainly bigger now, lively too. He got up and helped me off the boat. I gripped his hand a bit nervously as I looked up at the city gates, he exchanged words with the ferryman before walking towards the gate.

I kept close to him, and hugged his arm securely. He was calm though, like always, expertly avoiding contact with people. Even as a kid he despised being touched, I remember he beat up a kid for touching him everyday. It's like it's a pet peeve for him, something that drives him nuts. But he always initiated contact with me, I only reciprocated if he wished it.

He used his clearance to head inside Gluttony, the town was lively at this time of day, the shops were busy, lines out the door. Couples and friends alike.

"Mind a small change of plans?" Aubrey asked with a soft smile.

"Oh? Um, sure?"

"How's a bakery sound?" He asked.

"A bakery??" I tilted my head.

"Best in Gluttony, trust me." He led the way past the crowds and headed to a bakery, tons of people were seated in and out, a long line stretched down the sidewalk, just like the others. But I recall the symbol on the window.

"Oh! My brother brings cakes from here, he loves it."

"He's still gluttonous, hm?" He chuckled.

"Absolutely, he's been applying for chef jobs out here, we haven't heard back though."

"Well, if he's nice to me, maybe I can put in a good word." Aubrey joked.

I shook my head and swatted at his chest. He pushed in through the door, skipping the line. He walked to the side of the counter and grinned brightly, a short woman was buzzing around the counter, wings flapping as she took money and flew from serving customers to seating others. *That sure is one busy bee.*

"Hi Octavia, is Auntie in?" He asked. I looked at the floor, feeling the annoyed stares at us. The smaller woman buzzed and nodded.

"She's in the back, I'll call her up for you~" She hummed.

"Auntie?" I asked.

"Auntie Bee yea, she's kinda like my mom? Aside from Charon, they've been very active in my life since I was a kid." He nodded

"I see, you being Gluttony adjacent suddenly makes more sense, especially if she was one of your parental figures."

"Take it from me, don't ever eat her Nectar." He glanced down at me, "It's bad news."

I met his eyes, and they were serious. *Alright, no Nectar.. Got it.* I nodded and looked back down shyly.

"Aubrey~ now what brings you by sugar~" A small woman walked up from the backroom, she had big red eyes and bright yellow skin, same hue as the honey she sells, her wings fluttered and she squished his cheeks, she's not like any bee I've ever seen before.

"I was hoping I could get some pastries and coffee to go? On a date." Aubrey grinned.

"Oh?" Bee turned her gaze to me.

"H-hello Miss.." I smiled.

"You remember Keegan right? Mrs. Adams' daughter, her brother used to send me home with bruises in high school." He laughed.

"Oh! Yes, yes, I remember the family name. Nice to meet you dear." Bee turned to Aubrey, "I'll get a sample basket for you, but it'll take some time, go have a seat."

"Thanks Auntie." He smiled and led me to a table. He pulled the chair out for me, a gentleman as always. I looked around the small shop and smiled.

"This place is so cute, did you used to work here?" I asked. He shook his head.

"Dad would kill me if I ever worked here." Aubrey laughed and leaned back in his chair, "But I'd spend days in here when I got suspended or something. She always made me treats to make me feel better and whenever I did some fuck shit, I'd get a basket made for dad."

I laughed at that and shook my head, "Yea that sounds about right. You were something else in high school."

"I was a bastard, I know."

"Not to me." I smiled, "Now did my brother think so and tell me often? Well yes." I scratched my cheek with my finger. He laughed and shook his head.

"Yea, your brother was somethin' else."

"Why did you two have issues? I never understood it." I leaned against my hand.

"Oh he was mad at how cocky I was on the team, we butted heads often, he was the stickler nerd and I was the rash jock. Personality clashes mainly."

"Makes sense, he loves order, especially with competitions, he's always been weird like that." I said.

"Mm, so what have you been up to? Tell me something good." He smiled

I hummed, "Want me to tell you that I love you?" I joked then instantly got nervous, he blinked and then grinned brightly.

"I love that song, Ok, she can be funny, color me shocked!"

"Hey now!" I swatted at him, he laughed and leaned against his hand, "Well, something good?" I tapped my nails on the table in thought.

"Well, me and mom went shopping, I redid my closet, me and Orien spent a day together and we got a puppy!"

"Oh? A Hellhound?" Aubrey asked.

"Yep, we named her Oreo, she's so cute." I grabbed my phone and showed him pictures, his eyes twinkled and he looked eagerly, "She has little socks~"

"She's adorable, I love dogs."

"How is your Hellhound?"

"Lazy as hell." He snorted, "He's good, spoiled."

"Well he's a good boy, he should be spoiled." I hummed, Aubrey chuckled. "What have you been up to?"

"Got home a couple months ago."

"You left?" I asked.

"Uh, yea, college, didn't work out." He glanced away, "But I settled back in pretty well, got my old job back and Saint convinced me to go to the Sorcerer school, turned out to be a good thing. I met someone who's helping me with my magic, so I'm doing pretty well."

"Well that's great! You're an earth elemental right?" I asked.

He nodded. "Finally I can do more than vines, eh, sometimes. Still in progress."

"Well I wish you luck, can't imagine how hard it is when most people here are fire elementals."

"Yeaaaa, but hey I'm adaptable." He grinned. I laughed quietly as Miss Bee walked over and sat the basket down.

"Here you go dear~ enjoy~" Bee grinned, her sharp teeth lined up perfectly. Aubrey pulled out his wallet and handed money to her, she shot him a cold stare and he shook his head.

"Take it as a tip Auntie, let Octavia have it." He put it in her apron and stood up, grabbing the basket. "Thanks, I'll be back in a few days for a basket for dad, he's out of town, I'm sure he'd enjoy it."

Bee nodded reluctantly, "Fine, and alright, I'll keep that in mind. Have fun. But not too much fun." Her eyes glinted towards me and I stood straight.

"Bye Auntie." Aubrey threw his hand up and led me out, "Sorry 'bout that."

"It's fine, we can sit over there." I pointed to a bench outside a shop. He sat the basket between us and looked through the goodies.

"Two coffees, and a bunch of pastries, let's hope the coffee of the day is good." He handed me a cup and I blew on it instinctively. He picked up one of the muffins and took a bite. I sipped my cup and looked at the Demons passing by, all of them minding their business, enjoying beers, food, company, and just being out.

It feels nice doing something somewhat normal, and it smells wonderful here, the restaurants and the bakeries, makes your mouth water. I breathed in the fresh air and relaxed against the bench, feeling content wash over me. *This is nice.*

I took another sip and squeaked as it burned my tongue, and Aubrey turned his head to me almost immediately.

"You alright?" He asked.

"I'm fine, burned my tongue." I pouted. He took my chin in his hand and turned my head to him, moving his thumb over my lip. I could feel heat flooding my face, his eyes were narrowed, staring directly at my lips.

"Your lips are a little red too, I can get you some water?" He gently moved his hand and got to his feet, I shook my head and waved my hand quickly, glancing away.

"No no! It's fine really!"

"Don't worry about it, I'll be right back." He walked around the bench and headed to a store, I looked at the basket and immediately put a pastry in my mouth. *Girl, quit being such a loser. Get it together!*

I fanned my face and took a breath, he's so cute, what have I gotten myself into. I sighed and sat the cup down, nibbling the honey filled pie. The powdered sugar made it heavenly, certainly is the Gluttony ring, my gods.

I grabbed my phone from my purse and of course, Orien is already texting me. I rolled my eyes and scrolled through the texts, *gods if this man doesn't get a damn boyfriend or job.* I could feel my eyebrow twitch slightly and I sighed out, I noticed in the corner of my eye Aubrey exiting the store with a few waters, he was stopped by another Demon and they spoke for a little while.

He's so grounded here, I glanced to the side and nibbled the pastry,watching the traffic on the roads. Groups of Demons talking and enjoying their time and company. Just completely comfortable here. I looked at my lap and messed with my stockings.

"Sorry about that." Aubrey smiled and handed me the water, he sat on the bench and leaned back, sipping his coffee.

"It's no problem, thank you.." I gripped the cold bottle and glanced away, tapping my nails against the plastic, "Ya know… I'm kind of jealous of you if I'm honest."

"Hm?" He asked, turning his head to me.

"You're so alive here, you have friends, and history here. Everyone knows you.." I smiled gently at him. His eyes softened and he looked back towards the street.

"Yea, well, I grew up here.." Aubrey hummed, "Do you regret leaving?"

"Sometimes." I shrugged, "Sometimes I wonder what it would've been like if I stayed here..with you and Orien, got a job, a hobby, put my life on this track.. What would it be like?"

He looked at me, but stayed quiet.

"Maybe I'd be happier? I'd have friends other than my brother and you?"

"Well The Valley is a sleepy region, and you're phenomenal. If it wasn't the Angel academy, it would've been something else, a bird is going to fly, especially if the cage is open." Aubrey nodded.

I looked at him fully then smiled softly, "Yeah.. I guess you're right.."

"Besides! We can get you some hobbies and friends now, we are still kids kinda-? Not twenty-five yet." He grinned goofily. I laughed quietly and nodded.

"I look forward to it.."

"How's next Friday sound?" He asked suddenly.

"Next Friday?" I tilted my head in confusion.

"Want to go on a date with me Friday?" He chuckled. I felt my face heat up immediately. I stammered and waved my hand.

"Uh! Yes, sure.. That sounds fun.."

"We can do anything you want, any city you wanna go to, just let me know," Aubrey said.

"Any??" I asked.

"Any." He nodded.

"Even wrath?" I beamed.

He sucked his teeth as he leaned back and rubbed the back of his head before nodding, "Yea, I think I know a guy."

"You..know a guy?"

"A lot of guys." He chuckled.

I laughed and leaned back on the bench, "Well I'll dress my best to go to the wrath ring, I'm holding you to that.."

"I will do everything in my power to impress you darlin'." He smiled.

"Ahh, you don't have to do much.."

"I'm aware, but I will anyway, cuzzz I want to." Aubrey nodded with a grin.

I smiled then instantly felt dread as a black car sped up to us. We both looked towards it as a few Demons hurried out of the street and on the sidewalks, a few cursing at him, the blacked out window slowly rolled down and my brother's piercing orange eyes narrowed towards us.

I could feel my eyebrow twitching and fought the urge to scream.

"It's been 4 hours sis, let's go."

"Orien." I growled lowly.

"Hey Orien." I could hear the smugness in his voice and saw him do a wave in the corner of my eye, Orien opted to ignore him, barely flickering his eyes over to him. "What brings you out? You look cute."

Orien's eye twitched, he shot his head to him. "Don't address me you cretin."

"Ouch." Aubrey fake pouted and sat up, leaning against his knees, "I didn't know I had a curfew with your sister."

"She did." Orien muttered

"I am a grown woman." I growled, Orien rolled his eyes and motioned me in the car. "Go home."

"Mom is making supper, WE are going home."

"Orien!" I groaned.

Aubrey cleared his throat, then stood as he placed his phone back in his pocket, "Actually darlin', I have to run as well, something came up with a friend. It's important."

He smiled apologetically, I blinked in disappointment but smiled softly anyway, I stood and patted my skirt down nervously. He took my hand gently and kissed the top.

"Get home safe yea? I'll see you tomorrow and I'll plan that date." He winked at me and smiled.

I nodded gently and smiled a bit, "Alright.."

He smiled at Orien and winked at him as well, which Orien scowled at him. He opened the door for me and handed me my purse and the basket, "Text me later yea?"

"Yea.." I smiled. Orien rolled up the window and I groaned in annoyance, he smiled at Orien then stepped back from the car, hands in his pockets.

"Have a good evening, Orien."

With that we drove off, my annoying brother aside, I actually feel so happy. I looked out the window and leaned back in the seat, basically tuning out Orien. A date Friday.. Do I have a boyfriend?

23

TWENTY-TWO

"It's a girl!"

"A baby girl, Your name shall be Rue. For all the regret and ***anger*** *I feel."*

I like to think my mom loved me at some point. She never said it, but I like to remain hopeful. I mean, what mother hates their child? *Right*? They yell because they love you. They're hard on you because they want you to succeed. They want the best for you, *Right*? That's what I tell myself, how can a child comprehend being despised by the one person you're supposed to get unconditional love from? I have many memories, sorting through them has really been eye opening. I recall, when I was three, mom used to make me food and wash me, she would hum songs and put me to bed. Only after she's been ignoring me all day. Back then I didn't think much of it, I had a huge playroom, tons of toys, and infinite TV time. Why would I notice?

I started playing with the workers in the house when I turned six. They didn't get paid enough now that I'm thinking back on it. They were hired to cook, clean, or tend to the garden. Not deal with a neglected child but even then, they pretended to care more than she ever did. Isn't that something?

When I turned eight, my magic came in. That was the first time she paid actual attention to me. That's the most enthusiastic she's ever been to be around me. I loved her attention at first. I didn't realize I was deprived of it. That's when I learned, if I want mom's attention, I have to do something extraordinary and earn it. *What a joke.*

That happiness quickly soured though, I wasn't learning fast enough for her. I *was* **trying**, I mean I was only eight. What was she expecting? Full blown necromancy? The mastery of all eight magic forms she shares? *Nothing was enough.*

Years went by, I got older and more desperate. I worked. I worked *so hard.* I got the best grades, top of my classes. One of the strongest air elementals in our school. I even began studying mothers favorite form of magic, puppetry. And according to my teachers, I'm damn good at it too. She wouldn't know that though. She never talked to me enough to learn that. The moment I got a second to show my certificates or awards as a child, she just looked at me unimpressed. *How cruel is that.*

It was ridiculous in hindsight. But even so, I worked hard. *I worked so hard.*

I guess I kept it up because sometimes she'd reward me. She'd smile and tell me how great I was doing. That was only when she saw my magic ability. She always wanted me to perfect it. I practiced, I practiced at any opportunity I got. If I succeeded, I got attention. If I mess up I get berated. She was quick to anger. A hair on the trigger was all it took.

Like a switch. One moment it's:

"Perfect my love! I knew you could do it!" to,

"You are nothing but a failure of a child, how are you my offspring and you can't figure this out."

It should've demotivated me, made me hate her. It should've made me resent everything about her. But, I couldn't, I had to be the best. I **have** to be the best.

It got so bad I fell ill, the only one who cared was our staff, she couldn't be bothered to notice. When she was notified all she could say was, "Oh, what a shame."

No emotion, no care. Just indifference.

That should've been my sign. They say the opposite of love isn't hate, but indifference. *Hell I guess the constant yelling and insults were a sign too?* But she's the only mother I've got, *how was I to know this isn't normal?* That her behavior isn't normal? I still make excuses for her, I still want to be her perfect daughter. I still want her to love me.

I shook my head and looked at my lap.

"That's been weighing heavy on your chest hasn't it dear?" The soft voice across from me spoke up. I didn't realize how silent it's been. It was so deafening. I looked at the woman, she had bright pink skin, flower petals blooming from her. One of the best psychiatrists in The Valley. How a fae is living comfortably here? who knows.

"Yea. I guess so."

"Your relationship with your mother seems to be the stem of your current issues?" She asked.

I shrugged and turned my attention to the grand clock on the wall beside us. The armchair was elegant, like everything else in this house. I leaned my arm against it and pressed my face to my hand. All I could do was stare into space. What more is there to say?

"Now, Miss Rue. You know I'm paid by the hour. And I'm booked for three hours biweekly, courtesy of-" She began, giving me a look.

"Miss Petra." I glanced at her, her pink skin and white hair standing out against the dull blues of the room, "Yea. I know."

"It's been a month dear, I figured you'd be more open by now..." She spoke gently, "I've noticed a few things so far, but I don't have all the pieces, I can't help if you don't allow me."

I gave her a blank stare and sighed. The chattering and bustling out in the hall, the clock ticking, the birds chirping. All of it was so distracting. She just smiled warmly.

"Why don't you tell me about Miss. Petra?" She asked, I softened my look. I looked back at the clock and watched the red hand tick along, it's only been forty-five minutes.

I tugged at my finger absentmindedly, twirling my ring in thought. I can't remember a fond time before her arrival. I hummed quietly to myself in thought.

"I remember when I was a child, I was nine at that point, and I couldn't perfect my mothers spells, she yelled at me for hours." I trailed my eyes down to the window, the lava had a gorgeous glow to it at this time. It was calming.

"She complained loudly about how I was useless and not worth the effort. All I could do was sit there and cry, what else could I have done? But that seemed to annoy her." I said, " Shortly after that Miss Petra showed up."

Miss Petra was bright eyed. She was a slender woman, Her eyes were a beautiful baby pink and stood out against her brown skin. Her hair was short at this time, It was a simple dark gray. She spoke with kindness and grace. When she showed up, it's like everything changed. Mom was calmer, she was nicer, she was present.

Bare minimum still, but at least with Miss Petra here, I had someone to cheer me on. Someone to show my accomplishments too. Miss Petra was twenty when she began apprenticing under my mother, I believe she was meant to be mom's successor. I guess she gave up on me, gods forbid a nine year old couldn't figure out a level four copycat spell.

Miss Petra was a drastic contrast to mother, she was kind and had a smile that lit up a room. She was young and eager, mom liked that. Another soul to exploit I guess. Miss Petra basically moved in, she was training almost daily but still found herself becoming my nanny in a way. She'd cook for me, bathe me, put me to bed, play with me, show up for me. Mother couldn't have cared less, as long as she was doing her studies and not falling behind. She had so much potential, it's why she got to become Headmaster when mom retired. She worked hard and I was so happy for her.

She listens to my stories. She'd tell me how proud she was of me and my accomplishments. Suddenly I didn't need mom anymore, I began to slack up in my early teens, mom **noticed** that. She tried to crack down on me, but she couldn't do much when Miss Petra was around, she didn't want to taint her *oh so perfect* goddess image.

"So, You see Miss Petra as a family figure?" She asked.

"Yeah, I think so." I nodded, "She's always been there until recently."

"Recently?" She asked.

"The Headmaster position keeps her busy." I glanced to

the side, sliding the ring up and down my finger.

The pink fae wrote that down, nodding to herself.

I stared back out the window and fell silent again.

"I recall.." I spoke up, the silence disturbed, "My mother telling me the day I was born was the second worst day of her life." I laughed quietly and shook my head. The pink woman looked at me in shock and slight horror.

"That's horrible." She said carefully, "What was the first?"

"My mom, other mom, dying I guess." I shrugged, "She never talks about her, I don't know what she looks like, it's like moms personal secret you know?" I looked at her. "I went into mom's study when she left for a business trip once."

"I found a photo book, it's the closest I've ever gotten to seeing what my mom looked like, and that ain't saying much."

"I see." She nodded somberly.

I was in high school at that point, fifteen I believe? Miss Petra was still around, mom was on a 'business trip' so she was my primary care giver. I think that's when my rebellious streak began, I was getting love and attention from Miss Petra so I began to ignore my mother. I wouldn't step too far out of line, I still feared her. It's like if she couldn't make me as miserable as her, she couldn't be around me. Another red flag *huh?* Well, since she wasn't there, I couldn't ask questions. I guess she anticipated that now that I'm older I'd begin to wonder where my other parent was.

I knew better though, that was a spot incredibly too sore. It was still tender. So, I went in her study. I'm a ghost to her, it's not like she'd notice. When I was there I found a photo album, along with journals. All of it was pristine, like she never touched it but kept them spotless. When I picked the photo album up there was faint wear on the edge from use and the pages had tear stains. I felt nervous suddenly, what will be in this book? Why is she so caring of it? Why did she treat it better than me at *any* stage of my life? What if it's bad, what if it shows me something I don't want to see? Will it tell me if she *ever* loved me?

I'm still a child. I'm still her child. I just want to know. *Did she ever love me?*

I carefully opened the book, The photos were so bright and happy at one point, she was smiling, knitting baby sweaters and blankets. She had a radiance to her. Her blue eyes were so bright, even through the old sepia stained photos. She had photos of my baby room, of someone building a crib just off frame. There were photos of baby names, the name Persephonii circled, my middle name. I flipped through the book slowly, taking in the life I could have had. This is the mother I could have had. My heart hurt at that thought. What did I do wrong? What changed? She was still pregnant with me, she was so ecstatic to be pregnant, my first ultrasound, it's a girl stickers were all over the page.

Then I realized, it was the one taking the pictures that made her like this, the woman on the other side. My other mom.

As I flipped through, it changed. She was dull. The photos seemed gray. There was no joy in her eyes anymore. She was still pregnant with me, looked like she was ready to burst. But she didn't look happy. There's no photos of my mom in this house, all I got from that album was a glimpse of hair, or a hand in frame, but never her face. I don't even know her name.

I closed my eyes and laid my head back, taking a deep breath. I think I understand now. She died it seems. I noticed her hair was pink though, I guess that where I get it from, maybe this galaxy pattern as well? Is that from my other mother? My eyes? I know I don't look completely like mom aside from my hyper pigmentation and I inherited her magical ability. Maybe that's why she hates me? I was once a gift, now I'm just a reminder?

That hurt my heart even more, mom was just hurting. This whole time she's been hurting? Was I even helping her heal? Was I too much? I felt overwhelming guilt wash over me. I feel awful, I was so dismissive, I stopped trying. No wonder she left.

I closed the book and put it back where I got it. I walked over to her desk and looked through the drawers, looking for anything, the other journals just looked like notes and spells. I saw a strange pale purple book with gold trimming peeking from under the other journals in the bottom drawer. It was just a glance, but it still made me uneasy. It felt dark. *What is that?*

I gasped in fear as the door swung open, I looked up in utter shock. My hand froze in the drawer.

Mom stood there with her suitcase in hand, the hall light pooling around her. Her shoulder length blue hair looked darker in the shadows. Her icy blue eyes stared daggers at me. She was in an elegant white dress with custom ice shards dangling off of it, and a matching headdress. I guess she just came from a god meeting? I was caught red handed.

"Rue. What are you doing." Hecate asked, her tone unclear.

I looked down, closing the drawer softly. "I uh…"

"Speak up." She demanded.

I flinched slightly, I didn't look at her, "You… you left, so, I couldn't ask.."

Her eyes were harsh as she walked over, I placed my hands in front of me and dropped my head.

"What happened…to my other parent."

Her side of the room fell silent, I felt the tension heavy on my shoulders. I immediately regretted that sentence coming from my mouth, I quickly looked up and put my hands up to say never mind but before I could she spoke.

"She…" Hecate looked down, "She died."

"Died..?" I asked.

"A couple months before you were born, she was murdered." She said calmly.

That shattered me. Murdered? That's all I could think about. *Murdered*?

"She was falsely accused of a crime, and put to death." She looked at me, "She was the love of my life, after you were born and I recovered, we were due to marry." Hecate looked at the book I previously looked through. She moved her fingers over the front delicately. Her eyes and voice were soft.

"There was nothing I could do…"

I stayed quiet and looked down.

"I didn't have much time to grieve, you were due soon, and well babies don't raise themselves." Hecate adjusted the book properly.

"You couldn't even…" I felt my eyes well, that's so heartbreaking. And what did I do in return? Make things hard for her. "I'm so sorry momma.."

"Hm." She hummed and turned her head away, "What's done is done, life is full of disappointments. It's best to learn that now, I've grown accustomed."

That's all she said about mom ever since, that's mothers past. Mothers happiness. Something she's hoarded from me. What did I reasonably expect though? *A mother to love me? A mother to care for me?* Seems like high expectations from someone like mother, someone grieving so harshly. I'd be horrible to deny her pain and space. My mom was the love of her life. You know, I've heard mothers call their children the love of their lives. Never my mother though. She made it quite clear. Mom was the love of her life and I didn't stand a chance.

I don't know why, but I took that as an invitation to work harder. I got back to studying and went back to my old habits. It worried Miss Petra because I got sick again, but who cares at this point? By seventeen, I realized, I radiate magic. Just like mom. I have my own source of magic. I couldn't tell her that though, she was busy, if it wasn't mentoring Miss Petra, it was a business trip. I never got to tell her that.

"Rue?" She asked.

I blinked and looked over.

"You zoned out again." She smiled gently. I nodded and rubbed my face.

"Sorry, a lot of thoughts."

"Well I'd love to hear them." She said softly with a smile to match.

"I think I'm all talked out."

"You don't want to talk about your mother? You have an hour left dear." She asked.

"I am a child named Regret." I looked at her, "What more can I say?"

Even so, after all her cruelty and neglect, even now, I still wanted to please her. I wanted her attention, her recognition, and I wanted to prove I was worth loving. Worth her time and effort. I want her to *like* me. I want her to *love* me. What can I do to prove I'm her daughter? Then I ask, why do I have to prove myself to this woman. To my mother?

What is a mother?

To deal with these complicated feelings, I turned to poetry. It helped put my feelings into words, I carried journals everywhere I went, I eventually stopped crying and just wrote it down. It was and still is easier to talk to pages over another person. It made life easier to move through, at least, I thought so. Miss Petra didn't think so, she asked my mom to get me a therapist, she wasn't listening, she didn't care. She waved it off and opted to ignore her request. Miss Petra decided she'd pay out of pocket. She genuinely cared, why couldn't my mother?

Whatever, who cares right?

"Are we done here?" I asked, "I have to get ready for school tomorrow."

The small lady nodded hesitantly, "See you in two weeks… "

I bowed my head to her in respect then took my leave. I walked down the long empty halls, portraits of mom and I stared down at me. The lava glow was dim and the house was quiet. So quiet I could hear the front door echo close. At least I can see Miss Petra tomorrow? Maybe she's in a better mood? I began my bed time routine and laid in the cool satin pink sheets. I closed my eyes and tried to silence my thoughts.

Little did I know, my life was planned to the letter way before I was born. What was once happiness and excitement is now tainted with anger and pettiness. I'm still expected to do as she planned, but now it's out of spite.

Spite I don't feel.

24

TWENTY-THREE

I walked up to my gate and locked eyes with Rue, I locked my phone and put it back in my pocket. "I was busy rich girl. What is it."

She had a sullen look on her face, she looked at the ground and gripped her purse to her body. But kept her mouth shut. I raised a brow and tilted my head a bit.

"Hey, you alright?" I asked cautiously.

"I'm sorry.." Rue looked defeated, it's been a couple days, has she slept? She put a photograph to me and I blinked in confusion, "Miss Petra…would never do this…"

I looked at the picture, it was her holding a certificate and smiling wide with Headmaster Petra, she had soft and kind pink eyes, same as Rue. She couldn't be any older than fourteen in this picture.

I glanced up at her, "Want to talk about this?"

She nodded slowly. I sighed and motioned her to follow me inside, I unlocked the door and motioned for Iron to chill before she walked in. I tossed the keys in the bowl and motioned to the couches.

"Water?" I asked.

"Sure.." She spoke quietly as she sat down. "I thought it over.. What you said.."

"And?"

"You could be right… but it's not Miss Petra, it can't be…" She spoke.

"You two know each other well?"

"She's like a mother to me if I'm honest…More than my own mother." Rue looked at her lap. I walked over and handed her a bottle. I sat in the arm chair, draping my leg over the armrest and looked at her, she gripped the bottle and shook her leg slightly out of nervousness.

"She's always been there for me, um, she was meant to be her successor." Rue tapped her nails nervously.

"But, suddenly, she became distant.. My mom has been off on business in The Summit for the past couple of months, so Miss Petra was in charge of her affairs here, on top of being a Headmaster, even so, she was still Miss Petra."

I listened to her intently, sitting up properly.

"She just shut me out, it's like she was angry with me? Or something… I'd ask her for help with an assignment or ask if she was available to walk home together and she'd brush me off or talk down to me so coldly. Kind of like mom used too…" Rue's eyes began to well, "She's never treated me like that before, we haven't spoken since the day we met." Rue met my eyes and blinked the tears away.

"Even so, she wouldn't hurt anyone, ever."

"..Who's your mother, Rue." I asked, lifting my head up.

She fell silent.

"Rue…"

"Hecate.. Isn't it obvious?" She asked quietly. I nodded

and rubbed my face.

"So Miss Petra is Hecate's successor, and you're saying your mother hasn't been in town for months. THIS month she's still gone?" I asked. She nodded.

"So if not Miss Petra, and your mom isn't here, then who."

"I don't know, mom has made a lot of enemies, maybe it's a teacher at the Reaper school? She was bitter towards Reapers." She asked.

"That's a stretch, the Reaper school is doing its own thing, they don't even know about us."

"Well, that's not, fully true.." Rue trailed off.

"As in?"

"We have exams, events, etc with them. We're like sister schools, at least that's how Miss Petra put it." Rue spoke.

"Hm, events?"

"Like formals, or competitions, to show our magical abilities, there's one coming up actually.." She pulled her phone from her purse and showed me her calendar, "It's the Aides Moon event, for us it's a magic showcase. I've been practicing, I thought if I performed well, Miss Petra would be happy with me.."

"Send this to me." I asked, "I'll do some asking around, I'll see if anything connects." I sat up and got to my feet, "And if I'm honest, if your theory is correct, I doubt it's you she's unhappy with. She's probably stressed out."

"You think?" Rue asked.

"It's a possibility, especially if it was such a drastic 180."

Rue looked at her lap and gripped her hands gently. "Yea.."

I walked over to her and gripped her shoulder gently and gave a comforting smile. "And if you're Hecate's kid, that means this month is probably hard on you too, huh..?"

She fell silent. I sat next to her.

"And you're on your own, especially if your mother is gone and Miss Petra is being weird. How are you feeling?"

She dropped her head and I noticed her shoulders beginning to shake, a few tears hit her hand as she trembled to herself. I sat there quietly and hesitantly gripped her hand reassuringly.

"I'm sorry, Rue.."

"...I never got to meet her...Ya know..?" Rue spoke up.

"Hm?" I asked.

"My mother. My..other mother.. She died before I was born..." Rue sniffed and wiped her eyes, "I guess I look like her. I don't know."

"I know of *the...Altercation..*"

"Murder." Rue said firmly.

"....Murder... Of your mother, and why Hecate shut herself off, but I doubt anyone knew you existed."

"That's how mother wanted it." She shook her head, "She's so bitter and angry, even after all these years."

"Well, it's understandable, if my lover was taken from me like that, I wouldn't be the kindest, especially if you were on the road to get married and start a family. Her anger is justified, she just needs to start healing."

"You're preaching to the choir." Rue muttered.

"I'm sure... If you ask, the other Reapers will tell you about your mom, hell Jasper could probably tell you, they know their Reapers well."

She looked at me with red puffy eyes, she sniffed and wiped at her eyes. I grabbed a tissue box for her and sat it on her lap.

"Maybe it'll give you some closure..."

"I'm...I'm really not allowed around other Reapers.."

"Excuse me?" I asked in disbelief.

Rue shrugged, "I told you, she's bitter."

"Hm..." I leaned back and grabbed my phone, and spoke into it, "Hey Ibis, look up Ravona Genevieve."

She blinked in confusion and raised a brow. I looked through the articles and found an old one and pulled it up for her and sent it to her phone.

"My dad knew her." I smiled gently. She looked at her phone and read over the article, her eyes began to well again, I rubbed her shoulder in a comforting manner, she scrolled through the article and covered her face, a picture of her on the screen, She was a buffer woman, She has long dark pink hair and bright pink eyes. There was a moon shaped birthmark around one of her eyes and she was in her Reaper uniform. I pulled her into a gentle hug as she sobbed quietly.

Same pink hair and bright eyes as her mom, same warm smile, and her birthmark makes more sense now. I breathed out and rubbed her arm, shuddering uncomfortably as her tears hit my neck.

"I'm sorry... Thank you.." Rue grabbed a tissue.

"You're welcome. I'm really sorry for your loss Rue, I hope your month goes well, even if your mom isn't around. If you need anything you're free to come here."

"Thanks." She nodded.

I blinked slowly, a sudden wave of exhaustion washed over me, I shook my head and stood, making my way to the kitchen. As soon as I took a step the room began to spin, everything was disoriented, I felt my body collapse against the archway.

What is happening?

I moved my hand to my nose, it was bleeding.

"Wha… the hell?" I felt my words slur together. Before I knew it my body was falling forward.

"Aubrey!?"

25

TWENTY-FOUR

Few weeks before

It's hot, incredibly hot. I fanned my face gently and followed the taller male through the grand Hermes portal, shocked it still works. We got to a giant gate, a three headed dog was detailed into the gates, they were a bit rusted from use and probably bird waste. The lava had a dim glow to it and a small ambient noise as it flowed below us. It's so hot. A drastic difference from the chill on the surface.

My water won't be at much use here huh?

The Valley.

I looked around and took in my surroundings, Is this really where he ended up? A place like this? There were many formations from the lava, the rocks seemed to float around each other like islands, all occupying different things. It's huge. It's so otherworldly compared to the surface, a long beautiful trail streamed and weaved between and through all the rock formations. It had a stunning blue glow to it. Although it was bigger than expected, it was a sleepy little place. I assumed everything would be on fire, but in a crime scene way, not a literal way.

"Adonys..." I spoke up gently, the taller male glanced his bright crystal gray eyes at me, his skin had a subtle glow, he must be at home in this climate. His tail dragged on the ground behind him. He had his black hair pulled out of his face, a few stubborn strands rested against his forehead.

"Yes." Adonys stated, His eyes and sandy freckles shined in the dim lighting.

"You're sure..? This is where he is?" I asked cautiously. He gave a firm nod and opened the creaky gate for me.

"I saw her head this way after leaving the lab, it's only a matter of time before he shows up. If she figured it out, he might've too." Adonys spoke, he let the heavy gate slam closed behind us.

I looked over the cliffs and down at the spread out towns, it's like its own country, placed like an island in a volcano, how did he end up in such a place?

Adonys pointed towards the horizon, "Jonas, the scent is heading that way."

I nodded gently, he wasted no time and jumped down the jagged rocks. I followed close behind and landed on the ground below. I felt my eyes narrow in annoyance, if he's been here this whole time, why wasn't I notified? It took tracking Medusa to stumble upon him? How long has he been here? What will I say when I see him? Will he even remember me? Does he even know about himself?

I dropped my gaze to the dark brown rocks, he'd be so at home here with all this earth.

I still remember when he was created. Scorpio 31st, his final chaos injection, he opened his deep purple eyes for the first time, he couldn't talk, he couldn't comprehend, just look. He was beautiful. From there I *knew* he'd be the death of me, I saw our whole lives flash before our eyes. I would feed him, hold him, change him, spoil him. The whole nine yards. He'd smell like a brand new baby. His new skin would be so soft and his little cries would break my heart.

Then I remembered where we resided.

That sick man did it, *he made him.* He replicated *her* perfectly. He got what he wanted. How sick is that? Not only did he capture her likeness, he got him to *live*.

I remember staring him down, I felt so many emotions that day. Proud of my new sibling, then sorrow for the life he'll be given, to horror at the life he'd live. *He actually did it.*

Adonys had a horrified look in his sunken eyes, this is what all of this was for? Our suffering was for his new plaything, what about us now? Are we to be discarded, is this new being going to be a doll for nothing more than play? That thought made my stomach churn.

He was no more than a baby when the raid happened. Everything was destroyed, we were taken and he was left behind. So small and defenseless. I for sure thought he perished. His incubation was cut off and no one was there to complete him. Was it truly over? No way right? All that work, all those years of research, down the drain? No way he'd accept the end. He'd just start over right? I wasn't too far off.

We're considered abominations. We're illegal beings, considered crimes against the gods, Jezabelle the most. I assumed we'd be killed by now. The Summit would never allow us to survive, nor him. Not only did he defy Jezabelle, he did something despicable to a Goddess. Maybe that's why the raid happened, the gods requested it.

I wasn't made when all of his crimes began, but even if I wasn't programmed too, I could see the errors here. Nothing about this was humane, not only was it a crime. It was completely immoral. He was nothing more than a deranged obsessed person who wouldn't drop his foolish pride. They say pride is the deadliest and the creator of all sins. When one's pride is wounded, let alone crushed, it leads people to do unspeakable things.

His pride was crushed by a Goddess. What did he reasonably expect though right? What would a Goddess, *his maker*, see in him? What did he think? He'd confess his love and she'd be flattered and honored? You foolish ***disgusting*** man. You ruined so many lives over your delusions. You even managed to ruin mine, in the end he was taken from me. I felt an undoubted connection to him. I guess that's a given considering my DNA helped create him. I felt like a bird with an untimely empty nest. Like a predator came and destroyed all my eggs while I looked away for a second.

Years passed by before I received that letter. I always assumed he was gone. Adonys was reluctant, but it was photos of him, the same bright eyes and red hair. He's so big now. Adonys tried to talk me out of it but the more I looked at the photos the more my heart ached. I have to find him. It might not be a main priority over the children we saved, but it's still on my list of priorities. I **have** to find him. I'm his family, what if he needs me? And if he doesn't need me, well, I want to meet him. I need to know, what is he like? What does he do? Has he been safe? Does he have a family?

Will he like me?

I felt Adonys' warm hand pressing against mine, I met his gorgeous eyes. "We can still turn back, at the end of the day, the others are more important."

I glanced down at our hands and pulled away, "It's this way right."

"...Yes."

I'm finding my brother, I've put this much time and energy into him, I'm not giving up so easily. He's practically right there. And If I can help it, he will never get sent back there, especially by Medusa. I'll kill her before she ever got the chance.

We headed into the closest island, a lava river flowed directly down the middle of the beautiful town. There were tons of stores, beautifully built bridges and worn down stone streets. It felt so cozy here. Everything was so calming, I've never felt so at peace, is this what death is like for people? Warm and comforting? Just a long peaceful sleep?

I looked at the lava stream and felt uneasy, it's everywhere.

"This way." Adonys took the lead.

We made our way through the small town, Ravens and Crows sat perched on the gateway, cawing and staring down curiously, their beady red eyes seemed to hyper focus on us, like we didn't belong. The smaller birds were comforting though, something about them made me feel safe and comfortable? I've never been around Crows or Ravens before, I find them a bit unnerving considering where they reside. I dropped my gaze and gripped the bottom of Adonys' shirt. He slowed his pace and stayed close to me.

A few Demons passed us by, most were working and

others minding their own. Others waiting for the ferry or in line to rent a boat. The stores here were somewhat full, these Demons look strange to me though. Unlike the Demons on the surface, the ones here looked ethereal. A lot of them had fiery palettes while the others had starry aesthetics. Some of them had dark blue skin with stunning shimmering stars lining their bodies. No where near the grotesque creepers from the surface. Is this a new class of Demon? Or are they indeed not a monolith? *Strange. It's pretty lively for a graveyard isn't it?*

"We need to be quick, this heat isn't good for you." Adonys spoke up.

"I'm fine, just sniff her out big guy." I responded, fanning my face quickly before dropping my hand. Adonys turned his head to me and narrowed his eyes. The lava showing off his frown lines.

He went to open his mouth as if to protest then shook his head. He huffed quietly and turned his head towards a building, following a trail.

Adonys, no last name. I remember when we met the first time, He was so small back then, malnourished, sleep deprived, another one of that sick fuckers experiments. He was a trafficked Dragon if I recall correctly. He always had ways to steal a child, said their brains were easier to manipulate, easier to forgive. The amount of children he's caged and killed… all so he can make a meat puppet. All that death, all that pain, and it was all for *nothing*.

Adonys was his 64th subject. He put him through trials, altered his DNA, ruined his body. He couldn't have been anymore than twelve. Project Sleeping Beauty, want to guess why? He was curious if he could push a body to the brink of sleep deprivation. Every time Adonys was on the verge of death, he'd just revive him. Give him a day too cool off, then went right back to depriving him of sleep.

Adonys says he can't remember the last time he's slept, but he always feels like he's dreaming. I'm not entirely sure what that means. Sleep deprivation has a lot of side effects for their Earthborn bodies. Unlike myself, I have no need for sleep. But for Adonys, it caused cognitive issues, he can't function on par with other people his age at the time. He was prone to sickness more, so I had to clean his room often. He felt pain all the time too. He was just struggling.

One day his heart just stopped. I panicked. I didn't know what to do. He was the only kid around my age and he was always so sweet to me, he was the only friend I had left. I cried for the first time at that. I tried to fix him. I don't know what killed him, if it was the sleep deprivation symptoms, the sicknesses, or just pure exhaustion. I couldn't tell. I just cradled him in my arms and kept trying to wake him up. Father berated me when he saw me. He never taught me about death or how to prevent it. He revived him and he looked almost disappointed. Is this where he would've ended up? Here in The Valley? Would he have been happier here?

He said he didn't have enough time to see his Reaper, he saw nothing but darkness then that man's face.

After that he took his experiments a step further. I don't know what he did, but I could hear him screaming in agony for hours. It terrified me. I tried to calm the other children and take my mind off my friend's suffering. It didn't help, it was so gut wrenching. It made me feel sick to my stomach hearing such guttural screams come from him. Afterwards, he was unconscious in his room, laying on the cold damp floor. I wanted to check on him but father wouldn't let me. That was probably the longest time Adonys has ever slept in a long while.

I waited until father left for the night and snuck into his room. He was still asleep, his body looked different though. I couldn't quite pinpoint it. He had a glittery shine to him under the artificial lights. I kneeled next to him and laid his head on my lap. When I touched him, his body shifted like sand in a bowl. It felt disturbing. Just yesterday he was a solid boy. Now his flesh was squishy and shifting in my hands? I held him regardless. I tried to keep all the sand falling from him gathered together just in case he needed it.

When he woke up, that broke my heart. Heartbreak is so painful.

He screamed again, but this time it wasn't in pain. It was in pure and unfiltered anguish. He just kept asking over and over *"Midas! Where are my wings! Where are my wings! I can't feel my wings!"* I didn't have an answer for him. He sobbed for hours in my lap after that.

Project Sleeping Beauty was considered a *success*.

What a sick individual, how twisted is it to ruin children based on their favorite fairy tales? He always asked, he'd give them treats, ask them what their favorite fairy tale was, sedate them, then turn them into what they used to love.

Adonys was special though, he was a step closer to his wanted perfection. At Least that's how he explained it. He completely altered his body's cells, he's no longer bone and flesh, but sand. He glimmered in small lighting, flowed so effortlessly, at the cost of his wings and horns. A Dragon's pride. He was never quite the same after that.

Then there's me. I am Project Midas, the 40th subject. I was one of the only ones who survived and took to his alterations, because he made me from nothing. I'm a Homunculus, no soul, no clearance, no humanity. Just a test doll. He said since I came out so well, he's getting closer. He used me and my DNA since then, and now, Aubrey exists. His perfect doll, the one he did all of this for. I secretly hoped he'd be found, we'd be killed, and everything in those labs were forgotten. He ruined so many lives because he wanted to play god. Or get back at one. Who knows. His reasoning won't fix what he broke.

But of course we weren't so lucky.

After the raids, most of the children who got away couldn't survive, be it their biology was so destroyed they couldn't eat or drink, they gave up, or they had no survival instincts. Then there were the kids he was able to salvage. I looked for them for years, I figured Aubrey was a lost cause, so why not take care of those that are currently here right?

Then I got that letter.

"Jonas." Adonys spoke up, I blinked in surprise, his face inches from mine. He placed a cloth to my nose and shook his head, "No good. We're going back."

"No." I softly protested, "We need to find her, even if this is a lost cause, she can still tell us where the labs are. Either way we can help them, Vixen can handle it on her own." I motioned him away, he immediately stepped back but kept his lips pursed.

Even after all that, He's healed pretty well. His Dragon genes certainly kicked in as we matured. He got taller, took up exercising as a hobby and he helps me keep the kids safe. As long as that man is still alive and another lab is being run, those children aren't safe. No children are safe.

"Do you smell her anywhere?"

"It stops here, too many smells to pinpoint her…" Adonys spoke softly, he rubbed his nose and slid his eyes away from me in shame.

"I understand." I scanned the crowd around us, too lively. "Can you hear anything?"

"Just white noise." He cupped his ear and shook his head once more.

"Great…"

"Jonas." Adonys spoke up, "I need you to at least look after your health, stay on top of your water intake. Please."

"I'm fine, I will."

So worried. He always will be I suppose. Like it wasn't me always keeping him as safe as I could. I guess since we're older and he hit his growth spurt he decided the tables should turn. I certainly don't need the protection, but I'm flattered he cares so much, so I let his overprotectiveness slide from time to time. He's so cute when he's worried and serious. His face softens when he's worried about me, it's the least guarded I've seen him aside from small glimpses of him when I'm half asleep.

I blinked and looked up as a smell overtook me. A faint smell of hazelnut and pine? It was hard to pinpoint but I could tell from Adonys' subtle sniff and ear point that it's distinct. I stopped in my tracks on the sidewalk, ignoring the other Demons scoffing and moving around us. Adonys towered over most of the population here, they wouldn't dare raise an issue with me.

I scanned the crowd, I sniffed the air once more to try and catch it again. Adonys' eerie quiet told me it had to be him. In the crowd, across the river from us was a red haired boy. Even from here I could see his deep shining purple eyes. His hair was in locs and pulled into a low ponytail, he was in a compression shirt, his freckles were darker from the lava, maybe the sun he experienced on the surface?

I felt an immediate wave of calm wash over me, I wanted to desperately call his name. But at the time I didn't know it. He didn't have a name in the lab, just his Project name. No doubt he'd ignore such a goofy title. I put my hand to my chest and tried to ignore the welling feeling in my eyes. He's actually here. He's right there. *I desperately want to close the distance, but he doesn't know you. Be smart about this Jonas, don't make any hasty decisions.*

I wiped at my cheeks and sniffed quietly before nodding my head approvingly, I'll wait. I can wait. He's alive, that's all that matters, and he is here, that's all that matters.

* * *

"There you are." I spoke with venom. Looking down at her with malice. *Medusa.*

The petite snake haired girl jumped in shock, she looked up at us with confusion. "Midas. Beauty. Thought you died." Medusa grunted out holding her shoulder, Adonys led us straight to her.

"Good. We're gonna make sure your boss feels the same." I crossed my arms.

Medusa scoffed and collapsed against the building, her clothes were roughed up, her sleeves were a bit dirty and her jacket was falling off her shoulder. Her snakes rested elegantly past her shoulders, seemingly asleep. Guess she got into a little scuffle before us.

"You don't think I can send a message in death?" She scowled.

"Of course not, you're the failed Project remember."

She growled at that.

"The hell are you doing here, you stick out like a sore thumb you know. Especially with those disgusting snakes slithering around."

"Yea. Wouldn't you like to know." Medusa muttered. I hopped down from the roof, Adonys quickly following, he landed on the fire escape, the loud thud echoing in the alley. The vibrations slowly ceased as he perched there, staring down at her, I landed directly in front of her and kneeled to her level.

"Yes, I would." I moved my gloved thumb over her cheek, "Bit roughed up hm? Who did you bump into."

She moved her brown fingers to my wrist and tossed my hand aside, her hair hissing in retaliation. "Don't touch me."

"Why not?" I asked, moving my hands in front of me, "Why are you here.." I slowly slipped the gloves off my golden fingers, she instinctively pressed back against the wall.

"Hm." Adonys narrowed his eyes at her, watching her snakes intently.

"Is it Project EF." I stated.

She fell silent.

"Is. It. Project EF." I repeated harshly

She turned her head away, her snakes hissing lowly, "I'm just the exterminator."

I narrowed my eyes darkly and moved my hand towards

her, her snake went to bite but she pulled it down immediately.

She slid herself up the wall and dusted off her suit, "But hey, if you happen to find it, do tell me." She pushed past.

I immediately lunged at her with my free hand. As soon as my foot landed on the ground I felt myself stumble into the wall, I groaned a bit as the brick began to turn gold.

"Oh really." I pushed off the bricks and winced.

"I'm defending myself Midas. I underestimated one opponent, I won't do it again." Medusa turned her head to me and quickly put space between us.

I stood straight while staring her down then lunged at her once more, same trick pony, I flipped and grabbed her shoulder with my gloved hand and pushed her to the ground, she summoned more arrows and forced me back, I stumbled to my feet then felt my body jerk against another wall, I groaned in pain as it scratched up my shirt. *For fucksake I just sewed it!*

Alright, fine. I pushed off the brick once more and put my hand out, *it should be enough*. Water began to slip from my canisters, floating around me, she backed up instinctively and I hardened the water to ice instantly and began shooting them towards her, she tried to block, the spikes shattered against the ground and wall. Medusa summoned another arrow and propelled herself up then over towards the wall, running up it before Adonys could grab her. I growled lowly and wrapped the water around her foot dragging her back down, Medusa and her snakes hissed out in pain and she yelped as she landed on the ground.

"Where is the facility?" I demanded, freezing the water over her ankle.

"What are you talking about!" Medusa groaned, looking over her shoulder.

"Where is he? I know that's why you're tracking him down."

"I'm not at liberty to disclose that information." Medusa kicked the ground towards me and sent me back with another arrow, I anchored myself and stopped the motion, groaning in pain. Adonys jumped down but she sent him towards the walls, her hair began to grow and hiss, she got to her feet and breathed out.

She reached for her glasses and I instinctively looked away, freezing the ground under her making her slip. I hopped up and dove to attack, she rolled aside and elbowed me in my ribs, I groaned in annoyance and gathered the water back around me.

Make this quick Jonas, you're low on water.

she grabbed her gun from her pocket and fired. I dodged as quickly as I could and caught the bullets in a case of ice, and sent it back, Medusa blocked and growled, aiming her gun once more. I ran down and tripped her up, freezing the water around her, she groaned and fell to the side, I huffed out and walked over to her.

"I will only tell you this once, stay away from Project EF. If I see you again, I will kill you. Information be damned."

"Tch, I wouldn't tell you anything anyway." Medusa growled, her hair hissing and chipping at the ice.

"Stay away from him."

Adonys walked over and towered over us both. I melted the water from her and placed the small amount I had left back in my pouch. That was a rash move, I'm limited on supply here and it evaporated quickly. I sighed and walked off with him. He placed a hand on my upper back.

"She knows you're bluffing, we need to know where that facility is. Just, be calm alright?"

I groaned quietly, "Yea, whatever."

26

TWENTY-FIVE

I groaned in annoyance, *of course Midas and her lapdog had to be here*. I knew that damn letter was too risky. I walked down the sidewalk, clothes still soaked. I just want him dead, is that so much to ask? I guess so. Now he has body guards. He's definitely going to be harder to take care of than I expected. But he's certainly Project EF, looks exactly like her, and he wants it back.

What's even so special about you, I felt my eyes narrow and twitch in annoyance.

I want Project EF, I need Project EF, you are pathetic, useless, a waste of space, how many times do I have to tell your talentless ass. I NEED Project EF.

Project EF.

Project EF.

Project EF.

Project EF.

I let out a guttural scream and slammed my fist against the building. Project EF, what the hell makes you so special. You're nothing but a gutter rat playing house, what does he want you for? I can decipher any and all poisons, I'm immune, I'm intelligent, I'm strong, a perfect representation of everything he stands for yet? He still only cares about Project EF. Even after all these years. You're an abomination he created, something so illegal your death is imminent when you're found out. You have no soul, no purpose aside from being a plaything. You aren't Earthborn. And yet.

I groaned quietly as a few stitches popped, I gripped my wrist and groaned.

I guess you don't fall apart like I do, I guess you look like her *unlike me*. Your formula is probably perfectly balanced, *unlike me*. You aren't related to him like me. I cradled my wrist and gripped at the disgusting flesh, the bone worn down from all the years of exposure. Fuck, it's deeper this time. *Fuck*. I can't fucking think. All this damn noise.

"Shut up!" I growled, putting my hand up and silencing the insufferable hissing in my ears, I dropped my head back against the wall and closed my eyes. I'm wasting too much time. He'll try to reach out soon. He might replace me with another Homunculi. That's no good. I need him dead before then. It took me too long to find him that first time. This place is significantly bigger than I expected, I didn't send enough snakes out and they aren't growing back fast enough to send more.

I stumbled my way down the sidewalk. It's hot here. *Disgustingly so*. My heels clicked on the pavement as I trudged towards my hotel. It's a nice place though. And that makes me sick.

He got to live here? All these years? I was hoping he'd be dead. But no, he's alive. As well as ever. How frustrating. Why do you get to be saved and taken care of while I had to suffer in a cell I treated as a room. You got pampered and I got tormented. Oh congratulations you abomination.

I took my time going up the stairs, holding my wrist to my chest tightly, careful to not draw attention. I lazily used the key and used my body weight to push the door open and sat against the beige wall. I narrowed my eyes at the dirty brown carpet and dropped my head against it.

All that crosses my mind is, *How lucky are you? To be so desired, so loved, so protected*. Midas barely even knows you yet she's willing to protect you like this, while he's willing to neglect and send me off to get you back. He's willing to start another experiment period just to recreate you. How lucky are you.

I remember when you were made, I was no older than 5, before the raid began I heard him shouting in glee, while my mother lay rotting away in the bed upstairs, he couldn't have cared less. She was just another body to him, and so was I. The experiments began after that raid. He scooped me up in his arms and fled, I thought things would be different, oh boy was I wrong. I heard in the news that my mother finally succumbed to her sickness, he could barely remember her name. He looked at me and said, "W*ho?*"

He was cruel, every moment I've had close to death, he'd shock me back to life. I begged and pleaded and prayed I'd meet my first Reaper, but he'd never let that happen, I was too good of an opportunity to pass up, he says. His own flesh and blood that he can experiment on with zero repercussions? My body was a candy store for his childish self. *How disgusting.* All he did was take from me and foolishly expected me to be grateful for it.

I wasn't good enough though, the novelty wore off.

"Why can't you be more like Project EF, you aren't perfect, you are a disgrace."

Nothing was enough, nothing. I couldn't go to school, so I had to teach myself. I learned to read? *Well Project EF could've done it faster*, I learned to write, *Project EF would've done it better*, I grew an immunity to animal poisons, *Project EF would just tame the animals*, I made it to my 15th birthday, *well Project EF would have lasted forever*.

Project EF. Yea, *be Project EF or be nothing.*

I guess I'm nothing.

I pushed myself up to my feet and headed in the bathroom, tending to the scrapes on my face, the snakes sat quietly against my skin, their cold scales warmer from the climate, I placed my glasses on the sink and splashed my face and looked at my eyes. All of this because of Project EF. Just for me to be regarded as a failure. As nothing.

You are nothing.

You're barely a ghost. You are an abomination, a crime against the gods, you can't even fall in love, no one will ever want you, everyone will just die, the moment they look you in your disgusting eyes. He took so much from me, I can't even recognize my own face. I remember I was a brown skin girl, my mother was from the Middle Eastern region. I used to look just like her. She used to brush and braid my long beautiful hair. She told me I had the prettiest eyes she's ever seen. Now all I see is disgusting modifications. Scales, reptilian eyes, discolored skin, covered in bites and stitches. My body is on its last legs.

I bet Project EF doesn't have this problem.

I laughed quietly to myself in an annoyed scoff. *Comparison*, he's so happy here it makes me sick. He looks like he doesn't have a care in the world. Seeing his disappointment when he got to the facility was wonderful, but now I need to see him dead. I want the life to drain from his eyes so I can gleefully report that his perfect, precious Project is dead.

Won't be too perfect if it falls to a failure like me.

I took a breath and began tending to my wrist, I refreshed the stitches and slowly watched it begin its healing process. Once I got feeling back in my fingers, I grabbed a towel and patted my face. I have to be smarter, I can't be as reckless as I was. He's stronger than I expected, I'll keep my distance. Maybe poison will do the trick? A few more bites? Just for good measure. He can't still be alive after the bullet and bite right? I tapped my chin in thought.

I should check, you can never be too sure right?

I turned up the air and closed the blinds. This isn't the best environment for me. Summers on the surface? Sure. Staying in the middle of a volcano? Yea I'll pass. I sat on the old rickety bed and groaned in pain as I slowly detached one of my snakes, letting it slither on the ground. I used the towel to pat the blood.

"Find him, if he's dead come back." The snake hissed and slithered under the door, "Dammit."

I plopped down against the hard pillow. This is certainly a challenge.

27

TWENTY-SIX

"Aubrey."

"Aubrey wake up."

I groaned quietly, my eyes slowly began focusing, *fuck*. My head feels heavy. I could hear muffled talking around me, a few panicked words and muffled barks. My skin felt like it was on fire. Oh gods, am I sick? I tried to touch my nose but couldn't feel my hands. My body felt incredibly heavy and hot. *Oh, that ain't normal.* I tried to roll and sit up, but my head still felt heavy. What the hell happened?

"Aubrey!" I blinked and focused my eyes on Jonas, her bright brown eyes glimmered, but they were worried, Rue was panicking behind her.

"Huh..? Jonas...?" I squinted. Jonas pulled me up and adjusted my position then pulled me into a tight hug, which caused me even more confusion. Her fingers gripped tightly on my shirt, I just realized my jacket isn't on anymore. Then why am I still so hot?

"I-I'm sorry Aubrey she just burst in here and tried to inject you with something, I tried to stop her-" Rue said quickly.

"Inject-?" I asked, I wanted to push her back by her shoulders but my arms refused to move. Jonas pulled away herself and placed her hand on my forehead and frowned. Her gloved satin hands gave a slight chill, but it didn't last long. I held back an annoyed groan. I hope I don't have a fever, I'm so uncomfortable.

"Trust me. It's going to help." Jonas pulled a syringe from her pocket. I shot my eyes at her, they narrowed in warning but what the hell could I do? I tried to move away from her but my body barely fell an inch away.

"I don't think so." I muttered out.

"Aubrey, trust me." Jonas basically pleaded.

"He said no. You need to leave." Rue spoke up. Strangely, Iron wasn't on guard, he was completely calm, he'd bark and growl at Rue, but not Jonas? I watched him, he kept his eyes on me and didn't even flinch when Jonas moved towards me or touched me. What the hell is going on? This ain't like him. Is she safe?

"If anyone should leave, it's you." Jonas bit back.

"And leave you with an inebriated person to take advantage of!? I don't think so!" Rue spoke firmly.

The room is still spinning, why can I hear my blood in my ears? I groaned quietly and laid my head back against the couch, my breathing suddenly felt heavier, it felt like something sitting on my chest and crushing my windpipe. What is happening? *Am I dying*? I could feel the blood trickle down my nose once more. *Oh gods, I think I'm dying.*

My eyes stared blankly at the ceiling, their bickering was drowned out by white noise, I could barely feel Iron licking at my fingers. I tried to move my fingers once more, but nothing. My vision isn't clearing up either. *What is happening?* I feel like my body is shutting down? This has never happened before? Why do I feel so tired now? I blinked heavily and tried to focus, but all I could see were specs in my vision, everything looked like it had a gray film over it. Oh this ain't good, I knew my vision was bad but not this bad?

My head slowly began to turn to the side, I couldn't stop it. It's so heavy...

"Aubrey! Hey hey look at me honey-" I could feel Jonas' satin gloves cup my cheeks and she tilted my head to look at her, she seemed panicked now. "I'll explain, I promise I will, I just need you to trust me." Her voice sounded distressed and cracked like she was holding back tears.

Rue backed off after that. I could faintly hear Iron beginning to whine next to me.

Oh.. so I am going to die? Without getting to say goodbye to my dad first? I wonder what he's doing right now? Did he get enough metal mined? Is he on the way back? I can't even check my phone. What will they do without me, him and Iron? Would Mateo take care of him? Would they be content without me? Oh gods I'd hurt him. *Oh gods, And Saint?*

I jolted at a sudden shock through my body, my eyes began to water. I coughed harshly and doubled over in pain. *Actual intense pain.* That's new, and I'm not too fond of it. I grabbed at my chest once I felt my fingers move. I felt tears stream down my cheeks after every deep breath.

"It's Ok, it's Ok, lay down, give it time to work." Jonas soothed, laying me back down against the cushions. Rue gasped behind her. Iron whined and pawed at my stomach, his puppy eyes wide and worried, *I'm sorry.. I don't know what's happening either..*

I turned my head back up at the ceiling, my eyes still felt heavy. My vision slowly cleared up. Not by much. I blinked slowly and tried to calm my breathing.

"It's Ok.. It's alright.." Jonas breathed out and collapsed to her knees, dropping her head in her hands, "I'm so sorry, I was almost too late.."

"What the hell just happened, what did you do?" I mumbled, another heavy blink.

I shifted my heavy eyes towards Jonas, she kept her head down, face buried in her gloves, I could hear faint sniffs coming from her. Almost like she was relieved, *what the hell is going on*. I slowly flicked my eyes towards the door as the lock clicked, Iron's ears perked and he sat up, tail wagging.

"Aubrey?? I'm home!" Tartarus spoke up, tossing his keys in the bowl, Iron gave a small whimper bark but stayed close. I tried to turn my gaze to him but I still felt so tired. I tried to move my shoulder in an attempt to stretch but I feel so weak. I groaned quietly.

"Aubrey??" He walked down the hall and into the room. I tried to respond but could only muster another harsh coughing fit.

He dropped his bags and rushed over, tossing his gloves aside, "Aubrey!?"

His voice was panicked, I tried to calm my cough and looked up at him through heavy lids.

"I.."

He used his thumb to wipe the blood off my face and cupped my cheeks protectively. "What the fuck is going on here, who are you people."

TWENTY-SIX

Rue cowered back while Jonas hopped to her feet and took a step back, she quickly bowed her head in respect. Dad's body temperature was rising, his palms began to heat up my cheeks. He's defensive, I groaned and shook my head.

"M-my name is Jonas." She spoke quickly, "Aubrey was... He wasn't Ok, I helped.."

"What do you mean he wasn't Ok, his heart rate is low, he's bleeding and he's having a coughing fit." Tartarus let my face go gently and got to his feet, stepping between us protectively. Again, Iron wasn't on edge. He was eerily calm, even if he was worried for me, he wouldn't ignore dad's hostility like this. I could feel another cough brewing and the dryness in my throat isn't helping. I need water. I lifted my arm slightly off the couch.

"W...ater.." I croaked out.

Rue nodded and hurried to the kitchen, but dad didn't move, just clenched his fists.

"I.." Jonas cleared her throat as Rue hurried over, helping me drink, I could feel my body slowly functioning again. I weakly sat up, gripping dad's wrist, I gently tugged him so he'd look down at me.

"D-Dad...It's.. It's fine." I motioned to Jonas, "They're both school mates."

He narrowed his eyes and shot them a look. I pet Iron gently as he laid his head on my lap, whining quietly.

"What happened, Aubrey."

"I, I don't know.. I was talking to Rue.. then I got dizzy..I tried to get water but.."

"You passed out, you had a really bad nose bleed and you were really warm, warmer than usual.." Rue squeaked out, "Then she burst in, yelling at me to get away from you and started saying she had to inject you before it was too late."

"Inject." Dad echoed.

"Jonas." I slid my eyes over towards her, "I suggest you start explaining."

"I… My.. My real name, Is Project Midas." Jonas spoke bowing once more, I could see dad visibly tense, his hands and jaw immediately clenched.

"I'm your sister." Jonas looked at me, I blinked in confusion then surprise.

"What..?"

"We share DNA, um, you're a Homunculus right?" Jonas smiled gently, "I gave you an adrenaline shot, a little bit of electricity essence, uh, magic. Y'know? Like doctors use in the paddles?" She began to ramble. She dropped her hands in front of her and dropped her head in defeat, " I.. I didn't know what to do. It took all these years to find you, I can't lose you again."

"What are you talking about?"

"I…" She glanced at Rue, dad did too. I eventually looked at her as well. She isn't supposed to know. She was justly confused but kept to herself.

"I'm not sure what you're on about, but both of you need to leave." Tartarus growled out. He was on the verge of attacking.

"Wait!" Jonas quickly put her hands up, she quickly removed her gloves. Her hands were a bright shimmering gold, now that I'm seeing her in the light, her skin had a gold sparkle to it too, her eyes were two toned, like mine. She rolled up her sleeve and something was tattooed there. *'PM8'*

My sister? Is that why Iron wasn't concerned?

"You know exactly what I'm talking about, you were in the raid. That's how you found Aubrey right." Jonas spoke carefully.

I looked at my dad and back at Jonas, "Were you the one who sent me the letter…?" I asked quietly.

"Letter? What letter?" She asked.

"Four years ago, I got a letter telling me to go to the location of a lab. It was abandoned, no one was there, I never met who sent it."

"That's why you were on the surface..?" Jonas asked quietly, "I didn't send a letter, but, because you came up there, I was able to find out you were alive."

"Then who sent the letter?" Dad spoke up.

"I, I'm not sure.."

"Bullshit." Tartarus growled. He was on edge, "Who else knows about him."

Jonas took a moment to answer, "… Another one of the Homunculi." She spoke quietly and looked down, "He's still looking for Aubrey. He sent his daughter after you."

"Who?" I asked.

"Father."

28

TWENTY-SEVEN

"Tartarus, are you sure you can handle this?" Aides asked, I nodded to him. His presence was like a black cloud. His hand rested gently on my shoulder and I fought the urge to tense up. When he entered The Valley the cold front came in. Everywhere he goes a snowstorm follows. The walls began to frost over and the temperature dropped significantly, even I got a chill.

His voice was deep and commanding but he spoke gently to me.

"Jezabelle won't be happy if something happens to you. Understood?" Aides asked, his bright starry eyes stared directly at me, he gripped my shoulder reassuringly.

"Yes." I said quietly, "It shouldn't be too bad, sir."

Aides hummed and turned his head forward, the outside light illuminating half of his face under his black veil. He was in all black nowadays, mourning Lady Jezabelle. His sister.

"The intel says he should be on the surface, destroy all of it, I don't want Jezabelle knowing anything about these abominations, and bring that man to me. He will be tried for his crimes."

"Understood." I got to my feet, Aides nodded, his elegant hair flowing around him, his chiseled face was contorted in disgust, he dropped his hand to his side and directed his gaze aside.

"Why she made these creatures is above me. The things they do and come up with. New ways to *hurt* her. Now you make a mockery of her talents? *How disgraceful.*" He spoke bitterly, Aides. The God of Death, Death itself. He's a lot of things, Smart, deadly, sadistic, precise, and a good brother.

I was created by them. Mainly Jezabelle and *Terra,* with minor help from Aides. Jezabelle raised me as her own, and Aides treated me as his nephew. I was a successful Project for Terra. Creation from the very nature they adored, blessed with divinity, I was a trial. I was her claim to fame, the first being she ever made, I really help solidify her place as a Goddess. Jezabelle was so proud.

Sometime after my creation, Jezabelle fell ill. He's been angry ever since, he's more exhausted every time I see him. I know he was very excited to put an end to this immediately. One less pest, and maybe she'll wake up.

He's her polar opposite, unlike Jezabelle, He ran off and got married and started a family that way. While Jezabelle created all her children from her natural resources. Jezabelle created Terra, and Terra created the Earthens. With Jezabelle's encouragement and praise. He respected and cherished his sister and her daughter's creations but even then he had to put limitations, which is why he's regarded so poorly by the Earthens. He gives them short life spans, especially after their centuries long antics that caused Jezabelle's sickness to begin with. He says he always advised against them but his sister was so adamant, of her daughter's creations. She was so proud, and he couldn't tell her no.

He encouraged Terra to help make me as a test, carved from volcanic rock, cooked in lava, showered in ash and brought to life. That's how she and Terra explained it anyway. Terra was more than eager to help, she was the first thing I saw. Terra bragged about helping Jezabelle create me. She says I'm basically her son too. Maybe that's why she was so soft on me? Why she was so comfortable and happy with me? I looked up to her, I loved her dearly. Just for all of this to happen.

Maybe if I wasn't such a success, she wouldn't have wanted to make the Earthens next? Maybe if I wasn't here, maybe none of this would've happened?

I know Aides has regrets, he never, none of us ever… none of us thought a mere Earthen would get so bold. So arrogant and foolish to do something so heinous. I shook my head and tried to focus on the point at hand.

"You might gain another prisoner if I see it fit." Aides spoke and made his way to the door.

He tried not to show it but he was seething at the moment. His frost betrays him. His voice was dripping with malice. His back was to me, but I can tell his eyes were darker than usual. I understand though, all of us are angry. He's lost a daughter recently, then his niece, My sister. And now he's sending me into this degenerate's lab. I don't doubt my safety, but I know he'll be slippery and at this point, failure isn't an option. What other god could he be planning to do this to?

"…" I watched him go before following him out. The main room was filled with Demons, all suited up and ready to go. One in particular stood out, as he always does, his fluorescent eyes flickered to me.

"Got a stern talking to jail bird?" Levi's deep voice hummed, I glanced towards the taller male, his locs were pulled back, he had a cheesy grin on his face. His goofiness immediately erupted when Aides' presence exited the area.

"Stern?" I echoed, raising my brow.

"Isn't that the only tone his grace knows?" Leviathan chuckled.

"Oh haha. Lets get this shit over with, my orders are backing up by the second." I huffed out, rolling my eyes slightly. He laughed and patted my back.

"Lead the way entrepreneur."

I snorted through my nose and left the room.

Leviathan, the protector of the sea, Mainly Atlantis. He was created by her Goddess Cordelia, a little after I was. We've been friends for as long as I could remember. We both figured a lot of things out together and ended up living in The Valley with Aides. Leviathan isn't a Kovenn though, just works for the family. At least that's how he explained it and no one corrected him. After our school years he fell to the sin of envy. He was one of the first sins I believe, that's something I'm not too educated on. It was certainly a shock when a new city formed in the square and he was the only one allowed in.

He followed close behind and dropped his arm around my shoulders. "You're tense, big guy."

I blinked and glanced towards him, His bright blue eyes were so distracting. They always were to me, they matched the multitude of pearls he adorned. His deep dark skin complimented his blue accessories so well. He's handsome, he always was. And what's more dangerous than a man who knows his worth? I slid my eyes away and I shrugged him off but he didn't budge. He actually pulled me closer.

"Take a breath." Levi moved his arm and made me face him. I looked at him then away, breathing out.

"I'm fine."

"No, you're not. That much is clear." He spoke quietly for once, he's not good with emotions. If it isn't boasting, bragging or aggression he can't express much, he tries with me. He always has. He hesitated but moved his hands down my wrists and took my warm callous hands into his soft ones.

"She was your sister." Levi spoke gently.

I dropped my head. These moments were few and far between, so I knew he wouldn't drop it unless he heard what he wanted. I genuinely tried to not think about what he did. It's bad enough she's not here, I'm in her house and everything reminds me of her. Now I have to confront her stalker and murderer? Someone I failed to protect her from? I'm terrified, not of this man, but of disappointing and failing her a second time. What if we fail this raid? What if jail isn't enough? What if we were too late? The reports were horrific, who knows how many people and lives he's hurt or ruined? Finding out our family wasn't the only one hurt like a motherfucker.

"I just want to get this over with." I muttered.

"I know, but I need your head clear." Levi gripped at my hands, not too much though our body temperatures are very different. "You're in charge tonight."

"Yea. I know that." I went to pull my hands away but he gripped them tighter. I could see a flash of pain in his eyes and I felt a small wave of panic run over me. I tried to pull my hands away.

"Leviathan."

"Look." He said, "Just take a moment. Your family is under a lot of stress and I can tell you're under a lot of pressure. When was the last time we saw your uncle?"

"I don't know."

"A long ass time ago. This shit is serious, I can tell what you're doing and it ain't healthy, love." He said softly. "You read the reports, so did I. I don't need you freezing up when reality hits you."

"I won't, I'm not a child." I finally pulled my hands away, Levi's hands were red and burned on the palms. I immediately felt guilty and went to help him. He put his other hand up to stop me and I watched his hands begin to heal.

"I know you aren't, I know." Levi dropped his hand, "If it gets to be too much, just, tell me? I can stay with you for as long as you need."

"…" I had no words to say. *I just want this to be over.* I want him caught, I want him dealt with and I want to forget about this whole disgusting thing. I just nodded and walked past him. I felt his pitiful stare on my back. He eventually followed behind me.

The raid has been planned for weeks. I was the first brought in and I suggested Levi to back me up because I trust him. Aides didn't mind it, he just wanted this taken care of. Just go in, destroy the documents and equipment. Destroy everything. Leave no trace. He said such a power shouldn't be granted to those lowly insects, especially after Terra's death. I couldn't agree more. They lost all privilege to the art of creation as far as I'm concerned.

Terra's death...Something so heinous and sudden, all because of the lack of regulations, and ignoring the problem instead of cracking down on it. Along with my failure. It took one day. *One time* when I was busy, I couldn't protect her. I'll never forgive myself for that. But the least I could do was find him. But as a creation of Jezabelle and Aides, I can't act unless they demand it. Aides wanted to move smartly about this, so I was forbade from acting on my own. I guess thinking on it now, it was for the best.

I sighed out and rubbed my face then shook my head. *Focus.*

There's no room for error, if this checks out and the intel is good, we'll be able to recover many kidnapped and trafficked children and catch a member of the ring. I couldn't fathom doing something so disgusting. How her creations gained such a dark side is beyond me, it's almost disturbing in a way. And those habits bleed through the land and spread like a virus. Nothing but wars, arguing, hatred, and anger... It's upsetting and if she were alive to see how they turned out, it would break her heart. Terra never would've thought her creations could be this way, let alone one killing her and harming her mother. *What a mess.*

We ended up at a small cabin in the middle of nowhere. It was a lot of open land, probably belonged to some farmers and loaned out. It was pitch black and silent only the quiet sounds of pigs and cicadas. The pigs made my stomach churn. We slowly approached, Still quiet. The inside was dark, not a single movement. I kneeled down to the ground and placed my palms to the grass, closing my eyes. Focusing on the dirt and anything out of place.

The ground has been disturbed, a lot of shifting. "Hm."

"Find something?" Leviathan asked quietly, I nodded.

"Seems to be a bunker, I can feel some type of metal but it's faint."

"Can you flood them out?" He asked.

"Wouldn't be too wise. There could be survivors." I got to my feet, "We need to find a way down there, quickly and quietly without alerting anyone."

Levi flicked his wrist and motioned for the other Demons to search the perimeter.

"Do you actually think those kids are still alive?" He asked

"I'm hoping so, I know there will be child bodies down there. But not all of them could be dead right?"

Levi fell silent.

I wandered around the house, tapping my feet on the ground, looking for a hollow spot. I came to a window, the faint sounds of a TV filled the space between me and the room, I shifted my gaze up and met with dead eyes. A woman, her dark hair was basically falling out in clumps. Her dull brown reptilian eyes were sunken in, looking to the empty fields. Her brown skin was pale, even from here I could smell the death lingering around her. It's only a matter of time.

Her eyes flicked to the side, boring into mine. I broke the stare and looked back at the ground. Hollow enough.

I cleared my throat, "Leviathan."

The taller male made his way over, I split the ground as deep as I could, making enough space for the two of us.

"In the hole."

"Heh, haven't heard that from you in awhile." Levi tried to joke.

I shot him a look and pointed to the hole. He chuckled then turned his gaze towards the window. He made a face before jumping in, I followed quickly behind and led the way, following the heat signatures. There's a good amount of people still in here. And thank gods, it seems they're alive. According to the reports most if not all of these signatures are children, I can't handle seeing tons of dead children. Not tonight, not with this. Then a thought occurred to me. If any of these children died, a Reaper would have reported this location to Jasper, if not Erebus. I narrowed my eyes, well that's somewhat relieving, but also upsetting. These poor children.

"We should be coming up to a metal box soon, I need you to get it open." I mumbled close to his ear.

"Understood." Levi nodded.

I allowed him forward, he pressed his hands on the metal, he began to pull the moisture from the dirt around us and began cutting at the metal, one thing I can't do. I can make lava, move rocks, and make swords. But penetrating metal wasn't something I could figure out. He created a hole big enough for us to get in, I looked over his shoulder and moved around him. It was in fact a giant metal box of a facility. It spans a little past the house radius.

How did he even manage this? I got my hands ready and took the lead, I peeked around the corners and began to look in the different rooms. It was empty, all of it was empty. The rooms weren't clean though, you can tell something happened here. I tried to follow the signatures and motioned Demons to follow me. I carefully turned down the cold and dark halls, the artificial lights weren't doing much. I tried to brace myself for the vision of the kids, but I decided to just let the Demons handle it. I stepped back and motioned to the door and decided to clear the rest of the lab.

It was empty aside from the children. He wasn't here.

I swore under my breath and rubbed my face. *Aides won't be happy.*

"Aye, Tartarus." Levi's voice called down the hall. I turned my head and headed towards him. He was standing in the middle of a room, this one was cleaner than the rest. It was tidied and it was warm, he was here not too long ago. In the center of the room was a giant computer with files on it, *Project EF? What is that?* A few other files were noticeable but I could barely read them. There was a surgery table in the middle of the room and tons of wires leading to a corner.

In it was a baby. It was floating in this yellow liquid, its eyes were closed. It was so tiny, like it was just born? *What is this?*

"What do we do about all of this?" Levi asked.

I couldn't take my eyes off the tank, I had no words. What the hell is he planning? What is this? What does this mean? I was dumbfounded, how did these creatures get this level of intelligence to create life so carelessly like this?

"Tartarus. What do we do?" Levi asked once more.

"I..." I blinked and looked at him, "I don't know, I can't..."

"It's not real." Levi stated. "Don't let it fool you."

"Levi, it's a baby. So clearly." I shot back.

"It's not Earthborn, therefore it's not a baby." He said matter-of-factly.

"..." I looked back at it. It was so innocent, it was peacefully sleeping. I walked over to the tank and examined it. It was certainly high tech for their kind, not on par with Thoth's machinery in any way, but this is still incredibly disturbing.

I narrowed my eyes at the screen on the top. *Incubation twelve percent complete.*

Incubation? I looked back at the tank. It had the same colored hair and skin as Terra, it was so distinct it's hard to not recognize it. I placed my hand on the tank and watched it float there. I felt so many emotions overtake me. Disbelief, anger, sorrow, confusion. All of it. It looks just like her, down to the freckles.

Orders are orders, but I can't bring myself to destroy something so innocent. Why is he even making this?

I can destroy everything else, but I can't. No, I **won't**, Kill a child. No matter the circumstances.

"Leviathan..." Was all I could muster, all I could do was look at him in confusion and longing.

He met my gaze while at the computer. He furrowed his brows then glanced at the screen. It only took him a moment to think about it. He dropped his head and sighed then nodded his head.

"This is foolish." He muttered.

"It looks just like her..." I said, looking back at the tank.

"Seems that's the point." He motioned to the files on the computer. I looked at him. He motioned me over and pointed to the words.

"Project EF, Project number eighty eight, the perfect replica of the Earth Goddess, due to finish incubation in two days, should resemble Project Midas. Success?"

I narrowed my eyes in disgust, the fuck is this sick freak

planning.

"I'm taking it." I pulled out my phone and began snapping pictures of the documents. "He isn't here, this was a bust on that front."

"Tartarus." Levi spoke.

"There's a good number of children here, as far as they're concerned this child is one of them." I walked over and punched through the glass, the machine began to whine and flash red. The yellow liquid spilled to the floor and I gently grabbed the baby as it landed softly in my hands. I carefully lowered my body temperature and wrapped my jacket around it. The tiny baby slowly opened its eyes and oh my gods, they were the exact same purple as hers. My heart hurt.

I just fell to my knees and held the child to my chest. Before I knew it, I was sobbing. *Is this a second chance? Is this Jezabelle having pity on me? Or am I just delusional?*

Levi walked over and placed his hand on my shoulder, he kneeled next to me and pulled me into a hug. He didn't say anything, just sat with me. I'm glad he didn't say anything, I doubt I would actually form anything coherent. Then and there I decided, this is my second chance. I won't fail this time. *I'll make it up to you big sister, I promise, I won't fail you again.*

Everything after that was a blur, I destroyed as much information as I could. We got the children above the ground and treated them. I sent a letter to Aides to inform him of the results. Like I figured, he wasn't happy that the man wasn't there but he was pleased his "research" was destroyed. He was as disgusted as we were, he said those notes were horrific and borderline blasphemous. He went radio silent after that.

I took the child home with me, Levi was the only one who knew what I did that day. Once I came to my senses, I realized I can't take care of a child. I don't know the first thing about babies and childcare. I was just a walking prison with a baby crying its lungs out on my couch because I don't know what it wants. Iron wasn't too pleased with the noise or new addition.

I sat on the couch in thought, arms on my knees. At first I was just going to wait until it aged then put it up for adoption, but as he got older, he stole my heart. He'd grip my finger, cry if I wasn't around, call me daddy. I've never felt this... warmth, before. Maybe he truly was a gift from Jezabelle, what's the odds of finding a baby that heavily resembles my late sister? If not a mercy, then what is this? And who am I to question the will of the gods? If we weren't to meet, why was I put on this path? Maybe I'm delusional, not grieving properly, or just plain stupid. But, I can't deny the truth, I'm attached, I love him. *My little Aubrey*. Named after the auburn hair he adorned.

I couldn't abandon him. He was my son, my pride and joy.

I know, *I knew*, the consequences. And even then. I still never had, nor have, any regrets.

He's my son, and I'll be damned if anyone takes him from me. I won't fail to protect my family a second time.

I **won't** fail.

29

TWENTY-EIGHT

"*Father.*" Jonas' eyes were dark and somber, the word felt foreign off her tongue, her face was disgusted, almost like it pained her to utter that word. The room fell silent, no one moved.

Before I could react, dad swiftly darted at Jonas. I blinked in shock, as did she. He stopped short of her and towered over her, his hand shaking from anger. I've only seen dad angry once, and that's when I told him what my ex was doing to me back in high school, he was so angry. Even then I could tell he was holding back for my sake.

"Dad!" His eyes barely glanced at me before slowly raising his hand.

Jonas watched him cautiously and Rue kept her distance.

"You need to leave." Tartarus pointed towards the door firmly, "I won't ask again, and if you mention that fucker in my house and around my son again I won't hesitate to hurt you." His voice was cold and dark.

"Dad. Stop.." I sighed, rubbing my face, "Who is he."

"Aubrey, that isn't any of your concern."

"Like hell it isn't!" I closed my eyes and took a deep breath, putting my hands up, "I don't know what I am, you won't be honest with me, and Jonas has been nothing but helpful. I want to know."

He fell into a silent rage, he kept his eyes locked on Jonas but backed down.

"I've told you everything."

"No, you haven't." I shot back, "Who is he."

"He's a monster." Jonas eventually spoke up, "Your… Father…" She glanced at dad then back at me, "Took you from him. Years ago."

"He's a scientist, so he says. He wants you. You were everything he's wanted." Jonas said.

"What do you mean by that?" I asked, dad was still tense, but his face was contorted in disgust.

"He made you for one purpose, and I promise, it wasn't innocent." Jonas glanced away, "He ran experiments, killed many innocent children, defied the gods…"

The room was silent, I dropped my gaze to my lap, the heat from the room slowly aired out, I didn't realize how suffocating it felt, I took in a deep breath and rubbed my face.

"What does that mean?"

Jonas shook her head, "I'm sure you can finish the puzzle."

I placed my hand on my lower stomach and felt suddenly nauseous. If I wasn't sitting I'm sure I'd collapse and throw up, *I have a functioning uterus,* everything else in me is makeshift. I don't have a proper bone structure, I have a makeshift heart and stomach and lungs. Simple things that you need to survive, so Dr. Wynter said. He told me I was made to be *female*. I have a uterus.

I have a uterus.

I covered my face. I feel like I'm going to throw up.

"Nothing will ever happen to you Aubrey." Dad spoke soothingly, grabbing the cup of water, kneeling down next to me.

"So what. I was just supposed to be some doll on a shelf for this person."

"Basically. He either wants you back completely, or your formula." Jonas spoke gently.

"Formula?"

She raised her shirt gently, down her stomach was golden symbols similar to the ones on my back, I narrowed my eyes.

"He wants this. All of us have different combinations, and you were the only perfect one, I remember when you were made… He was so ecstatic." She shook her head, "I was the first attempt, but as you can see we look nothing alike. But I was good enough to use for samples and tests. I'm one of the only ones he made from scratch, the rest are experimented on kids."

"That's enough." Dad spoke up. I downed the water and moved away from his touch, Iron stayed close though, watching me intently.

"Aubrey.. Honey.. This is why I didn't want to tell you.."

"You're telling me, I was made, for such a horrific purpose. To be nothing more than a plaything on a shelf, and the man who made me, has been looking for me for the past twenty four years… And you didn't think that was something I needed to know."

"Why do you think I was so overprotective and made it clear to never leave The Valley?"

"Because you're a parent! Parents are protective! But this!?" I got to my feet, ignoring the dizziness.

"Aubrey don't-" Dad stood and went to steady me. I stepped back immediately.

"Don't touch me." I could feel the heat burning my face, I can't tell if it was a fever, or in disgust. I stared at the ground momentarily before turning around and leaving the house. *I need to get out of here. I need to fucking go.*

"Aubrey!"

I closed the door behind me, walking on autopilot. Staring at the ground as the dirt blew in the wind. Everything feels unreal, I wasn't supposed to exist this way. Was this even how I was supposed to look? Do I look and act like this on my own volition? Or am I just following specific coding? Does any of this even matter anymore? Is that really all I was made for? All I'm good for? *Am I even real?* Or just a sentient doll with no real purpose outside of pleasing a disgusting pig.

What was even the reason for this? Gods do I want to know? The implications are enough to make me vomit.

Everything felt so slow, so far away. Just a ringing in my ears and a blank stare towards the ground. I just kept walking.

Before I knew it, I ended up at Saint's. I looked up at the giant mansion, the lights were off. I guess Jasper isn't home. A harsh breeze passed by making the old manor creak. I made my way around the back and to Saint's balcony. I climbed up and tapped on her door. I didn't realize how late it was, I looked towards the horizon. The dark blue starry sky didn't feel as comforting as it usually does. The moon felt violating, it did nothing wrong but right now I don't like feeling watched. It peered down at me like a giant eyeball, cold and uncaring.

I turned my head as Saint opened the glass doors, her eyes were tired. She had a sleeping mask pushed up on her forehead, her hair was in a bonnet for bed. She was in her frilly black nightgown. She had an irritable glint in her squinted eyes. I couldn't say anything. I just stared at her and felt my eyes welling up. Lightning rumbled in the distance, clouds began rolling in, covering the moon and stars.

"Aubrey?" Saint asked, voice quiet, I woke her up.

"..."

"What are you doing here? It's late and it's going to storm." She said, she motioned me in without a second thought. I immediately pulled her into a tight hug. I desperately hugged her close and gripped at her sides. She blinked but returned the hug almost immediately.

"Aubrey?" Saint asked again.

"I..." I couldn't stop the tears, I just dropped my head on her shoulder, "I didn't know where else to go..."

"Oh honey..." She rubbed my back, if it wasn't her, I'm sure I'd be throwing up from the contact. But she felt comforting right now, that's what I need. She gently moved away and took my hands in hers. Pulling me inside she sat me on the couch, and lit a few of her candles to get dim lighting in the room. Her soft hands rubbed her eyes and she placed herself beside me. I stared at my lap while she gently gripped my hand and used her sleeve to wipe the tears away. I tried to stop her before my mascara and eyeliner messed up the fabric. She didn't seem to care though.

"What's going on?"

"I… I uh…" Gods how can I even explain this to her? How does anyone go about explaining such a thing? "I… Found out more about my origin…"

"What did you find out?" Saint asked, she gripped my hand reassuringly.

"I'm nothing more than a freak's abusive wet dream." I deadpanned, "A glorified sex toy."

"What?" She asked in disbelief, She made a face of disgust and glanced away.

"That's the gist of it." I sniffed, rubbing at my eye, "It's disgusting. I'm so disgusted…" I kept my eyes on my lap. I could hear how defeated my voice was.

I don't want to see the look on her face when I tell her this. I can't bear her looking at me differently, not Saint. She's all I have, she's my normalcy, my support, my everything. I felt another wave of tears washing over me, I can't deal with her being disgusted by me.

"I see…" She kept a grip on my hand. She placed her free hand on my shoulder, pulled me down to her, and rested my head on her shoulder then shushed me gently.

"It's Ok. It's Ok, take a breath Aubrey, you're safe."

I let her hand go and just pulled her close, she was completely relaxed, she rubbed up and down my spine soothingly. She didn't even flinch at the tears hitting her shoulder and chest. She just kept me close.

"Want to talk?" She asked, "Or is this enough for now?"

I thought for a moment. Will I get nauseous if I talk about this right now? I did as she said and took deep breaths. I tried to find the words. The room was silent. Her bird was asleep, and the house was quiet. All I could hear was my heart pounding in my ears. I went to open my mouth but immediately covered it, running in the bathroom, straight to the toilet. She squeaked quietly at me suddenly pushing her off but followed quickly after me.

I coughed and heaved as I threw up directly in the bowl. I feel disgusting. I feel fucking disgusting.

“Aubrey, here.” Saint kneeled down, handing me a tiny cup of water when I was done. She refilled it as many times as she needed too. She sat next to me on the bathmat while I dropped my head on my hand, staying close to the toilet.

She sat quietly and moved her legs up against her chest and just sat there. I took deep breaths trying to get the nausea to pass.

“I feel so disgusting.” I muttered finally. She looked at me, pain in her eyes. I could feel it on the side of my face. I stared at the mirror on the back of her door, it was angled to show half of my face. All I could do was bore into it and think about how it's probably not even my true face. Hell what does that even mean?

“I feel objectified. Violated?” I asked.

“It's understandable.” She spoke quietly, she kept her distance this time. “I can't begin to understand the turmoil you must feel, but I'm always here to help you.. So please.. Don't worry, just, talk to me…”

“I wish I could word how I feel..” I mumbled

“Take your time..” Saint said.

I closed my eyes, “My stomach hurts… so bad. There's this sinking feeling, I just feel overall disgusting.”

“I can imagine, how did you find out?” She asked.

“Turns out, that girl I wanted you to meet? Yea, she's apparently my sister.” I glanced at her. She blinked in shock.

“I thought you? Is she the one who sent you that letter?”

"She said she wasn't." I shook my head, "I still don't know who sent that."

"Well, what did your dad say?"

"Not much. He's pissed."

"I'm so sorry Aubrey…" Saint spoke softly.

She looked up at me while I dragged my hand down my face, ignoring my eyes welling up. The makeup was streaked down my cheeks, I wiped away at it. I sniffed and dropped my head in my hand. All I could think was; *A doll.* A doll is nothing more than a toy. Something inanimate. Something to play with. Is that really all I am? So many thoughts were swirling in my mind. It was so loud in here, I've never felt so distressed.

"Am I real?" I asked barely above a whisper, Is that what I am? I kept my hand over my mouth, staring into my hazy reflection, I blinked and a couple tears fell.

"What..?" Saint asked.

I didn't repeat myself, just sat in silence. She moved her hand to mine and went to touch my cheek. I glanced down at her with misty eyes. I could tell her heart was hurting, *gods Saint. I don't know what to do either. I don't know.*

"I'm sorry…I guess, I'm?" I looked at my lap, "Having a crisis? In a way?"

Saint wiped the tears away with her sleeve once more and touched my cheek, and turned my gaze to her, "No honey, you have nothing to apologize for."

"… I know..I…" I leaned back against the tub, "My mind is bouncing between, I was made to be an abusers plaything, to, am I even a real thing? Or just a sentient doll? This is too much."

"Aubrey, you're a real person." She said sternly, "Don't

think that way."

"It's fuckin hard not too!" I dropped my head against the tub, she just grabbed my hand in response. "What, do you think I'm overreacting?"

"No. Of course not." She shot back, "I just..."

She looked at her lap, "I'm sorry, I don't know how to help you..."

I looked at her, that hurt me. *Aubrey you idiot.* You wake her up in the middle of the night, info dump on her then snap at her? She didn't ask to be in this position. Why did I even come here, She should be asleep. It's storming. She hates storms. Yet I selfishly woke her up to deal with my problems. I wasn't thinking, *gods I wasn't thinking.*

"Saint... I'm sorry..."

"Stop apologizing! What could you possibly be apologizing for?" Saint asked, her own eyes were misty. I couldn't tell if it was from her interrupted sleep or distress. Either way it broke my heart. I immediately wanted to cup her cheeks and tell her it's Ok and just hug her. She moved before I could though.

"I shouldn't have come-" I tried to speak but she took my wrist and stopped my arm.

"I'm your best friend, if you don't want to be at home, you come here. What's changed?" She said.

"N-nothing I- It's just, this is a lot, I wasn't thinking-"

"You don't have to explain yourself! I know you're used to being a rock, I'm used to it too, but even rocks get cracks and wear down over time." She sighed out.

"I-?"

"I want you to talk to me, I just wish I knew how to help you..." She looked down, "I don't know what to say."

"You don't have to say anything, I shouldn't have bothered you…" I sighed.

"You aren't a bother." Saint looked at me, "The only advice I can think of is talk to your father."

"My dad?"

"Yes. He'd be the most knowledgeable about this, I mean all things considered?" She responded, I blinked and turned my head towards her, "He was made to be a prison no?"

"I?" I asked in confusion.

"He's probably asked the same questions. He was made for one thing, but He's more than that." She smiled softly, "He's a friend, He's a businessman, He's a father. *Your* father. Right?"

I looked away and at my lap, I guess she has a point.

"I don't really want to talk to him right now."

"Of course, I understand." She nodded.

I shook my head and wiped at my face once more. I took a deep breath and sighed, "I just, I'm sorry, I woke you up for this bullshit."

"Stop It's Ok." Saint said firmly, "You came here for a reason, don't downplay your feelings."

"I don't like this feeling…I wish I was never told.." I mumbled.

"No, it's your right to know." She said.

I went silent, I shouldn't have bothered her, what the hell was I thinking? What the hell am I thinking? It's too much, it's too fresh. It's too fucking much. I rubbed my face and stood up, moving past her and rinsing my mouth out again and leaning against the sink. I shouldn't have disturbed her, I need to leave, I need to think.

I sighed, "I should go."

"I think you should stay." Saint spoke and stood up, "It's storming, you know lightning is dangerous, and the brimstone can burn you." She placed her soft hands on my back and arm, "You know my bed is big enough, you need to rest."

"No, it's Ok." I said immediately, she looked at me in the grand mirror, her eyes were stern. I looked at her and felt myself beginning to cave.

"Stay." She said, I gripped at the sink then dropped my head in defeat.

"Fine, fine."

"I got my satin sheets on the bed this time." She hummed triumphantly, "My quilt is in the wash, I know you didn't like it last time."

"It's a sensory thing." I whined, "It made me feel itchy."

"Yes Yes, I know." She sat on the bed and patted the other side for me. She moved that old stuffed green Dragon to the night stand. I can't believe she still has that thing. I sighed and walked over, sitting down.

She stretched and checked the time, Three AM. Just until she falls asleep. She pulled her mask down and laid down. I laid next to her and glanced over, *you idiot I can't believe you inconvenienced her like this*. She placed her hand gently on mine. I adjusted to turn on my side to face her, I gripped her hand as lightning tore through the sky. I instinctively pulled her close to shield her from the noise, ever since we were kids, she never liked storms. They Are few and far between down here, but I always tried to stay by her side through them. I caressed the back of her head gently, letting her rest her head on my chest.

At least with her here, I feel calmer. I guess I really had to get some of that out, I still feel disgusting but at least Saint is with me, like she always is. I feel awful dumping all of this on her out of the blue, when I want comfort I think of her. She's always so consistent, she's always there. If I can't go to my dad I go to her, and right now I can't talk to him. I can't be around any of that.

I felt my tired eyes begin to close, this feels somewhat nice. It's a small breath of fresh air. Maybe this is enough for now.

30

TWENTY-NINE

Aubrey was gone when I woke up. His side of the bed was still warm. I patted my hand on the sheets and sat up, pushing my sleeping mask up. The morning lava light poured in through the windows. I immediately checked my phone, no messages from him. I can't tell if that's a good thing or a bad thing. I sighed out and moved my legs to the side of the bed. I got to my feet and headed to the bathroom. He cleaned it. *That dumbass.*

I sent a text to Rouge and called Mr. Tartarus.

I've never seen Aubrey so distressed before. It's certainly a foreign feeling, he was always so calm and put together. He always kept his cool. Yes he'd have his small moments of opening up to me, but that was about a cheating partner or a shitty work day or his growing stress over his schedules. Nothing *this* severe. I feel so useless, he came here for help, and I couldn't offer any.

"Hello? Mr. Tartarus?" I spoke.

"Saint, love are you alright?"

"I'm Ok sir, Aubrey stopped by last night, he left before I

woke up, um I thought I should let you know…" I rubbed my head.

"Did he say where he was going? I need to find him." He said urgently.

"No, I'm sorry, he was really upset and I got him to rest so, if anything he could be in Pride, or at the hills."

He went silent for a moment, "I'm going to send someone over to speak with you, We need to find him, it's very important, is that Ok?"

"What's so important? If I'm honest sir, I think he really needs space right now."

He went quiet again.

"You think so?" Tartarus asked.

"Definitely, he's never been so distressed like that, I got the bare bones explanation, but I think he needs a breather, I'd say send Iron after him and give him time to come home."

"…"

I waited patiently, I looked through my drawers and grabbed my toothpaste.

"Alright, I suppose that would be better…I'm sorry for all this, it's a lot right now." He said.

"It's Ok Sir, really, if you need anything just ask, if he doesn't come back soon I'll go find him."

"Thank you Saint, be safe now."

"Of course." I hung up and went on to do my routine. I hope that was the right call. He has so many thoughts up there yet can't word a single one, I want to run and find him too but I think this will be better for him, maybe he'll be calmer now. Gods, I just hope that idiot left in the morning hours and not during that storm. I patted my face dry and headed downstairs. Rouge was knocking at the door. I let her in and headed to the kitchen.

"Hey Hon, is everything alright?"

"Aubrey stopped by last night, I'm worried about him." I said, grabbing milk and cereal, "He was on the verge of a mental breakdown…and I couldn't help him." I looked down.

"What happened? Did he say?" Rouge walked over and rubbed my back soothingly.

"I don't know if I should say… He just, he came here and he wasn't all there… Ya know?"

She made a face, it was quick. She looked away and nodded, "Yea, I suppose."

"He's having an identity crisis, I guess that's the best I can explain it."

That seemed to please her. I'm not sure how much he's told her and honestly this ain't my business to tell. I do hate keeping Rouge out the loop like this but I value Aubrey's trust and privacy, and I know she does too. He will tell her if he feels it's right, oh gods I hope he doesn't feel more complicated when Rouge is in the picture.

I sat at the table with her and stirred the milk. *Why did I even make this? I don't even really like cereal.* For a distraction maybe? I guess so. If I'm honest I'm a bit shaken up, He's our rock. He's always the one taking care of us, but I can't comfort him in his time of need? What kind of friend am I? I feel useless, he came to me and I offered nothing but empty words and a bed. *What a joke.*

"You're quiet, love." Rouge said.

"I know…" I continued to stir the bowl, "His safety is just heavy on my mind. He ran off after I fell asleep. Should've known he would."

"It's not your fault hon, Aubrey has a unique set of problems we can't always help with, sometimes just being an ear or a shoulder is better than nothing at all."

"I guess so…" I shook my head, "He was crying, Rouge… It broke my heart seeing him so upset. Gods even after…" I trailed off, she knew what I meant.

He didn't handle the Hallow's Eve incident well. He was in shock, scared, and panicked. He immediately ran to my house to ask for help. He was terrified of what Mr.Tartarus would do or say. So I bandaged him up and helped him heal. He was in hysterics over Rouge not calling him, can you believe it? Forget being bitten and viciously attacked, he was more worried about Rouge feeling upset. How can you comfort someone like that? I surely don't know how, too selfless for his own good.

I cleared my throat, "He wasn't this bad."

She went quiet.

"I just…" I quickly changed the subject, "I just hope he's safe."

I blinked as a knock sounded. Who could that be? I got to my feet and headed to the front door. I blinked at the other woman. She had dark skin with a golden shimmer to it. She was in a denim outfit with white gloves. Her dark brown twists fell past her waist. Her eyes were distressed and tired. Her brown eyes were two toned like Aubrey's, her ears and pupils were small as well. She seemed to have a scar around her neck and lower arm, almost like stitches? I've never seen her before in my life.

"Is Aubrey here?" She asked. I raised a brow at her.

"And you are?"

"Saint…" Rue walked up beside her, she looked a bit upset

as well. *What's she doing here?*

"Rue?" I asked.

"May we come in?" She asked, clutching her purse, "It's urgent."

"Who is this? Why is she asking about Aubrey." I demanded, I could feel Rouge lingering behind me.

"Is he here?" Rue asked while the girl looked annoyed and impatient.

"He's not, he left this morning."

"Well where did he go?" The darker skinned woman asked. I raised my brow once more.

"Saint, This is Jonas." Rue motioned to her, "Aubrey's sister."

It all clicked. This is the girl he wanted us to meet? The upperclassmen he was raving about? I blinked in disbelief.

"Sister?" Rouge asked.

"Sister…" I echoed.

"Yes, I'm his biological sister." Jonas spoke confidently, "Please, tell me where he is, is he safe?"

"I'm sorry, I don't know where he is, like I said he left this morning." I stepped aside to let them in. Jonas walked in, she was nervously pulling at and messing with her gloves. They were Ironed and pristine, like she's never touched anything in her life. She stood a bit taller than me, with her heels, she's around Rouge's shoulders. Rue walked in shortly after.

"What's so urgent? Why do you need to find him?" I asked.

"He's… sick?" Rue asked, looking at Jonas.

"Sick." I stated.

They went silent and exchanged looks. This is making

me feel worse. Did I fail him again by letting him go? I try not to think the worst, but I know him too well. Something is wrong. Something they aren't telling. Oh gods was he attacked again? Is he injured? What happened before he showed up last night? I felt myself getting more panicky. I know Aubrey is strong and capable, and strange, but he isn't invincible.

"What's going on, you two came here for a reason." Rouge spoke, she had worry in her voice now too.

"Well, If you two have known him for so long, I assume you're aware of his... condition?" Jonas asked carefully.

I locked eyes with Rouge then cleared my throat.

"Yes, we're aware."

Jonas seemed relieved. She plopped on the couch.

"There was an altercation...." Rue spoke up.

"What altercation?" I asked.

Jonas cleared her throat, "Aubrey is, the best I can say? Sick?" She questioned.

"Sick how." I asked, annoyed.

"Aubrey and I are from the same...Origin.." Jonas glanced away.

"Where is this going, what is wrong with Aubrey." Rouge asked.

"I stopped by Aubrey's yesterday, and he completely collapsed, bleeding from his nose, and when she got there, he was...Dying?" Rue said.

Everything stopped at that moment. Did she say *dying*? I felt the room begin to spin. I felt lightheaded. Immediate panic rushed over me. What do you mean dying? He was just here last night, he didn't look sick, he was just upset. Rouge's silence was so loud, I didn't even have to look at her face to see the absolute horror there

"D-Dy-?" I felt the air leave my lungs, I couldn't even get the word out. Not Aubrey, not my Aubrey. He's everything to me, he's all I have. "What the fuck are you talking about."

"I-I don't know I-" Rue stammered.

"Aubrey is a very complicated being." Jonas spoke up, "He's made of Earth, Gold, Iron and Salt, amongst other things. When he was taken all those years ago, his research papers were taken as well."

"You may want to sit down.." Rue spoke quietly, she helped me to the couch. I can only imagine how pale my face is.

"What does that have to do with him dying?" Rouge asked, placing her hand on my shoulder for support.

"His father took his papers." She laid a file down on the coffee table, and pulled sheets of paper out, "He, after a lot of convincing, gave me permission to copy it."

She slid the papers to our view, "He wasn't done incubating, which is why he was a baby when he was found and grew along with you. But, I'm worried that had severe consequences."

"As in?" Rouge asked. She was more panicked.

"He isn't like me, I was fully incubated and don't have to worry about falling out like that. He's low on something, I just, I just can't figure out what. I gave him an electric shock, but that won't be enough."

"So you're telling me, he almost died yesterday, and you're just now telling us about it?" I asked, I couldn't hide my emotions in my voice, I'm distressed. I can't lose Aubrey, neither of us can. I gripped my nightgown, keeping my fists on my lap.

"Apologies." Jonas spoke. "I have been looking for him for

twenty four years, hoping and praying he was alive. And now that I'm here...Of course something goes wrong."

"Well where is he!? We can't just leave him by himself!" Rouge asked, fully panicked, her hands gripped my shoulder. I couldn't muster a reaction. All I can do is stare at my lap. I'm more than accustomed to death. I mean hell, I'm casket ready at all times. I've seen souls and death all my life. But this felt horrible, it felt like a dread I've never experienced before? It's so overwhelming, and if Aubrey dies, *what then?* He has no soul. He won't be here, there's nothing to reap or reincarnate? He'd be gone forever.

That made my chest tighten and I let out a small cry of anguish at the thought. Rouge immediately pulled me close.

"Mr. Tartarus sent the Hellhound to find him, all we can do is wait." Jonas said.

"Like hell we can." Rouge growled. I shook my head, I have to help. In any way I can.

"What is he missing? Is it something we can buy or pay someone to fix?" I asked.

Jonas read over the notes for a moment, "I'm worried it's the fluids he was incubated in." She shook her head, "Which is Chaos Essence, like, god essence..?" She asked almost in disbelief. She looked at her arm and seemed to come to a realization.

"Chaos?" Rue asked.

"That's... That's a problem." I spoke up. "Chaos is... dead? Gone? Who knows but she's not around, at least that's what dad said."

"Her essence might've been contained, maybe you can buy it somewhere?" Rouge asked.

"Unlikely...unless it's in some black market shit, you can't just buy god essence, it's a danger, that's how Icarus' are made." I explained, rubbing my chest.

"Oh.. right.." She looked down.

"Is there another way to fix this?" I asked.

"Well, there's someone here who's looking for him, the man that created him is still alive. She knows where his lab is, if she tells us, maybe we can go there and get something for him to fix this. And help the kids there… That's what I'm here for."

"Whoa, whoa, slow down." I spoke up and placed a hand up. "Kids? Lab?"

This is too much.

"It's a lot…" Rue spoke up.

Jonas went into a lengthy explanation, some of it was easy to comprehend, but honestly the only thing on my mind was Aubrey and his well being. I can't lose him, reaping him is something I can't bear. I got to my feet and left the room.

"Wait Saint-" Rouge called after me.

"I have to talk to him. Immediately." I spoke, heading upstairs to grab my phone and to get dressed. I sent him texts and called, no response.

That dread isn't leaving me. *Oh gods is he hurt? Is he in pain?* I tried to calm my breathing and stop my hand from shaking. I pulled on my clothes and left some feed and water for Opal. I'm not sure how long I'll be out. I don't care how long it takes, I'm going to find him.

I headed back downstairs, still trying his phone. While I stand by the notion of giving him space, I have to make sure he's Ok. This is so much more than I thought and I couldn't even help him. Does he even know? Or is he too focused on his own despair? I shook my head and walked to the door.

I have to find and help him. I can't lose my best friend.

I turned to them, gripping my phone. Rouge was already ready. Rue looked nervous as all get out and Jonas was distressed in her eyes.

"We need to get to him right now." We all nodded in agreement. No questions asked.

31

THIRTY

I don't know how much time has passed. I just know I hear sniffing and whines in front of me. Iron found me. I groaned quietly and slowly opened my eyes. *What time is it?* The storm stopped. I lifted my heavy arm and let my hand fall on my head, I rubbed at my eyes with as much strength as I could muster. Iron sat next to me, his tail barely wagging.

"Hey boy…" I glanced up at him and tried to move my other arm, but it burned. I groaned once more and looked at it, lightning burns.

What the hell happened? Did I get struck when I left? I sat up and rubbed at my arm, trying to ignore the burning sensation. That's gonna scar real bad. I groaned in annoyance this time and felt my hair fall around me and past my shoulders. I looked around and noticed the dried brown grass, the dead bare trees and rotting pumpkins. At least I made it to pride and didn't pass out in the square. Iron nuzzled against me, his ears pinned to his head. I pet him with my free hand.

"I'm Ok.. I'm Ok." I scratched behind his ears and closed my eyes.

Last night's events flooded my brain. I don't know what I was thinking, I just needed to get away. No one comes to pride anymore. It's been abandoned for decades. It used to be a thriving city way back when, I think in dad's youth? This is the only place with plants in The Valley, it looks the most like the surface. I always felt at ease here. If I was stressed I'd just come here and scream, or cry, or just make a fire and sit on a log. It's so peaceful here, a bit eerie since there's no Pride Demons here anymore, and the Sin of Pride disappeared so long ago. It's just abandoned now.

Only Saint figured out about this spot, but she only mentioned it in passing. She never came here. I guess she respected the need for space. I leaned back against a dead log and looked up at the tree obscured sky. The moon wasn't peering down at me anymore and all the clouds dispersed. *I hope she slept well, I shouldn't have left like that. She could've woken up and panicked. You're such an idiot.*

The lava's glow was dimmer, and the sky was brighter. It was morning it seems, or at least early afternoon. The pale blue river flow was not as noticeable from here but it somewhat peaked over the pride walls. I could feel the slow blinks of my heavy eyes every few minutes. I rubbed at them once more and leaned my head against the log and sat quietly. The silence set in, nothing but wind and maybe a few distant caws of the Ravens and Crows.

The reality is starting to settle in. I still feel disgusting. It's too much to entertain now, but I don't feel any better. My stomach faintly hurts but the nausea is gone at least. I don't want that man to find me, I don't want to imagine what he'd do if he got a hold of me. I'm fully grown and I assume I deviated from the plans? Would he even be bothered? Or would he label me as a failure and try to kill me for my formula?

I tried to shake that thought off.

"I guess I should go home." I sighed and checked my phone, Iron laid next to me and stayed put. Yea he can tell, I'm not getting up too quickly.

My phone screen was cracked, that irked me a lot. I huffed and rubbed the glass on my pants before it nicked my thumb. Ten percent battery life and tons of missed calls and messages. Some from Saint, some from Rue, some from Rouge and a ton from Dad. Hell even Mr. Mateo reached out? *Gods. My stomach hurts.*

I scrolled through the unread messages but settled on calling my dad. I guess Saint is technically right, he'd be the most helpful in this situation. I never noticed how similar we were. I never thought much on dad's creation, nor mine. I guess to be fair, I didn't have much information on mine, I was robbed of that privilege. I could feel myself getting angry then anxious again. I'm so *mad* at him, why would he keep this from me? Something so important? All he would say was *I'm different, I'm not like the other kids.* Yea but he didn't tell me I was supposed to be a freak scientist's plaything. I rubbed my stomach in disgust. I want to scream, I cried enough. I want to shower.

I sighed and closed my eyes, I called dad and tried to relax. The phone only rang twice before he picked up.

"Aubrey..?" Tartarus spoke up quickly.

"Yea dad. It's me."

"Are you alright? Where are you?" He asked in a worried

tone. I rubbed my eyes.

“I’m fine. I’ll be home later.”

He went quiet, I stayed quiet. I don’t like hearing him so distressed and I don’t like worrying him like this but, I don’t know. I’m so lost right now. I don’t know what to do. I know we need to talk but, is now a good time? Am I just being a brat? I don’t know what to do.

“... You know... You’ll always be my son.. No matter what..” Tartarus spoke up quietly.

“...Yea..” I blinked in confusion.

“And no one, I mean, **NO** one. Will ever harm you as long as I’m here.”

“Yea..” I echoed.

I felt my phone buzz against my ear, I glanced at it and noticed a message from him. I put the phone on speaker and looked at it.

“Did you get the picture?”

“Yea.”

“She was my sister? In a way?” He spoke.

The photo was of a red haired woman with bright purple eyes, her freckles noticeable, a beauty mark was under her soft eyes, splitting image. I looked at it as he spoke.

“Way before you existed, she was murdered, it blindsided all of us.” Tartarus shook his head, “We were close, she was always so kind and inviting, kinda like you.”

“...”

“When she died, the plant life here died too. She preferred living here, she said she felt so connected to everything here, balance, life cycles, all of that. Being the goddess of the earth will do that to you I suppose?” Tartarus spoke.

“What was her name?”

"Terra." He nodded, "She was the third oldest before my creation, she was Jezabelle's daughter I believe."

"When she died, we searched for decades for the killer, we put restrictions on Reaper weapons and cracked down on border hopping, and closed the Hermes portals. Things got more strict."

He gave a small sigh, "Then, we got that tip."

"A man, Salem, was at the end of a long line of child disappearances in Terra's cult region, some of those kids were found deceased. All mutilated in one way or another. Took a few months but we found him."

I made a face of disgust. *Mutilated?* How fucked up does this get? and how deep does it go? He was so obsessed he was killing children from her regions? I felt my stomach ache again.

"No doubt in my mind, he killed my sister." Dad spoke bitterly, "And I couldn't protect her. The least I could've done was catch the fucker. But I couldn't even do that right?" His voice was full of hurt and he laughed in disbelief.

"Dad.."

"Then I saw you." Tartarus said, my phone notified me that it was on five percent. I didn't want to rush him off though. "You look exactly like her, you were just a baby. I can't kill a baby… Especially not one who looked like her.."

"I figured this would've been my second chance to help her, to redeem myself? It's why I was so overprotective. I'm sorry, you have…Every right to be mad at me, but can you really blame me? I don't want to see you like this.. I didn't want you living in fear, constantly looking over your shoulder."

"…" I looked at the ground.

"But I know, I fucked up. I should've told you when you were of age, everything comes out eventually..."

"...I always felt like... Something was wrong...With me." I spoke quietly, "Yea, I knew I wasn't normal, but, it felt... Different. No one else understood how I felt, like that emptiness and confusion couldn't be comprehended, so I just..Ignored it."

Dad went quiet, I shook my head.

"Was that even my original feelings? Or was it some programming and I was subconsciously feeling it."

"Aubrey..." Tartarus said softly. "You are something none of us understand. I can't give you any sound advice that I can confidently say will help you, but I can be here for you."

"Yea.."

"You take all the time you need." His voice was softer, all that anger from yesterday was gone. Just full blown worry, "I will always be here, and I don't care what anyone says, or does, you will always. *Always.* Be my kid. And I am more than proud to be your father."

I looked down then nodded a bit, "Yea..."

I looked back at the picture and felt my stomach churn. He began to say something else but my phone died. I just stared at my reflection in the pitch black screen. All I saw was *her*. *Her* eyes, *her* hair color, *her* beauty mark. I'm looking at myself, but *all* I see *is her*. That is who he did all this for? He ruined so many lives over her? He ruined and stole her life? Then has the gaul to play god to recreate her? How sick can you fucking be. This is her face. Not mine. Yet here I am. *I feel so disgusting.*

"Gross." I muttered under my breath before putting the phone in my pocket. I glanced down at Iron and sighed quietly, rubbing my face. I don't feel like crying this time, I feel more confused and disgusted than ever. I want to scream, I want to punch, I want to forget.

Maybe dad was in the right? How am I supposed to just accept and move on from this information? I'm a doll based on a murdered goddess? Have I been hurting dad all these years? Was it a feeling of obligation?

I felt my chest tighten almost immediately.

'No, that's not true.'

I placed my hand on my chest and rested my legs against the ground. Yea, I guess that isn't true, how long can obligation go before It's genuine? It's been twenty four years?

"So, are you that little voice that's always steering me out of trouble Miss Terra?" I looked at the barren ground, the dirt blowing in a gust. Silence filled the area.

"I hope you're resting at least…I'm sorry if I offend you, I didn't ask to be made…I'm so sorry…"

The photo was on the forefront of my mind, I figured I got my earth connection from dad, but if I'm supposed to be a replica of you, is that where it comes from? I doubt it, who knows how he made me, who knows what he did or used, it's probably just a coincidence, like customizing your favorite doll. Find the wig, the clothes, the makeup, the obedience.

Is that why I'm so averse to authority? Why I rebelled so much as a child? I doubt I'm as nice as you, probably a little nightmare compared to you. Maybe that can be my purpose? Living up to you? Or would that be foolish and blasphemous, a doll made to replace you? How sick huh?

'No, not that.'

Are you still here maybe? Could I somehow give my life to you? Maybe then things could be better, and be as it were?

'No. you, are you..'

I laid down on my side, resting my head gently on Iron's stomach, watching the sky. This is too much. I'm exhausted.

32

THIRTY-ONE

"Hi sugar.." A soft voice spoke up.

I could feel light snowflakes falling on my face, landing on my eyelashes and cheeks. I slowly opened my eyes in confusion, Briar's ice cold hands rested gently on my cheeks. I squinted and allowed my eyes to adjust, my head was resting on her lap. I guess Iron went home, I probably fell asleep from exhaustion. Her eyes were worried, she was gently caressing my cheeks, her cold fingertips making delicate circles.

I sat up and rubbed my eyes, keeping my back to her.

How the hell did she find me?

"You alright..?" Briar asked gently.

"What are you doing out here Briar? How did you even?" I muttered.

"I was taking a walk and heard your pup whining.. He's very friendly." I looked over and Iron was laying down, head on his paws and looking up at me with those big puppy eyes.

"I guess he was trying to get a bystander's attention to help you, lucky it was me, huh? What are you doing out here?"

"..." I rubbed my eyes once more, "I'm alright..."

"You've been crying..?" Briar placed her hand on mine, and I slightly moved away. She seemed hurt by that but pulled her hand back anyway. She shifted her gaze to the side and rubbed her palms on her skirt.

"You know you can talk to me... laying in the heat probably isn't the best right now..?" I could hear the soft smile in her voice, but I refused to look up. Just went back to staring at the ground. Iron whined quietly and slightly crawled over with a defeated bark. I looked over and pet his head, scratching behind his ear gently. He pressed to my hand and wagged his tail.

"Yea, probably not."

Briar glanced away, "So, this place..?"

"Hm, I come here to relax sometimes.. It's calming, peaceful. Not many people come here."

"Is that so..?" She looked around.

"Mhmm..."

She stayed silent, but just like always, it was a comfortable silence. Her snowflakes flowed and melted off her, the intense heat making them melt faster, her cloud was bigger. I glanced up at it. She's going to overheat. Her face was soft, and she seemed content. She hasn't changed a bit.

"Hon, you need to head home."

"Will you escort me?" Briar asked with a slight glance. I looked away.

"I've been out here all night, I doubt you'd want me around you in this state." I rubbed the back of my head.

Briar shook her head, "If anything that's more of a reason to walk me right?" She smiled at me.

I glanced at Iron, his tail was wagging.

"... Briar..?"

"Yes?"

"If... If I wasn't... As interesting as your father believes, would you disappear..?" I asked hesitantly.

"Hm? What on earth made you ask that?"

I shrugged a bit, "I mean, isn't that why you kept me around? I was a mystery? *Something new*."

She turned to me and cupped my cheeks almost immediately, I winced slightly at the cold, our contact forming steam at her touch. Her face was completely serious, almost enraged.

"Is that really what you think?" Briar stated more than asked.

"Y'all are borderline scientists, with your business... It's what I always assumed." I muttered, gripping her wrist gently, but avoiding her gaze.

"Aubrey. You're a person. We don't see you as some commodity." Briar said, eyes a bit hurt. I glanced away in shame.

"I'm not a person."

"Stop that." She spoke.

"I'm *not*. A person." I went to move her hands from my cheeks but she doubled down.

"Stop that!" Briar had a stern tone in her voice. "Who told you that? Did someone say something to you? You've never talked like this before."

I kept my eyes away from her, her snowflakes melting on my skin. I could feel my eyes welling up, it's only a matter of time before she feels the tears. I moved her wrists gently and dropped my head on her shoulder, why isn't this feeling going away? How long will I feel this distraught? At this rate Rouge or Keegan will see me like this, they're going to be so worried. I'm the last thing they should be so concerned with.

I gently gripped her wrists, Briar was relaxed, her voice was gentle.

"Could… Your father fix me..?"

"You don't need fixing Aubrey." Briar said sternly. I let her wrists go and she pulled me into a gentle hug. She gently rubbed my back and cradled the back of my head. I couldn't stop my body from trembling.

"You are perfect." Her voice was sincere.

I gripped her skirt and felt the dam break, I don't want to feel like this anymore. I don't want to know this anymore. I want to go back to normal, my normal. I wish she never told me. I'm exhausted. I couldn't do anything but form basic responses, feel nauseous and cry. Is this grief? Or is this fear? Not the same fear as getting a D on my tests, or beating up a kid and dad was mad. No, this is so much more intense. I feel paranoid? Like I'm isolated. What is this?

My heart starts pounding, my stomach turns, my body shakes. Is this fear?

"Aubrey… It's Ok… You're safe… You're safe.." Briar pulled away and cupped my cheeks, "Take deep breaths, you're pale.."

I looked at her and slowly did as she said, I took a breath, I get it now. I've never felt this way before, of course it's so foreign. This dread, this fear of what could've happened to me? Dad was right, I feel like I need to keep my guard up, like I'll be taken away at anytime. Like I'll lose my autonomy, my will. I don't like this feeling.

"A few more love, you're panicking.." Briar caressed my cheeks.

She's always been so good to me, I never understood why. What does she gain from it? Someone of her stature. Rich, beautiful, intelligent, she can have anyone. Why would she settle for me? Why does she care so much. She was always so gentle with me, I never understood why. Love? Maybe, even then, I'm just.. Me, it's not something I fully deserved from her. Even now she's still so caring, putting her own needs aside to tend to me. Is this how Saint and Rouge feel about me? I let a small breathless laugh out, shaking my head.

"What so funny..?"

"Just…Thank you.." I took another deep breath. "I'll walk you home, your cloud is gonna dissipate here, you're too close to the lava."

"Mm… It feels nice.. the heat.. reminds me of you." I looked at her in slight confusion.

"That's why I kept you around." Briar looked towards me, "Yes, you intrigued me, but not because of your body."

I got to my feet and gently helped her up, she placed her hands in mine, "I can feel our differences, and that excites me. I wish I could see them."

I could feel my face heat up at that, her delicate fingers tickled against my palms, steam forming every time she lingered, she slowly trailed her hands up my arms.

"From your heat, to your muscles… You're just so different.. You're a rock, I'm a snowflake, a pretty interesting pair don't you think?" Briar's eyes twinkled, she linked her free hand with mine and I quickly caught myself, clearing my throat.

"Um, yea… I suppose that makes sense, I uh.. Should get you home, love."

"Lead the way…" She gently held onto my arm, I took a deep breath and led her out of pride, Iron following close behind.

"I need to be honest with you Briar.." I spoke up.

"About?"

"I'm not exactly single right now…"

"Oh?" She hummed, "Is it the vampire girl?"

"Rouge? Heh. No.. I fucked that up years ago.." I glanced away.

"I wouldn't be so sure.." She rubbed my arm gently, "Then the Reaper girl?"

"Saint? No. It's a childhood friend, I actually should call her, my friends, and dad.." I rubbed my face and groaned quietly. Then I remembered my phone died. I stayed up there for too long.

"I see, well, lucky her…" Briar smiled gently.

"More like lucky me. She's really a flower in a volcano." I chuckled quietly, "She's very much out of my league, hell you and Rouge are too but y'all have different quali-" I blinked, "Ya know, never mind."

"No no." Briar giggled, "Please tell me my *qualities*. I'm curious."

"I feel that's a set up.. So I choose to not speak."

She laughed quietly, "I'll let it go, just this once."

I smiled softly for the first time in the past few hours. She always puts a smile on my face. I looked up then stopped, I glanced over to the side, Iron began growling, tail still and faced the other way. I instinctively pushed Briar behind me and blocked the sudden bullets. She squeaked quietly in shock.

"The hell." I moved the vines aside, they feel weaker this time?

There stood that snake girl. She was in a more casual outfit this time but still clearly pissed off. I blinked slowly and kept her behind me. Iron was standing at attention. I finally comprehended what was in front of me. She held a bigger gun this time, snakes slithered around her. *Disgusting.*

"What's that?" Briar asked, gripping my jacket, I winced quietly from the burns and tried not to alarm her.

"A problem." I muttered through my teeth. "The fuck you want."

"Your head on a spike little lamb." She smiled, she had a giddy tone in her voice. I don't have time for this bullshit. Especially with Briar's cloud fizzling out. I glanced up at the cloud momentarily before a whir caught my attention, *what the fuck*, I shielded up and narrowed my eyes. Are those? Needles?

"Iron down!" I kneeled down, punching the ground in chunks, punching a few towards her to buy some time. Iron ran towards Briar and tugged at the bottom of her skirt, trying to pull her away. *Oh trust me Iron,* ***she's*** *not the one I'm protecting.*

She gained her footing and went quiet behind me. I could feel the snowflakes on my neck, sending a shiver down my spine. She was shooting like crazy at this point. Is this chick insane? I blocked as many as I could, trying to keep my vines sustained while trying to avoid those disgusting snakes. I tried to close the gap between us but that gun has a strong push. She cackled to herself. *She's not good at hand to hand, get closer.*

I blinked in shock as my body suddenly went flying into a window, I got enough time to protect my head. Iron was barking at this point. *What the fuck just happened.*

She was giggling. I sat up and winced at the uncomfortable feeling of a few shards stuck in my hands and side. I took it out and tossed it aside. I slowly got to my feet and cracked my neck. Alright, I see.

I immediately ran out of the building and launched myself, dodging her gun fire and landing a punch on her, she stumbled back but caught herself and went to shoot again. I kicked the gun to the side and went to throw a punch but her snakes began to hiss and nip at me. I immediately stepped back and moved my hand, she took that opportunity to break the distance between us, I put my hands up trying to block again, but ice took over the area. A wall of ice shielded me and Briar came above, slamming her feet down on her neck, she yelped as Briar kicked her away, the ice slowly traveled around her, orbiting her. I breathed out.

"You have gaul. I'll give you that."

Medusa sat up, still gripping her gun, her eyes narrowed as this five foot three girl stared down at her, she pushed herself up and sent out more snakes. I covered her and took as many out as I could. Briar was elegantly avoiding all the needles she could shoot, her grace was undefeated. The ice hardened around her into spikes, she got to upper ground and sent the spinning ice blades to her, controlling them like a symphony. I could hear her getting increasingly frustrated. While she was distracted I kicked towards the ground, making her stumble and one of the blades cut into her stomach, she groaned and held her stomach.

"Won't you just die already!" Medusa got back up, her hair suddenly extended in all directions, the snakes were bigger, I tried to dodge but one knocked me towards the wall, I landed with a crack.

I looked at her in pure annoyance, "The fuck is your problem with me!?"

Briar leapt and landed more kicks on her, flipping away to keep a good distance from the snakes, her blades still moving rhythmically. She's always been inspiring, she's mastered her craft, her element is all hers, I've never met an ice user with her capabilities, paired with her elegant ballet skills, I could barely land a hit on her. Sparring with her as a trainer must've been a nightmare.

Briar got knocked back, her ribbons slowed her fall, she flipped to a landing and brought the blades back to her. Before she or I could react, glass began to rain down. We both got a chance to block, Briar and I looked over at a loud thud. A taller man landed, his Dragon tail dragged behind him. His dark eyes were narrowed.

Is it the same guy from the campus? He threw out more sand and immediately they turned to glass and he shot them towards Medusa with no hesitation. I almost felt bad for her, she seemed like she wanted to surrender as soon as he made himself known. She squeaked and stumbled away, his hair was pulled back out of his face, he looked strange, he glimmered like Jonas. Is he one of us? Another Homunculi?

His presence commanded attention. Every step he took towards her felt deadly. She tried to throw dirt at him but that had zero effect. This is genuinely sad... Aubrey don't. *Don't fuckin.*

"Aye." I got to my feet. Adonys turned his head to me,

"Think that's enough? She's half your size."

His eyes were deadly, his face contorted in pure rage and disgust, I put my hands up to show I was unarmed.

"She's just a nuisance. Don't you think you've got bigger issues to tend to than a pathetic snake girl."

Said snake girl was sitting on the ground, her hand began to tremble and she quickly grabbed her gun again. "I AM NOT PATHETIC!" She shot immediately.

The Dragon blocked it with sand immediately and turned his attention back to her. She got to her feet, her face was red with anger at this point, she was basically shaking in rage. All I could do was stare at her. What the fuck is her deal?

I glanced at Briar, she immediately shot ribbons at her, tying her down. She squeaked and stumbled to her knees. The taller Dragon blew dust in her face, and she fell over shortly after.

"Don't ever address me again." His voice was deep and cold, he glared at me. I blinked and pointed to myself and looked behind me.

"Excuse me?" I questioned.

"You mean less than nothing to me, don't take this as a kindness." Adonys stared down at me with narrowed harsh eyes, "The only reason I'm here is because Jonas loves you, and I love her more than anything. But if you give me any reason to cut you down, I will take it."

I blinked in confusion, "I'm sorry, do I know you? The fuck is your issue."

"It's best to not threaten someone's friend in their face." Briar had an ice spike to his back, her voice was deadly.

He barely glanced back at her but kept that same cold

glare at me, "I won't repeat myself."

He stepped aside as Jonas and the others ran over.

"Aubrey!" Jonas immediately hugged me, I tensed up almost immediately, "Are you alright? Did she poison you? You're bleeding!"

"I'm fine.." I muttered.

"We need to get you bandaged, hon.." Briar spoke up. I nodded a bit and avoided Rouge and Saint's stares.

"Adonys? Can you grab her?" Jonas asked, the older male was already moving before she could finish her sentence, he has a calmer presence now that she was here. *What a fuckin bozo.* I narrowed my eyes at him.

"Is this the person who poisoned you Aubrey?" Rouge spoke up, motioning to Medusa.

"Yea, she keeps yelling about how she wants me to die. Who is she?" I looked at Jonas.

"She is Project Medusa, she's the one who knows where that fucker is, and we can finally put an end to all of this. She's slippery."

"She's another Homunculus? What the fuck. How many are there."

"Too many… but, since she's down, We can finally locate Father and get rid of him for good." She looked at me reassuringly. I nodded slowly and gripped my side.

"I have to take Briar-"

"We need to get you home, your father will worry." Jonas cut me off, she looked at Rouge and Saint, "Lead the way?"

Saint immediately came to my side and helped me out, and headed towards my house, Iron leading us. The silence was heavy, I know they're going to be so upset with me. Especially Saint, I was fine when she saw me a couple hours ago, now I'm injured. Oh Gods. And all these people coming to the house? Oh dads gonna be annoyed. I huffed to myself quietly.

33

THIRTY-TWO

I kept my mouth shut as Saint wrapped the bandages, the silence in the room was heavy. I avoided her gaze, I tried to think of a way to speak to her, but I know she's upset. What could I possibly say? Is it because I left that morning? Or the injuries? She looked so sullen. I looked down at my lap and tensed slightly as she tightened the bandages.

"You Ok..?" She asked, glancing up, I nodded gently. She grabbed the scissors and finished the bandaging, "Try not to move too much until it's fully healed."

I nodded as she began to clean up the supplies. I was able to convince them to let me shower first. As soon as I got home I let the boiling hot water cleanse me. Felt good, I was able to bandage the burns before anyone noticed, I caused enough worry for one day. They weren't as bad as they were earlier, that's good at least.

She closed the box and stood up and sat next to me on the bed,"Feel like talking?" Saint spoke up quietly after a minute. I shrugged.

"I..." I sighed a bit, "I.. I'm sorry for disappearing on

you..."

"I told you not to leave in that storm." She said.

"I know..." I said, "I'm sorry, I couldn't sleep...I just.. I couldn't stop thinking..."

"..."

"I just keep thinking..." I looked at my lap, "Asking myself, Am I real? Is any of this real?"

Saint gripped my hands, "Aubrey..."

"I'm not...Real... I'm not? I have no purpose outside of victimization." I sighed, "This isn't my face." I laughed in distress and covered my face, "These are her eyes, her features."

"Aubrey... Stop...Stop it.." She sounded so defeated and hurt.

"Why am I even still here? If I could give my life for hers, maybe dad..."

"Stop!" Saint shouted. I blinked and looked at her with welled up eyes. She's never screamed at me before. "Please stop."

She pulled me into a tight comforting hug. She desperately gripped at my shirt, I slowly wrapped my arms around her waist, laying my head on her shoulder.

"Please stop... Don't ever talk about dying, I can't bear that from you... I was so worried." Saint squeezed a bit tighter, but not enough to affect the wounds, "Jonas stopped by, she said you were dying, I've never felt dread like that...Now you're talking like this? Please stop. I can't bear it."

I blinked in shock, what? Jonas told her that? Was it because of the incident yesterday? I immediately hugged her as tight as I could, comforting her to the best of my ability. She seemed to relax against me after that.

"I hate that she told you, but it's your right to know." Saint said, "I hate how bad this news affects you. I hate how depressed you are right now. Aubrey you are a person, you're alive. And I can't stress enough to you, how much your creation nor your creator defines you."

"You, are you, and genuinely you are wonderful. I know this is too much for you, and I can't fully help you…I know that, but I will always be on your side. I'm here." Her voice was basically pleading, "You're a new experience. Something completely new, and you can do so much… or, you can be normal like the rest of us."

It hurt my heart to hear her this way, to see her so distressed because of me. I've never seen her this upset, and I'm causing it. Indirectly or not, her feeling this anxious is my fault. Even so, I still feel doubt.

"And the fun part, we'll learn more together." Saint pulled away, gripping my hands. Her eyes were welled up but she still had a soft smile on her face, I can't tell if it was forced or not. I love her so much, would I really cause such stress for someone I love? I tell myself no. But I couldn't stop myself from asking.

"What if I'm not…A good.. Creation?"

It's a thought that lingered a few too many times. I know I can't be Terra, I can't make up for what was lost. The logistics of my creation are a curiosity even to the gods, what if I'm not good? What if I'm just a ticking time bomb? *What if? What if? What if?* So many damn what ifs I never thought of yesterday. I wish I could go back to yesterday.

"If that was the case, I'm sure you would've snapped ages ago." Saint snorted quietly, rubbing my hands soothingly with her thumbs.

"Do you remember when we were thirteen?" Saint spoke up, "You took up jobs in lust, at that Goat Sanctuary, because my birthday was coming up. You went there every weekend, helped her with her goats, all for fifty dollars a day."

I looked at her, curious where this was going.

"All so you could buy me this super expensive ring I said I liked in passing, I remember it like it was yesterday, I thought you were mad at me and didn't want to be friends anymore, I was so scared." Saint laughed quietly, "Then you gave me that box, that beautiful ring. And you made them match? I still can't believe you did that."

I glanced down at her hand, the same ring there, that Cathedral ring she used to go on and on about. I bought her so many bows I wanted to buy something different. It was so her, it was by far my best gift to her. She wore it everyday, hell she still does.

"I can't believe how much you did for me, when you didn't have too. And it's so much more than material things. I never cared about that, you know I can get anything I want if I asked my daddy for it." Saint looked at our hands, "Yet you went out of your way to do nice and loving gestures to me anyway, and I treasured them infinitely more because they came from you. It's not just me you're super soft on either. Rouge is a given, but you're a good person. Always have been."

"Well, yea, I guess you guys would think so." I said softly, "If The Valley had a proper justice system, I'd have a record, you know that."

Saint shrugged and smiled, "You're just rugged. You might not be the nicest. But you are the kindest person I've ever met. You, are you, and genuinely I think you are wonderful.

I think you're a perfect creation."

I felt my eyes well up again when she said that. It was so sincere. I gripped her hands gently, pulling them to my lips and kissing the top. What I did to deserve her? I'm not sure, but I'm so happy I have her.

"You mean the world to me.." Her eyes began to well up, "And I can't begin to express how much you've changed my life." Saint smiled brightly.

I can't lie, it did make me feel better. The more I thought about it, dad being in a similar position also gives me a bit of comfort. I know we have to talk properly, and maybe that'll help me. I don't know, I don't think I'm angry anymore, or ever really was? Just confused and scared? I don't know. I kept her hand to my lips and closed my eyes.

"Thank you Saint…"

"Of course, Love." She smiled gently, "I'm always here for you. Always."

I let her hands go gently and laid back on the bed, looking at the ceiling, she laid on her side next to me, watching me expectantly. I folded my hands on my stomach and stared ahead.

"You… Really don't think I'm overreacting..?" I asked quietly.

"Not at all…" Saint said, "This is a lot to take in, your feelings are valid, your feelings matter. If it matters this much to you, I'll be here to hear whatever you need to rant about. I know it's hard to word it, but… I'm here…"

"I just… I don't want to be a burden… Or unreliable… I don't want you and Rouge..And dad… To worry about me…"

"Stop thinking that way. We love you, our relationships aren't one sided, baby." She rubbed my cheek gently. "You can't be strong all the time, rely on us."

I glanced away.

"You have feelings, thoughts, wants, needs, autonomy… You're alive. You not being Earthborn doesn't change that." Saint looked at me, her beautiful silver eyes were soft and loving, as always. "It doesn't change a thing, at the end of the day. To us and everyone else, You are Aubrey Kovenn."

"…" I pulled her close and rested my head on her chest. Her breathing was calm, she gently caressed my head and rubbed my back soothingly. The silence was still there, but it was more comfortable.

Maybe she's right? Who am I kidding, she's always right. I closed my eyes and slowed my breathing. I forced myself to ignore the lingering dread and tried to focus on now. I listened to her heart beat, I remember doing that as a kid, it was so strange to hear it. I've never had a heart beat, I thought something was wrong with her, but no, she was just asleep. I remember putting my head on her chest and just laying there and listening to her heart, it's so simple when you think about it? That one organ is keeping her alive, it was so fascinating to me.

I think that's when these thoughts of inadequacy began. At sleepovers I never slept. I don't think I've had to sleep since I was a baby, but laying there and listening to her live? That lulled me to sleep, then I realized, dad had one too, I was the only one.

I was the only one for a lot of things.

Maybe that can be a good thing? Maybe I'm just unique. And if there's others out there like me, maybe I can get a better understanding? Maybe knowing more will erase that dread of the unknown?

I closed my eyes and relaxed against her, I tried to silence my thoughts for now. Even with this dread and doubt, this made me feel a bit better. It's nice to know I have unconditional love around me. Why do I always doubt it? When will I learn? I breathed out after taking in the scent of her perfume, Vanilla and Black Cherry. Like always. It put a comforting smile on my face. Her heartbeat was music to my ears.

"Do you know how much I love you?" I asked quietly.

"Of course I do." Saint said softly, a smile was in her voice, "I love you too."

34

THIRTY-THREE

Dad softly knocked on the door and peeked his head in, "Hey kid.. Can I come in..?"

I nodded and sat up completely. Saint headed out a little while ago, I guess she went and told dad I was awake and fine. My body seemed to rapidly heal all of a sudden, It strangely didn't burn anymore if not at all? I decided to leave the bandages just in case.

"How are you feeling?" Tartarus asked quietly, sitting on the bed.

I shrugged, "Fine? I guess..."

"I wanted to apologize." Dad rubbed his hands on his pants, "I didn't respect your agency, I should've been more upfront with you... Especially if you could have possibly been put in danger.."

"It's alright.."

"It's not." He looked at me, "If I'm honest, I thought he was dead, I thought it was said and done. And I am, so sorry, for not being as responsible as I should've been."

"Now I feel like I caused a rift, I don't ever want you to

feel I'd lie to you, or that you can't speak to me.."

"I'm...Not angry anymore..?" I rubbed my arm gently. "I had a lot of mixed emotions with it, I just..."

"You can be honest with me Aubrey..." Tartarus said gently.

I looked at my lap and messed with my hands anxiously, my eyes began to water again. I willed it away with Saint, but the longer I thought about it the worse I felt. I opened my mouth to speak but closed it shortly after. It was overwhelming.

"Aubrey...talk to me kid.." Tartarus cupped my cheeks, a few tears began to fall, I felt like a little kid again, running to dad's room when I heard something in my closet or outside, I hugged him and broke down completely.

"I'm scared?" I gripped his shirt, "I..I'm terrified?"

He pulled me close and cradled the back of my head, the tears wouldn't stop, "And I don't know what to do dad... All I can think about is the past, and what ifs. I'm so scared..."

He had heartbreak in his eyes, he squeezed comfortingly.

"I feel so pathetic, I feel disgusting."

"Honey..." Tartarus spoke gently, rubbing his hand soothingly against my hair, "I'm so sorry..."

"You are not pathetic. The last thing I've ever wanted to do is make you feel this way." He looked away, "You are so much more than I ever imagined, you know.."

He chuckled quietly, "I was going to give you away when you turned three, I figured you'd be old enough to get adopted, and I'd just go back to life as normal. I'm no parent." He shook his head,

"Then you turned four, then five, then six, and every year I fell more and more in love with you, you are my pride and joy." Tartarus smiled, "And I'll do everything in my power to keep you safe, and to see you happy."

I looked up at him and rubbed my eyes. I laid my head on his chest, listening to his heartbeat, like I always have.

"Thanks dad…" I sniffed quietly. "I'm sorry.."

"Stop apologizing." He spoke gently, I sat up and rubbed at my eyes, taking a breath. "You have nothing to be sorry for."

"Can…" I started, He looked down at me in question, "Can you tell me about your creation?"

"Huh?" He asked, "Oh, well, of course…"

He adjusted his seating and thought for a moment. I laid my head on his shoulder.

"Well, I'm not Earthborn, a few of Jezabelle's children aren't. But not in the same sense as you." He tapped his chin, "If I remember correctly, Jezabelle said my sister, Terra, wanted to create something."

"It was like a mother daughter bonding thing?" Tartarus asked.

I tilted my head and raised a brow. "A bonding thing?"

"Terra said she wanted to create the Earthens and Aides was hesitant, but Jezabelle convinced her to start simple and to practice. She started off with little Claybornes they're like little clay statues she gave tasks to."

"Claybornes?" I laughed quietly.

"I never said she was a clever namer." Dad chuckled, "Then one day, Jezabelle and Terra made me. It's why Terra and I were so close, she's basically my creator. She treated me like her sibling, but Jezabelle said I needed a purpose 'cuz all the gods have one, and they wanted me to lock away someone." Dad seemed to instinctively place his hand on his waist, his eyes seemed slightly scared. "It didn't work out and I got injured but the idea of keeping prisoners in me stuck."

"So they're actually…In you?" I asked, "Does that not feel? Violating and gross?" I asked.

"The first few times it did, I wasn't sure how to go about it, I'm one of a kind." He looked towards the window, "I eventually got better, Terra convinced Aides to make me into a portal basically. They found a way to make my body more of a portal and lock, than a full time prison."

"Is that what that off limits place is that Charon told me about? Is that the prison you are linked with?"

"It is, I was going to take you when you got older, so you could see there's more to my job but Charon threatened me." He laughed, "They said it was too much for you."

I made a disappointed face, "Well now I want to see it."

He smiled and stroked the top of my head, "Maybe one day kid."

"So, you being made like this…It doesn't bother you..?" I asked.

"Not really, because I was raised like you. Once that first attempt failed, I wasn't really needed. Terra convinced me to try again."

"You really cared for Auntie Terra huh…?" I asked quietly.

"Of course, she was my family."

"You Miss her?" I asked, looking up at him.

"Everyday. She was irreplaceable, I like to think you were a gift from her. What's the odds I went to find the man who killed my sister and I end up adopting her mini me? I try not to dwell on the disgusting implications of it. I know if Terra saw you she would've taken you in a heartbeat." He chuckled.

I stayed quiet and sat up, looking at my lap. I could feel tears welling up in my eyes.

"Would you feel better if she was here instead of me…"

"What?" Tartarus asked in disbelief.

"If she never died I wouldn't have been created… Now she's gone and I'm here." I mumbled.

"Aubrey." He said sternly, "Stop that, none of what happened to her is your fault. The only one at fault is the man who did this."

"There isn't an Earth Goddess anymore, and now I'm here…"

"You are not Terra." He said, "You owe nothing to her responsibilities. You are not replacing her, to me you aren't Terra, you're Aubrey. You're my kid. I wouldn't want it any other way." He pulled me into a hug, "Look, sometimes people die, and we just have to learn to deal with that. No what ifs, or wishing will stop that. Yes it hurts, it'll always hurt to lose those you love, but we grieve because we love. That pain is there because we love."

"And if I lost you, it would hurt a lot more. Aubrey you are loved, just the way you are." He reassured me.

I felt tears fall and hit my hands, I dropped my head in my hands and sobbed quietly. Oh gods why did I say that, I hugged him immediately apologizing profusely. I feel like a stupid child again, saying stupid things with little regard. What if that made him feel like I was contemplating something? What if I worried him, what the fuck is wrong with me. I gripped his shirt and tried to calm down.

"I don't know what to say to make you feel better, but I just want you to know I'm always here, I'm not going anywhere. I love you very much Aubrey."

"I love you too dad…"

He kissed the top of my head and just rubbed my back soothingly. Honestly getting all these tears out feels better. I feel calmer, I'm exhausted but I guess emotions always are. I don't know why but hearing dad differentiate us made me feel secure, maybe it's because it was dad? Is that what that actual fear was? Abandonment? Fear of disappointing him? It's so irrational, He already knew right? He knew what he signed up for, but I guess it's relieving that he doesn't see me as a replacement for Auntie Terra. I know I can't be her, or live up to her, but maybe I can do right by her? I can take better care of her creations, learn more about her? Maybe then I can make up for everything? Or should I just leave it be? Gods I don't know, I'm tired. I honestly just want to sleep off these last two days and pretend it never happened.

I thought back on all the things Saint told me and now dad. Maybe I should take that into consideration? I'm alive, I have agency, autonomy, thoughts and feelings. I have people I love, people who trust me, who are worried. I want to grow. I want to continue to be me, no expectations, just like the day before. It won't have to define me, but it is something that's a part of me, I can't deny that. Hell, it's impossible. I love music, I love women, I love art and reading, I love my life.

If this is fear then I'll take that and use it to fuel me. Especially if this monster is harming and kidnapping other people? He can't be allowed to exist. I can't live like this. Looking over my shoulder and dreading a boogeyman peeking out the shadows. I won't live like a sheep in prep for slaughter. I haven't before and I won't now, I can't change what I am, and how I was made. But I can change his status of life on this planet. I don't have to forget, I can't forget. I can start to cope though, I think dad gave me that little push. I needed to hear that.

I'm Alive. I think that's enough for me. If dad can do it, then so can I, right? I'm a Kovenn after all.

"We can be more honest now if you want…" He spoke up, "Whenever you're ready, I'll let you read the files, or whatever you feel you need to do."

I nodded then smiled up at my dad. "Thanks, I feel better… Really.."

He wiped the tears off my cheeks and smiled softly. He kissed my nose and squeezed my cheeks like he used to when I was a child. I couldn't help but laugh a bit at how goofy it felt. I just let him, it's been a stressful two days, I hugged him again and breathed out.

A small knock caught our attention, Saint stood there, smiling gently, "She's awake now, everyone is waiting for you.."

I nodded and pulled away, dad roughed up my hair a bit and I swatted at his hands. He grinned and followed after me, we walked down the steps, Iron already waiting at the bottom, his tail wagging in eagerness. I pet his head and scratched behind his ear. The air was on full blast and It caught me completely off guard.

"Mind the cold." Tartarus said, "It's for your friend. She was very eager to meet me."

I blinked and looked up at him, "Oh, Briar? She's still here? Uh, heh. Yea she's my ex. So." I nodded and waved it off. He gave me a look but kept quiet.

There she sat, Medusa. Tied to the chair and swearing up a storm. She was hissing in annoyance and trying to wiggle her way out of the chair. Everyone seemed unamused while Jonas seemed outwardly annoyed.

"I can't believe you did that!"

"Would you prefer I break your nose?" The Dragon deadpanned, his eyes were dark.

"Where did you even pull that from! You are so disgusting!" Medusa yelled back.

"Don't even go there. You pervert." He muttered in annoyance.

"Who is this." Briar spoke up, she sat on the couch next to Rue, Rouge was staying close to Medusa, I could feel the heat radiating off her from here. She was angry.

"A nuisance." I said, "Who the hell are you, and why are you stalking me, I suggest you answer truthfully, you're severely outnumbered."

"Tch, aren't you lucky." Medusa scoffed, "A whole squad to protect your pathetic ass." She wiggled her dainty wrists.

"Seriously, what's your problem, I don't know you." I narrowed my eyes in annoyance.

"She's the daughter of the man that made us." Jonas spoke up. She had her arms crossed, the Dragon lingering. I felt a sudden dread wash over me.

"Daughter." I repeated.

"Don't call me that." Medusa shot back bitterly.

"Oh? Thought you wanted your daddy's approval. You've been running errands for him all your life." Jonas raised a brow.

She fell silent and looked away, "I don't want his approval, I gave up on that long ago. I'd never get it, Because *Project EF exists*." Medusa spoke with venom and rolled her eyes harshly, I could feel the bite in her words towards me.

"Project EF?" I asked, she groaned in annoyance and dropped her head against the chair.

"That's you hon.."

"Me?" I asked.

Jonas smiled and nodded, "All of us are projects."

"Projects…" I glanced at Medusa, then pointed at her, "But she's?"

Jonas nodded solemnly, "She was Earthborn, yes, so was Adonys."

I looked at the Dragon, he ignored my gaze, the others stayed silent, we all came to the same conclusion. These experimented kids are alive? I felt sick at the thought. Those poor children, and his own daughter was one of them? Disgusting.

"Which is why we need to find him, before he does this to even more children, but she won't tell us where he is." Jonas grumbled.

"But, why? That don't make a lick of sense, sugar." I looked at Medusa, "Why protect him, when he clearly has no care for you? What do you get out of it."

"…"

"Now you were just madder than a wet hen, now your cemetery quiet, what is your goal."

"I want him… to feel as much anger and disappointment I've felt. I want to kill you and any hope he has of reaching his disgusting goals." Medusa spoke up. I could feel the heat worsen from Rouge and my dad, Rouge immediately grabbed her by her shirt making Medusa's glasses slightly slip down her face, her eyes basically on fire with rage.

"Who the fuck do you think you are?"

"Rouge." I took her hand gently, "Look I get it." I slowly

moved her hand away and looked down at her. "You Are angry because you aren't me. And frankly, you will never be me."

Medusa growled out, her snakes hissed, I put my hands up before Briar and Rouge could jump. I kneeled next to her, and rested my hands on the arm of the chair. She was a petite and slender girl. Her snakes were a deep brown. She was in a low cut dirty T-shirt and jeans. Her body was covered in wounds. I sighed lightly.

"And that will never change, and doing whatever convoluted idea you conjured up in your mind isn't going to make you feel better. I could drop dead tomorrow, and you'll what? Go back there and go back to business as usual?"

I noticed her skin was significantly different from mine and Jonas'. Was she born this way? Or did he mutate her? I noticed healed over scars and bite marks. She had a lot of stitched up parts on her body. If this is how she looks, what do the other kids look like?

"Is that.. Really a life you want to live?" I noticed her hands were scratched and bruised, she isn't Ok. At first I felt anger, but now? All I feel is pity. This is a hurt child, a distressed child, an abused and battered child.

"Aubrey…" Saint spoke up. I looked at her then back to Medusa.

I stood up, Medusa kept her gaze away, her snakes rubbed against her cheeks, almost as if they were comforting her, she stayed silent.

"Look, you've tried to kill me, at least three separate times now." I sighed, "Even so, I can't bring myself to hate you."

"I don't need your pity." Medusa muttered.

"It's empathy." I spoke gently, "Something we can work

on."

"What." Medusa asked, finally looking at me, from this angle I could see just over her glasses. Her eyes were snake like, I noticed Jonas tense in the corner of my eye. Her eyes were mesmerizing, a reptilian swirl of brown and gold. She seemed almost surprised I held her gaze.

"Aubrey don't-" Jonas spoke up, she went to cover my eyes. I blinked and looked at her. "You..?" She asked.

"What?" I asked.

"You aren't stone." Medusa muttered, her snakes watched me curiously.

"Should I be?"

"Eye contact." Jonas spoke up.

"I see, is that why your eyes are so unique?" I asked, she blinked and looked down. "I'm losing my eyesight, might be a reason."

Medusa seemed taken aback by that.

"I apologize." I leaned over and adjusted the glasses properly on her face, "Are you more comfortable this way?"

Her snakes flick their tongues at me, I tried to stay calm and avoid any contact with them, she seemed less hostile now. Her shoulders were slumped, her gaze now fully hidden behind the glasses.

"Fighting isn't going to get us anywhere, so please, will you help us?" I put my hand to her gently after motioning Briar to retract her ribbons, she hesitantly did so but Rouge stuck close, "Do you really want more people to be subjected to that man? Children growing up like you and him?"

Medusa looked at my hand, the room was tense, everyone was waiting, but I tried to ignore them. I kept my focus on her, the more I looked at her the sadder I felt. Her body showed so much of her abuse, she needs help, not hostility and anger.

She eventually took my hand in her rough ones. I held her hand gently, and looked at dad. He looked away and breathed out.

"I'll... Fix up the guest room." Tartarus walked off.

I smiled down at her softly, gripping her hand gently and nodding to her respectfully, "My name is Aubrey by the way."

"I know this is a hasty decision, please don't make me regret it." I smiled, she looked at me then away.

This did nothing but solidify my stance. Your crimes won't go unpunished , you won't continue to get away with this.

Salem, *I will kill you.*

35

THIRTY-FOUR

I headed down to the kitchen, my eyes felt heavy and I can't stress how tired I am. My phone has been pinging all night, texts from the group chats, from Briar, everything. I huffed out and poured myself a cup of coffee after sitting my phone on the counter. Pinging *over and over*. I prepared my coffee and leaned against the counter, the house was silent, dad was working by now and I'm sure Iron is still sleeping, he huffed out of my room last night from all the notifications. I shook my head and picked up my phone, reading over everything.

'Aubrey! Have you lost your mind!?' Rouge asked.

followed by Saint's, *'She tried to kill you!'*

I groaned quietly and ran my hands through my locs a bit and began replying to the texts.

'I'm more than aware.' I leaned against the counter, *'This is better than her running around and shooting shit all crazy and hunting me right.'*

'What if this is a ploy, and she's trying to kill you in your sleep or something.' Rouge typed, I huffed quietly, do they

honestly think I'm that stupid?

'Iron and my dad are here, this is probably the safest place I'll be.' I waved it off, *'Even Jonas is more trusting and she just met me.'*

"We trust you, we're just worried.' Rouge typed

'And I distinctly remember her saying she didn't approve before saying she trusts your judgment, and threatened her life.' Saint replied

'Yea yea, it's fine, she's been docile.' I rolled my eyes and made another cup, glancing at my phone as another text came in, this time it was from Briar.

'Are you going to be Ok? Mentally..?'

I smiled a bit and responded to her, *'Yea, I think so, just.. Need to adjust to the changes.'*

She began typing and another text from the group chat flashed,

'Fine. If you need anything, please, just, call us.' Rouge spoke up.

'Good, I'm muting the chat now bye.<3' I shook my head and grabbed both cups, heading back upstairs, holding the mugs carefully and checking Briar's texts.

'Wonderful! Let us know if you need anything beloved, always here for you <3"

I smiled a bit and hearted her text before stopping outside the guest room. I knocked lightly and I put my ear to the door slightly and opened it, Medusa sat on the bed, covering her ears in what seemed like annoyance, her snakes were certainly lively.

"Morning."

She looked over, she dropped her gaze and sighed. "Yea."

"Here.." I sat the cup down for her and smiled gently.

"What's this. Poison?" Medusa narrowed her eyes, "It won't work I have immunity."

I raised a brow, "No, it's coffee, ya like coffee?" I asked

She glanced at the cup and picked it up, she sniffed at it cautiously, she's definitely like a child. She can't be too much younger or older than me, my rough guess is twenty two to twenty four. I shook my head and glanced away. She blew on the drink and sipped it.

"So, is your name actually Medusa? Or.." I asked gently.

She placed the cup on her lap and turned her head away, "Yes. It is, It's on my certificate."

"Oh? Well that's good, I don't want to call you a product number."

"Product number?" She questioned. I waved it off and rubbed my head

"Well, it's Saturday, I don't have school or work today, it's been a few days so… Would you like to head to town today?"

"Town." She questioned, "Are you luring me somewhere."

"No, not at all." I breathed out, "I figured you'd like some clothes, something to calm your nerves? Anything you need, you'll probably be here for a while…"

She looked at her cup and rubbed her finger against it, she looked almost ashamed? She had a small pout to her lips. "Why are you being so nice. I still don't know how I feel about you."

"I'm just a nice person." I shrugged, "Get dressed, we'll leave in 15 minutes." I nodded and headed outside the room, closing the door behind me.

I headed back to my room and looked through my closet. She definitely wouldn't like my style, but hey it's better than nothing right? I skimmed through a few of my clothes, I grabbed a few old t-shirts and shoes. I looked them over and thought for a moment, should be good enough for today.

I sat the clothes in the guest bathroom for her and walked back to my room before she walked in. I started my own shower and put the water on high heat. I stood under it. Taking a few relaxing breaths. What a long, exhausting few days. I laid my head back and closed my eyes.

A lot of changes too soon, I'm genuinely shocked dad allowed it. I figured he'd kick her out while I was out at school. Like an unwanted pet. He tried to talk me out of it a few times but eventually conceded. Maybe this is reckless, who knows? But leaving her alone in such a state, just to watch her hate and annoyance fester like that? It didn't feel right. She was clearly having a breakdown, or she was overstimulated, probably scared. She's been fighting all her life, maybe this'll be good for her.

I scrubbed down my body and got out, drying my hair and checking the clock. I pulled on my clothes and stretched. I walked in the hall after grabbing my boots and hat.

"You ready short stack?" I asked and knocked lightly on her door and pushed it open.

"Don't address me as such, my name is Medusa." She huffed, the shirt was way too big on her, but hey we can work with this. I walked over and picked up a belt.

"Yes ma'am, do you mind?" I asked, motioning to the belt.

"Huh? I haven't done anything?" She almost curled into herself, her snakes immediately got defensive. I blinked in confusion then looked at the belt and put my hands up.

"Oh! No! Gods no." I motioned to her waist, "I was asking if you were fine with me helping you with it.."

She looked down, her snakes slowly fell to her shoulders

but continued to hiss. Her eyebrows furrowed in annoyance, she muttered a harsh *shut up* under her breath, they're probably driving her crazy.

"My apologies.." I spoke gently. She nodded a bit and moved her arms up. I kneeled down and adjusted the belt for her, and fixed the shirt to cover her. "Alright, I can grab you some shorts if you'd like?"

"Sure.." She avoided eye contact.

"I'll be right back…" I left the room and rubbed my eyes. *How fucked up can you be? This is going to be a bit more complicated than I thought.* I looked through my drawers. Saint's shorts should fit her fine? I grabbed a few satin scrunchies while I was there and met back up with her.

"Here, and for your snakes, try this." I handed her the shorts and scrunchies, "I'll wait for you outside."

She took it and looked at it. I left the room and headed back downstairs, I grabbed my backpack and grabbed a few waters and checked my wallet. She came down stairs, her snakes were calmer, I smiled at her.

"Better?"

She nodded quietly.

"This shouldn't take too long, we can get you a few outfits, some snacks, what have you." I headed to the door with her.

"I don't have money.."

"Don't worry about it." I opened the door for her, "Dad! We're heading to the city!"

"Take Iron with you!"

I rolled my eyes a bit and whistled for him. He hopped up and took off for the door. I led her to the ferry and we made our way down to the city. Probably should've come out tomorrow, she might get overwhelmed, I glanced down at her. She stayed close, but she kept her eyes towards the town fountain. I bought two passes for greed and motioned her to follow.

"Like the fountain?" I asked.

"Yes, I like fountains, but where I'm from, water comes from them.."

"You're from the surface right?" I asked, looking down at her.

"I am."

"I've only been up there once, it was beautiful from what I saw, it wasn't a lot, but I still loved it." I opened the gate for her and let her inside. "How are you feeling here?"

"I'm Ok, I'm used to it I suppose." Medusa shrugged.

"Well, if you feel uncomfortable at any time, just tell me. Yea?"

She nodded and we headed to the town, I motioned to the shops. "Does anything stand out to you?"

Medusa scanned the area, her eyes seemed larger. Like she's never had this privilege, she probably hasn't, especially if that man is her father. She gripped my sleeve and pointed to a store. It had a cottage aesthetic to it. I'm shocked it's even in business, the tower was flashing red, so maybe we'll get lucky.

"You sure?"

"I am." She nodded.

I walked over and held the door open for her, she looked up at me and raised her brow, "Why do you do that?"

"What?"

"That motion, with the door." She pointed to it, "Do you assume I'm too weak to open a door? I should kill you."

I blinked then snorted, "Oh honey, welcome to the south.

That's a lil thing you're gonna have to get used to. It's what we call hospitality."

"Hospitality?" Medusa nodded slowly, "Oh, well, now I feel foolish."

"Most people up north ain't as civilized as we are. And you're strutting with me, I'm just polite." I motioned to the racks, "Choose whatever, I'll wait for you."

She nodded and I sat at the front of the store, checking my phone. A message from Keegan popped up and I felt my mood brighten instantly. I decided to call her, the phone rang only twice before her soft voice answered.

"Hello~" Keegan hummed.

"Mm, you have no idea how good it is to hear your voice, how are you?" I asked gently.

"I'm alright, how are you?? You missed a few days of school and didn't reply to my texts.. Then I didn't see you Thursday or Friday."

"Gods, I am so sorry." I laid my head back against the glass, looking up at the ceiling, " I don't even know where to start. The past week has been a pain in the ass."

"Are you Ok?"

"I…think so?" I rubbed my hand on my pants, "I wish I could tell you, but it's a long complicated situation at home right now. I'm sorry for missing our date, not too mad for a reschedule?"

"Well, I should be mad. But you sound so exhausted…"

"I am." I chuckled, "I'm sorry, I can definitely do the date tomorrow? I'd love to spend some time with you, you always put a smile on my face."

I could hear the bright smile in her voice, "I'd be delighted, as long as you talk to me Ok? You don't have to bottle anything up hon.."

"I won't burden you, but, today I'm in town, uh. Helping out a family friend who stopped by suddenly?" I glanced to the side at the small white lie, "I've been coming straight home to her to make sure she isn't face down in the bathtub." I joked

She laughed quietly, "I see, don't stay out too long? Make sure you rest, I want you at your max energy tomorrow." Keegan giggled.

I smiled, "As she wishes, I have no idea what I did to score you, but gods I'm happy I did it."

"Oh stooop, you're a wonderful person."

"..." I looked down at my lap, eyes a bit distant, "I'm glad you think so."

"Hm? Oh, sorry momma is calling me, you be safe yes? And I'll see you tomorrow?"

"6?" I asked

"5:45." Keegan joked back. I chuckled and nodded, rubbing my head.

"Perfect. Tell them I said hello."

"I will~ see you~" She hung up and I dragged my hand down my face and breathed out, Medusa walked over with a few clothes in her hands, a small amount. I raised a brow and looked up at her.

"That's it?" I asked.

"I don't need much.."

"You're gonna need more than A dress and a shirt and a pair of pants. Love, pick out as much as you want." I motioned her towards the racks. She looked slightly uncomfortable before nodding obediently. I sighed sadly and watched her go.

She came back over after a minute, holding more.

"There we go." I stood and looked through the pile, "Lets try these on and whatever you like, we can get."

"You're being serious right?" Medusa asked, looking up at me. I nodded almost eagerly.

"Absolutely. You are safe here. I will kill that man, if I have to, I'll learn exorcism so he won't even end up down here in death." I felt my voice get cold, "You don't have to leave here unless you wish too."

She looked down, before nodding, "I will, *consider*, trusting you."

"I'm not here to force anything on you, you have freedom to do as you please, hon."

"Yea.." Medusa nodded and walked in the dressing room. Gods, this is painful. Rouge and Saint would be infinitely better at this than me. They're the outgoing ones, this'll be a long process, but hey, at least I'm patient. I glanced out the window at Iron, he was laying on the sidewalk, growling at random people passing by, I shook my head and checked my phone while I waited. I leaned against the wall and tried to relax, bright side, I'm not shopping with Saint.

She always takes forever. Such a beauty queen. Then people assume I'm her boyfriend and try to fight me, the hell did I do. This place is strange sometimes, but she's always so happy to spend that time with me and vice versa. I looked over at the clothes and put my phone away and skimmed through the clothes. Red hm? That's more of Rouge's color. I looked through the different dresses, would that even be appropriate? I'm not her boyfriend anymore. And Keegan is not a red girl, she loves baby blues and whites and none of this is her style. Maybe a different store.

THIRTY-FOUR

"Ok, I'm ready." Medusa walked over, her shoulders seemed relaxed now, progress.

I looked up from the clothes I was looking at, "Tried them all on?"

"I don't want these." I took them from her and put them back on the racks. I took the clothes she had and headed to the register, paid and left with her and Iron. Now would be best to get essentials, I headed to a store and motioned her inside after putting my card to her.

Medusa blinked in confusion and looked at my hand then back at me, "Uh?"

"I'm going to trust you to do this, alright?" I spoke gently, "I won't linger over you while you get essentials, I don't want to make you uncomfortable. Get whatever you need, and I'll be out here."

"And you're trusting me so easily?"

"Gotta start somewhere right?" I grinned. Medusa raised a brow before taking the card cautiously. She headed inside and I motioned for Iron to stay and wait for her. I went a little ways up the strip and into an electronic store, if she's gonna be down here she's gonna need a phone. I looked over the older models, they won't break as easily and have a more simple style and they're cheaper. This is gonna definitely break my bank. I pushed the thought back and went to purchase the phone, a sim and a simple case.

I walked outside and started setting it up, and put mine and dads number in it. What else would she need? I looked down at the clothes bag and thought for a minute.

I can let her borrow some of my chucks for now, I doubt she'd be out and about for awhile. I started my walk back down to the store she was in until a record store caught my eye. I looked in the windows and walked in, a little detour can't hurt right?

I looked over the different albums. Most I already have, but I don't have them all, and we're out and about. I can get one? Why not. I skimmed through the vinyls and read a few of them. My MJ collection hasn't been added to in a long while.

I walked over to the player and looked over the tracks, until I felt a presence behind me.

"There you are." Medusa said.

"See, you gained my trust." I smiled and took the card from her. She rolled her eyes.

"What is this store? I don't need anything in here."

"Oh, this was for me." I chuckled and sat the headphones down, "I like to collect records."

"Why? For what purpose."

"Fun." I shrugged, "Do you like music?"

"Music.." She tilted her head, then thought to herself, "I haven't listened to music..since I was a girl…" Something looked distant in her eyes. "I remember a player, it had a funnel on the top, and I remember my hair being brushed… It was a faint sound…" She rubbed her head.

"Oh?" I looked at her intrigued, "Do you remember the melody? If it was playing through a phonograph then it's probably in here somewhere."

Medusa rubbed her head once more and looked at the ground. She was concentrating hard, she began to hum quietly, it was a soft lovely tune, familiar too. I turned to her.

"Mm…Mmm… Rose…" Medusa shook her head, "No good, that's all.."

"No, that's perfect." I hummed the same tune over and over again while looking through the tracks, "I love music, it's one thing that always made me feel something, isn't that just phenomenal?"

She looked at me curiously.

"Music is heavenly, it makes a mood, tells a story, describes a feeling, It's a gift. Hm... Kiss from a Rose, right?" I nodded and motioned her over, handing her the headphones, "That song stuck with you because it gives you a feeling, right? How's it make you feel?"

She took the headphones and put them on, and I played the song for her, "Is this right?"

She took a moment to listen, before I knew it, her eyes were welling up. I panicked slightly and went to turn it off, she placed her hand on mine, stopping me gently. She gripped my hand and nodded solemnly.

"Yes, this is the song... It...Reminds me of my momma..." Medusa spoke softly. "That's who was brushing my hair..." She put her hand to her head and gripped at the snakes. "Before this." She took the headphones off quickly and basically threw them down before abruptly exiting the store.

Way to go dumbass.

I felt a pit in my stomach, I looked at the track and put the headphones back, made my purchases and followed after her. She was sat in a nearby alley, she wouldn't get far with Iron around, her legs were pulled to her chest and she was rubbing at her eyes.

I slowly approached and sat next to her hesitantly as she trembled.

I'm not good at this. I laid my head back against the bricks, thinking of what to say. She was shaking, small cries coming from her. I just sat silently, sometimes, that's better than speaking. I just sat and let her get it out, she's clearly got so much on her chest she was never allowed to get out. The grief she must feel for her past life before he ruined it. Nothing more than a pawn in a game she never asked to play.

Once she calmed down, I gently gripped her hand, rubbing the top reassuringly. She looked up at me with glistening eyes, rubbing at her eyes with the sleeves. I smiled gently at her.

"It's Ok..."

She trembled once more and looked down.

"I can't begin to fathom what you've been through, or what horrors you had to endure... I won't pretend to know." I rubbed my nails on top of her hand gently. "But if anything my dad and friends taught me, it's that listening and being an ear is more helpful than doing nothing."

She rubbed her eye, and sniffed quietly.

"And I've been told I'm a good listener." I looked at her, "If you need to talk, or cry, or scream, whatever... I'm here.."

"But why. What have I done to make you give a shit." Medusa looked at her lap.

"Everyone is deserving of compassion and understanding." I shrugged, "If people wrote me off based off my first and second impressions, no one would like me." I shook my head, "In all honesty, I think Rouge and Saint make people give me a chance." I chuckled.

"They do look nicer than you..." Medusa sniffed and wiped her cheek. I laughed quietly.

"So I've been told. I think I get it from my dad." I smiled.

She sniffed and looked at her lap, "I'm sorry, I don't know

why I reacted this way… I can't even… Remember her?" Her eyes began to well again.

"That's why…" I gripped her hand, "Let it all out love."

"I… I Miss her…" Medusa hugged her legs to her chest. I rubbed her back and let the calming silence fall over us again. She slowly calmed down again. I put the CD and a player to her.

"It's just that song." I smiled gently.

She took it gently in her hands and looked at it, a brief smile flashed on her lips, she looked up at me. Her face was significantly softer, no scowls or angry furrowed brows, just, a woman.

"Thank you…" She spoke softly and smiled.

"You're welcome Medusa…"

36

THIRTY-FIVE

I couldn't help but glance at the clock, it's been hours and these people still haven't left yet. I like this job but *Jezabelle*, I hate the clientele sometimes. I checked the clock once more and went back to cleaning the tables. The den is a nice vibe but gods it sucks when niggas don't leave the fucking establishment before closing. At least I'm getting overtime? Shopping for Medusa and taking Keegan out directly after really broke my bank last weekend. I huffed quietly and picked up a few glasses and put them in the bust bucket

"Are they still here?" Blanche spoke up.

I grunted in slight annoyance, "Yea, dad is gonna kill me if I don't get back home soon."

"He still doesn't know you're doing night shifts?" Blanche asked, counting her till.

"Nope, that vein might pop." I wiped the tables down and popped my neck. "You're the boss, can you kick them out already?"

"You know that's not how we do things, these pests complain about anything."

"What if I call Auntie and offer them as ingredients." I muttered in annoyance. She laughed and waved it off.

"Oh behave, just give them the check." Blanche handed me the tab and I huffed quietly before walking over.

"Evening, just dropping off your check." I smiled gently, the woman immediately turned her head to me with a look of amusement, the man seemed annoyed but reluctant.

"Evening, how much would it be for your time?" He asked in a venomous tone, I blinked in confusion and tilted my head.

" 'Xcuse me?" I questioned.

"It's our anniversary and she wants a-"

"Oh, whoa, sorry, I'm just wait staff sir, I'm not a sex worker, they have all gone home for the night, and I ain't into men, a threesome won't work out." I said almost passive aggressively. I could see the staff snickering in the corner of my eye and I could feel my eyebrow twitch in annoyance, but kept a polite smile.

"That's a shame, well, I guess we'll be heading out."

"Yes, well, have a nice night." I bowed my head and quickly walked off.

"Ya know, you'd make a killing as a consort, I can get your own room and everything. The patrons seem to love you." Blanche leaned against her hand

I rolled my eyes, "Yea I'll pass. And last time I booked a room, one of the workers tried to force himself on me, I ain't doin that shit again." I pushed down a disgusted shudder, ever since I learned about that fucker, being objectified and lusted after like this feels, *icky*. To put it lightly. Something turns in my stomach, I wasn't too fond of it back then either but now? Especially not.

"And he was fired and taken care of, but It is 100% your choice my love, but I know you've been tight on cash lately.."

"Yea, well my current choice is home. They're gone and I'm clocking out."

"Enjoy your night Aubrey." The cook spoke up. I threw my hand up as a goodbye and clocked out before grabbing my jacket and heading outside. I pulled a pack of cigarettes from my pocket and lit one and took a deep breath.

I looked down and counted through my tips and nodded to myself, "Oh not bad Kovenn, not bad at all."

A throat clear immediately put me on guard, I got in a defensive position then breathed out in relief.

"Medusa?" I asked, walking over to her. She was in one of her new dresses, she was leaning against the bricks, she was slightly shivering, "What are you doing out here? It's late, and sloth's cold front is pushing down." I pulled my jacket off and draped it around her shoulders.

"I wanted to come get you, Mr. Tartarus told me you'd be here..."

Of course he did, They've been friendly lately. Hell I'm starting to think he gets on better with her than I do.

"It's quiet when you're gone..." She spoke the last half quietly.

"Ah.." I nodded, "Well, thank you, hon... usually I'm home by now, but late night customers." I motioned her to follow as we began to walk.

"Are you... doing sexual favors..?" Medusa asked, glancing up at me. I blinked then laughed quietly.

"Not at all, got a girlfriend remember?"

"Oh, yes, the blue one."

"Her name is Keegan, be polite." I pat the top of her head

and looked up at the stars, a few clouds began pushing this way, Briar must be comfortable, I remember she mentioned vacationing here during the cold fronts, very cute to think about her coming to this hot ass place in ski gear, all 'cuz someone left sloth's fridge open. I popped my neck and breathed out.

"Yes. Um, I'd like to go somewhere."

"Tonight?" I asked.

She nodded, "If that's not too much to ask..."

"Is it out of the way?" I asked. Medusa shook her head and pointed to a shop, the only shop with its lights on, I raised a brow reading over the sign.

"A bookstore?" I looked down at her. She nodded eagerly.

"I saw a notebook I want..." Her voice was eager, well that's enough for me. I checked my watch, she knows what she wants and I can use card, it shouldn't take too long. I opened the door for her and let her walk ahead. I gave an apologetic nod to the cashier and waited for Medusa. She B lined directly to an aisle and looked over the notebooks.

I checked my phone and sent dad a quick message, he's probably worried. I'm shocked he didn't send Iron after her. Her chunky heels clicked on the wooden floor and I looked up from my phone.

"Just this." She sat a book down with a frog and mushroom design on it and a mushroom pen. The cashier rang it up quickly and I paid with my phone, leaving with the smaller girl.

"Mushrooms?" I asked. Medusa nodded, she had a slight bounce in her step.

"Yes! I discovered them while testing poisons here, we don't have any where I'm from." She pulled out her phone and showed me multiple pictures, some blurry, some too close and others just right. I smiled gently at her.

"They have so many uses! I can make so many poisons! Oh and I discovered these little cuties! I love them!" She showed me a few pictures of frogs and salamanders, *ah, a slimy creature enjoyer.* I gave a forced smile and nodded.

"Well that's great..."

"I learned some of these little hopping things can be poisonous too!" She held her bag, "I wish to calculate my findings in this cute journal. I'm bored when you leave, so Mr. Tartarus told me to find a hobby, he gave me some advice but none stuck out..."

I looked at her and rubbed my eyes.

"Then I saw the field of flowers by your house, they smelled poisonous. So I began studying them but I couldn't record my findings." She said.

"Oh, be careful with those, they're Death Flowers." I said between yawns. "They're Nightshade or something? Or Belladonna, something like that."

"I see!"

"I'm sorry, wait, you can smell poison?" I asked.

"I can smell it, taste it, make it, cure it, anything." Medusa nodded, "My snakes are very venomous. I grew an immunity. So for fun I find new ways to make poison. My body itself is toxic."

"Is that so?"

"Mhmm." She went silent after that. I nodded and led her home.

"I see." I spoke quietly. "So the bullets and syringes you shoot?"

"All poison! My poison to be specific! I can ooze it or

expel it from my fangs."

I shuddered in discomfort, "Does that imply you shot me with your poison when we first met?"

Her face lit up with a red blush. She quickly shook her head in embarrassment, "Don't say it like that! Sounds intimate! I just wanted you dead nothing more!"

I raised a brow and shook my head, "So, you're a full blown snake yourself?"

"Technically, Father and Mother were Earthens. I just take after father." She glanced away after that.

"This father is a snake too?" I made a face.

She nodded once more, "Mhmm, his snakes are different from mine."

"Disgusting." I blinked then put my hands up, "Uh! Respectfully- I don't like snakes much haha.."

She laughed quietly, "Yes, I noticed your aversion, it seems Ironic, almost like it's a subconscious fear for you, how fascinating."

"Aht aht, don't you go trying to experiment on me." I shot her a look and opened the gate for her.

"Better me than a stranger right?" She gave a grin, oh that's a first. I chuckled quietly.

"Not sure, ask me in the morning." I unlocked the door and kicked my shoes off. She took hers off and stood behind me. "Enjoying the clothes?"

I asked, glancing at her and unbuttoning my shirt and taking my hair down.

She blinked and darted her gaze away, "Um, yes, they're comfy."

"Great, if you need anything else just let me know, right?"

"Right.."

"And you've been behaving, so maybe we can go shopping this weekend?" I asked. She gripped at the bottom of the jacket and kept her gaze away but she responded quietly.

"Um, maybe..."

Oh hell, I hope I didn't upset her. I went to touch her arm but she moved aside and lowered her head a bit awkwardly, "Um, I wasn't completely truthful..." She said suddenly.

I blinked in confusion.

"Do you mind if we chat quickly?" Medusa asked, her cheeks slightly red in the lighting. I nodded a bit and motioned to the couch. She sat and I sat next to her, she kept her distance though.

"What weren't you honest about?"

"The Earthens part." She rubbed her legs, "The most I had was my mothers eyes. Momma used to say I'd grow into my tail in no time! She died before she saw it happen though." She spoke quietly.

I looked at her sadly, gods I can't imagine all she's been through.

"I've been listening to that song, I think it's helping me remember things I've forgotten." She nodded, "I was told I looked a lot like my mom... before this."

"So none of this was..?" I asked quietly.

Medusa shook her head, "All from his experiments. I remember the pain of the snakes growing out of my scalp and my hair falling out."

I cringed at that.

"Momma used to say I had beautiful hair." She gripped at the snakes again, her eyes focused on the floor, "She used to brush it for me, she'd sing to me in her native language, I never got to learn it..."

"Thank you for giving me a second chance Aubrey…" She said with a gentle smile.

"I?" I tilted my head, "But I didn't do anything?"

"You let me stay, you took pity on me and helped me…" Medusa shrugged, "I wanted to kill you for so long, up until our shopping journey I still did. I planned to let my snakes bite you, or poison your food… Anything to complete what I put my life towards. Then I thought of your words…"

I felt my eyes soften, I just let her talk.

"I really sat down and thought, I thought about what you said and what I'd gain from your death. Temporary satisfaction? A brief feeling of accomplishment? Then what? I never thought about that." She gripped at her dress, "Then listening to the song, remembering her… She'd be so disappointed if I hurt you, I know she isn't here, but…"

"Hey…" I touched her hand.

She looked at our hands with welled eyes. I try not to touch her too much without her permission, I know unwarranted touching is annoying, I personally hate it. But I notice she responds when you connect with her like this. She never shies away from my touch, so I take it as a good sign, her hands always catch me off guard, without a locket her snake features are front and center.

Her hands feel scaly, her eyes are reptilian, and her skin patterns are remarkable. She's genuinely beautiful to me, her features feel unique to this region, her slimmer nose to her full lips and her round eyes. I could only imagine how she would've looked without these experiments, it's a shame that her unique beauty is probably seen as a disgrace to her. I hate that she achieved this uniqueness through torture and abuse, it feels disgusting to complement her so wholeheartedly but I also believe she should hear it because it's her reality. While I'm not fond of snakes, I'd never make her feel lesser.

"She would have really liked you…" Medusa said quietly as her welled up eyes looked at me, "I'm sorry, I know you're tired." She went to move her hand away from me but I gripped them gently.

"Stop, no it's Ok." I kissed her knuckles gently, "I don't mind, I have all the time in the world to talk to you, just let it all out."

She looked down, the shadows in the room tinting her face. She was relaxed in my grip.

"I Miss her, and I want to make her proud…Even though she's…"

"That's normal love." I said, "We always want to make them proud, and I think if you keep it up, you will. You'll know. You'll feel it."

"Do you think she'd be down here? Could I see her again?" Medusa asked.

"It's hard to tell if I'm honest, I'd have to ask Saint."

"Oh." She looked away and shook her head, "No, never mind."

"It's Ok Medusa…"

"She dislikes me." She said.

"I can still ask, it could give you closure?"

"No, it's Ok." Medusa stood up, "You've done so much already, I just wanted to be honest with you."

"Well, I'm not mad about the uh…*Thoughts.*" I questioned, "Of killing me, but I appreciate your honesty."

"Mr. Tartarus says honesty is a good thing."

"It is, but uh, don't tell him your thoughts. He won't like

that very much." I chuckled.

She looked at me with kind eyes then gave a small smile. I stood and rubbed at my face. I felt her stare lingering and I turned my attention back to her. She seemed to snap out of it and turned towards the stairs, seemingly hiding her face.

"Goodnight, thank you for taking me to the shop. And listening." She then turned and hurried upstairs, Iron walking in her room before she closed the door.

"You're welcome." I waved my hand a bit and rubbed my face. This is a good sign, she's opening up. She's trusting me. I'm just happy it took a couple weeks for her to relax and work with me. I tried to be more excited but, *Ugh, I'm tired*. I made a quick snack then got ready for bed.

This weekend hm? Maybe we can all do something, and I can invite Medusa, it's been about three weeks now. It's probably the best time, she needs to work on her social interactions and she can't be cooped up in this house all the time, especially if me and dad work all the time, on top of school.

Speaking of school. I checked my old text thread from Rue and checked the event she sent me. I nearly forgot, I'll have to keep an eye on that, and I have to meet Jonas for my lessons as well. *Ugh, I'm tired.* Maybe getting a job was dumb, I plopped down in the bed and sent a quick text to Saint then lazily grabbed my bonnet. Too tired to tie it up, silk bonnet is enough. I dropped my head on the pillow and closed my eyes and immediately fell asleep.

37

THIRTY-SIX

The morning lava shone bright in the window. Iron was already awake, his brown eyes staring up at me as I sat up. I rubbed my head and enjoyed the peace and quiet before the snakes woke up. They've been calmer since my stay here, that's a relief. The past three or so weeks with them has opened my eyes to a lot of things. I'm unhealthy. I was in a dangerous situation and I was too one track minded. Aubrey and Tartarus' kindness has been so refreshing and mind changing. I can't believe just two weeks ago I planned to still kill Aubrey. After speaking to him at the record shop I had to accept, there's no reason to fight when there's nothing *to* fight. I fear I'm growing fond of him and this family he's built.

"Morning Iron..." I hummed and moved my legs over the bed, slipping my feet in the frog slippers Mr. Tartarus gave to me. I shuffled to the bathroom and began my morning routine, I heard Iron plop down outside the door. He's been glued to my hip since my arrival. At first I believed he was just keeping an eye on me, But now I think he just liked me. I won't complain. I kind of enjoy his company. He's impressive. He's a very smart creature and very interesting that's for sure.

I exited the bathroom and pet the top of his head. The wall clock caught my attention and I felt myself perk up. *Mr. Tartarus might be awake already, maybe I can help with breakfast this time.* I hurried down the stairs and saw the Mouse man sitting at the table while Mr. Tartarus made him a coffee.

I gripped my skirt at his presence and glanced away.

"Oh, morning Medusa. You're up earlier than usual?" Mr. Tartarus said with a soft smile.

"Yes, I wanted to help cook?" I asked quietly, he seemed to light up at that.

"Oh? I'd be delighted!" He motioned me over, "It's not too much since I have to head to some meetings today, so just eggs, bacon and waffles."

I walked over curiously and looked at the stove, "Alright?"

"Here, I'll let you do the waffles." Tartarus grabbed a bowl and plugged up this black machine. "Did you speak to Mateo?"

"Oh, um, Hello…" I spoke quietly and looked away.

"Hello." Mateo responded kindly, and nodded his head then sipped his coffee.

"It's polite to address the room, unless the people in the room pissed you off then fuck em." Mr. Tartarus sat some ingredients down.

"Oh, Ok.." I nodded.

"Honey." Mateo spoke up.

Mr. Tartarus has been teaching me the etiquettes down here, it makes me feel like a child who's learning how to socialize for the first time. There wasn't much etiquette and class where I'm from. Just pain, death and misery. Mr.Tartarus has been more than eager to teach me his recipes and show me around when Aubrey isn't around. He took to me surprisingly well and honestly I'm grateful, he's incredibly kind when you get past his dark eyes and harsh demeanor.

"Ok honey, I'm going to make the batter for you, and I'll let you cook them in the waffle machine. Do NOT touch this part." Tartarus pointed, "It's hot."

I nodded eagerly and watched him make the batter. Along with etiquette he's been teaching me "Basic life skills". Obviously something I lack. He started with cleaning then cooking. The cleaning part didn't go too well and I'm glad Aubrey wasn't home, I would have been even more embarrassed. Last time he taught me how to make omelets. This seems a bit more complicated though. He's adding a bunch of ingredients I've never heard of before, he'd usually explain them to me as we went but I guess he was in too much of a rush. I followed his instructions to the best of my ability, the first few didn't come out too great but Mr. Mateo ate them anyhow. Iron ate a few of the worst attempts before laying down in defeat. It took a few attempts but I made about four good ones, one for each of us.

I don't think cooking will be one of my strong points.

"Those are perfect!" Tartarus nodded, "Next time I'll teach you how to make french toast."

"Oh, that sounds delicious," I beamed.

He smiled and patted the top of my head and I felt prideful. He told me he's never had a daughter before so he's very eager to share home making things with me. Apparently the only thing Aubrey took to was cleaning and basic cooking, I was genuinely shocked by that. I assumed he would have been able to learn almost like a computer does. I'm realizing everyday, I don't fully understand Aubrey. I never got to fully read his files so most of my information is based on common sense and loose assumptions.

Speaking of which, I realized Aubrey never came downstairs.

"Here darling, you can eat outside with Aubrey. He's got errands to run today." Mr. Tartarus said, handing me two plates, except one lacked bacon. I blinked in confusion. I guess he eats too? Why? He has no use for it? I looked towards the window and noticed him working. He was loading up a trailer with some stuff, I tilted my head in question. I looked back at Mr. Tartarus and nodded with a smile.

I headed outside to Aubrey. He was loading more of that stuff, throwing them and stacking them. He was grunting and sweating. I felt something tighten in my chest. I shook my head and closed the distance between us.

"Morning Aubrey, Mr. Tartarus requested me to bring you food." I said. He seemed shocked to see me. He used his gloved hand to wipe sweat off his cheek. He was breathing a bit heavy. He then smiled that typical warm smile.

"Mornin' I appreciate it." He said. He took his gloves off and plopped down on one of the bails on the ground. He motioned me over with his finger and patted the hay. I walked over and handed him the plate and sat next to him. The material was firm, and a bit painful. I tried not to make a face and just focused on my food.

"Of course..."

He began to eat and I watched him curiously.

"Aubrey? I have a question." I spoke, he said I can ask him things. I try not to abuse his kindness and openness but his existence here is still a bit strange to me, he acts like Earthens. He eats, He sleeps, He attends schools and jobs, why? Even now with his new knowledge. I guess it's hard to change what you're used to, It took awhile to stop subconsciously calling him Project EF.

I've been outwardly studying him. I learned fairly quickly that I can't measure up to his pure muscle and strength, which is partially why I didn't even entertain the idea of attacking him. He also seems to have a bit of discoloration with his eyes and mouth. His tongue is yellow, along with his eye whites, teeth and gums. Is that from his insides being golden? He came after Project Midas, yet he seems like a first draft? Or is this purposeful? I don't want to over step his boundaries so a lot of my questions will most likely be unanswered.

"Shoot." He said, biting the waffle.

"Why do you eat?" I asked.

"For fun." He shrugged.

"Does it do anything for you?"

"Nah, not really." He leaned against the other bails, "I can't really taste anything, but it feels nice to participate? I guess?"

"I see…" I looked at my plate, "Wait. You can't taste?"

"Nah, Doc Wynter said I don't have normal organs, he says my taste buds ain't developed."

"You've been to a doctor?" I was astonished. How interesting, he doesn't have normal organs? Why? I narrowed my eyes as he spoke.

"Kinda." He took another bite, "He's a surgeon and he said I was weird, he did some checkups on me and noticed I ain't exactly normal."

I nodded, "I guess that makes sense, If what Midas says is true, you weren't fully incubated..."

Aubrey shrugged, "Hey, I got a question for you now."

I gulped quietly but sat to attention, "Yes?"

"Lightening. How would that work on my body?"

"Lightening?" I asked. The question caught me off guard.

He nodded, "Before you started staying with us, I got struck by lightning I believe? It was weird. Jonas mentioned she gave me a shot of lightning to fix another issue prior."

"Yes, well." I thought for a moment, trying to recall what I was able to read in Aubrey's documents, I tapped at my lips and sat my plate on my lap gently, "If I recall. In your notes he used lightning to help your incubation process. It helped stimulate the essence you were incubating in."

"Stimulate?"

"Activate it to give you life per se." I said, " I guess lightning can react to your body strangely?"

"Like healing?"

"That's definitely a theory." I nodded.

"Well, when we fought, I got cut up pretty bad, I fell asleep and they were basically healed, along with the lightning burn I got, coincidence?"

"Fascinating..." I gripped my chin in thought, "It seems your body can attract and harness lightning, although I won't be able to know more without running tests on you."

"Tests..?" Aubrey asked, a tone shift in his voice.

"I only got to see a few of your files, and honestly from your development. They're obviously outdated or flat out useless, you're basically an anomaly, you're your own thing." I tried to explain, then looked towards the sky, the giant moon peered down at us. I pursed my lips in thought. He could be like a battery? The lightning could've given his body a bit of a boost. Or it could've been a coincidence. *Gods I wish to know, he's so fascinating.*

He went silent for a moment and I glanced at him, "What kind of tests?"

I thought for a moment before listing a few, "In all honesty, it should work in your favor, what did Jonas have to fix?"

"Not sure, she just said I wasn't feeling well, and I passed out."

"I see. Yes it might be in your best interest to run more tests and document your changes." I said, "Although at the end of the day that's completely your decision. I would highly recommend it, but if you don't want to, it's fine."

"Would it be..." He looked at his lap, "I don't even..."

"Well, If you wish for me to do it, I'll make it as comfortable as possible." I smiled.

He moved his eyes towards the ground, seemingly in thought. He didn't give me an answer though. He instead stood up and motioned to the tractor.

"Want to come with me to Saint's?" He asked.

"The purple one?" I asked, "What for?"

He got a slightly annoyed glint in his eye, "Yes, her name is Saint."

Aubrey shook his head, "Got some errands to run for her, Her dad needed a bit of help on the Ranch."

"A Ranch?" I asked.

"Her family owns a horse ranch, She asked for the Hay." He wiped the sweat off his face and pointed his thumb back at the stacks.

His bright purple eyes were so kind but tired. His brown skin glistened with sweat. His eyes were sharp and hair pulled back in a ponytail. His muscle was noticeable, his biceps were huge. He was in a worn out black shirt and green overalls. *He's so handsome.* He's definitely not what Father expected. Hell he isn't what *I* expected. Especially when he was intended to look like *her*. He's a stark contrast. How did he get this way?

Medusa, you're staring. I blinked then nodded and he smiled that sweet smile.

He climbed up on the tractor and started it up, his boots moving to the petals. He put his hand to me and pulled me up with little effort like I weighed nothing. I couldn't help the sudden squeak of surprise that left my mouth.

"But the plates?" I asked.

"I'll clean them up, don't worry 'bout it." He started driving the giant machine. It was an old thing, it was green. The paint was faded and chipped, the wheels were huge and the seats weren't the best. The old trailer creaked behind us, it wasn't very fast, but it was nice to see the scenery he lived by. We had to go through The town and towards a giant house, there were fences all around the property with these horses. They had four deep eyes. Their manes were made of lava, or fire, or stars. They're certainly beautiful animals, bigger than I expected.

Saint was standing near a horse, feeding them an apple. I felt my eyes sparkle at them. I wish to feed one.

"Hey baby girl, sorry, I'll have to make two trips." Aubrey hopped off the tractor and motioned for me to come down as well, his hands gripped my waist as he helped me down and I patted my skirt down.

"That's fine." Saint hummed, she was dressed down more than usual, she was in a worn out shirt as well, looks like they match. *Peculiar*. Her hair was in a bun and she was in jeans and boots. She's definitely not the one I'd think about when I hear the term Rancher. She turned her gaze towards me and raised a brow.

She cleared her throat and Aubrey looked at me then back at her.

"Just letting her see the horses." He smiled.

"Sure. Thanks for the heads up." Saint rolled her eyes.

"Where you want these?" He asked.

"Couple out here, the rest in the barn."

Aubrey nodded and got to work. I stayed out of the way but watched him. He tossed a few of the bails off the trailer then unhooked it and began to pull the heavy trailer towards a barn. He's strong. Like very strong. What is his endurance like? I could tell Saint was staring too, but for a different reason. I looked at the ground and rubbed at my arm.

"Aye. want to feed one?" Saint spoke up suddenly.

I looked up at her.

"It's fine." She motioned me over, "Grab an apple, He's friendly."

I hesitantly walked over and did so. She took my hand in hers and gently lead it to the horses mouth and he began to eat at the apple, taking big bites. I felt my face heat up at her gentle touch, she's a bit intimidating. Even dressed like this she's opposing. She radiated power and dominance.

"His name is Chapel, He's mine." Saint nodded.

"You ride horses?" I asked, "Excuse me but, you seem… " I trailed off, I tried to remember Aubrey's advice on socializing, "High maintenance?"

She blinked then raised a brow, "As in?"

"You're so frilly and stuff. I didn't think you'd enjoy this kind of stuff." I said quietly.

She closed her eyes and sighed quietly, "I've been helping with the ranch since I was twelve, I love my dresses but I also love horses."

"I enjoy your dichotomy."

"Thank you?" Saint turned her head away, "How are you enjoying Aubrey's house." She stated more than asked, I can tell she still doesn't fully trust me. Her voice was very cold, she barely even made eye contact with me.

I can't even blame her. Especially with the version of events she might've heard, and she's clearly very close to Aubrey. At least she's more approachable than the red one. She makes me more nervous versus this purple one. She seems more calculating and cunning, like a snake in the grass. While the red one is a provoked bear. I don't look forward to seeing her face again.

"It's fine, he's kind to me." I said.

"Mhmm."

Aubrey walked back over and dropped the trailer back by the tractor and hooked it back up. I backed away as he walked over to us. He breathed out and petted the horse.

"All done with that, gimme a sec and I'll get the rest."

"Thank you, I'll have lemonade and pie ready for you when you're done big guy." Saint smiled.

"You're so sweet." He grabbed the water from her pocket and downed it. He breathed out and wiped at his mouth then leaned against the fence.

"Oh, I've been thinking."

"About?" Saint asked with a smile.

"How's a kickback sound? In Pride."

"Pride?" She asked.

"Mhmm." Aubrey propped his arm on the fence, his eyes and face were so soft towards her.

I observed their banter and body language. He's so comfortable with her. His voice is deeper, his eyes are loving and his demeanor is different, I guess I understand. They interact so casually, is that the word? No, intimately? He'd do little things with her that I've noticed he'd avoid and scowl at with others. He nearly got violent with a man who touched him at the store, that was very eye opening. He's so complex. He truly is *alive*.

I tried not to stare at him too frequently, I can't begin to imagine how he must feel about it. He never mentions it, but who genuinely likes someone staring constantly? But, *My gods he's handsome.* He's probably used to it. At least he isn't too off model, he has her breathtaking beauty and allure, just in his own way.

Looking at the purple one next to him, She's stunning as well. They are so beautiful together. I could see them as a pairing most definitely. *But he chooses that blue girl? Purple compliments green significantly better than blue? Is that too literal and logical?* That confuses me. He's clearly infatuated with this girl, yes? It's as clear as day. Maybe he's just softer with me because he pities me? He's never addressed me or the blue girl this way. I rubbed at my head and looked away.

"I want to introduce y'all to my girlfriend."

"Girlfriend?" Saint asked, taken aback, "Oh fuck you, Mr. lets stay single for awhile."

Aubrey chuckled and grinned, "What? She asked me out.

Was I supposed to say no?"

"And who is she." Saint rolled her eyes and crossed her arms.

"Keegan, Keegan Adams."

"Adams?" Saint tilted her head, "Adams…?"

"The Angel I went to high school with. Me and her brother were on the basketball team together."

"Oh! Yea you had a crush on her?" She asked.

"Yea, I also want Medusa to come."

I looked back over at the mention of my name. I felt myself shrink back as they turned their gazes towards me.

"…" Saint pulled him close and they turned from me. I just looked back at the ground.

"You sure 'bout that? With Rouge around."

"She's a friend now, and she's chill. Genuinely." He spoke, "She needs to get out more, she's basically only interacted with us, and out of the three of us, one is a dog."

Saint sucked her teeth, "I guess."

"Just, be nice? She's trying."

"Yea. I can tell, she called me high maintenance." Saint huffed, I looked away in guilt.

"Medusa?" He looked over at me, "Did you?"

"I meant it as a compliment…" I rubbed my arm.

"Yea."

He just laughed and shook his head, he put his gloves back on and went to walk away but stopped in his tracks. Almost like a light bulb sparked behind his eyes. He pointed his hand up then turned his gaze back towards her. We both watched him curiously.

"Saint, I need a favor."

"Sure baby, what's up?" She asked without hesitation.

"How's your lightning?" Aubrey asked, I looked at him in question then narrowed my eyes.

"Better."

"Can you strike me with it?" He asked. I felt my eyes widen at the same time as Saint's. When I said run tests I didn't mean it like this? I went to say something but Saint spoke up first.

"Excuse me?" Saint asked.

"I have a theory, and well it ain't gonna storm anytime soon, I got lucky? The first time I guess." He trailed off, heading towards the tractor. I guess that was for the best because her calm body language quickly got aggravated.

"The first time!?" Saint exclaimed.

"Oh- shit." Aubrey muttered and sat on the tractor. "I wasn't gonna tell you that-"

"Aubrey! Did you get struck by lightning that night!? I told you to stay!"

He seemed to casually shoo the concern away, "It's fine, it's fine, I think that actually helped me? Medusa could probably explain it better."

"I will do no such thing." I stated firmly, "Such a foolish idea."

Maybe his creation ain't that remarkable after all. I shook my head in disbelief.

Aubrey huffed, "Gods, it was just a thought."

"Yea a horrible one!" She reiterated.

He pulled me back up on the tractor and tipped his hat to Saint. He's very charming isn't he? His face was so serious yet it was so round and soft. He started the tractor up as Saint cleared the path for us, she waved her hand then checked her phone once we passed her. I noticed her face slightly fell before she put the phone away. I looked away then at Aubrey. He was quiet now, I guess the idea being shot down took a bit of wind out of his sails. He should've known the purple one would never. I doubt she's capable of hurting him in any capacity on purpose.

I wanted him to feel better though. I took a moment to think of my words, "Aubrey, I think you're fascinating, you're very handsome."

"Huh? Oh, thanks?" He glanced back towards me and seemed to perk up a little bit and gave a small chuckle.

"It's so strange to me, I guess it makes sense. Scientifically you are designed to be beautiful because of your base."

His face slightly fell at that, I noticed and cleared my throat and looked away. *Dammit.*

"By that I mean, you're supposed to look like someone, but instead you look more like an offspring, uh, of said person…" I trailed off, "You're so uniquely you, it's kind of baffling."

"I'll… Take that as a good thing." Aubrey muttered.

"For me, yes! For…." I didn't finish the sentence, he knew what I meant.

"Your friend is very pretty too, do you two not have relations?" I asked. He seemed shocked by my question, I immediately felt dumb for asking. *Oh my gods.*

"Me and Saint? nah. She's my best friend. We've known each other since we were kids. We're just really close."

I nodded, "Huh, is that why you choose the blue one over the purple one?"

"Why do you refer to people as colors?" He raised a brow, "Her name is Keegan, and there was nothing to choose between, Saint and me are just friends."

"I see. Well I refer to you as green in my head." I said matter-of-factly, maybe I misread the situation. I do struggle with cues, maybe I looked too much into it, maybe that's normal for friends? I hope he gets that comfortable with me one day. That thought made me happy. I turned my head away, leaving the conversation at that.

He shook his head at my statement, "Hey… can you… run some tests?"

I turned my head towards him with wide eyes, "Are you sure?" I asked almost too eagerly, but he nodded anyhow.

I can't stress how interested I am to see how he ended up this way and how he's developing. It's like he's read my mind! Obviously I wouldn't force this on him but I won't dissuade him either! This is such a golden opportunity to dissect him like this, and maybe I can figure out what issues he had with Midas as well? Maybe I can help him and make up for my prior transgressions. I could barely contain my excitement.

"I'll even record my findings in my notebook!" I nodded.

Aubrey laughed quietly, "Ah, well I'm honored to be the first thing in it."

"I'll even share my findings with Mr. Tartarus, I think he'd be proud!" I smiled.

"I think so too, Just, go easy on me yea?"

"I promise, you're safe with me!"

"Alright.. I trust you." He smiled back at me briefly but his eyes were filled with unease. I'll do everything in my power to make this a pleasurable experience for both of us, and I will get something useful out of it. Imagine his disdain when he finds out his failure of a daughter was able to fix ***HIS*** mistake in his perfect creation. He'll never have him, that's for sure, and he may never know. But I'll take this as a win. Aubrey trusting me is a Win.

"Um, that's why I've been staring by the way…" I said quietly, masking my excitement, my face hot in embarrassment.

He laughed, "Yea. I figured."

38

THIRTY-SEVEN

"Aubrey, tighten your stance, earth is just as much strength as it is power." Jonas spoke up, her arms were crossed, she sounded annoyed but she remained patient.

I groaned and slammed the rock down on the ground in frustration, unintentionally scaring away the birds, "I'm trying, I'm just tired."

I rolled my shoulder and stretched before plopping down on the ground, closing the book. Her little Dragon boyfriend kept his distance but lingered close enough to keep an eye on Jonas, I'd assume. What a weirdo.

"And why are you so tired? Have you been exhausting yourself?"

"Not with practice, just... Medusa has been running tests, and no she isn't hurting me before you ask." I said, " My anxiety is just spiked. Then there's school and work, and now trying to learn these forms? What a fuckin joke." I groaned and laid back against the ground, looking up at the sky. A few crows flew past.

She made a disapproving face, "She's... running tests." She

swallowed her disdain and sighed quietly, "Well, nothing is ever easy, I didn't get to where I am by accident. Took a lot of practice, dedication and discipline." Jonas spoke gently.

"Yea but you had a reason to learn, I don't."

"Is self improvement not a valid reason? Didn't you want to learn more?"

"I suppose so?" I sighed and sat up, "I'm sorry, I'm just frustrated. I've been practicing these forms and it's like I'm not even progressing. I thought having you here to critique me would help but I'm just getting irritated."

"We should take a break then…" Jonas rubbed my shoulder, "This isn't supposed to be a negative experience."

"Yea.." I sighed and rubbed my arm, "Say, Jonas, do you know about that Reaper and Sorcerer event coming up?"

"Event?"

"Yea, Rue told me about it a couple weeks back, will you still be here?" I asked.

"Oh Aubrey, I took this long to find you, Death themselves would have to pull me from you." Jonas nodded, "But why do you ask?"

I laughed a bit awkwardly, I'm still getting used to the fact she's technically my biological sister? In a way? It's cool as hell 'cuz she's phenomenal, and it helped me pinpoint why she felt so familiar. While on the other hand, I've never had a sibling before, not a bad change, but a change nonetheless.

"I…have a bad feeling about it." I rubbed my head.

"What do you mean?"

"It's… A lot to explain. But long story short I think the Reapers might be walking into something they aren't prepared for, I'm still putting the pieces together."

"Reapers huh? Why them in particular?"

"Well, Sorcerers are Hecate's creation. Hecate was engaged to a Reaper way back when, but the other Reapers sentenced her to death for a crime she didn't commit, I'm sure the rest writes itself." I shrugged, "At least that's how the history books relay it."

"Is that so? And you're technically related to this *'Hecate'*?"

"Yea, dad's a Kovenn, so I'm related by adoption, I'm legally his child."

"Is that so?" Jonas trailed off and leaned against her hands, "What's it like?"

"Like?" I asked.

"Having a family like this?"

"Ah, well, it's normal, it's all I've ever known, Dad, Auntie Bee, Charon, Jasper, they've all been parental figures, going out of their way to care for and protect me, it's wonderful, genuinely."

"Maybe I'm a little jealous." She laughed a bit, "All I've had was smaller children to look out for and only had Adonys to talk to…" She glanced over at the Dragon.

"Ah, yea, what's his deal by the way?"

"What do you mean?" Jonas tilted her head.

"He's… kinda a dick."

"Nah, he's just guarded, he's sweet when you get to know him." She smiled.

"Ah, so he's your passion Project or your boyfriend?" I teased. She got red in the face and quickly shook her head.

"No noooo he's not my boyfriend! What makes you say that? Did he say something?"

"…." I glanced away in thought remembering his coldness weeks back. Something tells me she won't be too fond of that, "Uh, nah, nothing really-"

"Ah.." She glanced away.

"If you like him you should go for it, why wait?" I asked.

"Complicated if I'm honest." Jonas huffed quietly, "Too many responsibilities."

"Jonas." I looked at her.

"It's fine, if it were meant to be it would happen right?"

"Something like that." I glanced down at my phone then hopped up, grabbing the book, "Sorry, I gotta head out."

"Already?"

"Yea, I promised I'd meet Saint and Rouge for lunch, and I got a couple errands to run." I packed up my backpack, "But I'll keep practicing." I grinned at her and hurried off towards the house. I quickly showered and headed back to Sin City, Saint and Rouge were already waiting by the fountain, talking. I huffed out and waved my arm in exhaustion.

"Hey you two, sorry sorry, I had a training session with Jonas."

"Training?" Rouge asked.

"For my earth magic, she's hella educated on it. But that's not important." I waved it off, Saint was looking at her phone and didn't even acknowledge me. I waved my hand near her face.

"Hey hon, you in there?"

She blinked and looked up, locking her phone immediately, "Oh, sorry."

"You good?" I asked.

"Yea, yea! Anyway." Saint stood up.

"Since we're heading to Gluttony, mind if we stop by a store?"

"Sure? Which one?" Rouge asked, she walked with me, Saint trailing behind. That's not like her. She was fine the other day? Now her energy is low and dull. I narrowed my eyes as I glanced back at her, she's still on her phone. Might be overthinking it, if something was wrong she'd talk to us right?

I turned back to Rouge.

"Oh, just Woodland." I pointed to it, "I think they'll have what I'm looking for."

"Woodland?" Rouge tilted her head, "Didn't take you as the cottagecore lesbian type." She giggled at her little joke, I snorted and rolled my eyes playfully.

"Haha, real cute. It's not for me, it's for Medusa." I nodded. She blinked and her expression soured almost immediately.

"Medusa?"

Saint came to attention too, "What about Medusa?"

"He's buying her gifts now." Rouge said with an underline of bitterness. I raised my brow at her and crossed my arms.

"Oh yea, they're close now. She's practically swooning."

"Knock it off, she's just socially awkward. Gods are y'all still mad?" I huffed, waving my hand in dismissal.

"She tried to kill you!" They said in unison.

"Water under the bridge I built." I waved it off and headed to the store, "She's actually kinda cute, like a dork, she's apparently really into frogs and mushrooms."

"Is that so?" Rouge glanced away.

"I'm serious guys, she's chill." I glanced at them, "And I'd appreciate if y'all would be nice to her, if dad can, y'all can."

"..."

"Aubrey wants to invite her to a kickback." Saint mentioned. I shot her a look. I wasn't going to just blurt it out like that. I rubbed my eyes.

"What." Rouge asked.

"Don't be like that." I said, "She's fine, I just want her to socialize. She can't be cooped up in the house all day."

"I don't think any of us are too fond of having her around." Rouge said matter-of-factly, Saint agreed.

I rolled my eyes, "Guys. Please."

Saint sighed and crossed her arms, "She did seem…Tame, last we spoke."

I smiled a bit hopeful, but Rouge was a bit hesitant.

"Arms length." Saint nudged Rouge and she huffed and rolled her eyes.

"Fine."

"I'll take it." I grinned and walked in the shop, looking around and heading to the shelves, looking over the books. "Hm…"

"They're fairly priced…I could get two?" I muttered to myself.

I looked over the different books, then glanced over at Saint, her phone catching my attention. Hm, what the hell is she so interested in, she isn't even talking to Rouge, she ended up wandering off. I stood and held the books in my hands and walked off, but keeping note. This store is really cozy, very cute, it certainly fits her vibe. I looked at a few of the furniture and accessories, *she'd probably love fairy lights to go in her room, which might relax her a bit.*

I picked up the box and looked over the price. *How cute they are mushroom shaped.* I put it under my arm and glanced over at Rouge, she was looking over some clothes, pushing through the racks. I made my way over and leaned opposite of it and quickly caught myself after slipping before she noticed and smiled awkwardly.

She turned her head to me then laughed quietly, "Don't

hurt yourself."

"I'm finneee" I waved my hand, "Didn't take this as your style, not enough bats."

She laughed quietly and held a flowy dress to herself, "Whatcha think? Can I pull it off?"

"You pull off literally everything." I smiled a bit, "Uh, in a neutral friendly way-"

She laughed and put it back, "Take a breath, hon."

"Sorry, feels so weird being normal again, it feels nice though.." I messed with one of the shirts.

"I agree, I missed you both like crazy.." She moved her hands over the clothes and moved closer while looking at the clothes, "I was worried we'd grow apart after all those years apart."

"Well, four years ain't that bad… right?"

"A lot can change in a person in 4 years… I mean, look at you, you're certainly more mature." Rouge said.

"Ahah." I shook my head a bit with a chuckle, "Should I say thank you or?"

She nodded, her long lashes framed her bright green eyes, *gods she's so beautiful,* I could feel my breath catch, *she's certainly matured in those four years too. Stop it, you are grown and capable of being friends with hot women without panicking. You loser.* I glanced away.

"Take it how you will, sugar."

I hummed and stood straight, and cleared my throat. I glanced back over at Saint, still on her phone.

"So…" Rouge spoke up, "That Briar girl..?"

"Hm? What about her?" I asked, tilting my head.

"How long have you known her?"

"I met her about two years ago, why?" I asked.

"She's very pretty."

"You think? I'm sure she feels the same about you." I blinked then smirked at her, "Oh wait..is that the little green eyed monster peeking through?"

She rolled her eyes.

"You're so much like your daddy." I laughed quietly and messed with the pearls around her neck, she placed her hand gently on mine, her warm hands were so soft. Her eyes had a small glint in them, as much of a glint as you can get from being a vampire. I felt myself gulp slightly.

"Should I say thank you? Or..?" Rouge joked.

I laughed a bit awkwardly and pulled my hand away as my phone went off, saved by the bell, and of course, it was my girlfriend. I moved away and checked the message and breathed out. I read over the message then a thought crossed my mind, why not invite everyone? Rouge and Saint need to properly meet Jonas, Rue can get out of the house on top of meeting Keegan. Plus If Medusa tags along she can *maybe* start mending some bonds. I sent her a quick text and nodded, walking over to the register and noticing a cute mushroom hat on sale. Oh she'd love that.

I paid for everything and nodded. "Alright, we can get lunch now." I smiled.

We left together, Saint still glued to her phone, she seemed more distressed. I narrowed my eyes but before I could speak, Rouge spoke up.

"Hey hon, you alright?"

Saint looked up then nodded, "Uh, yes."

"You look panicked." Rouge said. She quickly locked her phone and put it in her pocket instead of her purse. Yea that definitely ain't like her.

I glanced away and opened the restaurant door for them, motioning them inside. Rouge walked in first and I rubbed Saint's shoulder as she passed. I checked my bank account and nodded approvingly and waited as Rouge got a table for us. Immediately the shameless Demon tried to hit on her, oh you have no idea just how uninterested she is. I rolled my eyes and glanced towards Saint. She looked like her fingers were fidgeting. She wants to check her phone again, I can hear the vibrations.

We headed to the table, Rouge and Saint on one side and me on the other. I leaned back and breathed out, sitting the shopping bag down and looking over the menus. *Another vibration.*

I glanced over the menu at Saint, she was checking again. I snatched her phone from her hands and raised a brow.

"Seriously. The fuck is wrong with you?"

"Aubrey!" Saint exclaimed, she sounded exasperated. Rouge raised a brow as well.

"Who's got your attention this much." I held the phone away from her, "It ain't giving positive."

"Give me back my phone please." Saint basically pleaded.

"Are you being harassed?" I asked.

"Aubrey." Saint said sternly.

"Do I need to hurt someone?" I narrowed my eyes. She hesitated before snatching the phone back.

"It's nothing."

"Obviously it's something." Rouge spoke up. I nodded in agreement.

"It's just my ex, he's been texting me since last week, going on about nonsense, I don't know. He sounds like he's having a breakdown." Saint muttered.

"Your ex." I deadpanned, "You know what ex means right."

"Whatever that loser has going on, has nothing to do with you, stop responding." Rouge rolled her eyes and picked up the menu, "Block him."

"Literally block him." I waved my hand, "Unless I need to hurt him." I looked at her.

Saint didn't speak up that time, just eventually shook her head. She hesitantly silenced her phone and put it back in her purse. Rouge smiled and rubbed her hand, then handed her the menu. A waiter came over and took our order and brought drinks.

"Lunch is on Aubrey today~ cheer up! You love when he plays sugar daddy."

"Ahaha." I rolled my eyes playfully, "Sugar is runnin' low princess, choose wisely."

Saint laughed quietly and looked over the menu, "Well, I do love free stuff…"

"As do I~" Rouge giggled.

"About that kickback." I spoke up.

"What's up?" Rouge asked.

"How about tonight?" I asked.

"Tonight?" Saint asked.

"Yea! Why not? I kind of want to invite everyone instead of us four Y'know?" I asked hesitantly, "And I want to introduce y'all properly to my girlfriend, Briar and Jonas. Y'all mean the world to me."

They exchanged looks then made sour faces.

"Hon, Medusa is already a lot…" Saint started.

"Please?" I asked with a slight smile, "How 'bout this, my birthday is coming up and it's been four years since we celebrated my last one together…" I slyly pulled the pouty card.

"Oh, Scorpio is right around the corner huh..?" Rouge said quietly.

"..." Saint made a face. The waiters brought our lunch and I put my straw to my lips, nibbling on it. I know Saint won't say no. She's the more lenient one. Now Rouge, that's a different game. If I can convince one of them I'll eventually have both. Maybe a *lil nudge* in the right direction.

"And it's been a tough month, but.. If it's too much of a request..." I glanced away.

"Well, it can't hurt..." Saint elbowed Rouge, "Right?"

Rouge huffed quietly, "Fine, only because I have new outfits I can show off."

"Yay~" *success.*

"Wait, back up, girlfriend?" Rouge spoke up.

"Hahaaa" I bit on a fry, "Yeaaaaa"

"Who?" Rouge asked.

"Mr. 'lets be single for a while' bagged an Angel." Saint teased, "Can ya believe it?"

"Look, I'm weak for a pretty face." I grinned, and leaned against my hand. "It's Keegan, Keegan Adams."

"An Angel?" Rouge asked. "Is that wise?"

"Yes, and yes." I sipped my drink, "She's not like the others, clearly, I mean she's back down here so... She rejected me because of the Angel program."

"Is she nice at least."

"A *literal* Angel, love you'll adore her." I smiled at Rouge, "Put that cute lil devil away."

"You think she can hang though? We're Demons." Saint gave a look.

"I guess we'll see. Be easy on her. Heavy chance her

brother will come too, he's protective and still hates me. Heh."

"Oh? Is he cute?" Saint asked.

"For you."

"Fuck you." Saint rolled her eyes.

"Love you, sugar." I chuckled, and sent a text to Briar. I also sent a quick text to Medusa. I couldn't help but feel a bit giddy. It feels nice to finally relax with my friends. It feels like we haven't had proper time since we got back in school, at least in high school we had parties and shit, now it's just work and school. I nibbled my fry and glanced at Rouge, she sat her phone down.

"Is your dad cool with it?" I asked. She won't go anywhere without notifying him. And trust, I learned that the hard way. I rubbed at the back of my neck instinctively. Her dad stresses me out.

"Yea, he said not to stay there too long." She nodded, "It's his date night anyway."

"Date night?" I asked, then laughed, "You're deadass? Your dad?"

"Yea, surprisingly, He got a boyfriend when we moved back, he's so nice. He's been taking me shopping and doing girly stuff with me. He's very open about his intentions with my dad."

She slid the phone to us. I let out a whistle, and nodded.

"Damn, Ok, ain't that Greed?" I asked.

"He's stunning, damn how lucky is he." Saint spoke up.

Rouge and I gave her a look.

"What? Not my fault both of your dads are hot." She shrugged. "I have no shame."

"Clearly." I said.

"We noticed." Rouge snorted at the same time, "Well, I'm actually kind of excited, it's been so long since we've kicked it."

"And it's the weekend so we can get fucked up without consequences." I grinned, "I got some good shit from Sloth yesterday." I grinned and sipped my soda.

"I'm game." Saint said, "We gotta share, though."

"Say less." I hummed, leaning back in the booth.

39

THIRTY-EIGHT

"Hey Medusa, did you get my text?" I asked eagerly. She nodded, looking at me from the couch.

"Yes but I don't understand, what is Pride-?" She asked.

"Just get dressed!" I grinned, "Wear anything you want, something comfortable but fashionable."

"Oh uh?" She looked at Iron then stood. I walked over and took her hands gently. She blinked and looked down at our hands, her cheeks got a bit red.

"Let's get you some friends, and I figured you'd enjoy doing something outside for once. Fair warning, all of us will be there, including Jonas."

Medusa made a face, "I don't know.."

"They'll be nice, especially if you Behave." I smiled, "Think of it as a birthday gift for me." I winked at her.

She dropped her head then nodded, "Alright, fine…"

I grinned brightly, "Fantastic~! I have to get ready, Rouge and them will be here soon."

I let her hands go and headed upstairs eagerly. I showered, fixed my hair and got dressed. I packed a speaker, a few blankets, and a few essentials. I guess we can order food, a bit short notice. I checked my phone and naturally, Briar is already by the gates with her brother, cute, can't wait to see Blaire again. I sent Jonas the address and sent a text to Rouge, Saint and I's group chat. Sent a text to Rue, Then texted Keegan, as I thought, her and Orien will be there, she'll meet us. Perfect.

I felt that familiar giddiness, like being a kid again.

"Um, Aubrey?" Medusa knocked lightly, I was mid spray of my cologne and looked over. She was in one of her fairy dresses with a black corset around it, and some tree print leggings, she looked comfortable and happy. She messed with the bottom of her skirt, her snakes resting behind her.

"Is this Ok?" She asked.

I nodded, "Won't feel uncomfortable in a few hours?" I walked over and rubbed the top of her head.

"It's comfortable.."

"Oh, I got this for you today." I smiled and handed her the bag, in my excitement I completely forgot.

She took it gently and opened the bag, looking into it, her eyes sparkled, she pulled out the two books and grinned brightly. "For me? Really?"

"I hope they'll interest you, I don't know much about mushrooms and frogs, so I hope you get a use out of them."

"I sure will!" Medusa exclaimed, hugging the books to her chest. I smiled gently, a feeling of pride washed over me. She's growing so much. She's certainly happier and expressing herself better, she's more comfortable around the house and dad. I'm happy I took a chance on her.

"Oh, and this." I pulled the hat out of the bag and placed it on her head, "It clashes with this outfit, but I thought it was cute."

She blinked and glanced up before touching the hat and smiling, "It's perfect, I'll treasure it forever.. Thank you for listening Aubrey.."

"Hm?" I tilted my head, "It's just the bare minimum."

"Yeah , but you didn't have to do this, or listen to my interest, or be so nice to me. Yet you have been. I genuinely appreciate this, all of this." Medusa smiled softly.

I felt a ping in my heart and grinned cheesily, "Well, I'm happy to hear that." I picked up a few satin scrunchies and motioned to her hair, "May I?"

"Sure.."

"Not gonna harm me are you?" I looked at the snakes before taking a breath and putting her hair in pigtails, they looked uncomfortable, there's even indents on their bodies from the ties shes been using, they need to be kinder to each other if this will work for them. I held back a shudder of disgust, moving my fingers over their scaly bodies,a few of them hissed at me but they aren't hostile. They seemed almost relieved at the softer hair ties. I moved my hands away and smiled.

"Maybe they aren't too bad."

"Oh?" She touched the ties and then rubbed the snakes. They're quieter, "I suppose that's why they keep me up all night."

"Probably, you guys need a kinder relationship. I know they aren't ideal, but they're yours, and it'll hush those annoying hisses and let you rest. I can give you some more tomorrow."

"Well they like the bonnet." Medusa nodded, then glanced away.

"Well, I'm happy to hear that." I looked at my phone as it buzzed, "Oh, they're outside, let's head out."

"Oh, alright." She stepped back and waited for me by the top of the stairs. I walked to dads room and knocked.

"Dad we're going, if you need anything call me yeah? It'll just be you and Iron tonight."

"Oh? Well, y'all have fun, keep an eye on Medusa." Tartarus said.

"Of course, don't do nothing crazy on your own." I joked. He snorted.

"Ima be out like a light, keep me updated."

"Gotcha." I nodded and pulled the door closed. We headed outside and was caught by surprise at Leviathan's car parked on the street. We walked over and Rouge rolled the window down.

"Sorry, Daddy insisted on dropping us off." Rouge smiled apologetically, Saint sitting next to her with a wide smile.

"Oh Uh, that's cool… Evening Mr. Levi." I nodded to him and got in the car after Medusa.

He narrowed his eyes in the rear view mirror, glancing at me. "Aubrey."

"Yea." I looked away, he had a smaller male in the passenger seat, his cat ears flickered and he turned to face me.

"Oh! You're Aubrey~?" He purred, "I heard a lot, you're Tartar's lil son?"

I blinked, "You know my dad?"

"Oh we all go back wayyy back." Scotus laughed and waved it off, "I'm Scotus, a pleasure to meet you finally."

"You as well… um, this is Medusa, a friend."

"Hello." She spoke quietly.

"Hello." Scotus smiled, his eyes seemed to narrow, but he turned around before it was noticeable, snakes and cats, how fun.

"Well, Briar is already waiting for us, and Keegan and Orien are gonna meet us there, and I think Jonas is on the way. Rue said she can't tag along, we'll have to hit her up another time."

Rouge nodded, slightly disappointed about Rue but smiled anyway, "We should do dinner, that might be more her speed."

I nodded in agreement.

"I wonder what Jonas is wearing~ I noticed her wonderful fashion sense. I'm so jealous!" Rouge said, looking at Saint.

"I think she's the only person I've met to pull off denim like that, you know who she reminds me of?" She asked,

"Osun, The super famous fashion designer~?" Rouge answered quickly.

"Oh shit, she does?" I said and nodded, "I wonder if that's on purpose."

"Oh it's gotta be? Think if I asked, she'd make me an outfit?" Saint asked.

"Probably, she's very proud of her skill, she offered to tweak my uniform but I forgot to go to her dorm, haha…" I rubbed my head.

"Oh I NEED a uniform modification by her, imaggiinnee!" Rouge grinned.

"Ask her, she thinks y'all are gorgeous, she'd probably do it for y'all for free." I leaned back.

"Oh I could never accept something free from her." Saint spoke.

"Oh that's rich." I raised a brow.

"Oh hush."

Rouge laughed. Medusa remained quiet, she was looking out the window. I glanced at her and rubbed her hand gently and smiled a bit, she looked at me and blinked before slightly smiling. I'm an idiot, we did not work on social interactions. I mentally face palmed.

We got to the gates, I got out and helped Medusa out of the car. She looked up at the black gates, It was quiet, the dead trees rustling by the slight breezes. The moon shone down on us, silhouetting the birds. She looked a bit disturbed.

"Uh, is this pride?" Medusa asked.

I nodded eagerly, "I come here a lot."

"Oh." That's all she said. I will take that in stride.

"If you get too overwhelmed, let me know and I'll take you home. Ok?"

"Ok.." Medusa stayed a bit close, her snakes hissing at any and every sound.

"It's just a bonfire, it hopefully won't be too overwhelming." I smiled then looked up as Briar made her presence known.

"Aubrey!" She waved, she was in a corseted lace shirt with a ruffled mini skirt and long white socks, dressed to impress like always.

"What the hell is this?" Briar asked, taken aback. She looked up at the scenery then back at me.

"My happy place that I'm choosing to share with y'all." I grinned.

She pursed her lips and shook her head. Blaire stood beside her, matching her style with ease, some of his braids pulled back out of his face. He gave a gentle wave and a smile. I walked over with the others and grinned, putting a hand to Blaire, he slapped my hand and pulled me into a hug. I laughed quietly.

"Nice to see you Blaire, you remember my friends right?" I motioned to the others, "Rouge, Saint and this is Medusa."

"I certainly remember Saint." Blaire said quietly and scratched his cheek with his finger. I raised a brow and grinned.

"Oh? Well, she's single."

His pale face went bright red. He waved it off then greeted the others with Briar. I kept an eye on Rouge and Briar, if I'm honest I'm not too sure how they'll interact. I know Briar has no filter when she feels threatened and I know Rouge is territorial. All things considered. That'll be a bit of a headache.

"So are we just waiting for Jonas and Your girlfriend?" Saint asked, "I can go ahead and order some stuff for the night. That's about eight people right?"

"Uh, yea, I doubt Jonas is bringing that Dragon freak, and if she is, he can pay for his own shit." I muttered.

"Aubrey." Saint elbowed my back. I rolled my eyes.

"He's a dick."

"Yea, pot and kettle." Saint rolled her eyes, "Be respectful of Jonas."

"I ammmm." I huffed.

"Order... Are you paying?" Blaire asked gently and walked over to her, Saint looked up at him then gave a sweet smile.

"Yea, it's no big deal." Saint waved it off, "In all honesty I was gonna make Aubrey do it."

I whipped my head around to her, seeing her covering her mouth with her fingers and giggling quietly.

I could see it in Blaire's eyes. He was fighting back a

flustered blush, "Oh, no need for that, I can cover it." Blaire turned his attention towards me, "If you're Ok with that of course Aubrey?"

"Oh baby, I am more than Ok with that."

"Oh, That's so nice of you…" Saint smiled, urging for his name.

"Oh-" He cleared his throat and rubbed the back of his head, "Blaire, Blaire Wynter…uh Briar's twin brother… uh Rowan or Blaire is fine, uh Rowan is my middle name uh…"

"Well, it's nice to meet you Blaire Rowan Wynter." Saint smiled, her tone softer.

Her eyes had a sparkle in them. I know how her smile affects the knees. I could see the slight buckle but he smiled it off politely. I couldn't help but snicker to myself. Now that's a pair I wouldn't be too mad at. I know Blaire, he's as sweet as they come. That way she can actually date in her standards instead of below it. I nodded approvingly.

"Aubrey!" I looked up at the familiar voice and met eyes with Keegan, Jonas and that asshole Dragon not too far behind. I smiled at her and opened my arms, she walked over and practically jumped in my arms, she pecked my cheek and she giggled quietly.

"Sorry, I hope we aren't late…"

"Not at all, we just got here." I put an arm around her shoulders, she was in a semi flowy blue dress, the top off the shoulders. She had tights under it and tennis shoes. I waved at Jonas and smiled.

"Guys, this is Keegan, my girlfriend." I grinned. "Keegan, this is Saint and Rouge, my best friends, Briar, her brother Blaire, Jonas. My sister, that guy, and you remember Medusa right?"

"Oh, wow.. Lot of people.." She waved awkwardly, she bowed her head, "It's a pleasure, he speaks highly of y'all, um, this is my brother Orien."

Orien's arms were crossed and I could feel his glare on my temple. I flicked my middle finger at him which annoyed him further.

"Ain't ya momma tell ya staring ain't polite." I grinned, "I know she did."

He rolled his eyes and turned his head away.

"Wow, look at you, an Angel?" Saint asked. "How's your… stay?"

"Oh, it's wonderful! I'm native here so.." Keegan smiled.

"To Sin City?" Rouge asked, her arms crossed.

"Yes, my mom lives here in the Lust city actually, fallen Angel and all that.." Keegan messed with the end of her dress and glanced away. I rubbed her lower back comfortingly.

"You're so beautiful! Aw Aubrey, I'm happy for you~" Jonas spoke up, she clasped her hands together with a small bounce, her Dragon companion stayed silent, eyes more annoyed than anything.

"Gods, Jonas! Your outfit is everything!" Rouge gasped.

She grinned proudly, "Oh! Thank you~ made it myself~"

She was in a hand sewn denim bodysuit with a few strategically placed fabrics on the bell bottom pants, she still wore her white satin gloves but had white boots and a white bandanna to match.

"Phenomenal!" Saint's eyes sparkled.

"Y'all we should head in before people ask questions." I spoke up, interrupting the girl talk before it began. I pointed towards the gate. We all walked through and headed towards the old abandoned courtyard.

I kept an eye on Medusa then smiled at her. I nudged her shoulder "Try compliments, to break the ice." I smiled.

She glanced away then nodded lightly.

I began setting up the bonfire and the speakers. Logs were already arranged from my previous stays. I sat the blankets over them for the girls though.

"Ok, food should be here soon. I chose the raven option so keep an eye out." Saint nodded.

I sat on the log and stretched.

"So this is uh..." Jonas spoke up, "A place."

I chuckled, "Pride, yea. It's long abandoned. But as you can see lots of plants."

"Yes, is that normal?" Jonas asked.

"Just for pride and the king's place." I nodded, "Pride is a bit of an anomaly."

"Why is it abandoned?" Keegan asked, "It's been like this since before us, mom told us not to come here. Like ever."

I tapped my chin in thought, "Well, how dad explained it, it's kind of a love story in a way?"

"Huh?" Saint asked.

"Yeah, turns out Pride disappeared centuries ago. People have their speculations, be it death, stepped down, what have you. Me personally? I like the idea of them leaving for love." I smiled, "The plants are here because of their love for their partner, allegedly. No one really knows why pride is like this."

Rouge snapped her fingers, "Oh! You mean the old Hades and Kore story? Dad told it to me."

My eyes sparkled at her, "Oh?"

"Yes, he said Pride ruled here for years, one of the first Sins to appear. He was ruthless. Not many people messed with him because you know Pride tends to birth the other Sins. They all intertwine in some way. Well sometime later, he met Kore, some say he kidnapped her, or she got stuck here when trying to exorcise him, dad said She succeeded and left." Rouge said, "Not sure about the love story aspect though?"

"Ah, nah, for me. Dad said the first half, but Kore and Hades fell in love, she grew all of this because she was stuck here but she wanted to share the beauty of life with someone so accustomed to death, she declared to him that she will learn his true name, it's implied she did and they ran off together. He didn't want this anymore, he wanted her." I smiled, "I always loved that story, it kinda reminds me of like soulmates yea?"

"You believe in soulmates?" Keegan asked.

"Of course, not too corny is it?" I laughed quietly.

"No, no, not at all." Keegan had stars in her eyes. I smiled a bit then glanced towards Rouge, She seemed to turn her gaze away as I did.

"I definitely never heard that version, it sounds beautiful." Rouge spoke.

We looked up as a raven cawed down at us. Saint motioned the bird down and took the food from them. She happily gave the bird some treats for their work. The bird flew off happily. Saint sat the pizzas and wings down, and dropped the case of beers.

Oh, now that's what I want. I grinned and went to reach for one but Saint swatted at my hand.

"Aye, food first."

"Saint, I am grown."

"Yea and dumb. Eat a wing 'cuz then you'll be texting me

at 2 am saying your stummy hurts." Saint rolled her eyes. I narrowed my eyes at her and snatched a wing. Rouge and Keegan giggled quietly to themselves.

Briar grabbed one of the beers and made her way over to me and sat next to me. She handed it to me with a smile on her face. I smiled and took it from her. I flipped the cap off with my bottle opener and took a sip.

Saint and Rouge watched her. She sat quietly while eating her pizza.

"Ya know, it's so quiet here." Briar said, looking up at the sky, "I can't believe I've never been here before."

"Probably ain't really a tourist spot." Rouge said, taking a bite of pizza.

"Nah, probably not." Briar said back.

I cleared my throat, "Uh, anyway. In all honesty no one ever comes here, it's why I love it. This is where I was when you found me with Iron."

"Oh?" Briar asked.

"It does fit your vibe." Keegan giggled.

My eyes softened at her, "Oh is that so?"

"Absolutely, only a creep would enjoy this typa scene." Orien said slyly.

I shot him a look, he's lucky his sister is sitting next to me or I'd do something harsh. I just smiled at him and picked up another wing, taking a bite out of it.

"Aubrey? Would it be Ok if you walk me around, it's woods here right?" Briar spoke up after a while. Most of the food was gone and my phone playlist was playing softly in the background. I nodded.

"Yea I definitely can."

"Actually, how 'bout we all stretch our legs?" Saint said, I raised a brow at her and Rouge stood beside her.

"Just girls, ya know?" Rouge smiled.

"Oh? That sounds nice." Briar smiled, she placed her cold hands delicately on my shoulder and stood, I sat my beer down and immediately went to put my arm to her out of habit.

"Just be careful, Briar is blind, it's a bit dark as well so she's way out of her element." Blaire spoke.

"I can walk with you." Keegan smiled sweetly, she put her arm to her and Blaire took it gently with a smile on her face. Rouge and Saint shared a look before walking off with them.

I raised a brow, "Y'all behave out there now."

Saint threw her hand up.

I glanced towards Medusa and she looked less stressed than before. I think the food and calming atmosphere helped her relax. I doubt she'd enjoy wandering with the girls so I didn't bother asking her too. If I'm honest I'd prefer to monitor their interactions with her. I know she's still a sore spot. Briar and Keegan can handle a little heat, Medusa? I'm not so sure.

***

Keegan's eyes were bright, she was looking up at the moon with Saint. Answering any and all her questions with pure happiness. Saint seemed to loosen up towards her since she was being so honest. Maybe she isn't a stick in the mud? In all honesty she was more worried about Keegan than Briar. Briar is an ex, someone his type. The usual. But this Angel?

Who knows what her motive is. Saint's dad has made it very clear, angels are exorcists. What if she was just trying to get close to him to take advantage? He's her best friend. It's only natural to be a bit wary.

They all came to realize, *she's sickeningly sweet.*

Rouge and Briar on the other hand. Polar opposites. Fire and ice. They were in their own world, talking amongst each other. Rouge had that green rage to her words while Briar had cool and collected responses.

She spoke up after her barrage of questions, a coldness to her tone, "Ya know... You're all he ever talked about, you and Saint." Briar looked towards the moon, her snowflakes chilling Rouge's shoulders. "I hated it."

Rouge scowled, "Well he is my best friend."

"Oh please, you and I both know, that's not the case." Briar practically laughed, "If he didn't announce he was dating the Angel, you'd be throwing yourself at him as much as I would."

"I don't like your implication."

"Your attack of questioning and those pretty green eyes tell me all I need to know darlin." Briar said, "I know you love him, I love him as well, sadly I lost him once, and it seems I've lost him a second time. But unlike you." Briar turned her head to Rouge, "I wish to be cordial, I have no ill will towards you. We're both losers here it seems."

"..."

"You're everything he said." Briar laughed quietly, "You're tall and beautiful, I didn't think he meant you had green eyes literally. Kinda Ironic ain't it?"

"How'd you-?"

"Hm? Oh, my snowflakes work as my sight, in a way. It's

not perfect at night, but hazy is better than nothing in this environment." Briar hummed, she put her hand to Rouge, "Anyway, If I'm honest. I've been dying to meet you both."

"Why. To compare or brag." Rouge Said.

"Gods no, I love women, more than I love men. I can't lie. I see no woman as competition, but how softly he speaks of you, I might be humbled." Briar laughed quietly. "I don't know of your past with him, but I wish to be a part of his future, and I'm willing to admit my defeat."

"Defeat hm." Rouge rolled her eyes.

"Look, I'm not too fond of the events either. I came here to win him back, but it seems things didn't work out. So for his sake I will be cordial, if you will be." Briar pulled her hand back

"Tch." Rouge sucked her teeth and turned her head away, "I'm only here for him."

"As am I, so I guess we agree." Briar nodded. Rouge pursed her lips and stayed quiet. They turned their heads toward the other pair.

"Well, she answered all my questions enthusiastically, she might be a keeper babe." Saint said.

Keegan was practically beaming, she had the brightest eyes. Stunning blues, especially under the moonlight. Rouge turned her gaze away. Keegan rubbed at her arm and cleared her throat.

"So, The ex girlfriends? Oh wow.." Keegan said nervously. "I guess I'm not exactly his type.."

"Oh please sugar, he don't got a type." Rouge snorted, "Don't sell yourself short, you seem nice."

"Um, thank you.." Keegan responded.

"Just. Take care of him. Yea..?" Rouge smiled gently, but it was distant, she patted her hand gently, blinking away a few tears, maybe she should admit defeat too? She seems sweet, she's beautiful, shorter, curvier, he looks at her so lovingly. *I guess it's over?* She thought to herself. She moved her hair out of her face and breathed out.

The girls began to walk once more heading back towards the bonfire. Keegan had her hand on Briar's as they walked side by side. Briar gripped at her sleeve at the same time as the girls turned their heads toward a sound.

Medusa emerged from the trees and looked shocked to see them. Rouge immediately narrowed her eyes and Saint got defensive. She rubbed her arm and hesitantly walked over.

"Um, sorry to startle you, I decided to try to catch up to you.." Medusa spoke.

"Why." Rouge demanded.

"Well, Aubrey would like it if I tried to socialize with other girls." Medusa said, "And he really likes the bl- *uh*- Keegan. I wanted to meet her properly." Medusa looked at Keegan, she blinked in shock then pointed to herself.

"Me?"

"Yes, you're his partner right?"

"Yes." Keegan smiled and put her hand to her. Medusa hesitantly took it. Keegan's smile didn't falter. She seemed almost eager to meet Medusa, which confused her.

"Aubrey told me a bit about you, he seems to really care about you." Keegan said.

"Oh, yes, he's helping me out… Thank you for understanding, the other ones don't get it." Medusa said a bit passive aggressively. Keegan laughed it off awkwardly as Rouge narrowed her eyes and Saint rolled hers.

Medusa glanced at them and remembered what Aubrey suggested. He told her to start with compliments. She already complimented Saint once and it didn't go too bad. She took a minute to think while the other girls stared at her. She felt nervous and felt her face slowly becoming hot from embarrassment.

Medusa cleared her throat, "Um. You're a good friend to Aubrey." She said to Saint then looked at Rouge, "And you give the fungal beauty of a Schizophyllum Commune." Medusa basically stuttered out. The other girls seemed confused, again just staring at her.

"I'm sorry?" Saint asked.

"Fungal-?" Rouge tilted her head.

"Well, that's um…" Keegan said hesitantly.

"Well, uh, Schizophyllum Commune is my favorite mushroom…" Medusa looked down then rubbed her arm. "Oh! Should I say you remind me of a Centrolenidae? That's a glass tree frog! That is my favorite frog, they're very tiny." Medusa smiled.

"A frog." Rouge deadpanned. Briar snickered and glanced away.

Saint dropped her head in her hands.

"Maybe we should head back, the boys will be worried." Briar spoke gently with a smile, "Especially my brother."

"Of course." Keegan led the way, Medusa following behind the group quietly. She tried, she didn't do that right. Aubrey will be disappointed.

40

THIRTY-NINE

"Well, I have to tinkle~" Jonas stood and dusted off her spotless skirt, "Anywhere I can squat or something?" She asked.

I motioned towards the woods, "I put a makeshift bathroom a few trees back."

"Sounds great." Jonas motioned for the Dragon to stay put. He looked slightly distressed at that but stayed like an obedient dog. She wandered off and he sat quietly.

Should I extend an olive branch? I mean, he's a dick, sure. But clearly, Jonas is into him for whatever reason and I want to support her. He avoided any eye contact. Now looking at him, he looked exhausted. His eyes had dark bags under them, but his iris' were a piercing silver. They practically glowed in the darkness, they were a stark contrast to his black sclera. It's what makes him easy to pinpoint. Strangely he's very silent for a six foot Dragon. I looked away, it's just Orien, Blaire, me, and this Dragon. Orien ain't gonna say shit, and Blaire is nibbling the last of his pizza. I huffed to myself and rubbed the back of my head.

Can't hurt to try right?

"Ayo. You want a beer or you gonna stand over there all night?" I spoke up and held a beer up. His bright eyes flickered towards me then he rolled his eyes in annoyance.

Yep that's enough for me. I waved it off then tossed the beer towards Orien. He accepted it and took a sip, turning his gaze to the trees. He and that Dragon ain't too far off. I shook my head with a small chuckle.

"What are you giggling about." Orien said.

"Ah, I was gonna do something outlandish and ask you to soften up thing two over there. I feel y'all would get along." I took a sip of the beer, "Then I remembered you're you."

Orien narrowed his eyes, "Yea I see why he doesn't acknowledge you."

"Nah he got his own problems he can't address. You, on the other hand, are just so fun to poke at." I grinned.

"Can't address?" The Dragon spoke up, his voice catching us all off guard. "I definitely can, I just choose not to."

"And that's fine babe, I couldn't care less if ya paid me." I shrugged.

"Why do you assume you have any type of entitlement towards me?" Adonys said, offense laced in his tone. Now I'm confused, 'cuz when did I ever give that impression?

"Excuse me."

"You talk like you're hot shit. Like you deserve an explanation for a disliking towards you. You talk like you're the best thing since oxygen. So yea, excuse me if I ain't too keen to "chill" with you and your loser friends." Adonys narrowed his eyes.

"Nigga, calm down." I felt my eyebrow twitch, "We had a total of two conversations and half of them you looked like a stick was parked permanently up your ass. I don't know nor care what your beef is, but I suggest you squash it."

"Or what." Adonys challenged.

"Oh you got balls now?" I asked.

"Ok, Ok don't start anything you can't finish you two, Aubrey just let it go." Blaire said gently. He smiled and waved his hand awkwardly. Orien already knew not to say a thing to me. Blaire on the other hand was too sweet, I took a breath and nodded.

"You're right. I'll drop it."

"We're here for your friend right?" Blaire said, meaning to Medusa.

"Something like that, she ain't used to socializing like this."

"I see, how did you two meet?" Blaire asked, "She's so unique, very pretty. Where's she from? Is it nice?"

I smiled, but Before I could answer, The Dragon scoffed. Sounds of twigs snapping behind us as the girls emerged from the tree line.

"It's nice if you like suffering and freaks like her and her shitty ass father." Adonys mumbled.

The area fell silent for me. They all just stopped and looked at me. I gripped the bottle in my hand. I suddenly felt hot in the face. I'm happy she decided to leave because clearly he has no filter. Her hearing that would have destroyed all that confidence and reassurance and that ain't something I can look past. Talking about me is one thing but what he ain't gon do is talk slick out his neck about Medusa.

I laughed quietly and sat the bottle down.

"Are you fucking serious."

"Aubrey, I'm sorry I didn't-" Blaire spoke up, I put my

hand up to stop him but kept my gaze on the Dragon.

"Aubrey-" I heard Saint's voice behind me momentarily.

"Look, I don't care what your problem with me is, but keep Medusa out of it." I narrowed my eyes, "I was gonna bite my tongue and tune you out because you and my sister got something goin on. But I don't play about mine. *At all.* "

Adonys stood up, almost like he was trying to intimidate me. That pissed me off even more. All I could do was laugh at the audacity. I rubbed my head.

"Are you tryin' to press me right now?" I scoffed, "You get a lil too bold when my sister ain't around, and honestly I'd advise you to keep your mouth shut. If I stand up I guarantee imma knock your teeth down your throat. 'Cuz If you got such a fuckin problem, nigga we can solve it."

He seemed to falter slightly at that.

"You can't step to me. Don't puff yo chest out now that Jonas ain't here. You a bitch. You got a fuckin' problem you address me directly. Don't you ever talk to or about her like that again, especially in my face. This is your only warning. And that goes for ALL my girls. ALL of my friends. You talk to damn slick out yo mouth, I'll knock your fuckin' jaw loose. Bitch ass nigga." I narrowed my eyes. In all honesty it's taking everything in me not to knock him in his jaw right now.

The area was quiet after that. Adonys seemed to back down completely. He pursed his lips and just walked away, opposite of us. I sucked my teeth and threw the beer bottle in the fire making it shatter on impact. I stood up and turned, the girls were standing there. But I didn't see Medusa.

"Aubrey, hey. What was that about?" Saint asked. I looked

down at her and she seemed worried. I forced a smile then shook my head.

"Where's Medusa? Wasn't she with you?" I asked.

"She was just?" Saint and the girls turned around, but she wasn't there.

I felt panic start to set in. Did she hear what he said? Did she hear all of that? I immediately walked past them and towards the trees to look for her. I can try to somewhat salvage the situation.

"Medusa?" I asked, looking around the area, she won't go too far. I checked behind a few trees before seeing her snakes peeking out at me. I breathed out and walked over. "Hey Rose, you Ok?"

"No." Medusa said, rubbing at her eyes, the moon light highlighted the streams on her face. I frowned and walked over to face her.

"I'm sorry you had to hear that..."

"I'm Miserable, all of this is miserable!" Medusa had her head in her knees.

I could see the glint of tears on her cheeks and that genuinely broke my heart. "Medusa."

I kneeled down next to her, she was trembling and sniffling.

"Just stop. You're clearly in the minority. You're the only one who can even look at me." She sounded devastated.

"I can't socialize, I look like a monster, people hate me. He ruined my life." Medusa covered her face with her hands, "I can't make friends with your friends, I can't be normal."

I genuinely don't know what to say. I wish dad was here. He's way better at this stuff than I'll ever be. I just sat next to her and pulled her head to my shoulder. She sniffed and wiped at her cheeks. I rested my head on hers and looked up at the moon. If I'm honest I didn't think he of all people would get under her skin like that. Hell this was probably a bad idea, she's probably overwhelmed. I sighed and closed my eyes, letting her calm down.

"He's just a bitter asshole that needs his ass beat. If it wasn't for the occasion I would." I said quietly, "You aren't a freak, you're just unique. All of us are. For fucksake, I'm a sex toy at worst. Jonas is a sentient creation, Rouge is a vampire, Keegan is a fallen Angel. None of us are normal. You fit in more here than you will anywhere else. I know if they got to know you like I did, they'd love you as much as I do."

"..."

"Did the girls say something to you?" I asked.

"No, no." She shook her head, "But I think I upset the red one..."

I blinked then raised a brow, "Rouge? What did you say."

"I said she was pretty, like my favorite mushroom..." She shook her head once more, "I didn't do it right... I'm sorry..."

"Medusa..."

"You've done so much for me, and I can't do something as simple as befriend your friends. I don't care what they think about me. I care what you think. And how you feel. I just... I don't want to disappoint you.. Or make you regret me..."

"Whoa, whoa." I rubbed her shoulder, "I'm not going anywhere, you're stuck with me I fear."

I smiled softly, "You're one of my own now. You're just as important to me as the other girls are. You are safe here. Hell you're the daughter my dad didn't know he wanted." I laughed.

"We're immensely proud of you, you took to change really well. You're opening up and trusting us. That's more than enough.." I laid my head back against the tree bark. The moon peering down at us.

"I was a bit of a dumbass pushing you into this setting so fast. This is normal for me, I didn't consider how overwhelming it could've been."

"Yes. You didn't." Medusa huffed. I chuckled and closed my eyes.

"Seems I'm the one who should apologize?" I pulled away and rubbed her back, "I'm sorry Medusa, I didn't mean to put you in this position. We can take a minute. Just… breathe rose."

She nodded and wiped her eyes, "Ok.. It's Ok.."

She looked at her lap, "You don't have to call me that. Rose implies beauty."

I glanced down at her, "Well, I think you are beautiful. And it's the name of your favorite song."

She looked up at me, "That's why you say that sometimes?"

"Felt it would be more comforting." I smiled.

She nodded, "Oh, I see. I guess it's Ok then…Thank you."

"Of course, Rose." I smiled softly.

* * *

"What happened?" Briar asked, sitting back down.

"Well we were talking, Jonas went to the bathroom and the big guy just started getting really hostile. I tried to de-escalate by talking to Aubrey and well…" Blaire said, he rubbed his neck.

"Should we go after them?" Keegan asked.

"Nah, she might be overwhelmed, Aubrey can handle her better than any of us." Saint said, "Thank you for trying to keep Aubrey calm Blaire. He's protective."

"Of course, I've never seen him get angry before, he's usually more calm than that."

"I think he's going to get mad at us." Saint said, her eyes sad.

"We didn't do anything. That's all him." Rouge said. Saint shot her a look.

"He wants us to care and be kind to Medusa, we've basically ignored her all night." Saint said.

"She called me a mushroom then a frog!" Rouge said.

"I doubt she meant any harm, Aubrey said she's docile and we should trust him." Saint said.

"I do. I just-"

"We have no problems, if Aubrey has no problems. Yea I'm not too fond of her either, but I care about Aubrey and this is important to him, so put that green eyed monster away and let's start building a bridge. Yes?" Saint said, smiling gently at Rouge.

She sighed and looked at her lap, "Fine. Sure."

"How about we make S'mores? Aubrey loves them!" Saint stood, "I can run to the store, it's just a city over."

"Oh, I can walk you. It's late." Blaire immediately chimed in. Saint looked at him then smiled.

"Sure, it shouldn't take too long."

Blaire stood and put his arm to Saint and led her away.

"Well, Seems he's a gentleman." Rouge said, watching them go.

"Always has been." Briar said with a small laugh.

Saint led the way towards the Gluttony city. Her heels clicking on the concrete. The moon was high and most of the square was crowded. She tried not to stare up at Blaire, but she couldn't deny. He was certainly handsome. He was very kind as well, and it seems Aubrey is fond of him so he isn't a creep. That's a nice change of pace.

"So, you and Aubrey are friends?" He asked.

"Since elementary." Saint nodded.

"And you never been to his little hang out spot?" Blaire asked.

"Oh no. He knows I don't do creepy." Saint laughed, "But I do love a good kickback with him and Rouge."

"Ah, well, that's something I was never fond of." Blaire chuckled.

"Yet you came?" Saint asked, tilting her head.

"My sister insisted." He shook his head, "Sadly I'll do anything for her."

"Sadly?"

"She knows." Blaire laughed. His smile was so charming. Saint laughed along quietly.

"Well, I've never had siblings, so I guess I wouldn't get it." Saint said.

"Yes, you're a Sawyer right?" Blaire asked. Saint rolled her eyes and glanced away.

"Yea." She said coldly.

"We're a Reaper family, so I promise I only know because of your distinct features." Blaire put his hands up. "Your hair color is kinda a dead give away."

"Oh- Heh, right.."

"You Ok?" Blaire asked cautiously.

"A bit tired of that damn name right now." Saint said, glancing away. She decided to leave her phone on silent for the night, the amount of texts she's gotten is getting tedious. She huffed quietly and looked forward.

"Well, If it makes you feel any better, I ain't too big on my name either. Most definitely for different reasons. Heh.." Blaire chuckled awkwardly.

"Wynter?" Saint asked.

"Kinda notorious if you know my dad, but on the surface it's… Different…"

"The surface?" Saint perked up, "You've been there-?"

"We live there." He nodded, "Born and raised."

"Really? What brings you down here? I mean, y'all ain't very equipped for this scene." Saint watched a few snowflakes elegantly flow off him, his pale skin illuminated by the street lamps, his desaturated eyes having an inhuman glow to them, Saint could feel her cheeks heating up.

"Dad is from here, so we visit a lot. We're mainly visiting our brother this time, momma likes to intrude." He said.

"Who's your brother..?" Saint asked.

"Erebus, he runs the-"

"You're related to Erebus?" Saint asked, looking up at him, "He's my dads successor."

"Heh, yea" Blaire smiled, "It's why he stays here."

"Wynter.." Saint put her fingers to her lips then snapped, "Yes, I remember, Mr, Erebus isn't proud of his family name, he actively avoids using it."

"Sounds about right…" Blaire said.

"What does your family do?"

"Errr uh-, I don't like talking about it." He glanced away.

"Oh, my apologies.." Saint smiled apologetically.

"Uh, me personally though, I'm in med school." Blaire said.

"Really?" Saint asked, looking at him.

"My dad is a neurosurgeon, I'm studying to become one as well."

"Fascinating!" Saint bounced a bit then smiled awkwardly, "Sorry, heh, not many interesting guys around here to talk to."

Blaire chuckled, "well I'm glad I hold your attention."

Saint smiled, her cheeks becoming rosy. He opened the Gluttony gates for her. She walked ahead and bowed her head respectfully.

"So, you're in Med school, handsome, and single I'm assuming?" She asked with a smile.

"Sadly, it takes up a lot of time. And my family is a bit hectic, hard to date."

Saint's smile slightly faltered but she nodded in understanding. "I'm sorry to hear that, I'm sure you'd make a lucky person very happy."

"Heh, thanks." Blaire's eyes were soft, She's only seen that sweetness from Aubrey. That stunning passion in his eyes. She looked away, shaking her head and taking the hint.

'You already got a nutcase blowing up your phone girl, you don't need a crush.' She thought to herself. She fanned her face and took a breath.

"Want to blow Aubrey's mind?" He spoke up.

"Huh?" Saint asked.

"He doesn't try new things often but." He picked up a spice jar, "Cinnamon and sugar on a S'more is delicious, he might like it. Especially since he's a weirdo and prefers dark chocolate on his S'mores."

"Dark chocolate has always been his little quirk, he says he can actually fully taste it, so I guess that makes sense, whatever that means."

"Oh, from how Dad explained, he has a hard time tasting certain things, he really put me through challenges to cook for him, I tell you."

"You cook too?" Saint asked.

"Hobby." Blaire grinned, "Now my sister…" He trailed off. "Yikes. Anyway."

Saint laughed, "Got it."

He bought the supplies before Saint could get her card out. Her eyes were practically sparkling in the Supermarket lights. He held the bags for her and stayed close to her as they walked. Gods he's everything her ex wasn't. She didn't have to train him, nor did she have to worry about her status and her image. He's a man of class and gods. What's more mesmerizing than a man with goals, ambition, class and charm? Is this how it feels to not worry so much? She was absolutely entranced.

"There y'all are." I said, watching Saint and Blaire walk towards us, a bag in their hands.

"Let's make some S'mores." Blaire smiled, holding up the bag.

41

FORTY

That was so stupid, what the *hell* was he thinking.

The dragon sat on the old abandoned stairs. The area farthest from the bonfire and a lot quieter. He was beating himself up. He's never lost his cool like that around Aubrey before. That's something he swore he'd never do. But gods he *hates* him and his stupid carefree smug attitude. Everything he does feels like a personal attack. He knows he can't beat Aubrey, especially when he's mad.

Why Jonas cares so much? He'll never know. He gave up questioning long ago. At this point it's above him. He just loves Jonas, and that's all he's here for. His head was resting on his hand, he sighed out and tapped his heeled boot on the old dry rotted steps. How much longer do they have to stay here?

How much longer do I have to tolerate him and the snake. He thought to himself. Is this really what Jonas wants?

He shot his head up as a twig snapped. He calmed himself once he saw those stunning brown eyes. Her cheeks were red and she had a carefree look on her face. Gods, she's divine.

"There you are! We're making S'mores." Jonas smiled, her walk was a little off. Seems she drunk one too many. She hummed and sat next to him, he tried to stop her because of the dirty wood but she didn't seem to mind much.

"I made you two." She put a napkin to him.

"Nah, that's Ok." Adonys spoke quietly.

"You sure hon?" Jonas asked, looking up at the taller male. He gave a small smile and nodded.

"Fine, fine , suit yourself." Jonas took a bite out of the treat, "You feeling Ok? Aubrey said you walked off to get some air."

He didn't tell her, why? Adonys grunted to himself, turning his gaze away.

"I'm alright."

"Did he say something to make you upset?" Jonas asked.

"..." How can he even begin to explain his disdain to her? "No... I'm alright."

"Alright, we don't have to stay too much longer, Aubrey says his dad gets worried."

"Mhmm." Was all he could muster, He hates his name. He hates him.

"What do you think it's like?" Jonas asked quietly, laying her head on his shoulder, "Having parents?"

"I wouldn't know." He said, looking away.

"I think I'm jealous of Medusa." Jonas laughed quietly, "I guess she has some sort of a parental figure now? I wonder what would've happened if he took both of us."

Adonys looked at her, her eyes were dreamy. He gave up on those types of thoughts years ago. It's So distant. He's an orphan, he never thought of the concept of parents. Who needs them when they can abandon you and leave you to the wolves so easily? Titles of superiority mean nothing when we're all the same. A parent is still a person, and a person is still useless.

"..."

Jonas shook her head a bit and balled up the napkin. She got to her feet and slipped, Adonys was at her side immediately. He gripped her hand and wrapped his arm around her waist and steadied her. She blinked then laughed quietly. "Sorry sorry."

"Please be careful." Adonys muttered and slowly let her go, his touch almost lingering. She nodded and moved her hair behind her ear.

"Um, I might've had a little too much... Not drunk, don't worry..." Jonas glanced away, her cheeks red. "I was kinda eager to show you how to make S'mores, Saint makes it look easy. But that's Ok..."

Jonas turned her head towards the fire, the taller male looked down at her, his stare almost desperate. He gripped at his shirt and glanced away as she turned to him.

"I'd be...." Adonys cleared his throat, "I'd be delighted for you to teach me."

Jonas blinked and smiled, putting a hand to him. He hesitated before taking her hand gently in his. Her eyes had a sparkle to them, a sparkle he used to love. Something that he was so fond of, it felt like a distant memory now, but this felt new, a new memory to replace all the ones he's lost. But he would never forget her smile, that was something worth more than anything to him.

He let her gently lead him to the fire. He ignored their looks as Jonas motioned to grab some food. She walked over and sat next to him. Adonys gently started a small fire for her to show him. It's the little things, she looked ecstatic. Jonas put a crudely made one to his lips, He smiled and chuckled lowly. He took a bite for her. She grinned in embarrassment.

"Maybe they aren't that easy?" Jonas laughed quietly.

"It's perfect." His eyes were soft and loving.

"Ya know, you look so much more approachable like this." Jonas joked.

"Mm.." Adonys hummed. "I only care if you approach me."

She looked up at him, gripping his hand gently. Her face was warm but the shadows hid it.

"You have always been all I care about." Adonys glanced at her, "Always Jonas."

Jonas felt her breath catch, she squeaked and dropped her cracker, he tried to catch it for her but she put her hands up in shock. His face was inches from her red one. Jonas closed her eyes and took a breath.

"Sorry! Sorry!" Jonas fanned her face. "It's Ok, it's Ok, I have plenty?"

"Sorry, you sure?" Adonys stayed close to her, his hand placed firmly on the ground to keep his position. "Didn't mean to startle you."

"No, no, it's Ok." She smiled.

They both looked up as a presence approached them. Adonys cleared his throat and sat back. Medusa stood there, she ignored the dragon's presence but she kept her eyes on Jonas.

"Midas." Medusa spoke up, she messed with her skirt. Jonas looked up, holding her bag of crackers.

"I wish to build a bridge."

"A bridge?" Jonas asked.

"You asked for the location of the labs, yes? I will tell you."

"Really?" Jonas raised a brow, "Are you expecting me to trust you? Because you're playing house with Aubrey?" Her tone was hostile now, Adonys sat straight as well.

I kept an eye out from afar, I couldn't make out the full conversation from here and I didn't want to intrude. I noticed Medusa seemed to tense. I narrowed my eyes at the Dragon but it didn't look like he opened his mouth. *He better fucking not.*

Medusa slightly backed down, "I offered because I respect Aubrey, and strangely he's fond of you."

"Tch, I'm his sister, and no matter how much you play pretend princess I'm not trusting you further than I can throw you."

"Well, that's fine by me, I'll just keep my information to myself and tell Aubrey you were unwilling." Medusa huffed.

"Very childish." Jonas narrowed her eyes.

"I could say the same for you." Medusa growled, Adonys immediately stood to attention, nearly standing. Jonas motioned him down and rolled her eyes in annoyance at her.

"Look." Medusa sighed, "If I'm being honest, I was going to tell you anyway... I don't want more kids to be a *freak* like me."

"..." Adonys diverted his eyes.

"So, I'd rather do something right for once, especially since it would make Aubrey happy, and those kids will be free and safe. I couldn't care less of your feelings towards my actions, but I care what Aubrey thinks." Medusa put her hand to Jonas, a slip of paper there. Jonas raised a brow then glanced at the paper with narrowed eyes. She hesitantly took it, reading over it.

"I'd be careful, who knows who's guarding. I'd imagine you're rusty." with that Medusa turned back towards us, she looked proud. I smiled gently.

Jonas looked at the paper and felt a wave of relief wash over her, she covered her mouth and breathed out.

"We can finally find them..."

"We can finally leave?" Adonys spoke up.

Jonas didn't respond, just looked at the paper.

"Did you apologize?" I asked her with a smile. Medusa just somewhat nodded and sat back down, her eyes were tired. The beers were gone, most of the S'mores were gone and it was late. I finished off my blunt and tossed the last of it.

"Are you tired?" I asked, looking down at her, she looked sheepish. I smiled gently and nodded.

"Y'all ready to head out?"

Saint nodded, "Absolutely. I wanna sleep!"

We cleaned, then rounded up everyone and began walking back home. At this point I'm sure Leviathan was long asleep, especially since Rouge didn't call for him to pick us up. Aside from that fucker, Tonight was fun. Saint really put everything back on track with the S'mores. Keegan seems to have made a good first impression. Saint and Rouge are being nicer to Medusa, and it was wonderful seeing Blaire and Briar. This is something I'll definitely never forget, I hope I'm able to have more moments like this with them.

I leaned against Medusa as I felt myself begin to lose balance, the drinks and drugs were kicking in heavy. She squeaked quietly and Rouge propped her up.

"Easy there, you might have to help him home.." Rouge smiled gently.

Medusa huffed but adjusted her stance and gripped my wrist. I threw my hand up with a grin and waved.

"I'll call y'all tomorrow, maybe?"

"Night Aubrey… Saint you can spend the night at mine if you want?" Rouge smiled.

Keegan went to say goodbye but Orien quickly swept her away. She smiled apologetically but blew a kiss, I caught it and waved at her, the crowd dispersed and we headed home. I tried to walk straight but kept feeling myself lean against Medusa, *fuck I'm tired.* She huffed every time my weight got too much for her. But she didn't complain, I breathed out and patted the top of her head.

"I hope you had some fun.." I said, she looked up and smiled softly.

"Yes… I did. I like your girlfriend, she's very sweet." Medusa said.

"I'm happy to hear that…Ya know, I'm proud of you Rose, you did great." I nodded and nuzzled the top of her head, "Maybe one day we can do something like this again."

"Yea… maybe one day.."

My eyes got heavier, I felt them slowly close and felt the soft scales of her hair against my cheek, she began to slow down as I dozed off against her, she groaned out and whined, I grunted a bit and picked my head up.

She helped me to the porch and unlocked the door, I stumbled over to the stairs and headed up slowly. She pushed my back from behind, keeping me upright, she had a slightly annoyed look. Heh, cute.

She steadied a table I bumped into and shot her head towards dads room. She then opened the door for me and I collapsed on the bed. I dropped my head on the pillows and felt sleep creeping in,

"Mm, night Rose.."

"Night Aubrey.." She said softly and slipped out towards her room, I heard her door softly click closed, and with that I was out, not too bad, hopefully we can do this again.

42

FORTY-ONE

A couple weeks passed by, Scorpio has settled in and the school seemed more lively. Tons of events for students, but also tons of tests. I opened my eyes and sat up, rubbing my face and checked my phone. The group chat has been silent lately, mainly on Saint's end, I should check in. It's been a few days since she's texted, she could have that Reaper flu again? She's sickness prone around this season.

I sat up and groaned quietly, I don't feel like going back to that god awful school, weekends don't last long enough. For the past few Sundays, we've been having hangouts with Medusa, I think the girls are finally warming up to her. She's a lot happier now, Rouge doesn't scowl at the mention of her name and Keegan is more than eager to spend time with her. And Saint naturally goes above and beyond. My mind lingered on Saint.

She texted me a few days ago saying she was enjoying Blaire's company, then she asked about Medusa's favorite color. I guess she wanted to get her something to show she was actually trying. She never responded to that message though. I checked my phone once more, her location isn't on either, that's explainable right? *Don't over think, she's probably just at home. Yea, she's probably just at home.*

I swung my feet over the edge and headed to my bathroom to shower then headed downstairs, Iron was already laying at the end of the stairs by the kitchen, his tail wagging. The smell of breakfast filled the area and Medusa was on the couch. I waved at her and she smiled brightly, waving and going back to her book. I turned the corner to the kitchen and stopped in my tracks.

"Morning dad-?" I blinked at the taller gray haired male, he let out a high pitched squeak and turned his head like a kid caught dipping in the cookie jar. He was shirtless and his hair was a mess, *Ok that ain't my dad.* I narrowed my eyes tiredly.

"Mr. Mateo?" I asked.

"Uh, heh- Morning Aubrey-" Mateo rubbed the back of his head, "Sorry, I thought you were already at school, uh your dad is still upstairs."

"..." I blinked slowly, "Did you spend the night last night?"

"Any who~" Mateo turned back to the stove and whistled a tune, plating the food, "Please enjoy~"

"Aren't you supposed to be at work? Ain't there Reaper events you gotta plan?"

"Mm~ touch your nose little field mouse." His ears twitched towards the stairs and dad shuffled in, his robe was disheveled and his PJ bottoms were loose, he looked well rested but still tired in the eyes. He stretched and threw his hand up.

"Morning Aubrey, I thought you would've been at school by now?"

"Y'all, it's 7. School don't start till 9." I rubbed my face and shuddered in discomfort, "You two are gross. Medusa's in the house."

"Oh please." Dad waved his hand, "Medusa honey, come eat something."

Medusa closed her book and made her way in the kitchen, dad patted the top of her head and she took her seat at the table.

"Are you going to school today?" Medusa asked. I sat next to her and nibbled the food.

"Mhmm, I think Rue is back from her little 'vacation' trip, thing, to the surface. I'll have to talk to her."

"The pink Reaper, yes?" Medusa asked. Mateo placed a plate down for Iron. He ate it happily, his tail wagging.

"Yes." I nodded with a smile.

"Reaper?" Mateo asked.

"Oh, yea, Mr. Mateo, do you know Rue Persephonii?"

"Persephonii?" He put his hand to his chin in thought, "I don't know any pink haired Reapers, well, at least, not anymore."

"Anymore? You knew Miss Ravona?"

"Knew her? We were friends! Her death anniversary is coming up." Mateo shook his head in disappointment, "Senseless murder, all that really was."

"Oh, my apologies." I glanced away.

"They're still paying for that bad call, we aren't allowed to do death penalties anymore, all things considered."

"What was the crime?" I asked, tilting my head. Dad glanced over from the coffee pot, raising a brow.

"She was accused of being a Harvester."

I blinked and tilted my head, "A what?"

"Harvesters are Vampire infected Reapers, they lack Reaper values. Basically disrespects and has no care for the dead, a major taboo. They're rare, but they exist."

I pursed my lips as Briar crossed my mind, I guess that's why her family doesn't live here anymore.

"It was bullshit from the jump, yes she worked on Moonstone, but they couldn't harm her, she never said she was infected and most vampires can't see Reapers anyway, there's nothing to reap from those monsters."

"I see..." I cleared my throat awkwardly and looked at my food. Dad handed Mateo a coffee mug and gave him a soft look.

"Oh- err, not all vampires of course-" Mateo tried to correct, I glanced at my phone and narrowed my eyes.

"Um, anyway, I should head to Saint's. She's been MIA for a couple days, she could be sick." I stood up and gave the rest of my breakfast to Iron and grabbed my backpack.

"Should I call jasper?" Dad asked, placing a hand on my back, I shook my head.

"Nah, she's probably Ok."

"Bye Aubrey! Have a nice day!" Medusa said through spoonfuls. I laughed quietly and waved, leaving the house and heading towards Saint's.

I have a bad feeling, hell not even Rouge has mentioned it. I know she dropped her off back home last weekend? I checked our texts then scrolled through them. I tried to call her once more and sucked my teeth.

Voicemail this time.

I headed to the Ranch and noticed the horses seemed unkempt, that's not like her. I headed up to the house and knocked, the house was quiet. Jasper was back to work, usually when they were gone Saint would leave the porch light and Jasper's room light on as a source of comfort, neither were on. I put my hand up and touched the bulb. *It's cold.* Hasn't been on for awhile. I narrowed my eyes. I backed up and walked towards the back of the house, I climbed to her balcony and tried the doors.

Luckily it was unlocked. I walked in and looked around, everything was untouched. Her bed was still made, her vanity was slightly unkempt, her closet was partially open and more importantly her Raven's food and water wasn't full. That's a major red flag. I hurried over to her and pet her head gently.

"Hey there Opal.." I said, she looked tired. I quickly filled her water and food bowl. Saint loves that bird more than anything, no way she'd miss a feeding day, let alone three. Rouge said she dropped her off on Sunday. It's Thursday now and it's clear she never made it in here.

I swore to myself and quickly checked her drawers. I messed up her covers a bit. I don't know what I'm looking for but I'll know it when I see it. I touched the bulbs of her vanity, cold. It's like she left it. I clenched my fist and opened her room door, looking down the hall. Maybe she slept in Jasper's room? She does that sometimes?

No. Stop being delusional. Sleeping in their room doesn't stop her from feeding opal, nor ignoring my calls.

I called her once more and this time it rang a few times then voicemail. I didn't even hear it ring in the house. I pursed my lips and breathed out of my nose in annoyance.

Alright.

I walked down the stairs and called Rouge. She picked up immediately, "Hey love."

"Hey, sorry to call so early, you at school yet?" I asked.

"On my way, why?" She hummed.

"Can you see if Saint is there when you do?"

"Saint?" Rouge asked.

"She's not home. Seems she hasn't been for awhile."

"I dropped her off a couple days ago, what do you mean." Her voice was worried.

"Did you see her go inside?"

"No, she got out and my driver took me right back home, Aubrey should I-?"

"Just keep an eye out, love." I said gently.

"Alright." She hung up.

I know she isn't at Briar's. She would've been gushing to tell me she spent the night with Blaire, and he's way too reserved and shy to get under her skirt so soon. Hell he'd ask me permission first so he shows he means no disrespect, that's just how he is. For the love of everything in this *godsforsaken* place, I better find Saint. **Unharmed**. Or I'm leveling this place to the ground, starting with that fucking school.

I headed towards school. A few people were pooling in, all fourth years. they always got in early. I raised a brow as they walked in through the side door Rue and I went in that night, odd. Why not use the front door? It's unlocked by 8, it's 8:15. I watched a couple of them look around before heading over, a few of them had posters in hand.

It is Scorpio, a really important Reaper time. I checked my calendar, that event Rue sent me. It's this month, I narrowed my eyes. *Can't be a coincidence*. I sat a little ways away and kept my eye on the side door. I tried to tune into the plants near the door.

I sat and took a few deep breaths and began to concentrate, deciphering through the different conversations from the green and tried to hone in on the plants by the door. The training with Jonas has been paying off significantly, my growth with my magic is impeccable to say the least, it feels like something clicked when she suggested pulling magic from earth instead of Hecate, it's been tough but I think it's worth it. I strained my ears, catching every other word. Something about a ceremony and Scorpio.

Come on, give me a little more.

I took a few breaths.

'Ceremony...flyers...Scorpio... Ceremony, ceremony ceremony.' Dammit a ceremony for what. I jumped as a voice suddenly spoke up next to me.

I opened my eyes and turned my head to see Jonas, she looked shocked and waved her hand slightly. Jonas?

"Hey, hon, you alright?" Jonas asked gently.

"I... ?" I asked, "Something is wrong."

"What's wrong?" She asked, her voice stern.

I got to my feet quickly and headed to the entrance, Jonas followed quickly behind.

"Saint is missing."

"Missing?" Jonas asked.

"She isn't answering my calls and she hasn't been at home." the clock began to chime, it's nine. I looked up at the ocular shaped clock peering down on us.

The other students began filing in, the halls became crowded with chatter and bodies, I made my way through the crowd towards our lockers, hoping to see Saint there, bright and early. All I saw was Rouge, I closed the distance between us, she had a flyer in her hand and she looked upset,

I took a breath and carefully spoke.

"Hey hon?" I waved a bit. She looked up at me with misty and red eyes.

"Hey, Rouge. What's wrong?" I asked, touching her shoulder gently. She gripped the paper and handed it to me slowly, almost like she was hesitating.

"It's Saint..." Rouge spoke quietly. I immediately took it and read it over. The poster was her face, full name and dead language written all over it, *that's definitely not a nice word.*

"Where did you get this?" I narrowed my eyes.

"Some girls in the bathroom were talking about a Reaper being in school, something about a ceremony, an event? She'd be perfect for. I pressed them about it and took this from them. They know she's a Sawyer. These are all over the fourth year halls. Do you think they took her when I left?" Rouge was on the verge of tears, I could feel my hands slowly crumple the paper in anger.

I pulled her into a hug, and shushed her calmingly. I noticed her locker, it was vandalized. This isn't good. I took a deep breath, patting the back of Rouge's head to calm her down. I closed my eyes and took a breath. Turning around and heading to the headmasters office.

"A-Aubrey-?" The girls asked in unison.

All of it clicked. I know that old bitch is behind this. But how did she find out? Saint has always been careful, no way she'd slip up like that. I could feel that fiery feeling of wrath on my neck. I pushed through and basically stomped towards the office. I knew it. I knew she was planning something, And she was so emboldened to *kidnap* a Sawyer? *Weapons trafficking my ass.* What the hell will a Sawyer do in that regard?

I opened the door and Rue was sitting at the desk speaking to Petra. She seemed shocked when I entered. She got to her feet.

"Aubrey? Is everything-?"

"Where is she." I demanded, narrowing my eyes at her, Petra sat there, hands folded on the desk. Her long hair rested on her chest, and down her back.

"Whom?"

"Saint." I growled out.

"Saint?" Rue questioned.

"Not sure what you mean." Petra spoke, her voice was quiet but it was venomous.

"Don't give me that shit. What the fuck is this." I slammed the paper on her desk, "Don't fuckin play in my face."

"Oh, yes, I was informed about the Sawyer girl." Petra waved her hand, "Who am I to interfere with student discourse? This is a space for freedom of speech and ideals. That's something you'd have to take up with the students."

"You can at least pretend to give a fuck about your job. Listen here you *old bitch*. Fix this or I will call her father down here, will that encourage you."

"If I were you, I'd watch your tone."

"Well, shame you ain't me then ain't it." I narrowed my eyes, I couldn't help but bare my teeth in pure anger, Rue gripped my arm and pulled me back away from the desk.

"Aubrey, calm down, stop."

"You can go." Petra spoke up. "Rue."

"Huh? Me?" Rue asked, looking at the taller woman as she stood.

"I believe me and Mr. Kovenn have some things to

discuss." She walked around the desks and rested her hand on Rue's shoulder. "Head to class won't you."

Rue glanced towards me but I kept my eyes on Petra, Rue nodded hesitantly before grabbing her backpack and leaving the room silently. The room fell silent between us. Petra walked towards the book shelves, circling me. I followed her with my eyes.

"Well, aren't you a fiery one." She spoke up, "Weren't you Kovenn's raised better."

"Yea, well I don't take kindly to authority figures, especially ones like you."

"Ouch." Petra had her back to me, moving her hands over a few of the books, "You have a very slick jaw. Maybe I should fix that. It would be a shame to send you home that way wouldn't it?"

"Is that a threat."

"Is it?" Petra glanced back at me, her pale blue eyes seemed to glow under her bangs. Her eyes weren't blue in the portraits. *She's a damn fool.* In every photo she was proudly showing her face, now this year she's blue eyed and shady? Yea, I ain't buying that. It's all falling into place.

"Sounded like it, and if it was I'll react accordingly, *Hecate*. You hear me."

She blinked then laughed, "Oh, you're far too observant." Hecate hummed,"You're the Blacksmith's kid right? Not a *real* Kovenn." She turned to me and shook her head, she stayed in front of books, covering one with her body intentionally. I narrowed my eyes and tried to glance around her.

"..."

"How was his departure?" Hecate asked.

"How is your stash."

She laughed quietly, "Oh, so that was you? Who was lurking around in the closed off wing?"

"You are aware, that's illegal, correct. Even for you." I clenched my fists, "All it takes is one heads up."

"Oh?" She hummed, "You wouldn't do that."

"I wasn't aware I wouldn't?" I raised a brow.

"Well, you'd want to help me help you right, *Nephew*?" Hecate walked over and placed her freezing cold hands on my shoulders. Her energy was dark and disgusting, her fingers dug into my shoulders passive aggressively and she had a faux smile on her lips. "It would be a shame if your little Sawyer friend got hurt? Or ended up missing? This is a pretty hostile environment for those...*Reapers*."

"Don't address me as family, I see how you treat family. Where is Saint." I growled and gripped her wrist as tightly as I could, I could feel her slight flinch then pulled my hand back at a sudden surge.

"Play nice, and you will be rewarded." She pet the top of my head and I jerked away.

"The bell has rung, I suggest you go, you'll be late and I'll have to give you a demerit." She sat back at her desk and grinned. She rested her chin against her gloved hands.

"Look here." I placed my hand on the desk and leaned down to her level, "I'm not Rue, I can see thru your bullshit clearer than a bird on window cleanin' day. Tell me where Saint is."

She just smiled. I felt anger boil in me. *So you really want to play this game with me?* I narrowed my eyes darkly and stood.

"Head to class, dear."

"…" I walked out, slamming the door behind me and left the school. Oh this bitch is mental. I could hear footsteps following quickly behind me.

I just kept walking and headed down towards the town. I Know exactly who told that bitch about her, and his stupid ass wouldn't leave too quickly, he was probably expecting Saint to come crying to him in desperation. *Oh nigga you better hope I don't fucking catch you.*

"Aubrey! What happened!" Rouge asked, panicked, she kept her distance though, I just kept my gaze forward.

"Aubrey please! I need you to communicate!"

"It was so fucking obvious from the jump." I muttered, "The posters, the secret classes, the Death Metal. The fucking school. Looking at the curriculum. It's all dark magic, it's Hecate. It was *always* Hecate."

"What? What are you saying?" Rouge asked, I looked at her. She stepped back, I could feel the heat on my face and the panic causing my eyes to water in frustration.

"I need to find the fucker that leaked her information." I looked at her and softened my expression, "I *need* to kill him."

"Aubrey…"

I turned away and walked off, she followed behind and I made my way downtown. I checked the restaurants, the bars, the convenience stores, anywhere. I could feel my anger and anxiety rising by the second, until I saw him, sitting in a run down bar. All I saw was red. Before I knew it I threw the biggest fucking rock I could manage through the building, towards the back of his head.

That pathetic snake shrieked. I climbed in through the rubble and walked towards him, he stumbled to his feet and his eyes widened in fear as he looked at me, the room stayed away from us, the bar owner cowered behind the counter. I gripped him by his shirt and lifted him to my face.

"Adam. You motherfucker." I growled out, "Do you have any idea WHAT YOU'VE DONE!"

"A-Aubrey!" He shrieked. He tried to pry my hand from his shirt. I closed my fist and immediately hit him in the face, over and over again. His nose was broken, blood and tears were streaming down his face.

"WHY DID YOU DO IT YOU LITTLE BITCH!" I threw him through the destroyed window, I followed him down like a predator cornering its prey. He was nothing more but a sleazy asshole with zero self respect. He gets dumped and thinks this is the way to go?

Vines formed around me, whipping up from the ground. He tried to run away. He wasn't going to get far. I won't allow him too. I put my hand out and lifted a few rocks around me, I chucked as many as I could at him. He fell to his side and curled up, the rocks beating and bruising him.

I walked closer to him, every step causing the ground to crack. *I wasn't in control, this was a new feeling,* I've never done this level of magic before. It was like I was on autopilot. Is this what I'm capable of? What all that training has unlocked? *It felt good.* This power feels *good*. I could see yellow surging through the cracks. He scrambled desperately to his feet but I grabbed him by the back of the head.

His face had snot, blood and tears running down it. It disgusted me. He was begging and groveling for forgiveness. *Is he serious?* I lowered myself down, his swollen eyes staring into mine.

"P-please Aubrey, I-I'm sorry!"

I moved my hand to his throat and began to squeeze. Forget the rocks, forget the magic, forget the long distance. No, I want to *feel* the life leave this man's body. My vision was dark, I could tell my face was emotionless, just a dead frown. There's nothing left to say. You should've *stayed away.*

I gripped his throat tighter, I could feel my muscles flex. I was determined to crush this fuckers windpipe. I need him to feel an ounce of the pain I feel right now.

"Aubrey!" Rouge called out. She fell to her knees, grabbing at my wrists. Her eyes were terrified and she was shaking. I tried to control my breathing.

"Stop! You need to stop! This isn't right!" Rouge sounded desperate, her eyes were wide and welled, she was panting and gripping my hands. I glanced at her momentarily before letting him go with as much reluctance as I could muster. He rolled over and coughed desperately for air.

"He…he told her…" I stared him down, "Saint could be dead. Or hurt. All because of him." I felt the anger begin to boil in me again.

"What..?" Rouge asked. She looked towards the pathetic worm, begging her for help. Only because he saw a woman and thought she'd offer solace. No. She loves Saint almost as much as I do. You fucked up. More than your pathetic mind can comprehend.

Rouge gripped my hand and turned her attention to him. She looked hurt, almost like she was in disbelief. I doubt she even remembered this fucker, she had tears streaming down her cheeks. She parted her lips and uttered one simple word.

"Pain." A surge of red emitted from her. He yelled out in agony, he fell to his knees, begging and crying like the pathetic waste of space he is. She said nothing after that, just stared him down as he screamed. She kept that spell on him for as long as she could. *She won't kill him though.* She's not that kind of girl.

I took a few deep breaths, I felt my body getting heavier, and something began trickling down my nose and chin. I touched my nose and my vision began to blur. I stumbled before I could catch myself and fell forward.

Everything drowned out around me.

43

FORTY-TWO

"Aubrey.."

Everything sounded drowned out, like a conversation underwater. I tried to open my eyes but everything was hazy, like a dream. I could hear the blood rushing in my ears, I could *feel* my heart pounding. It was deafening, a loud, tragic pounding.

"Aubrey..."

I tried to hear what was being said, I tried to see where the voice was coming from. All I could see was a hazed scene before my eyes, a pool of red slowly spread towards me, I looked down at my body, I'm not me? My hands weren't mine? They were two toned, one of my hands was green and rotting. My chest was flatter, and my vision was fading. But the blood was so loud. I felt my eyes widen, my hands and clothes were covered in it.

"Aubrey, why did you do this?"

This voice? Why is it familiar, why is my heart pounding in fear. Why am I terrified?

"Why did you do this to me?"

I looked up, teal hair was slowly noticeable in my vision, bloodied teal hair. I looked down and saw those familiar green eyes, lifeless, her eyes weren't looking at me though. They were dead and empty. I could smell the blood on my face and clothes, my hands, the whole area smelled of blood.

It was Rouge, she was on her side, facing me, blood pooled around her, some trickling from her mouth. She was dead. Flower petals fell around her, like some kind of sick joke, then I noticed the vines through her torso.

I did this?

"You loved her... and you did this to her...?"

No. No, I wouldn't. I'd never? Not to Rouge. Not to anyone. I felt my body begin to shake. Wake up, this is a nightmare, it has to be, Did I lose myself?

No. I'd never.

Wake up.

Wake up.

Wake up!

"Rouge!?" I jolted up right with a loud scream, I looked around the room panicked, I could hear my labored breathing and quick footsteps in the hall. I looked down at my hands, shaking. It was a dream… It was just a dream.

"Aubrey!" Medusa hurried in, laying me back down and placing her hand on my forehead. "Don't move too much."

"What… What happened? Where's Rouge?"

"Easy.. she's downstairs. She's talking to your father, you passed out." Medusa turned on my desk fan and pointed it towards my face. I gripped the sheets taking deep breaths.

"There's…bad news.." Medusa spoke carefully. "I called Jonas from your phone, it's best if you all hear this…"

"Bad news? I know. Saint is Miss-"

"Bad news about *you*." She cut me off. I blinked and turned my head towards her.

"Aubrey, you're dying…" Medusa said carefully, all I could do was stare at her, I was speechless, baffled. What do you mean dying? I rubbed my neck instinctively over the scarred bites, glancing away. No, that doesn't make sense, if that was the case I would've died when it happened.

I shook my head, "What are you talking about?"

"Remember those tests I had to run? It might just save your life. I noticed your body wasn't right. In the sense of, your genetic makeup is not what it's supposed to be. Then I realized, your cells are slowly dying, you're losing an immense amount of energy. Your life essence basically. The more you output this chaotic energy, the quicker you speed up the process."

Medusa shook her head, "I reread the notes, you never finished incubating. That means you aren't up to standard like Midas is. You're supposed to be 'fully cooked' like she is. You're the equivalent to a half baked rotting pie. Excuse the metaphor."

I blinked slowly, trying to process everything.

"May I check you?" Medusa asked. I nodded. She walked over and placed her hand on my forehead, then checked my hands. My fingertips were blackened, she must've removed my locket. Is that really how I look right now? I can tell my skin is paler. *What the fuck?*

"Oh, yes. This isn't good.." Medusa took my hands, "You aren't supposed to have blackened fingers like this, and you're so cold…" She tapped her lips with her fingers in deep thought, she then touched my face, her hands were freezing, I flinched slightly as she stared into my eyes.

"I'm hot." I muttered.

"Ok, you have a fever. Your eyes are dulling too, open your mouth."

I made a face, "Medusa…"

"Aubrey, I need to check." She tilted my head back as I opened my mouth, she moved my lips to look at my teeth, and lowered my jaw to check my tongue, she narrowed her eyes.

"Your teeth?" She asked.

"Huh? Oh, vampire venom sharpened them when I was 17." I said, she nodded.

"That explains the cells then, it's the venom attacking them but your body is so makeshift it doesn't know what to do with it, I can help you." Medusa stood, "You'll be alright, you should rest."

"Rest-?" I asked, "Medusa, I'm so confused-?"

Medusa put her hand up, "Yes, basically you're using up too much of your life essence. I'm shocked you haven't completely depleted it in the past 24 years. Since you never finished incubating, your body is falling apart and dying. Understood?"

"U…Understood…" I said in disbelief, "But, I'm sorry, what do you mean falling apart? That's a bit much isn't it? I know you're literal-"

Medusa took my arm, tugging it slightly, I could feel it slowly detach. I grunted and yanked my arm away quickly.

"I am very serious."

I just stared in disbelief. *What the fuck?*

"You need to rest until I can find a way to finish incubating you or you'll die. And you have no soul, when you die, that's it." Her voice got shaky.

"I can help you." Medusa nodded then left the room before I could respond.

I sighed and dropped my head and looked at my arm. The skin was ripped, looked like stretched Swiss cheese, no blood, just metal? I narrowed my eyes and tried to focus, isn't there supposed to be bones inside? Well, most people aren't able to remove their appendages like a mix and match game.

I held my arm in place and shuddered in discomfort as the skin slowly fused back together, I moved my fingers down and rubbed my wrist. I messed with my fingers and pulled. My middle finger popped right off and stiffened almost immediately, like plastic, I couldn't even feel it coming off? I bent the finger and it moved like a ball joint. Is that what I am? Is that what's under my skin? I felt my eyes widen and nausea settling in. *What... what the fuck did he do*. I put my finger back and moved it,opening and closing my fist. Now that I'm thinking of it, is this why I never experienced pain before? At least, not pain like this. I can feel pinches, shocks, intense heat or cold, things like that. I thought that was normal. Until I sent a kid to the hospital for the first time, he was crying and screaming, I didn't understand it then.

That's normal. *And I'm not.* I felt that sinking feeling creeping back in. Just when I thought I was over it? I thought I was going to be *Ok*. I took deep breaths trying to ignore that pit in my stomach.

I sighed and laid back against the pillows, looking up at the ceiling. How deep does this go? I touched my face and gripped, there's something hard in there, is it metal too? I closed my eyes and touched around them, that's hollow, like normal people.

I just don't understand. I opened my eyes tiredly and stared at the ceiling once more.

I grunted quietly and moved the covers off myself, it's hot. She did mention a fever, guess that checks out. I glanced towards the mirror and blinked, eyes hazed, but the reflection seemed off? I could barely make out my reflection, but I could see the hair was different colors, and the blobs of clothes were black white and red. What?

"Seems you're awake." The voice was deeper, I tilted my head in confusion.

"Wha.." I asked, *oh I gotta be trippin.*

"Listen to me. You need to get that book."

A book? What the hell is it talking about? What book? Why would I get a book? I narrowed my eyes.

"If you don't, Rouge will perish. Do you hear me?" I stood to attention, I felt a low growl rumble in my throat, *"You'll know it when you see it, kid."*

"Who the hell are you?" I mumbled out, dropping my head back on the pillow.

"I'm someone you know well." Condescending fucker. *"Just get that book, and don't fuck it up."*

I moved uncomfortably, I feel like I'm being watched. I turned my head away from the mirror and stared at the ceiling. I swear I saw a multitude of eyes staring down at me, most of them being a deep yellow, others being swirled. *I'm losing it.*

I closed my eyes, falling back asleep.

* * *

"What do you mean Aubrey's dying!?"

I sighed lightly and rubbed my temples. "I'm sure it was a very straightforward statement, Midas." I tried to stay calm and scientific. My shaking hands aren't noticeable if I keep moving them.

The room was quiet aside from that outburst, Rouge was sitting on the couch, covering her mouth, Jonas was shaking, Mr. Tartarus was quiet but his eyes were heart broken. And the moronic lizard stayed quiet like always, just a brooding shadow looming over Jonas. *Why are you even here?*

"I think I can fix him, I know what's wrong with him."

"What's wrong with him?" Mr. Tartarus spoke up, his voice was softer than I was expecting.

"Um, well, he's basically losing his life energy, the thing that's keeping him alive." I nibbled my nail in thought, trying to find the right words, "The way he made Homunculi was with god essence. Aubrey and Midas are made from chaos essence, when you found Aubrey, he was incubating and was supposed to mature like Midas but you stopped that incubation, which is why he stayed a baby and grew like normal."

"His essence is depleting, his eyes are duller, and his mouth is off. And in all honesty I'm shocked he's lived this long. Especially with vampire venom inside him, that should have destroyed his essence immediately like the venom always does."

Rouge began to tremble but Tartarus seemed taken back by that. He glanced towards Rouge then moved his hand down his mouth and looked away. I glanced away and cleared my throat awkwardly.

"Um, but he can be helped, I believe if we get more essence

we can simulate an incubation process? Like we can inject him with what he needs, the equations for him should still be available. Or I can go by Midas's equation, all things considered."

"And where can we get chaos essence, chaos hasn't existed in centuries." Mr. Tartarus spoke up, I smiled and put up a finger.

"At his old lab! The one he abandoned, there should still be some essence there, we can get some and bring it back. When we do, I can run some tests and figure out how to properly continue his incubation process without interrupting his current biology." I tapped my lips, "Putting him in the tube isn't a good idea, it could make him age incorrectly, or start him over completely...That's my biggest concern."

"So if we get this essence, we can help him. Yes?" Rue asked, the pink haired girl was rubbing Rouge's back.

"Yes. I'm determined." I nodded. "We may be on a timer, I'm not sure why his body is failing all of a sudden? Rouge, what happened when you two were together."

"He got angry..." Rouge shook her head, "About the Headmaster, She found out Saint was a Sawyer. And now she's missing..." She looked at the ground. "The guy Saint was dating told her."

"Angry..." I tapped my lips, "It must be his magic then? Somehow it's weakening his body, has he done anything different?"

"Well Aubrey didn't use much of his earth magic, he could only understand plants and use vines, but today his magic felt different, he was throwing rocks, making the ground quake, he's never done that before..."

"Felt different?" I tilted my head.

"It didn't feel familiar, like if I or Rue uses magic, it's like he's on a whole other level, his glyph was even different."

I glanced at Jonas, she had her mouth shut for once I narrowed my eyes, "What did you do."

"Excuse you." She narrowed her eyes.

"What did you *do*." I repeated, "Because whatever you did you put him in danger, you idiot."

"How dare you, you're the one who tried to kill him!" Jonas pointed at me.

"Yet I'm not the one who's killing him now am I?" I growled back. Her eyes widened in rage, I turned my head in annoyance.

"You don't actually expect any of us to trust you do you!? Do you honestly think we believe your delusions. Or that any of us give a fuck, we're here for Aubrey." Jonas said, poking my chest, I stumbled slightly from the force and felt my snakes get defensive.

"I'm the only one trying to help and offer solutions! What can you do! You don't know shit about the Homunculus procedures! You didn't even realize he was pushing himself too much!" I raised my voice and poked her chest just as hard.

"Girls." Tartarus spoke up, his voice booming in the room. "Stop, do you really think now is the time for this." He pinched the bridge of his nose and sighed.

"Look, Medusa, we need to get anything that will help him. If we get you to the old labs, will you help."

"Of course. I'll do anything." I bowed my head to him respectfully.

"Good, I'll go with you. I'll also call Jasper, they need to know about Saint, if something happens to her it won't be good for any of us. Split up, figure this shit out before I get off the phone." With that he walked upstairs. The room fell silent almost immediately, Iron was up and alert now, watching Jonas. Her eyes were locked on me and Rouge and Rue stayed quiet.

Rue silently spoke up, "This is deeper than I thought, she's planning something, something sinister, and now that she has the son of *THE* Reaper… I'm worried she's going to do something drastic."

"Mr. Tartarus is right, we need to split up."

"I'm not going to be of any use on the surface, so I can stay here and look for Saint." Rue said, "It shouldn't have gotten this far."

"I'll stay too." Rouge said, wiping her eyes, "Maybe we'll find something that'll make all of this make sense."

"Alright, I'll be going to the labs with Mr. Tartarus."

"I'm going too." Jonas spoke, her voice dripping with venom. I grimaced and looked away.

"You can stay here." I muttered.

"As if, I'm not leaving Aubrey's safety to the likes of you. At all." She crossed her arms.

I rolled my eyes and crossed my arms, how tedious.

"Alright, Jasper was notified. We're on a clock, work fast. What's the plan?" Mr. Tartarus came down and crossed his arms.

"Rouge and I are going to search Miss Petra's office and find some evidence. We're going to figure out why she took Saint and where she's holding her."

"You'll need help.." Mr. Tartarus tapped his chin, "I'll call Mateo." He sent a text to the male, "Now. Medusa."

"We're going to have to head to the labs, I remember the location, but we'll need to be on guard. I've been gone for a while, he could have left someone there in case I failed."

"Alright, there's a Hermes portal by the gates, we can head up now. Let's go."

I will make all of this up to him and Mr. Tartarus, even if I'm stuck with Jonas lingering on my back. I'm so happy he trusted me to run tests, and I'm glad I'm slowly getting answers. I'm just so happy there's a solution. Him and Mr. Tartarus are all I have, I'll be damned if he takes them from me. It's not about spite or hatred anymore, if I'm honest I think it stopped being that a long time ago. I will be better than him, *I am better than him.* Aubrey has been doing so much for me, this is the least I can do for him. I will protect Aubrey this time, I won't let him have his way. I won't let him destroy my happiness again. I'm choosing him, I'm choosing Aubrey.

44

FORTY-THREE

I was happy once.

I'm the youngest of my sisters, we were close. My sisters and I outnumbered our brother, Caelus, much to his dismay. Though unlike my sister's and cousin's, my following and cult wasn't much to brag about. I was often overlooked in favor of Terra, Cordelia, or Helios. I mean I can't exactly blame them can I? The Earth, Ocean and Sun? Over the *Magic* goddess? I gave magic for free. It's normal for them, they need the sun in the sky and earth beneath their feet. It's something I've grown to expect. I was on par with lower level gods like Love and War. Something that exists but isn't something desperately needed. I was never picked, or preferred when it came to universal gifts. At least that's how it felt?

Cordelia was blessed with a beautiful son, a flourishing kingdom and the Ocean itself. Terra had mother's attention. She could do unimaginable things, she proved her Celestial power by creating a new species. While I stayed in The Summit at one of mother's shrines. I had no partner, no children, no purpose, no direction.

Then Ravona showed up.

Thirty some years ago, I met this woman. She had the *most* beautiful pink starry eyes I've ever seen on any woman. I'll never forget them. She was a muscular woman, covered in scars and had a unique moon shaped birthmark on her face. Her long pink hair was always braided behind her. I feel she knew she was attractive, kind of dangerous. She always wore the first few buttons undone on all her work shirts. She had tight pants and kept her sleeves rolled up her strong arms. *She made me breathless.*

I met her on one of my visits to The Valley for Terra. I visited often, she refused to leave The Valley. At the time I didn't know why, I never asked. It feels like forever since I've seen her. Now my memories of her are few and far between, I remember how she used to smile so wide when I visited, after Cordelia's passing we decided to stay in touch. Maybe it was out of guilt? Or regret of the little time we spent with Cordelia. Terra used to show me around her home, and while we were out I'd notice that stunning Reaper. Terra would catch me staring and tease me endlessly. She'd go on and on about how her little sister had her first crush and was finally growing up. She used to drive me crazy with that. *I miss my sisters.*

I remember when Ravona first spoke to me, It was so hard to contain my excitement.

I was in a bar, waiting on Terra to show up and show me to her home. Ravona and a few other Reapers came in and got a table in the back. They were a loud bunch, laughing and telling jokes. I kept stealing glances towards her, I think she noticed.

She approached me and leaned against the bar. It wasn't lost on me that this position amplified her muscles.

"Evening, You finally gonna tell me your name? Since we keep meeting like this." Ravona smiled.

I was taken aback by her bluntness. She approached me like any woman on the street. I tried not to stare and half expected her to just order a drink and move on. Her speaking to me caught me off guard completely. I moved my finger over the rim of the glass and smiled softly at her.

"If you tell me yours first." I responded desperately trying not to trip over my words. *Come on Hecate, you're a Goddess for goodness sake.*

She laughed and shook her head. She was more dressed up than usual. She had a few cross pendants dangling from her jacket and a black hat on her head. She was in black pants and boots and her undershirt was a dull pink and she wore black gloves.

"Ravona." She said, she messed with her earring and glanced towards her table of friends before focusing on me again. I eyed her and looked her up and down. *"Now you."*

I felt a bit anxious at her side glance. I couldn't tell if it was harmless or not. Her friends seemed to go back to speaking amongst themselves. I looked back down at my glass and messed with a strand of my hair. She looked at me expectantly, she tilted her head waiting for my response.

"Hecate." I said quietly.

Her pink eyes flashed in intrigue. She didn't back down though. She grinned and nodded, *"So I was right. The Hecate, in our humble town?"*

"I'm shocked I'm recognized down here. I'm not too well

known." I said.

"Well, without you there wouldn't be magic in the world, yeah?" Ravona smiled, *"Plus, Your beauty knows no bounds, I mean what Demons or Reapers look like you?"*

"Ah, well I guess my appearance is a bit hard to miss?" I giggled.

"Yes, and I've seen you around town with Lady Terra, I figured you must've been of some higher standing, she rarely leaves her home." Ravona nodded.

"Yes, she likes staying to herself." I said and moved my hair behind my ear. I glanced away from Ravona and took a deep breath, trying to calm my nerves.

"Am I being disrespectful holding your attention like this?" She asked. I shook my head almost eagerly.

"I don't mind." I responded.

She hummed and turned to the bar, *"Can I buy you a drink?"*

"I have one?" I tilted my head and tapped my nail against the glass.

"A refresher can't hurt? It's free." She tapped the bar. I glanced over as the Bartender began making another. *"I'm in a celebratory mood. I graduated AND I'm being graced with a Goddess' presence? I'm beside myself."*

I giggled, *"I think I'm more enamored with you, than you are with me."*

"You think?" Ravona asked, baffled, *"I highly doubt that your grace."*

"No, No, I'm sure I am. Have a seat?" I asked and motioned to the bar stool next to me. I sent a quick text to Terra and let her know I was preoccupied. We talked until the bar closed that night. I was smitten. She was confident, funny,

intelligent, and had a smile that stopped me dead in my tracks. Terra couldn't help but tease me when I finally got to her house. She just kept chanting *"My baby sister has her first girlfriend.~"* I didn't mind it this time, I couldn't get that damn smile off my face.

I spoke to Ravona daily after that. I sent her letters, visited any chance I got. Hell I even bought a home down here to be closer to her. She spoiled me in every way. Then I got the news of Terra's passing. That shook me to my core. I was a wreck for what felt like centuries. Ravona stayed by my side that entire time. She never once judged or downplayed my feelings. She was always there. That's when I knew she was the one I wanted to marry. I even spoke to Mother Jezabelle about making her a prophet so I could be with her forever. Mother never got back to me on that though, entirely too sick.

From then, days turned to months to years. We were so happy, *Until she was stationed in Moonstone.*

I think that was the beginning of the end for us. Moonstone was contaminated. I heard talk of Aides' artifact causing an outbreak there. It was a catastrophe. All the people there died and got infected by this ancient Moonstone, they had an insatiable craving for flesh and blood, they couldn't tolerate the sun, they thrived in the cold and worst of all they were plague spreaders. Once one was bitten, they turned and could bite more. There was mass panic, everyone was on edge over this new plague. Accusations got thrown around, and somehow Ravona ended up on the receiving end. All she did was work and now she's being put on trial?

I was beside myself. I tried everything but the Reapers

swore it was *their* matter and 'A *simple Magic goddess had no say in their affairs'*, only Jasper had a say. Jasper's region, which means they automatically trumped my status. A foolish ideal, *A god is a god.* Regardless of cults and regions. Turns out Jasper was unavailable. *I was so angry.* Ravona needed my help and I couldn't do *anything.* They killed her. They deemed her guilty and **killed her.**

'To set an example.'

I was furious. Heartbroken. Empty.

I couldn't save her. I couldn't revive her, I couldn't do *anything!*

I was so desperate, Death wasn't something I could interfere with without Divine intervention. I knew Caelus and our cousins wouldn't help. To me, that was the love of my life. To them that was just a random Reaper they have no obligations to. I was alone. *I felt so alone.* Everyone was speaking over me, talking down to me, downplaying my feelings, and ignoring me. Terra never would have treated me this way. She would've been in my corner. I had no one.

Helios was my breaking point. We had another meeting, I once again brought up Jasper's incompetence with the Moonstone situation and was met with silence or disdain. None of them cared. None of them understood this *pain* this *grief.* They all exchanged looks. It seems no one else wanted to be the bad guy. Thoth turned his luminescent green eyes away from me. Nyx remained silent and Caelus went to move along the meeting.

Then Helios spoke up. His yellow eyes stared down at me in pure annoyance. His blonde locks shined from the sun radiating behind him. His dark skin was flawless. He was wearing all black, *in solidarity* he said. In reality black has always been his preferred color. He claims it amplifies his beauty. He had the *audacity* to have his Werewolf husband by his side as he told me, *"Hecate, It's been a decade. It's time to get over it."*

How dare you*. How dare you say such disrespectful words to me with your husband by your side.*

Caelus went to reprimand Helios, but the damage was done. I haven't been home since then. They were dead to me as far as I was aware. How heartless can you be? A decade to a god is nothing, my pain is *still fresh.* I should be married with a child right now. Yet I'm here, in a big house *alone*, Pregnant and depressed.

I was so desperate. I went to the royal palace in The Valley. If one artifact can cause this, maybe another can fix it? I snuck onto the island and entered the palace. I tried to move past the unfrozen prisoners on the island, Aides' hasn't been down here in centuries. I can imagine this is bliss for the souls he traps here. At least when he's gone they aren't frozen. I quickly realized they couldn't be bothered with me. They rather wander the outskirts of the island.

I headed inside and looked at the big abandoned main hall. It was strangely empty here. There was dust, cobwebs and pure silence inside. He had portraits of himself, his wife and his children between the grand staircases. Barely any furniture. Sadly there were a multitude of rooms in the manor. I went from room to room searching for something. *I didn't know what, but I knew it would stand out to me.*

I ended up in a grand library. It was two stories, and a wrap-around balcony was in the room. The shelves were floor to ceiling. There was a giant globe in the middle of the dark room and around them were a few chairs and lamps. Everything had gold accents, Aides' main staple. The energy in here felt significantly darker than the rest of the abandoned home. It sent a shiver down my spine. It felt unsafe here.

I cautiously entered the room and looked around.

This way.

The feeling of unease intensified the more steps I took. I whipped my head around as the giant golden doors slammed shut behind me.

This way.

I slowly walked over to the globe, it had a faint purple glow to it. Aides is so mysterious to us. He's only my uncle so I never get to see him, let alone be in his home like this. The globe was turned to one of Jezabelle's shrines, I didn't dare touch it.

Your grief...

I walked past it quietly and looked up at the book cases.

Your pain...

I wasn't sure what I was looking for, but something was telling me it was in here.

I want it all.

I felt uneasy but my feet moved on their own.

Give it to me.

My feet lead me to a closed off room. The wood looked old and fragile. Some of the planks were falling off and the old curtain was barely on the rack anymore. I gulped and peeked in the room. In the center was a singular pedestal. It looked like a book was chained on it. I tilted my head and pulled the planks down.

Your grief and pain. Give it to me!

I slowly entered the room and felt a heavy darkness

around me. It felt like walking into an abyss. Nothing but black and emptiness. All I could see was this book. It was a pale purple with gold trim. It had an intricate design, there was a golden apple decal on the front with an eye carved into it. The aura around the book was black and harsh.

Everything in me was screaming, *turn and run away.* Even so, my hand slowly reached out to it. Dread was on my shoulders but I couldn't stop myself.

Give it to me!

I picked up the book. I couldn't explain what was in the book. I don't even know what I read. I just knew it told me what I needed to do. It told me what I needed to hear. For once I felt heard. I felt understood.

Everything fell into place after that. Trade their lives for the life I desire back.

That's past now. I need to focus on the present. I breathed out and headed under the school. I headed down the old stone steps and followed the torch light towards the abandoned catacombs. It was silent aside from the echo of my heels. Most of the Reaper staff has been acquired, and I surprisingly lucked up on a Sawyer. I can't believe she was under my nose this whole time. How fantastic.

I waited so long for this, It's simple. Lives for a life. Everything is going according to plan, just like *she* promised. And now I have an even better offer on the table? Make and example out of the only daughter of Death? Basically the princess of their people? Oh they'd feel as hopeless as I did. If Jasper can't protect their own daughter, how can they protect you all? I felt a bitter laugh creeping in my chest.

Fucking Jasper.

Jasper was the worst. I begged them to fix this. The

transgressions their people levied against me was entirely too great and all Jasper could offer was temporary pacification. Empty promises. In the end those involved just got demotions, or stripped of their titles. **That isn't enough.** Not so much of an apology. How heartless can you be? None of them even care that she's gone. It's like she never existed to them at all. It's a disgrace. You all will pay.

This will teach you a lesson. One you'll *never* forget.

I came to a stop in front of the small girl's cell, she was chained up and sitting on the floor. She looked up at me then narrowed her eyes.

"Evening Sawyer." I smiled.

"Miss Petra? What is the meaning of this!" Saint exclaimed. She looked around the cell and went to move her arms, "Let me go!"

"I can't do that. I have special plans for you."

"You are aware I'm a high profile woman, People will notice I'm missing. My friend will notice immediately." She warned.

I waved my hand, "Where is your father."

"My father?" Saint asked.

"I want to know If i should kill you now, or wait for their arrival." I said.

Saint stiffened at my words, her face fell, "What are you talking about!"

"Your father has incurred an impossible debt with me. And I intend to collect soon." I muttered, I glared down at the girl. Sorry child, it's nothing personal with you, But everything to do with your *kind.*

"..." Saint's eyes narrowed at me, "Are... Are you Rue's mother?" She asked cautiously. It was like her thoughts were calculating on her face.

"Mm. That child." I sighed and looked away.

"You won't get away with this." Saint said, she seemed to back down this time, "My father, Hell my *friends*, aren't ones to take lightly."

I narrowed my eyes at her and waved my hand, "Just sit tight yes? I'll be back for you soon."

With that I walked away. I've planned for twenty some years. Nothing will stop me now. *Ravona soon you'll be back home with me.* In my open and loving arms. I can see it now, we can finally get married, we can move and start over. We could have the baby we always dreamed of. I'll hastily make up for lost time. I'm treading the abyss as fast as I can my love, just continue to be patient with me. Just a little longer. I could feel tears streaming down my cheeks. They won't get away with this, I promise.

"Miss Petra!"

I turned my heads to a few boys closing the distance between us. I raised my brow in annoyance as I watched them. They hastily bowed their heads and took deep breaths.

"We have a problem."

45

FORTY-FOUR

"Evening Mr.Mateo..." I bowed my head respectfully. He smiled and waved slightly.

"Oh, Aubrey, what happened kid? You look rough." Mateo said with worry in his voice. He then turned his head towards Rue and Rouge.

"I'm fine, dad called you here for them." I motioned to the girls with a heavy arm. I feel like I did before that injection Jonas gave me, I guess I really was, well, *am* dying? *That's a bummer.* Rouge was doing everything she could to keep me comfortable. Her hands were shaking. I wanted nothing more than to comfort her. I hate seeing that sullen look on her face. I sighed and closed my eyes.

"Oh, are you the kids Tartarus told me about?"

"Yes sir." Rue spoke up, "We have a big problem. My name is Rue Kovenn, Hecate's daughter."

"Oh? Miss Kovenn? Yes, what can I do you for?" Mateo asked politely, nodding his head to Rue. Rouge was sat on the bed and I propped myself up against the pillows.

"The Headmaster of the Sorcerer academy is committing

a serious crime and we need to protect our friend, it's... a*lleged*... she kidnapped Saint Sawyer and she may be planning to hurt her." Rue spoke carefully.

"A sawyer? That's a pretty bold accusation." He crossed his arms.

"She was notified by an outside source that she was a Sawyer and she went missing shortly after." Rue sighed lightly, "I'll have to notify my mother, but she's on the surface, I doubt a letter can reach her so soon..."

"Your mother?" Mateo tilted his head, "Well, Miss Kovenn, I fear your mother hasn't been on the surface in decades."

"What..?"

"I just got back from the surface, I go there everyday, she's never been around. The gods have been talking about how she hasn't visited in years and magic is weak on the surface. She ain't been up there in a very long time."

"That's not... that's not possible.." Rue said in disbelief, "She left 3 months ago. Where could she have gone."

I blinked in realization, *I forgot.*

"Didn't Aubrey say..?" Rouge turned her head to me. I nodded.

"When I was talking to Petra, I noticed. Her eyes were blue." I shook my head, "It was already weird that her bangs were obscuring her face. But I remember in her photos, the photo Rue showed me in particular, she had clearly pink eyes. She said I was observant when I called her Hecate."

"What are you saying?" Rue asked, sounding distressed.

"Maybe she never left... She lied." I spoke up. I looked at Rue and furrowed my brows, "You said your mother's anniversary is coming up, yes? And there's that event in a few days."

"Yea.. but mom never celebrates momma's anniversary." Rue said, "What does that have to do with Miss Petra."

"Maybe because she was waiting for a perfect opportunity. You were right when you said that wasn't Miss Petra." I said, "You said Petra suddenly started acting different and ignoring you, that can't be a coincidence, from how you talk that's your mamas favorite pastime. She was also your mother's successor right? That means..."

"She would be able to withstand Hecate's magic." Rouge finished and I nodded.

"Possession 101. Saint is a possession student, remember." I grinned, "Maybe school is good for something."

Rue grunted and looked away, "Even if that was true, what opportunity could she be waiting for."

"Well what makes this anniversary so special this year?" I asked, "Especially if she planned a student event around it, on top of kidnapping Saint."

"The date..." Rouge spoke quietly, "Check that date again."

Rue pulled out her phone and checked, "The 13th?" She asked.

"The 13th?" Mateo spoke up, "Well, Scorpio 13th this year is on an alignment." He smiled, "The Reapers were going to celebrate with a party because it's the aligning of Aides and Hecate and Thoth." Mateo pointed to the ceiling, "Aides being in front is a rare occasion and considering he made us, it's a pretty big deal to honor him that day."

"Alignment..."

"Oh... yes, I remember that.. I was invited..." Rue's voice went quiet.

"I remember that, daddy told me about the alignments." Rouge spoke up, "He always told me, Helios, Aphrodite and

Caelus is the most powerful alignment for fire elementals."

"I don't know much about alignments, dad never taught me those, but he did tell me the moons can amplify the elements they correlate with, and that annual Sorcerer event happens on Hecate's new moon right?" I asked, trying to remember.

"Yes that's correct, it gives sorcerers a buff, and it just feels nice~ basking in the moon and all." Rue nodded.

"But the Aides moon is always noticeable here, why is the alignment so important Mr. Mateo?" I asked, looking at him.

"Well, as Rouge said, alignments are wonderful for the corresponding elements. For you, Terra, Jezabelle, and Helios would be a perfect alignment to enhance your earth magic, the Aides alignment makes Reapers stronger, but, since Hecate is in the alignment, it can also make sorcerers stronger, maybe more powerful because sorcerers have Hecate's magic, while we do not."

I rubbed my head in thought, leaning into my hand, thinking this over. She's angry, that we know for a fact, her fiance's anniversary is coming up, she had Death Metal, the special trips for four years. *That book.* A light bulb flickered. I sat up, almost in disbelief.

"She's going to commit a genocide..." I spoke quietly.

"Huh..?" Rue asked.

"It all makes sense now." I rubbed my head, "The weapons, the special trips, the fourth years? Fourth years are hand selected based on their skills, not their time like the rest of us, and the alignment making them stronger? She knows the Reapers celebrate the alignment, she can wipe them out without them fighting back. She could be trying to make an example out of Saint."

"That's... That's crazy.." Rue shook her head.

"Yea, well, so is your mother."

Rouge cleared her throat, "It's worth looking into, there's too many coincidences, at the very least we can warn the Reaper school just in case."

"Mr. Mateo, will you accompany us to confirm our suspicions?" Rouge asked as she stood.

"Absolutely." Mateo nodded firmly. Everyone seemed on board except Rue, this is going to be hard for her to accept. I went to get up, but immediately felt nauseous.

"Aubrey, no, rest. We can handle this. Alright?" I glanced over at Rue, "I called Briar, it's not good for you to be on your own right now. I figured you didn't want Keegan to see you like this."

"Oh..." I looked at my lap, "Yea, thanks... keep an eye on Rue?" I said quietly. Rouge looked over then back at me and nodded.

"I will."

I nodded and laid back. I tried to focus my vision on her, it was too dark. I sighed as they left the room and placed my hand in front of my face, I can barely see it. Ever since I woke up, I noticed I can't see my Peripheral Vision, and my eyes aren't adjusting, it's spotty. I don't know why I'm shocked. I dropped my head back against the pillows, dropping my hand on the bed.

I knew this would happen one day, it was already starting. I guess it was a sign of my life essence depleting. How annoying, how was I even supposed to know that? How could I have prevented it? I guess it's not the end of the world? I've already heavily relied on hearing, what's the difference?

I sighed and closed my eyes, taking deep breaths. Let's hope this is the only side effect.

46

FORTY-FIVE

I couldn't explain what I'm feeling right now. Fear? Panic? Paranoia? Worry? All of the above? I haven't even begun to imagine my life without Aubrey in it, and now I'm being told I can lose him because of my ignorance all those years ago? Has he been suffering this whole time? And I was ignorant to that as well? How selfish of me. Would he have been better off if I was strong enough to kill him? I looked up at the dark purple sky, the moons high, the stars twinkled, it was cooler up here, almost harsh. I forgot about fall. How chilling it felt compared to The Valley.

Would he have loved this? All this earth? This variety? Maybe I can bring him up here on a trip, like I should've done. I glanced at the Aides moon, then glanced away. *Oh yea. I remember why I never come up here with him.* There's eyes everywhere, and they'll jump to make an example of him. I can't allow that to happen. But how long can I protect him? He's grown now. I closed my eyes and took a breath.

"Not too much further now." Medusa spoke up. She was leading the way, I felt a pit in my stomach. I honestly thought that man would have perished by now. He got away all those years ago, and even then he's still managed to weasel his way back into mine and Aubrey's life. Nothing can ever be simple. He's a fucking Earthen, their life spans aren't even that long yet he managed to cause so many problems. *I won't fail this time.*

Jonas and her man friend stayed silent, but they kept their eyes on Medusa. I understand their aversion, it took awhile for her to grow on me. Then I saw what Aubrey saw, a traumatized, abused child. Lashing out at the wrong person. She went out of her way to get in my good graces, she took this seriously, and honestly I thought it was because Iron was glued to her side and she was scared. But no, she was genuine, it took her awhile to get used to my presence, but she's so much more lively than before. I'm proud of him for helping her. But I don't like that I'm basically following her into danger like this.

"This way." Medusa pointed, the more familiar the area, the more my nerves worsened.

We eventually came up to the ruined building, I tried to mentally prepare myself for what I'd find in there. I buried those memories. That bunker was disgusting, I tried to forget the conditions those kids were in, I couldn't forget. And now that I've got my own? I really don't want to see it again. Medusa entered the ruined home hesitantly, I noticed the same hole I left there when we first came. But from the other side. The house smelled of death and expiration. But the window was still untouched. I remember that woman in the window, she stared past me, like Jasper themselves had her attention. *Was that Medusa's mother?*

Medusa opened a hatch and I helped her down hesitantly,

then Jonas and went in after the Dragon. Dust clouded the area as soon as our shoes hit the ground the girls coughed and the Dragon was tense. He must've come from here. These kids have been through entirely too much. I sighed lightly and tried to pull myself together, I'm the adult here.

"Medusa, where should we look first?" I asked.

"Um.. The lab..." She pointed down that same dark hall. I let my hand warm up and used the lava to light the way, papers were scattered on the floor, most too faded to read, others crumpled. Lots of water damage from Levi's abilities, it smelled of mildew. I tried to ignore every room, *cages*, just so many cages. I fought back a disgusted growl. *Stay focused.*

"Sir, it should be in there. I remember the computer." Jonas spoke up. I headed in the direction she pointed and the memories hit me immediately. The machine he was in was still shattered, papers all over the floor, dried blood on the floor and beat up furniture. He should have died that day. Cobwebs littered the place. Medusa walked over to the tube and began to inspect it, while Jonas stayed to herself, like she was trying to disappear. She stayed silent while Medusa searched, I kneeled down and picked up a few of the pictures, trying to make anything out. Seemed like equations. I sat them on the computer.

"Ah ha!" Medusa mused, she tapped the side of the tube, "The settings are still here!" She pulled her phone out and took pictures, "Look around, his notes could still be in here."

"Right.." I looked around at the scattered papers, Medusa did too, she patted blindly in the dark and squinting at text. "Honey, don't read in the dark, I moved my hand towards her."

"Apologies, I think this is one of them, it's a bit faded but still somewhat legible. Look for anything with PEF88 on it." She flicked on her phone light.

I nodded and skimmed the legible papers.

"Jonas, I need you to find the essence, it's in the testing labs." Medusa turned her head to Jonas, she remained silent.

I looked over and glanced away. "I'll look for them, Jonas honey, come look for the papers."

"Yes sir.." Jonas nodded. She walked over and kneeled next to Medusa, Medusa muttered a small apology to her as I walked off, I left the room and headed down the halls, peeking in the rooms. *Chaos shouldn't be too hard to spot right?*

I was so occupied I didn't even notice the Dragon boy deviated from the group. He was standing outside a room, his fire illuminating his hand. He looked out of it, all he was doing was staring at nothing. I slowly walked over and cleared my throat quietly.

"Uh kid?"

"Do you honestly think all of this is worth it..?" Adonys spoke quietly. I raised a brow. "Maybe he should just die with this place, like he should've all those years ago."

I narrowed my eyes and stopped myself from snatching him up, *he's a kid Tartarus.*

"Excuse you."

"Why do you care so much, Jonas I can understand, she's basically his mother. But you? Why." He didn't sound malicious, more defeated, "Why..?" Adonys echoed.

I looked into the room, it was a cell it seems? It had tally marks and scratches all over the room, like something was trying to get out. A few walls were dented and what looked like sand was scattered in the room.

"Because he's my son." I said, "I know you're young, but imagine if it was your kid in this situation. You wouldn't try any and everything to save them?"

He fell silent, "You have no idea how far I'll go for someone I love, how far I've already been. I've tried *so hard* yet every time it feels useless, and now I'm here, aiding. All because I love her."

"Well, they say trying the same thing over and over again and expecting a different outcome is insanity, if you want change, you have to *make* a change." I touched his shoulder gently, "The funny thing about love though, you have to be willing to let go at some point. I'm not there yet, and maybe you're not there yet either, but it's important to keep that in mind."

"You're a father, I never had one of those." Adonys finally dropped his gaze, "All I've known was this. Torture, experiments, just pain. Then she came along. Do you know what it's like to fight so hard for someone, just to lose them?"

"I do." I closed my eyes, "Sadly, my sister was the beginning of all this, I did everything I could. I stayed by her side, I stayed with her at home, even if he couldn't come to The Valley, I validated her, I fought for her... But it took one time, one slip up. And now she's gone."

He blinked and looked up at me, "I still haven't let her go, and I'm not ready to let Aubrey go either."

"Oh... I'm so sorry..." Adonys said.

"No, I should be apologizing to you, he shouldn't have been able to do this, I won't pretend to know what you've been through, but if anything, Aubrey dying most likely won't fix your suffering kid. Maybe... If you took a chance, you might have some stuff in common." I smiled gently.

"...Adonys." He said.

"Hm?"

"That's my name sir, so you don't have to call me kid." Adonys laughed awkwardly.

I chuckled, "You got any idea how old I am? Y'all are practically sperms compared to me."

"Well I prefer kid over sperm." I let out a loud laugh and patted his back.

"Well, let's find this essence stuff and get out of here, I know you kids are uncomfortable."

Adonys nodded, he led me towards the labs. I looked through the drawers and disheveled items until I came across some vials. *Ain't no way.* I picked them up and smiled.

"I think these are it."

"We should go." Adonys said. I double checked the space then headed out with him.

"I'm sorry for telling you to go to the labs, I wasn't thinking.." Medusa spoke quietly.

"It's fine, I can tell you didn't want to go either." Jonas responded, straightening up the papers.

"I don't want to be here, but if my hypothesis is correct, Aubrey should be fine. At least for a couple decades." Medusa handed the other papers to Jonas. "At least until I find a perfect way to complete his incubation."

"You're serious about this?" Jonas asked.

"Absolutely." She responded without hesitation, "I owe Aubrey everything. Do you have any idea what he would've done to me if I went back." She spoke quietly.

"...Yea..." Jonas said.

"He gave me so much grace, patience and space. No one

else has done that before." Medusa looked at her lap, "And Mr. Tartarus, they both helped me, this is the least I can do."

"..." Jonas looked at her, "I'm sorry too.. For being so hostile."

"It's alright. I get it." Medusa shrugged, "I understand what's so special about him now."

"There was nothing special about him, at least not in the way you're thinking." Jonas shook her head, "He's just a good person."

"I think that makes him special." Medusa nodded, "Look at where we came from, can you really blame me for finding that rare?"

"Well when you put it that way..." Jonas looked at her lap.

Medusa stood and put her hand to Jonas. Jonas took her hand and stood, brushing off her skirt.

"Truce? Jonas?" Medusa spoke.

Jonas blinked in surprise, "You actually called me by my name?"

"I figured it was better than a product number." Medusa said softly.

Jonas looked at her then smiled gently, "Ceasefire."

Medusa smiled then turned her head towards the door, I held up the vials.

"These it?"

"Yes! That should be more than enough to experiment with, for now we can inject at least two of them in him to get his fever down and revive his body."

I breathed out, "Excellent, lets get the fuck out of here."

I handed the vials to Medusa and patted the top of her head and let the kids walk out ahead of me, Adonys leading them through the dark. I looked back at the room and debated if I should burn this place to the ground. It's nothing but pain and bad memories. My eyes suddenly focused on something. I walked over by the tube and picked up a feather. Everything fell silent. I felt dread immediately fall on my shoulders.

It was her feather. It was distinct, It's undeniable. It was a woodpecker feather, no other woodpeckers are this big. I felt my fist close around the feather.

"He had her here…" I could feel anger rising in me, I began shaking, I couldn't stop myself. A deep guttural scream left my mouth before I could catch it. All I could do was punch the wall. The dam broke, I could feel the tears pouring down my face.

I'm burning it all.

All of it.

I wiped my face and stomped the ground, lava pooling below me. I spread it everywhere as far as I could get it. I gripped the feather and turned away, making my way back up the hatch, and joining the kids outside. I watched as the house caught fire, I just watched it burn, like we should've done all those years ago.

I'm so sorry Terra, I'm so sorry.

"Let's go."

47

FORTY-SIX

I am angry. Honestly I can't even begin to explain why. Or do I feel betrayal? Foolish? I'm not shocked. Sadly I know that. Maybe I always knew? I think that's what scares me most. I never had the best relationship with my mother, she was stuck in the past, fixated on her grief and never appreciated what was in front of her.I thought maybe we made an inch of progress. Then I have to remember, I'm the one in therapy. Not her.

I guess I thought, she didn't hate me that much?

How heartless can one be? How long until the explanation becomes an excuse? How far is too far?

Is this what she was doing when she was ignoring me? Plotting to harm a group of people for a decades old grudge? She missed when I won awards, had talent shows, and made my best accomplishments. She missed being my mother, all so she could do *this?*

I don't know, maybe a small part of me wanted to believe my mother did love me, or that she cared enough. Even if a small amount, just in her own way. A small part of me wanted to believe she was trying. I suppose other children don't have to wonder that? Aubrey surely doesn't, neither does Rouge or Saint. They don't have to go above and beyond or play a guessing game. I thought it was something all kids had to deal with, tough love for attention, any praise was good even though it was dismissive. For so long I thought this was normal. I'd come to my senses, then fall right back into the same trap.

Not this time. *I can't do it again.*

Especially when it's Miss Petra's life on the line. How long has she been possessing her? How long has she had this planned? I'm so disgusted.

"Ok Rue, you'll have to be quick. We don't know how long Mr.Mateo can get away with keeping the halls clear." Rouge spoke. I looked over and nodded.

"Right..."

"I'll be right outside alright?" Rouge smiled gently and squeezed my shoulder. I nodded once more and headed into the office, tip top shape like always, every book in order, papers neat, chairs pushed up. Nothing out of place. Makes more sense now I suppose? Miss Petra was always a bit unorganized, she'd lose things so easily.

I laughed quietly to myself and checked the small places, anything that looked out of place. There's still a small piece of me that's hoping this is just speculation. And that there's a good explanation. I guess that's a normal feeling when a parent is accused of genocide? How pathetic.

I looked behind the books, placed my hands under the desks and chairs, I even tried the drawers, nothing in them, just office supplies and paperwork. A small amount of relief seeped into my chest. Until I noticed the hollow bottom,

I used to have one in my drawer, two actually, to trick my mother after she read my diary when I was thirteen. She was so angry that I didn't perceive her as a divine goddess, she dared to be angry her second thought didn't worship her. She punished me for that.

I slowly opened the bottom and felt my heart sink.

I gently put the contents aside and fully opened the drawer, inside was an astrology book, made by Thoth himself, with a bookmarked chapter, the alignment. She had receipts, logs, and scheduling. Dating back before Petra was even in the picture. All I could do was stare at the logs.

Scorpio 5th, she found out about the alignment, almost twenty years ago. And soon after she hired Miss Petra. She noted how strong she was, and how she passed Puppeteering and Possession down to me, but I was too weak. She couldn't *possess me.* I felt sick. I could feel my eyes welling. I panicked. I didn't know what else to do, I just took them. I took the book and the logs, all of it, I put the bottom and contents back and left the room. Rouge was standing there waiting for me like she said, she smiled softly.

"Find anything?" Rouge sounded almost hopeful that we were wrong too, I nodded and held up the books.

"Aubrey was right…" I could hear the defeat in my voice. She wanted to possess me? She never loved me. *Just a means to an end.* I guess that was the wake up call I needed. I'm exhausted, I'm out of emotions to feel for that woman. I'm done, I have nothing left to give.

Rouge's eyes saddened and she pulled me into a soft hug, rubbing my back gently, I held back the tears and gripped the logs.

"What do we do now?" I asked.

"I suppose we should give this to Jasper and Tartarus, this is serious, this is a horrendous act. This is above us." Rouge said. "But first we need to get Mr. Mateo and warn the Reapers. She no longer has the element of surprise."

"Sorry girls, but I can't let you leave." We both turned our attention to a fourth year walking around the corner, opposite of us. Rouge immediately got defensive. A few more fourth years joined behind him.

"Be good girls and give us that back, Headmaster would be upset."

"And if we don't." Rouge said, she narrowed her eyes.

"Then we'll kill you." He shrugged, he got in a defensive position, Rouge laughed quietly then glanced back at me.

"Stay close, understand." I blinked then nodded, "Protect the documents, take pictures if you need to."

The area around us suddenly got hot. The boy laughed and shook his head.

"Do you pathetic little first years seriously want to do this, we're fourth years for a reason."

Rouge didn't speak, her hand glowed a soft red, her glyph was tattooed to her hand, I never noticed, she doesn't have to draw them out. Suddenly a wave of fire burst between us. I squeaked in shock, she sent the wave towards them with no hesitation. And sending three more immediately after, she didn't even break a sweat.

"Run to Mateo while I hold them off." Rouge stepped forward. I nodded quickly and hurried off, trying to ignore the heat in the hallway. *What the hell is she even doing in this school? I'm sure most fourth years couldn't stand a chance against her.*

"Mr. Mateo!" I called after him, he turned around and

smiled.

"All good?" Mateo asked.

"We got caught by some guys, Rouge is holding them off, she told me to come to you.

"Fourth years." Mateo looked towards the hall. "Stay here."

Rouge placed glyphs around her and sucked the fire back towards her. "Get the hint yet."

"Oh, you got a little pyrotechnics. That ain't gonna stop us."

She smiled, a sinister smile, "Then come here."

The five boys charged her, she dodged most of their attacks and deflected or parried the attacks coming her way. She used her glyphs as a shield and a way to get them out of her space, she rhythmically moved away from them as they tried to land a hit on her. She made notice of the Death Metal, they tried to mask it. How long have they had these?

She flipped back and landed a little ways from them, getting back to her feet and setting her glyphs around the halls.

"I do hate fighting, so I'll give you one more chance to tuck your tails and go. Or else."

Two of the boys slashed at her glyphs, shattering them. Rouge's eyes widened in surprise then narrowed. *Noted.*

"Fine." The glyphs on her hands began to glow, she moved them in front of her then up slowly, a giant glyph forming above all of them, the corridor raising in temperature. The glyph spun quickly as she moved her finger elegantly.

"Summer kitchen." Her eyes darkened significantly, the boys froze, their bodies began to tremble in pain, a few of them falling to their knees before the flames shot out at them, cooking them alive. She took a breath and deactivated her power. Mateo showed up soon after, noticing the burnt bodies.

He blinked in shock and glanced back down at her.

"Uh, well I can see you're Ok." Mateo said.

"I am my uncle's niece, and I don't take too well to threats." Rouge fixed her afro'd hair and nodded with a kind smile, "We need to go before someone catches us here, we need to get this information to the Reaper academy."

"Uh, yes, agreed."

I looked up as the two hurried out, I got to my feet.

"I took pictures, I sent them to Aubrey." I said.

"Great, I didn't hurt you, did I?" Rouge asked, looking my body over. I blushed a bit and waved my hands.

"N-no I'm Ok."

"Ok good, I know my magic is very… Hot…" Rouge said a bit hesitant, "I try not to use it with allies so close."

"I see, I'm alright."

We followed Mateo to the school, he used his key card to enter and we stayed close to him. But the area felt…*off*. The halls weren't as lively, there were barely any decorations for a supposed celebration happening soon.

"Wait. Something isn't right." I stopped.

"Huh? What is it?" Rouge asked.

Mateo stopped as well, he looked around then, put his hand up to silence us, "She's right." He suddenly pulled his scythe and blocked a hit. More fourth years. He grunted as blood dripped from his cheek. I gasped and stumbled back.

"Girls, you need to go. Now." Mateo pushed the guy back and spun the scythe, "I got this."

"Sir-" I spoke up. Rouge grabbed my hand and pulled me along.

"He's a Reaper. He can handle their weapons better than us." We tried to head to the exit but got stopped by more fourth years.

"Not so fast."

Rouge grunted in annoyance and she immediately got defensive. I'm not much of a fighter, that was never my strong suit, I stayed close to Rouge, she summoned her glyphs again as they lined the walls, she shot fire from each glyph and got a few of the fourth years. Her eyes were dark. I tried to move out of her way and bumped into another fourth year. I squeaked and ducked before he could tackle me, I quickly scurried past him as Rouge pointed at him and spoke.

"Pain."

He began to scream and double over.

She's a pain sorceress, but that seems so minor to her element. Her fire is on par with Dragons. She's mastered her element for sure, I've never seen this much fire, and hell we live in The Valley. She was holding her own but I can tell those other boys tired her out a bit. Her motions were getting slower and they seemed to notice too.

I need to help her, I can't fight, but maybe I can amplify her magic? Give her a boost? I've never projected it before but I'm the daughter of Hecate, how hard can it be right? I tried to take deep breaths and focus, I closed my eyes and tried to harness the energy I felt. I gripped the papers and felt sweat slowly running down my brow. Then I felt gloved hands rest on my shoulders. I opened my eyes quickly.

"*Tsk tsk tsk.*" The familiar voice.

"You know better, child." I felt my body tense up. I tried to call out to Rouge but she beat me to it.

"Sleep."

FORTY-SEVEN

"Here hon, you should drink this." Briar handed me a cup of ice water, "It should help the fever."

"Thanks." I laid my head against the pillows, "This sucks."

"Would you like me to call dad? Maybe he can give you something?" Briar asked sweetly, tilting her head to the side. "Or he can do a checkup on you, how are you feeling?"

"I'm alright, love. Don't worry." I looked back at the ceiling, "Well as alright as you can be with a fever."

"What exactly is wrong with you?" She sat on the edge of the bed.

"Uh, something about me being under cooked." I shrugged and rubbed my head, "I need something to fix my 'incubation interruption'. I'm a chemistry guy, not a mad scientist."

"Huh..." Briar tilted her head, "I'm going to call dad, maybe he can alleviate the fever." She grabbed her phone and sent a quick text to him. I dropped my hands on the bed and huffed out.

"This sucks."

"So you've said." She laughed quietly.

"Haha." I rolled my eyes and smiled softly, "Thanks for coming over, I'd imagine you were busy."

"Nah, we're on vacation so, not much to do. We're waiting for the alignment event~" Briar nodded.

"Oh? Your family goes to that?"

"Yep! Every year it happens~" She hummed, "Dad gets drunk there every time and we have to drag him home, then mom yells at him the next day, good ole traditions~ and it's the only time Erebus actually seems to enjoy our company."

"Oh, yes you're related to Mr. Erebus, I forgot, why say that?" I asked.

"There's bad blood, daddy tries, but Erebus won't budge. Blaire and I are the youngest so whatever happened between them to make him go low contact is beyond us."

"Does he talk to y'all at least?"

"From time to time." She nodded, "I noticed he didn't use our family name down here, I assumed it was because of the family business, but I don't think that's the full extent of it. He just seems angry."

"Well, hopefully it'll get better? He's the oldest isn't he?"

"Yep." Briar nodded, messing with her dress.

"Having a big family seems complicated…" I said.

"Sometimes." She shrugged, "Anyway, yea we're waiting for that and we'll be heading back home afterwards, so~ enjoy me while you have me~" She flicked a few snowflakes at my face and I laughed quietly.

"Don't I always?" I hummed and breathed out, "So, do you mind if I ask you a question?"

"Sure hon."

"Mr. Mateo mentioned something called 'Harvesters', is

that what you and your family are?" I asked.

She nodded, "Yep, I was born a harvester, daddy became one because of mom. Dad said he was stationed in a place called Moonstone?"

"Really." I raised a brow. *That name again.*

"That's where he met my mom, he was supposed to 'dwindle' the vampire population, but he met my mom and chose her over the organization. It's why we live on the surface."

"So how do you enjoy the alignment events and vacation down here? Can't he get in trouble?" I asked.

"Daddy said he won't be found out because nothing about his appearance changed, he's always been albino, we just aren't allowed to talk about it, as far as they know he just quit, or retired." She leaned back on her hands.

"I guess that makes sense, I remember you said the bites could cause albinism." I rubbed my neck over the bites.

"Well, depends, but you're different, your body doesn't even react to our venom, I doubt you'd lose your melanin." She giggled.

Briar looked up as a knock sounded, "Well speak of the devil." She got up and headed downstairs then came up with her father in tow.

"Evening Aubrey." Belial smiled and bowed his head respectfully.

"Hello sir."

"So, what seems to be the issue? Not poisoned again are you?" He joked and sat his doctor bag down.

"Nah, this time I'm dying."

Belial stopped what he was doing and whipped his head towards me, eyes wide in shock. "Huh."

"It's a lot…" I sighed.

"Daddy, he's got a fever, do you have anything that can soothe it until his father comes back?" Briar asked.

Belial opened his bag and looked through his medications, "I don't exactly have fever before death, medicine." He picked up two pill bottles and read over them, "But I guess we can try this."

He gave me two pills and I picked up the water, taking them immediately.

"I'm not sure if it'll help or not, but worth a shot right? Was that all?"

"Um, actually, if it's not too much to ask…" I sat up and rubbed my neck, "Do you mind doing a checkup on me?"

"A checkup?" Belial kneeled by the bed, "In all honesty I'd be delighted, your body is very interesting, I'd love to see what's in there…"

I stiffened and cringed, "Sir, you're being creepy again."

"Dad." Briar shook her head.

He just smiled, "What in particular are you requesting, what has you curious?"

"Uhhh well…" I moved my arm up and grabbed my wrist, pulling it straight off with no effort this time. He gasped and Briar covered her mouth with wide eyes.

"I don't think this is normal."

"Certainly not…" Belial gently took my hand from me and studied it, "It's light, almost like plastic." He looked through it and raised a brow. "You don't have bones…"

"Are you able to see inside? I noticed that too."

"I brought my portable x-ray." He gave my hand back to me and I reattached it. He grabbed his tool and walked back over, checking my arm with the device. It took a minute to register but on the screen popped up a cylinder in my arm. I tilted my head.

"What's that mean?" I asked.

"Hm." He rested his hand against his chin, "It's almost like you have a casing inside, like your skin is pulled around it. Like icing on a cake."

Briar looked over his shoulder at the monitor as well, he moved the x-ray around my upper body.

"Yet, you have a skull… A humanoid one. You're bizarre.. The best way to understand your design, is to make you a cadaver, but I doubt you wanna test if ya got that chicken luck." Belial moved it back down, "Then of course your makeshift organs, such as your heart thing, it's like you're missing some, like whoever made you forgot to put them in."

I touched my chest and sighed quietly. "So, a doll. I'm basically a doll."

"That would explain your casing and how you move without bones. You must have ball joints, you're so advanced yet crudely made. Your outside is flawless, but your insides are a nightmare, it's a miracle he was able to bring you to life and you kept living after the fact."

"…"

"Wow.. Aubrey, you are genuinely fascinating…" Briar said, her eyes bright.

I looked at my lap and stayed quiet. *That's definitely not the word I'd use.* I leaned back against the pillows, looking back at the ceiling.

"Whenever you come back to the surface, I'll give you a more thorough check up." Belial smiled and patted my hand. I nodded and looked down at my phone as it buzzed.

Rue's name flashing, the clock saying 3 am. It's been a day already? Gods, how long did that fever knock me out.

I picked it up, scrolled through the pictures and narrowed my eyes. "This bitch is deranged." I muttered.

"Hm?" Briar and her father looked over.

"Yea, y'all might not wanna go to that event this year." I sent the photos to my dad and tried to call Rouge. No response. I raised a brow and called Rue, this time straight to voicemail. She just texted me?

"What?" Belial tilted his head.

"Why, what's wrong?" Briar asked, standing straight. I tried to call a few more times then grunted, trying not to crush my phone out of frustration. This ain't gonna fly, how bitter do you have to be to plan a fucking genocide, what? Does she think this is some kind of gift to her ex. I groaned.

"Uh, Hey hon."

"Yes?" Briar asked.

"Something ain't right." I groaned quietly and got up, my body felt weak and heavy, it was hotter than normal and the room was spinning. I balanced myself and took a few breaths.

"Aubrey! You can't be walking around right now-" Briar sounded panicked. I waved my hand and grabbed one of my hoodies and slipped my sneakers on.

"You're not too hot are you?" I asked, looking at her. She frowned but shook her head. She knew there was no point in arguing, I might regret this later but one friend already went missing, now two more. And dad's gonna want his boyfriend safe. Who knows how long it'll take them to get back, I looked at Mr. Belial and smiled a bit.

"Can you tell my dad we're at the Reaper academy?" I

asked, He pursed his lips and looked at Briar, she nodded.

“Of course…” Belial said reluctantly.

“Alright let’s go.”

49

FORTY-EIGHT

I groaned quietly, slowly waking up and shaking my head. My eyes slowly adjusted to the area, I looked around in confusion.

What the hell happened?

I went to move my arms but felt them shackled down, I blinked and looked up, my arms were chained to the wall. Rue was sitting next to me, she was calling my name but it didn't register till now.

"Rouge! Are you alright?" Rue asked.

"What the fuck happened." I muttered.

"We got captured." She said and sighed, I looked around once I fully woke up and noticed the bricked cell.

"Huh? Did this bitch put us in a dungeon!?"

"Seems so, I believe we're under the school, these used to be training rooms for necromancy till it was made illegal." Rue shook her head, "It's no good, I tried to get the cuffs to budge, but they're strong and there are guards who come in every five minutes."

Her voice sounded so defeated. I looked away then up at

the shackles.

"Lightwork." I said and placed my hand on top of the shackles, "We need to get out of here and get to Aubrey."

"I sent him the documents, so he probably already knows. And Saint could be here too."

"Wait.. You're right.." I kept heating the chains.

If Aubrey has the information that means it's a good bet that Jasper has it now, the least we can do is find Saint before heading back, that way Aubrey won't be as stressed until Medusa can figure out the death situation. We both looked up as footsteps approached, the tall curvy woman walked in, her bangs situated perfectly over her face, I narrowed my eyes and lowered the temperature of my hands. Rue went silent as she looked down at us.

"Well, I see you're both awake." Hecate spoke coldly.

"What is your problem." I narrowed my eyes at her.

"Currently? Well, even at twenty-four, I have to ground you children, because you constantly stay in grown folks business. How much do you know."

Rue and I stayed quiet.

"Where's Mr. Mateo."

"Hm? Oh? The mouse. He's a teacher, yes? He's with the other teachers, you know they've got a big party to plan for." Hecate smiled, I scrunched up my face.

"Something ain't right with you."

"Why are you doing this…" Rue spoke, her voice was smaller, the taller woman turned her head towards her, almost like she was offended at her speaking. She scoffed.

"It's been twenty five years mom…" Rue said, looking at the woman.

She scowled, "Grief knows no time."

"This isn't grief." Rue said, tilting her head up slightly. "This is nothing but revenge, a festering wrath that should've been let go decades ago."

"I wouldn't expect you to understand, you didn't even know her."

I noticed Rue's slight flinch.

"You were supposed to do this, but you were *too weak*. And got too attached to Petra. I should've known you'd ruin this." Hecate sighed and rubbed her temple.

"Watch your mouth." I growled at her.

She shot me a look, "Watch your tone."

"Well my love, you certainly lived up to your name." Hecate smiled, I could feel the impact that had on Rue, she stayed quiet. She turned around and left the room, I looked over at her, her shoulders were slumped but I could see subtle glints of tears down her cheeks. I felt my heartbreak for her. I can't imagine the turmoil she's going through. I went back to melting the chains and pulled my hands through.

I hurried over to her and began melting her chains. "Don't let her get to you Rue." I muttered, working as fast as I could.

"That's what she wants."

"She rarely spoke to me…And that's all she had to say…?" Rue shook her head, "And hearing it in Miss Petra's voice…"

I broke her chains and pulled her into a tight hug, I rubbed the back of her head gently. After a minute I pulled away and gripped her hands.

"Water over stone." I used my thumbs to wipe her tears, "Your name is also Persephonii. Know what that means?"

She blinked and looked at me in confusion.

"Bringer of destruction." I smiled, "Now is the time to live up to that name. Your mother is too far gone, but the least we can do is save the Reapers and Miss Petra."

"I know hearing that from your parents hurts, trust me, I have few memories before my dad adopted me. But I remember the words useless, pathetic, waste of space. Any demeaning name you could think of," I gripped her hands once more, "It hurts. Words hurt."

"But, the words from those who love you are louder, and sweeter." I helped her stand, she sniffed and wiped her eyes.

"A small part of me knows that I think…" Rue looked away, "But I guess I kind of always held this small glimpse of hope that my mom loved me, in her own way."

I felt my eyes sadden, I rubbed her hands with my thumbs, she closed her eyes tight and shook her head.

"No, I know, not the time.."

"Oh sugar. Let it out…" I smiled gently. "I can't imagine what you've been through, just take a moment."

She nodded and dropped her head, I rubbed her hands with my thumbs, humming a gentle tune.

"Ok, Ok.. I'm Ok.." Rue rubbed her eyes. "We should find Saint and the teachers, they're probably held in the same place, can't be too far, the event is tonight."

"Tonight-?" I asked. I grunted and rubbed my face, "Yea we need to move fast."

I took her hand and slammed my foot on the cell door, breaking it down instantly. I immediately put a defensive glyph in front of us and filled the room with flames as footsteps came running towards us. I took Rue's hand and hurried down the halls. I tried to focus my nose and tap into my bat sense.

I took a few deep breaths. I think I remember the scent of

Mateo's cologne. I doubt I can sniff out Saint at this point. I sniffed the area and closed my eyes, footsteps approaching us. I can't concentrate. I summoned more glyphs on the ground and torched the hall.

"We need to split up."

"H-huh?" Rue asked, "N-no I'm not a f-fighter-"

"Baby girl, we gotta find them, you're a Sorcerer and top of your class, you can do it." I smiled. "Go right and I'll go left, I'll try to be quick."

Rue hesitated before nodding and running off.

Gods what time is it, what day is it? It's so damn dark down here it's disorienting. I ran down the halls, scanning the area and trying to pick up any scents. A few fourth years tried to stop me, but they were nothing more than fodder, this is tedious, she'd catch us off guard at this point. This was a maze like catacomb. Too many turns and entrances.

I searched the hallways and came across a roped off section, noise was coming from there, commotion. I creeped towards it quietly and peeked around the corner before noticing vines. I blinked and narrowed my eyes and followed them. I turned the corner defensively and had my hands up, ready to fight. I blinked then smiled as I saw Aubrey and Briar.

"Rouge!" Aubrey dropped the guy he was interrogating, he hurried over and pulled me into a tight hug. I fought the urge to melt into his touch and patted his back before pulling away and cupping his cheeks.

"What the hell are you doing down here!? How did you even find this place!?" I asked, feeling his cheeks. He's so warm. His eyes were so dull. It hurts to see him so gray like this. He shook his head.

"I tried to convince him to stay in bed." Briar sighed, her own eyes worried.

"You know I got good hearing, what's going on, why is the school basically empty. Where's Mr. Mateo." Aubrey asked.

"I'm not sure, I was looking for him, Rue went that way." I pointed back from where I came. "She implied all the teachers are being held too, we came here to warn Mr. Erebus, but she ambushed us."

"So we're sure she's Hecate." Briar asked, "She's a goddess."

"Absolutely. She acknowledged Rue." I said.

"Alright, Briar, how are you feeling?" Aubrey asked, turning to her.

She crossed her arms, "I should be asking you that."

He gave her a look and I gave him a look.

"Not over heating yet?"

"No baby, I'm fine." Briar waved it off.

Aubrey turned his head towards the other direction and narrowed his eyes, "Rue is calling you." He ran off in that direction, I stressfully followed after him, Briar not too far behind. He came to a stop and Rue was standing there with Saint.

"I found her!" Rue smiled brightly. "But I couldn't find the teachers."

"Erebus...?" Briar asked, her eyes fearful.

"Saint!" Aubrey hugged her immediately, practically scooping her up in his arms. He looked her over then cupped her cheeks, "Are you Ok? Did any of them hurt you? No scrapes, bumps or bruises?"

"Oh. I'm fine." Saint's eyes and tone were angry, I hugged her tightly as well, breathing out in relief. "But I'm fucking pissed."

"We need to go, your dad should be back soon, he can put an end to this." Aubrey spoke up, we all turned around at a loud noise. Heels clicked behind us, her presence making the atmosphere darker.

"Couldn't just sit tight now could you." Hecate's arms were behind her back.

"We need to go." I muttered, "We can't fight her."

Briar nodded, "I agree."

"Didn't your mothers teach you it's impolite to mumble." She spoke sinisterly.

"Hasn't yours told you genocide is bad." Aubrey shot back. She scoffed.

"You slick mouthed heathens." Hecate moved her hands and I got defensive. Lightning sparked between her fingers as a bow slowly materialized in her hands, she aimed and pointed the arrow towards us, "Allow me to teach you some manners."

"Everyone stay close!" Aubrey got in position right as she shot the arrow, I got disoriented as soon as the explosion went off, I felt my body go airborne and hit through the ceiling, I heard all of us thud on the ground and rubble. I groaned and rubbed my head.

I tried to focus my eyes as her footsteps echoed again, she made her way up the hole they made and started to close the gap between us.

"Hold still now, this'll be quick."

50

FORTY-NINE

"Hold still now, this'll be quick."

I groaned in annoyance as the floor crumbled around us, I got to my feet and narrowed my eyes. I groaned, the heaviness in my arms wasn't as prominent. I shook my arm and bounced on my toes a bit to get my energy up. Gods, let's hope this doesn't take long. I don't know how much longer I can stay awake. I took a few breaths and looked at her with a dark glare.

"Ya know, I never liked you." I stomped on the ground, summoning my glyphs. Maybe using her magic will lessen the energy I use, pulling from her seems smarter now, the green glyphs lifted the rocks. Hecate seemed taken back.

"Oh, you can actually use your magic, your grades were not very impressive. I suppose I have to try now." Hecate put her hand up, but before she could I sent all the rocks towards her. Rouge and Briar got to their feet, dust clouded around the impact but I kept my guard up. Rouge summoned her glyphs around her wrists and waited. Lightning began to surge through the dust clouds and I tried to dodge. Rouge countered it immediately, absorbing it in her glyph and groaning in pain.

"Ow..." Rouge muttered quietly.

Hecate had a bigger dull blue glyph floating behind her, "You little heathens." She hissed out.

Briar glanced at Rouge and she motioned to her, I noticed their looks and kneeled down, summoning the glyphs again and cracking the ground. Briar and Rouge darted on either side of her and tried to attack, Hecate stumbled slightly at the ground cracking then growled in annoyance, she flipped the glyph and split it, lightning shooting out at them both, Rouge absorbed hers and Briar ducked out of the way, she iced the ground and Rouge warmed it up, creating steam, I used that as an opportunity to close the gap. I let the rocks fly towards her.

Hecate looked up and put her hands up, shooting us back towards the walls, Briar landed elegantly and Rouge slid to a stop. I caught myself and landed, kneeling down, panting. *Too fucking slow.*

Both girls turned their attention towards me and I got to my feet with a slight stumble, this is gonna be close.

She changed the glyph's hue and muttered under her breath, conjuring up bodies. Of course she has multiple abilities, we'd be foolish to expect any less. These weren't fourth years though. I squinted, that's necromancy. I sent a quake through the ground interrupting the glyphs. She retaliated by sending a shadow towards me.

"Don't think so!" Rouge canceled it out, her fire illuminating the area. She seemed slightly impressed, she used the blood from the disrupted conjures and began to projectile them. I pulled up a wall and the others ducked behind it.

"This is ridiculous. How the hell are we supposed to fight her, she's literally magic itself." Rouge complained, covering her head.

"We need a plan, we have to attack at once." I said, ignoring the sweat trickling down my temple.

"We need to go, you're not Ok..." Briar said. I shook my head and waved it off.

"We can't leave now. She'd just follow us or she will kill the teachers. We just have to hold her off until our parents show up." I wiped my forehead.

"Ok, so what's the plan?" All three of them looked at me, while Rue stayed away, I looked at them confused, "You're the brawler here Aubrey, we'll follow your lead."

"..." I took a moment to think, she can control all 8 classes of magic, she can counter most of our attacks. I can defend and make walls at most right now, Briar and Rouge would have to pull most of the weight for any of this to work. I thought through multiple possibilities.

Rouge can absorb her lightening, Briar can make it too cold to use her lightening but that'll fuck up Rouge's power. And Saint can do possession. I rubbed my head, I peeked over the rock as the blood slowly stopped,the ground began to shake again, she's conjuring again. More bodies, more effort. Ugh. I tapped my forehead then looked up and nodded.

Then I remembered what happened to me in pride. I guess now would be a better time than ever to test that theory?

"I got it." I peeked back out and counted the glyphs, "Rouge you have to counter the conjure spells."

"How?" She asked.

"You're a marksman, I'm sure you can figure it out." I nodded, "If we can get her out of this area and outside I can use more earth to trap her. But in order to get that to work, we need you to freeze the room Briar."

"Freeze? But wouldn't that hurt Rouge?"

I looked at her, "Rouge, you gotta be quick."

Rouge nodded, "I can handle it."

"Saint, I need you to shoot lightning at me."

"What!?" She exclaimed, "Aubrey I told you I'm not-!"

"Saint, I can barely feel my arms. Jonas AND Medusa says electricity could help. It's better than nothing. I'm the brawler right."

Saint went quiet, her eyes conflicted. I could tell Rouge and Briar wasn't too keen on the idea either.

"I trust you, Saint." I said.

Saint sighed quietly then nodded, "Alright, Ok. I'll try…"

"Great, Rue-"

"I'm going to wait for the others, I'm sorry I won't be of much use." Rue's voice was quiet, almost indifferent.

I blinked, "Hon, that ain't gonna-" I grunted as the wall got shattered. "Fuck."

I motioned Briar ahead. She got up and ran around, tapping the ground once before gliding around the room, Rouge began summoning her glyphs.

"Hotspot." Rouge put her hand out as her glyphs began to shoot out fire like bullets, I covered us and helped Saint and Rue outside before stumbling and panting. Saint took a breath once the room was fogged and used the cover to generate as much lightening as she could. Her hands were shaky and eyes nervous. I gave her a reassuring smile.

Hecate let out a yelp of surprise as she slid to the ground, she sat up and growled loudly. Rouge joined us outside. Rue was trembling, she was terrified. I made another wall and began shooting chunks out towards her and Briar also sent her ice towards her. I could feel my motions getting slower as Saint worked. She looked like she was ready to shoot before Hecate yelled out in frustration.

"Enough!" Hecate grew in size, she was almost as big as the school, is this what all the gods truly look like? Even dad? She put her hand out and Briar gasped as her ice dried up and she was thrown across the courtyard, Rouge's and Saint's magic fizzled out and their keys shattered. Rouge looked at her hands in shock.

"Don't forget who you're dealing with!" Hecate growled, "I can give you magic and I can take it away!" A giant glyph was behind her, too big to even read it. My rocks collapsed on the ground. I panted out, *this is impossible.*

"Rue-"

"I-I'm sorry." Rue hugged her legs to her chest, curling into a ball, "I'm useless, I'm sorry I can't help. My powers aren't-" She muttered.

"Rue, you're a Kovenn" I fell to my knees, *it's so hot,* "Which means, your magic and power will always be more than ours." I panted out.

Rue looked down and trembled.

Hecate summoned more glyphs, all lightning. This might be my only chance. The moons were becoming noticeable in the sky, and we're running out of time. I groaned and leaned against Saint as she tried to help me up. I made a small barricade for Rue and stepped forward. I summoned the vines, they wrapped around my hands like gloves, and put my fists up. She looked down and laughed.

"Really? Do you *really* want to do this?" She put her hand up, the glyphs lighting up. "I almost feel pity."

"Well, I guess we're on the same page."

"You... *pity* me." Hecate seemed offended.

"Well. What else can I give a grieving widow." I glanced up at her and slightly past her, I held back my grin. "Other than a reality check." I slammed my fist on the ground and summoned a bigger glyph. Her eyes widened. She lost her footing and the glyphs disappeared. I swore to myself but pushed through.

"What!?" Hecate went to stand forward. I lifted the rock and flipped off it and kicked it towards her. She put her arms up to block, but I sent three more towards her. While she was distracted, Jonas had plenty of time to muster up her water, she jumped down and landed, landing iced slashes down her back.

Hecate screamed out and stumbled forward, panting out. "What is the meaning of this!?"

Jonas didn't say anything, she just attacked, every attack harder than the last. I shook away my dizziness and joined in, overwhelming her. She groaned out and sent out a waved of darkness, sending both of us back. Jonas caught me as gently as she could but we both tumbled down, she charged up another lightning strike and shot it directly at her water, sending a charge through both of us. I could feel myself nearly passing out.

Rue was trembling, but she looked over at Aubrey then back at everyone else. If Jonas is back, the others have to be just as close right? She gripped her hair and trembled more, she didn't know what to do. *But Aubrey will die if we don't end this, all the Reapers could die. Her friends could die. Miss*

Petra could die. She covered her face.

"Pesky insects. I will give Petra this, her lightning is surely useful." Hecate composed herself and walked over to us, kneeling down, "But your magic is certainly strong." A glyph appeared on her palm and she went to touch us. Until her hand stopped suddenly.

"Huh..?" Her hand began to shake, she gripped her wrist with her other hand and jerked to attention. Hecate turned her head towards Rue.

"Mother!" Rue yelled, sending her back towards the building. She had tears of frustration streaming down her face, her stance wasn't solid. Everyone was stunned. Rue hesitantly walked out from behind the shield. Pink glyphs shined behind her, strings shooting towards Hecate. Her magic basically illuminated the area in pink. Almost like she was a beacon.

"How dare you." Hecate knocked the strings away as she stood up, dusting off her dress, her hair was more disheveled. Before she could get close, the winds picked up, pushing her around and making her stumble to her knees, more strings tied around her arms and yanked her around, controlling her movements.

"How dare I?" Rue asked, she put her hand out, "How dare you!" Rue tossed her aside and trembled, her voice was shaking but she was still angry.

Rue kept the winds high, as the moons began to align. Her eyes grew brighter and she summoned a bigger glyph, conjuring a giant hand. She was completely still. Hecate looked at her in disbelief.

"What is that.."

"If you ever paid any attention to me, you'd know I was

a conjure student!" Rue used the hands to summon more strings, attaching onto her wrist, pulling at her either way, "And that I'm top of my class! And I can do something you never thought weak little pathetic Rue could ever do."

"I can create magic too!"

Rouge, Saint and Briar could suddenly do magic again. A new glyph appeared on the ground, Rouge wasted no time and got to her feet.

"I don't know what you're doing Rue, but keep it up!" Rouge summoned more of her glyphs, she was tired and they were slightly weaker but this was better than nothing.

Saint quickly joined in, she quickly began to cancel out the remaining lightning glyphs. Hecate's hands were bound and being pulled towards Rue's summon. The hand kept inching her towards them. Hecate tried to dig her heels in the ground. She got over her shock as quickly as she could.

"That might be so. But you are still weak." Hecate slammed her foot on the ground, shattering the new glyph, and just like that the magic dried up once more.

"If you weren't so fragile, maybe you could have learned how to become magic. Just like your Momma." Hecate yanked her arms from the wires, she ignored the pain and created a bigger glyph for herself, the area shook as the winds picked up.

The shaking got to me. I groaned quietly, moving my hands. I suddenly felt full of energy. I could feel the lightning coursing through me, I felt like I got a major boost. I sat up and looked over, Jonas was still out, I looked towards Hecate and noticed her third eye, maybe that's her weak spot. I got up and stretched once more. I'm not wasting this second wind.

"You idiot." I grumbled and got to my feet. "You have no idea what you've just done."

I concentrated and summoned a few more glyphs, I put my hands out and let the rocks shoot like bullets, cutting through her glyph. I started adjusting the field, using multiple glyphs to split and rearrange the ground, isolating her as quickly as possible. Hecate was too slow to react. She had a look of shock and confusion on her face. I hardened rocks around my fists and took off.

"Rue! You're a fuckin badass!" I grinned at her and dashed past her, jumping from rock to rock, shooting as many at her as I could. I began shooting them at her like bullets and kept shifting the ground under her. I was slowly closing the gap but she was desperately using any spell in her arsenal. I cut down the shadows, dodged the conjures, fought through the telekinesis. I could feel lightning surging through my body and *gods did it feel fantastic.*

I jumped up, and darted myself towards her, slamming my fist directly into her face. She gasped and fell back, I straddled her and gripped her face.

"Seems you underestimated me. I'm a fucking *witch* you old bitch." I moved my hand down, ripping the third blue eye out of its socket. she screamed and clawed at me trying to get me to stop. I pushed through, her spells began to fizzle out, just a little more.

I yanked it out and threw it aside, the eye bounced down the rocks and landed by Rue's feet. I dropped the rocks and felt the high slowly wearing off.

I backed up and stumbled to my feet, panting and fighting back the exhaustion.

The eye began to twitch and move before forming into

Hecate. Her pale blue hair fell to her shoulders as she sat up. Her white dress was disheveled. She was on the ground, panting as the alignment shined above her. A book materialized by her. It was a pale purple with gold trim. It had an intricate design, there was a golden apple decal on the front with an eye carved into it.

Rue looked down at her, her eyes were sad, pitiful. "Mom..."

Hecate looked up at her and scowled, even now, she won't care. And I think Rue noticed, she closed her eyes and looked away.

"I hope time is kind to you, and heals you." Rue's voice was quiet. I hurried over to her, Hecate looked infuriated.

Before she could react, chains wrapped around her wrists. I looked up as dad, Medusa and Adonys jumped down, she looked back in fear.

"No!" Hecate tried to struggle but dad just pulled her in, she clawed and screamed, all Rue could do was look away.

"No! Please! Not there!" Hecate was pleading, I rubbed Rue's shoulder comfortingly but narrowed my eyes at her. She reached her hand towards me, tears of fear and panic streaming down her face.

"*Sister*!" I blinked in shock and was taken aback.

Dad's form became clouded before she was swallowed up, sent to Tartarus. Rue immediately broke down. She trembled and fell to her knees. I kneeled next to her and comforted her. Saint ran over to Miss Petra and checked on her. She was still breathing, and she'll be Ok. Jonas sat up and rubbed her head, right as Adonys closed the gap between them.

"Aubrey!" Medusa shouted, running over. I looked at her

tiredly and smiled a bit.

"Just… In time…" My eyes felt heavy.

"Hold on, hold on." Medusa quickly caught me and injected something in my body. I groaned and closed my eyes. My body instantly got heavy. *I'm so tired.*

51

FIFTY

The place was destroyed, but luckily, Mateo was able to free the teachers and Jasper was able to warn the other Reapers. The alignment slowly parted in the sky, Aides' moon shining as bright as it usually does. The deep blue stream was passing in front of the moon so beautifully. This will definitely be an alignment they'll never forget.

Saint ran over and hugged Jasper tightly, burying her head in their chest. Jonas recovered and began healing Miss Petra. Jasper said she should be able to make a full recovery, Rue stayed by her side. Her tears were a mix of pain and relief.

The blood in his ears slowly stopped, Aubrey could feel his body again and slowly opened his eyes. Everyone was crowded around him, watching him expectantly. He blinked. Rouge made the first move.

"You idiot!" Rouge pulled Aubrey into a tight hug.

He smiled gently and rubbed her back, "Did we do it?"

"Yea, she's going to be imprisoned for a long while, she committed unspeakable crimes. No trial is even needed." Tartarus pet the top of Aubrey's head. Aubrey closed his eyes and breathed out, nodding.

Saint hugged him as tight as she could, relief on all their faces.

"Now about my school." Jasper raised a brow. They all laughed.

They helped him up and began to migrate out, Aubrey took Medusa's hand gently.

She blinked and looked at him, her eyes misty.

"You did good… You really saved my life." He smiled, "Thank you Medusa."

She blinked and wiped her eyes, "I didn't…"

"Without you, we wouldn't have known what was wrong with me, or where to get the fix."

"It's temporary…" Medusa rubbed her arm, "But it should be more than enough until I can-"

"Aubrey?" A small voice spoke up. Aubrey glanced towards the door and noticed Medusa standing there, she seemed shy, she was practically folded in on herself, the hall was dim from her bedroom light. Aubrey sat up in his bed and nodded.

"Hey, you alright?"

"Yes." Medusa nodded, "I would like to apologize for today, I didn't mean to mess up the washer..." She messed with the bottom of her PJ shirt. She looked embarrassed.

"Oh, Heh. Don't worry 'bout that."

"Mr. Tartarus seemed upset..." She said.

"He just don't play 'bout the house. And I got it all cleaned up, really it's no worries." Aubrey waved it off, and yawned while stretching. "It's late though, you should head to bed."

"I'm sorry.. Are you tired?"

"Eh, kinda, but." He shrugged.

"Do you mind..." Medusa messed with her shirt, "If I talk to

you until I fall asleep...?"

Aubrey blinked then nodded a bit, "Sure..." He patted the bed and moved the covers, "You sure you Ok?"

"She climbed in the bed and pulled the covers over her legs and hugged her legs to her chest. "I think so... I just feel bad."

"Sick?"

"No... Inside." Medusa shook her head, "When it comes to you.."

"Why?"

"I hated you.. So much, for years I was compared to you, I was angry..." She gripped her shirt sleeve, "My main drive was killing you. And you're so..."

Aubrey tilted his head.

"Kind..." Medusa looked at him, "Why?"

"Well, to be honest, because you're letting me. I can't give what you won't accept." Aubrey laid back against the headboard and moved his arms behind his head.

Medusa looked at him, then looked down. "That's not an acceptable answer."

"Then what is?" He asked.

"..." She shrugged, "A part of me wishes you'd just hurt me. To atone.. To make myself feel vindicated in my hatred towards you. But I know you won't..."

"Well, you're right, I'm not." Aubrey sighed a bit, "Look hon, you dealt with some horrible stuff, your mental state, your body responses, your body... I don't ever want to contribute to that."

"And honestly, I'm glad that you feel guilty." He said, she shot her head towards him, "That means you're changing, for the better."

Aubrey smiled gently. She dropped her gaze and looked down.

"Everyone's gotta start somewhere, and the only reason this

was able to work, was because you wanted it too. And I'm proud of you."

Her eyes began to water and she nodded, "Thank you.."

"Of course, hon." He laid down and turned his side lamp off, and patted the pillow for her, "You can rest."

She hesitantly laid down, turning to face him a bit, he closed his eyes and breathed out quietly.

"Ya know, I've noticed something in you."

"Have you...?" Medusa asked.

"Mhmm, you're very smart, like hella smart... you have so much potential to be more. I genuinely can't wait to see what you'll become in the future, especially with that new little err.." He took a moment to think, "Mycology......." Aubrey narrowed his eyes. They glinted in the dark.

Medusa laughed quietly and nodded, "Yes, Mycology."

"Mycology hobby, I did more research on it, did you know you can make medicine out of mushrooms? Crazy."

She smiled, "Yes, I did..."

"And with your knowledge on poisons, your horizons are bright, hell you can make so many life changing antidotes or cures..." Aubrey closed his eyes. Medusa's eyes softened as she looked at him.

"Dr. Medusa got a nice ring to it don't it?" Aubrey spoke quietly before slowly falling asleep.

I see, I guess this means I'm dying? Remembering something so precious with a sudden pain in my head? Aubrey please don't be sad.. Please don't make that face. I'm so sorry to worry you. I guess in another life I can be a doctor, and we could meet and be friends again? Thank you for making this life better, even if it was for a little while. I'll always cherish this. I'll always cherish you.

Project EF, you truly were perfect, in all the imperfect ways.

BANG!

It happened so fast, there was barely any time to react. Suddenly she was bleeding on the ground, the ringing of a gunshot was in the air, her snakes went limp almost immediately, her eyes began to dull as blood pooled around her head.

The area was silent. Everyone stared in disbelief.

Aubrey's body began to shake as he fell to his knees and cradled her close. All the noise around him was drowned out, what just happened. *What the fuck just happened!?*

"Did you really think I wouldn't have put alarms in my old lab?" A voice spoke up, he was a good ways away, his accent was strange. He had snakes down his back in a loose braid. He had on a lab coat. Pure dread filled the area with his presence. When he spoke, Aubrey slowly turned his head towards him. Time felt frozen. He had on chunky glasses. He tossed the gun aside without a care in the world.

Is this him? Is this her father?

"Seems she was good for something for once. She led me straight to you." The man grinned.

Aubrey couldn't comprehend what he was seeing, all he felt was *impalpable, unwavering, unfathomable* **rage**. His hands slowly gripped Medusa's lifeless shoulders, she was in one of her favorite sweaters, the green one with a frog on the back, mushrooms trailing down her arms. The same sweater she requested Aubrey matched with her. It was still on his bed, he wore it just for her. Everything was hot.

All he could ask himself was, *Is this what pure wrath feels like?*

52

FIFTY-ONE

I remember the day he was created. It was a very joyous day for *him*. The energy was kinder, the halls were quieter, aside from his cheers of success. I can't remember what day it was at that point. I've been awake for so long. I was at the point that my cognitive function was down to zero. I don't know how many days it's been since I slept last. It's so dark down here, we never see the sun rise or set, we never breathe fresh air. The days all blended together, they all felt endless. Hours and hours of nothing but pain, torture, and trauma.

The only thing I could look forward to was Jonas. Seeing her face was my sunshine. When I tried to remember what being outside felt like, all I could imagine was her. Her face, her smile, everything. She was perfect, something that should be unfathomable to the normal mind. Her kindness knew no bounds. We were the same age, she was always so gentle with me afterwards. Her warm hands bandaged up any wounds I accumulated, she watched over the other kids the best she could.

She was the first iteration of *Project EF.*

When he was made, I had no idea my life would plummet so drastically. He was the beginning of the end. As they say hindsight is 20/20. I wish the signs were.

Shortly after he perfected him, the lab was raided, Jonas ran to find me. She helped me up and exclaimed over and over that we're safe, the kids are safe. If I'm honest I could barely understand anything she was saying, but her eyes and face were so relieved. Men barged in, they gathered us up, did a headcount and began discussing what to do with all of us. Some of us had families, the rest were orphans, he picked a lot of us carefully. I was sold to him, I remember my parents leaving me on a shady doorstep and they trafficked me. I was passed down through so many hands before falling in his.

His was by far the worst. Every inch of me is scarred, my pride is shattered, my dignity is non-existent. My genetic makeup isn't even the same. He said I was the most successful, the perfect Project, the first Earthborn child he altered. He thought he was a god, or at least deserving of the title. *He disgusted me,* he kept me isolated in a cell, running tests on me, once I lost my wings and horns I began to dissociate. My parents used to tell me that it showed a Dragon's pride, something we'd boast about. I'm never getting mine back.

I thought us getting found was a good thing, it was for the other kids, and Jonas and the Project. The taller man, he looked like The Valley, he cradled the Project in his hands and Jonas desperately tried to get him back. She was hysterical. I suppose that makes sense, they share DNA, genetics?

That man adopted them both, I ended up with Jonas, I refused to part from her. She was all I had. Over the years, I thought things were getting better. The man, Tartarus, took care of us, he let me stay with Jonas, he raised the Project and her as siblings, he gave me food and enrolled us in schools. Before I knew it, the Project was fifteen and we were twenty three. She had been my girlfriend since high school.

All my good memories involve her. Jonas was my world, my moons, my sun, my air, my waters. She was *everything*. She was my best friend and the love of my life. How did I get so lucky? Jonas was very active in the Project's life, he was a good kid, wanted nothing more than to impress her and Tartarus, a real *'watch this!'* kid. He had Jonas wrapped around his little finger. He was the only competition I had. And I knew if it came down to it, I'd always lose. I came to terms with it. Especially if it means I can stay by her side in the moment.

"Sandman~" Jonas hummed, she snapped her fingers in front of my face and leaned down. I blinked and met her stunning brown eyes. She had a wide grin on her face. "Awake?"

I raised a brow and gave her a look, "When am I not?"

Jonas smiled and sat down next to me with a bounce, she was excited. Something good must've happened on her outing. Jonas was a teacher this time around. Her love for the Project and the other kids showed her calling. With my mutation, most jobs never stuck. Not much you can do for too long before your low cognitive function and alertness becomes more noticeable. I remember one of my bosses calling my depression and anxiety *infectious*.

Jonas didn't seem to mind it though, she never got angry or yelled when I lost another job. She never gets irritated when I sit for hours staring at nothing. She never punishes me for my issues, she just embraces them, and makes it clear she's happy. That's all I want. That's all I've ever wanted. Since we were 9. After every time she bandaged me up, gave me food or water, or gave me hope again. I wanted to be that and more for her.

"I got more letters~!" Jonas beamed, she sat a stack on the table, "A lot of the kids are doing so much better." Her voice and eyes softened, I smiled gently at her.

"That's wonderful…" I looked at the stack, "Any job offers for me in the mail?" I joked.

Jonas swatted at my arm and shook her head, "Oh hush, you're a house husband, that's plenty of work."

"Ah?" I asked, feeling my cheeks heat up, "You think so?"

"Of course~ why ya think I pay so well." Jonas grinned. I cleared my throat and glanced away with a heavy blush on my face.

"I'm teasing~!" Jonas giggled and kissed my cheek, "But really, you don't need a job love, you do more than enough here, and I'm so grateful, and I rather you safe here than at a dangerous job when your symptoms are still prevalent."

I glanced away and sighed lightly, "Yea, I suppose so…"

"Oh…" I rubbed my head and glanced around, "I forgot to make dinner for you.."

"Aw don't worry about it, I can do it tonight." Jonas stood and I gripped her hand gently.

"Jonas…"

"You do it every night, one time won't hurt." Jonas smiled sweetly. I felt my heart flutter. I let her hand go gently and she walked to the stove. I hold this memory dear, her long hair flowed gently behind her as she walked away from me. It was such a small moment, but it was something I'd always go back to during the night times. While she slept peacefully next to me, I stared at the ceiling reliving my happiest moments until she woke up and made my day all over again.

Not too long after that, I was able to scrape up enough cash to get a ring. I can't imagine my life without Jonas in it. I never want to. I often forgot to ask, sometimes I didn't even realize when she got home. Not until she was actually in front of my face. I chickened out a few times, too many voices screaming at me that this is a bad idea.

But this time I was going too. Until *he* came knocking.

He was eighteen now. I always felt indifferent to the Project. He was often forgotten to me until she mentioned him or he visited. Still her pride and joy. This time he wasn't so joyous.

One thing I never liked about him was his anger. It was so explosive and destructive. It was rare, but when it happened it was loud. He was talking to Jonas, can't remember what about, but he was shouting and she was trying to calm him down. That's something I hold dear as well, for another reason.

That was the first time he *hurt* her. It was an accident and he immediately apologized and tried to help. She never held it against him. But *gods* if Jezabelle offered a sign, that would've been it. Rose tinted glasses I suppose.

She was my wife now, of course she said yes. I started looking into methods to alleviate my symptoms, so I could be more functional, I felt myself slowly slipping from her.

My mind was scattered, memories and thoughts were few and far between, it felt like a hike to get to my next thought. After an incident with the stove, Jonas said enough was enough and started encouraging me to find some remedies for my own safety.

I wasn't concerned with my safety, but hers.

I couldn't feel a thing, nothing but a tingly numbness and unrest. The grains of sand continuously shifting and reforming below my skin felt normal. Unless she touched me, then I felt warm. Like I could turn into glass. Silly I know, she said it always felt like a hot summer beach day, and she found that comforting but hated cuddling too long because it started to feel itchy.

That's dear.

Where was I?

Oh yes, the memory nearly left me again.

The Doctor came back, none of us held it together. Especially after he kidnapped Aubrey. She was a mess. We figured he was dead, we hoped he was dead. Turned out he just escaped, laid low and went back to kidnapping and buying kids to experiment on. Apparently that didn't sit well with the Project. His *star* Project.

He was done in by the same thing he adored, how befitting.

As quickly as he was gone, he was back. But something was clearly different. He wasn't the same bumbling, well meaning, love struck kid. His fuse was significantly shorter, his tongue was sharper and his actions harsher. It was such a dramatic turn. Jonas feared the worst happened when he left, but he never gave clarification. He never even spoke about it. I think that's what went wrong, he bottled all that fear, anxiety, discomfort and trauma up until it exploded.

And when it finally did, *I lost everything.*

He went on a rampage, he went no contact with Tartarus, which he raised concerns with Jonas about. She said she'd talk to him. I asked her not to, I told her to just give him space. She reassured me he just needed a shoulder. That memory hurts. *It was the last time I saw her alive,* I held her while she bled out. And even then. She told me

"Don't be mad, it's not his fault. I'm so sorry."

No.. no I don't understand, what are you apologizing for? This isn't your fault, none of this was your fault. That's when something dawned on me. She's always felt this pressure to perform, to be the mom that everyone could look up to. To be the one to take responsibility. Ever since we were kids. She took it upon herself to treat the children, to treat me.

I held her close as the shine in her eyes died out. I was hysterical, I couldn't comprehend it. He disappeared after that.

I had to come home to an empty house, lay in a cold bed, cleaned for no one. I was alone again. The sun was gone, I found myself coming to in corners. Sitting in the corner of the bedroom until my eyes adjusted. I could see her sometimes, that was a plus. Then I'd remember she's not really there, *just another symptom being cruel.*

I was alone again, but this time I had no one to bandage my wounds. No one to smile at me and tell me everything will be Ok. And it was his fault.

I screamed. I cried, I broke things, I stared at nothing. I did everything.

I was too weak to protect her. Eventually I got tired. I tried to join her. But how cruel, I couldn't. Nothing worked.

I gripped at my hair and felt tears staining my cheeks, no more sobs were coming out, just tears. I was losing sand, I hoped that would kill me. Maybe if I deteriorate I can finally sleep and dream of her?

What's it like to sleep? I haven't done that in twenty years. I curled up on the floor and watched as my sand slowly blew from my body, watching my arm get smaller and smaller with every gust of wind.

Then I noticed something was wrong. I blinked and watched my arm some more, it's almost like my sand was on loop? It blew from me then came back, over and over, it was never getting smaller. I sat up and inspected my body, I never disturbed my sand, I hated thinking about it if I'm honest. I staggered my way to the kitchen and began to cut away at my finger. As soon as it detached black sand poured on the table. I blinked and inspected it. It had a glimmer, I rubbed it between my fingers and glanced towards our engagement photo.

That's when I realized, I can do more. *I can try*. I did a few experiments. Before long I realized my sand had more uses. I could make things sleep, or stay awake, or control the sand and harden it to glass with my fire, I can do *more.*

More importantly, I can create a special kind of sand. It was an accident. I still don't fully understand what I did, but I remember hearing her voice and looking towards the bedroom. The moment I turned my head, everything flashed before my eyes.

She walked over and was slipping on her earrings, she had a bright smile on her lips. "Ready to go? Aubrey will be upset if we're late."

I couldn't tell if this was fiction or reality. The house was clean, the lights were fluorescent. All I could do was reach for her. I placed my hands on her soft warm skin and she blinked in confusion.

"You Ok? It Looks like you had a bad dream." Jonas smiled.

I had a second chance, I won't let this happen again. I pulled her into a tight hug, Jonas hugged back but she was confused, she pulled away and patted my shoulders.

I can't remember how many times I failed at this point. Every jump she died, every time at his hand. Every Time I got more and more tired. I trained harder, found remedies, and even then I still couldn't beat him. He was so strong. I got smarter, every charge to the sand makes a jump, it took some time to hack and control it though. But I finally figured out how I could fix this. I just have to go back further. Starting here already has her fate sealed.

Things got easier once I got a better control on the sand, yet I still failed, some things changed, but the ending always stayed the same. I was getting frustrated, holding her and watching her die over and over *and over again*. I couldn't do it anymore. *I couldn't.*

He was horrible, he ruined everything. *Over. And over. And over again.*

At this point I'm tired. All my optimism and hope died out. I got more patient, colder, more calculated. I'll do this until my body dies. I'll do this until I save her. I won't let her die again. I looked down at the glass and gripped it, flipping it upside down after adjusting the dials.

"Alright. One last time."

I was starting to have hope, this timeline was so different. She was still Jonas though, she wasn't mine, but that was

Ok. Being close to her like this was more than enough. For a while, It was just us, he was nowhere in sight, I don't know exactly where I landed, but I was content. Until she got that letter.

He was alive.

I tried so hard to talk her out of it, I tried so hard. **I TRIED SO HARD.**

He showed no signs, it was like he was a completely different person. He didn't even look the same here, he was rude, but well meaning. He had more friends here, a small tinge of hope sparked in me, until Medusa announced his problem. I was hoping we'd fail. *Would the world be so bad without him? Mine wouldn't.* I'd have my wife, my happiness, our safety. I'd have a future...

"If you want change, you have to make a change."

I will. I will make a change this time. I won't hesitate. I won't wait. I know this can cost me Jonas, but at least she'll be alive. And if there's a future where she's alive and well, then that's good enough for me.

Oh? Is that my lives flashing before my eyes? I guess I thought I was safe.

He held Medusa in his hands, he was shaking in pure rage. That same golden spark danced around him, I felt my heart sink. Before I could stop myself, I shot a string straight through his necks, everything moved so slowly. Jonas's eyes widened in pure horror, the sound was sucked out of the area. Everyone was too stunned, so was I.

All the sound dropped with his body. All I could hear was a gut wrenching.

"Aubrey!"

FIFTY-ONE

To be continued....

53

EPILOGUE

I sat at the computer, phone to my shoulder. My fluffy earring tickled my neck and jaw. The ringing filled my ears and the clicks of the keyboard echoing in the dark room.

"Yes, I found him. He's in The Valley." I said, "His name is Aubrey."

"Aubrey?"

Her sultry voice sounded excited, *"Oh my Angel, I knew you wouldn't let me down. Find him for me, my love."*

"I will. I'll bring him to you, as soon as possible. I won't let you down."

"I know my little dove." Her beautiful voice sent a shudder down my spine.

I've been away from her for so long. It feels like eternity. I know it's wrong but I long for her. I want nothing more than to be with her. I also want her to succeed. I knew being away was benefiting her. All I have to do is find him and I can go home to her. I can rest in her arms. In her paradise.

"Work quickly and diligently. I can't afford to lose you dove." She spoke.

I nodded foolishly like she could see me, "I understand."

"Hurry back."

With that, the dial tone droned in my ear. I sat the phone on the receiver and looked up at the cork board. His auburn hair and bright purple eyes. He's hard to miss. The school uniform really washed him out. I nodded to myself. If he's what she wants, then that's what she'll get.

"I'm coming for you, *Aubrey Kovenn."*

www.ingramcontent.com/pod-product-compliance
Lightning Source LLC
Chambersburg PA
CBHW020327030826
48979CB00021B/466

* 9 7 9 8 9 9 1 8 7 4 1 0 6 *